PAUL E. HORSMAN

THE SHARDHELD SAGA

Book 2

RUNEMASTER

Cover: Jos Weijmer, JW Art Studio

For more info: www.paulhorsman-author.com

There are a glossary and a list of names at the back of the book.

Paul E. Horsman's books:

Zilverspoor Uitgeverij (Dutch Editions):
Rhidauna – Schaduw van de Revenaunt #1
Zihaen – Schaduw van de Revenaunt #2
Ordelanden - Schaduw van de Revenaunt #3 (2013)

Red Rune Books (English Editions):
Shardfall - The Shardheld Saga #1
Runemaster - The Shardheld Saga #2
Shardheld - The Shardheld Saga #3 (2014)

Rhidauna - The Shadow of the Revenaunt #1
Zihaen – The Shadow of the Revenaunt #2 (2013)
Ordelanden – The Shadow of the Revenaunt #3 (2014)
Shadows Under Nadril - A Revenaunt novelette

TABLE OF CONTENTS

CHAPTER 1 – MUUS

Muus opened his eyes to the sound of a rough song in the distance. He groaned, feeling gravel stinging his cheeks. For a moment he lay there, getting used to the hazy world around him, before he tried to sit up. He was on a beach, a man's length past the surf, facing a long row of pale dunes. He remembered the storm - the heart-stopping sounds of a ship running aground on a reef - the broken mast carrying him to safety through the dark. Now it was day. Icy cold water soaked his clothes, but he felt too tired to move.

Again, he heard the song and he forced himself into a sitting position. The sea was still rough, sending rows of foaming waves to chastise the land. On their backs, the rollers bore a large wooden platform shoreward. Muus caught his breath as he stared at the incoming raft, with its posts sticking in the air. On top of it huddled two small figures, Hraab and Prince Ottil. The boys clung to each other, singing a bawdy warrior song. Muus shouted and ran into the surf.

The waves, angry at being robbed of two lives, grounded their raft with a crash, throwing the boys into the water. They rose spluttering, their song forgotten, and waded ashore.

Muus spread his arms and caught his young friends in a fierce embrace. 'You're totally mad,' he said, tears pricking in his eyes.

'I wasn't scared,' said Ottil firmly, as if continuing an earlier conversation.

'You were,' said Hraab.

'Not.' Then the prince started to cry. 'I was. Damn. So what? Anyone would be scared by a shipwreck,' said he defiantly.

'Of course,' said Muus, holding him close. 'It's no shame to be scared; you're not made of stone.' Looking over their heads, Muus searched the beach and the sea. Where were Birthe and her baby, the paladin and Kjelle? They couldn't have drowned. It wouldn't be fair. He sighed. *Don't fool yourself; the Fates don't care about fair.* He turned his thoughts back to the boys and managed a smile. 'What a grand boat you were sailing.'

Ottil wiped his nose. 'It was the forecastle,' he said. 'The wind blew it into the sea after the crash, right under our noses. We jumped and off we sailed.'

Hraab plucked at his soaking wet tunic. 'Ehhh, I'm getting clean.'

'That wouldn't be a bad idea,' said Muus. 'I don't think you've washed anything since this whole thing began. At least take them off and wring them out.'

The boy lowered his eyes. 'No need, they'll dry.'

'Well, I will,' said Ottil, stepping out of his knee-length tunic. 'Help, will you?'

'Wait, someone's coming,' said Hraab. He pointed down the beach, where three riders came galloping their way, kicking up the surf around them.

'If we're in Brytanna, Nords won't be popular here.' Muus glanced at the two boys. 'Hraab doesn't look Nordish; he could be my little brother. You...'

'I don't look like a proper Nord either,' said Ottil, slipping his tunic back over his nakedness. 'I know. Other boys told me the same, before I bloodied their stupid noses.'

'Well, don't try and bloody mine. From now on you're a Gaul. Do you speak Gaullish?'

'Of course I do, plus a mouthful of Brytan and Old Rom.'

Muus heard a distant yell and knew the riders had seen them. 'Listen,' he said hurriedly. 'We're escaped slaves, our master Kjelle drowned. Remember that.'

'Only you hope he didn't,' said Hraab.

Muus shivered. 'He can't have.' Then he turned to watch the three riders coming through the surf. They were young, he saw, and in good spirits. They didn't look threatening at all, in spite of their spears.

As they came near, the riders reigned in and surrounded them. One, a young man of Muus's own age, with close-cropped, reddish hair, planted his spear in the sand and said something in a foreign tongue.

Muus understood what he meant. He hadn't spoken the other's language for years, but automatically his mind formed answering words. 'We are ship racked,' he said. 'No, wrecked. We ran on the rocks.'

'Shipwrecked?' The young man looked surprised. 'Last night's storm? Where is the wreck?'

Little Hraab looked up at the rider, his eyes large as if in remembered fear. 'We drifted all night, like storm-tossed trash, unable to see. It was scary.'

'I bet it was.' One of the other riders made an averting move with his free hand. 'You were blessed; it was rough last night.'

Muus looked back at the sea. No wreck, nor any reefs to be seen. 'Perhaps the ship sank. The rocks had torn out her bottom.'

'Whence do you come?' asked the first rider. 'You are clearly of the Un-a-Dach, but your words are strange.'

'I haven't spoken our language for ten years,' said Muus. 'We were slaves of the Norden.'

The young man nodded gravely. 'And now you return to your homeland? I wish you joy! How did you escape?'

A breeze coming across the sea set Muus shivering in his wet clothes. 'We were underway to Harflot with our master. I was standing at the mast when we struck, and went overboard with it. I held on to it and kept my upper body out of the water. My master was on the quarterdeck, so he must have drowned. Now we've returned, free at last.'

'Woo!' The rider gravely lifted his spear. 'The Fates were surely with you, friend. What is your name?'

Muus frowned, surprised. 'All these years I had forgotten my name, but now it has returned. I am Terrel, son of Slade, from the village of Owwich.' He felt as if he was talking about someone else.

The riders exchanged glances. Then the redhead smiled. 'I've never heard of Owwich. No matter; my father will know, or else the druid. Who are your friends? The little one could be your brother, but who's the other? He isn't a Nord?' he asked anxiously.

Muus smiled. 'This is Ottil, from Gaul. The small one is Hraab.'

'A Gaul, that's good,' said the rider, relieved. 'We have no quarrel with the King of the Gauls. Why, one of merchant Theodgard's peddlers passed through yesterday. They sell the finest wares of Harflot.'

The young rider sat up straight, as if he'd come to a decision. 'Well, it's all very strange. But you and young Hraab are clearly of the Un-a-Dach, and those are to be trusted. You are heartily welcome, friends. We'll take you to our village. I am Gillach, son of Cardoc chief of Windiss.' He gestured to his companions. 'We can ride double. It's not far to the village, but you look too tired to walk.'

Muus glanced at Hraab and saw him nod. *Un-a-Dach? It feels as if I should know that name but I don't,* he thought. Then he shrugged. *I can't do a thing about it.* Weariness enveloped him and everything about him was bitter cold. Thankfully, he mounted behind the rider, clutching at the latter's saddle.

The horses walked a twisting path from the beach through a stretch of grass-grown dunes to a broad stream, with cultivated lands beyond.

'Here's the Winde River,' said Gillach, as they forded the running waters. 'Our village lies behind the bend.'

Muus felt tears sting his eyes. It was like coming home. He knew how the village would look, the round huts under thatched roofs, with chickens, pigs and playing children. His eyes sought a man in a red mantle, and a small woman with black hair like his own. They weren't there, of course; they came from his dreams. He saw Hraab watching him, but for once the boy remained silent.

At the entrance to the village, they were met by a burly man who bore a resemblance to Gillach. He watched their coming impassively and as they came near, lifted his hand in greeting.

'Do you bring us visitors or slaves, my son?' he said, without moving an inch.

Muus stiffened, but Gillach chuckled as he reined in his horse. 'Visitors, father. We checked for flotsam on the beach. Instead of valuables, we found these three. The storm had plucked them from their ship on the reefs somewhere and brought them here.'

Muus clambered stiffly from the horse. 'Thank you for your help, Gillach,' he said. He turned to the burly man, showing his open hands. 'Greetings, I am Terrel, once from the village of Owwich, now an escaped slave of the Nords. My friends are Hraab, and Ottil from Gaul.'

The man spread his hands. 'I'm Cardoc, chief of Windiss. The Un-a-Dach are always welcome in our village.' He turned to his son. 'Our guests appear in need of food and warmth. Take them home to your mother's care.'

Gillach dismounted and sent his mates away with the horses. He smiled broadly. 'She will be pleased.'

'That's most important,' said his father. 'I'll see you later, friends.'

As they walked through the village, along paths muddy from the late storm, they were halted by a tall, green-robed man. He looked at Muus with a strange expression on his face. 'I dreamed last night that a stranger came. Now you arrive and the world is in balance once more. But...' He peered at Muus. 'What is your purpose here?'

Gillach frowned. 'Druid Ewynn, with respect, our guests have just survived a shipwreck. They need food, drink, and a chance to rest.'

'A strong mind can overcome the weakness of the body,' said the man dismissively.

'We would be pleased to speak with you, master druid,' piped up Hraab. 'But our brains are dull from lack of sleep and the roaring of the sea in our ears. We wouldn't do your wisdom justice.'

The druid flinched at that. 'You are right, child. I am overhasty. You will answer my question later, when you are fed and rested.' Then he walked away, with the hem of his green robe swirling around his bare legs.

Gillach grinned. 'He's very wise, but not entirely of this world.'

Hraab and Ottil glanced at each other, but neither said anything.

The chief's house, next to the mead hall, was a squat building, constructed of rough logs. Inside, in the dim central room, a corpulent woman looked up from her work. She held her stout arms out to them. 'Oh my poor boys, but you look terrible. Such a nasty thing is a shipwreck. Sit by the fire and make yourselves comfortable. I'd say you'd like a bit of my stew, and fresh bread?'

'Yes!' said Ottil eagerly. 'Please,' he added and the woman laughed.

'It was a nasty storm,' she continued, while she filled three bowls. 'You should thank the Gods you survived. It blew so hard; many of our houses got damaged.'

Muus found her chatter peaceful and while he couldn't understand everything she said, her words soothed his mind. He sopped up the remaining stew with a crust of bread and propped in his mouth. For the first time since long, he was content. A loud burp escaped him and the woman smiled. 'Bless you.' He leaned his head against the wall and closed his eyes.

The press of small bodies woke him. As he opened his eyes, a half-circle of children stood staring at him with awe on their dirty faces. He quickly closed his eyes again.

'Truly,' said Hraab. The boy was standing beside him with his hands lifted, in the middle of some tall story. 'Lightning sprang from his fingers to the tops of the mountains. Its mighty noise roared as a dragon's breath between the cliffs. The deadly machines shooting at us from the summit shattered, raining debris and bodies for the waiting fjord sharks. The lightning followed them down, to the ships that were thinking to kill us. Fires spread and the wails of the dying echoed off the fjord walls, as the enemy drakkars smoked and sank away into the bottomless depths. The sharks ate well that night.' Hraab's voice had taken on an unexpected storytelling power, and even the chief's wife had stopped babbling to listen. 'That's him,' said the boy in a dramatic voice, pointing at Muus. 'Behold Terrel of Owwich, master of lighting. He is soft-spoken, but his anger is terrible. Truly, a high and wise worker of magics is Runemaster Terrel. Windiss is doing well in aiding him and the Gods will bless Windiss in return.' Then he brought his hands together and fell silent.

Their hostess sighed and shook herself. 'What's this?' she said, putting her hands on her hips. 'Shoo, children! Go pester others, but leave the Runemaster in peace.' With a last, awed look at the mighty visitor in their midst, the children hurried into the sunlight.

'What did you tell them?' said Muus in an agitated whisper, his eyes still firmly shut. 'What nonsense tales where you spinning that no one will believe?'

'He gave them the truth,' said Ottil, dropping down beside Muus. 'He wasn't really exaggerating either. Bards will sing of your deeds that night.' Then he closed his eyes and fell promptly asleep.

'But why tell it here?' Muus opened his eyes, blinking against the light.

Hraab frowned at him. 'It will be better for you, and for us, when everyone knows you for a powerful Runemaster. And the children will spread the word even faster than our hostess could.'

'A fine Runemaster I am! I can't even control whatever power I have and I burn myself whenever I use it.'

'Help will come,' said Hraab, sitting back.

Muus looked around as a long shadow fell over him. He recognized the lanky figure of the village druid.

'Good day,' said Ewynn absently. 'I came to see how you were doing.'

'He's doing fine.' The chief's wife frowned at the intrusion. 'If they'd all leave him alone. First all those pesky infants come, ruining his sleep and now you. The poor dear needs to rest.'

The druid ignored her protests and sat down opposite Muus. 'The children are babbling nonsense about you being a Runemaster. You are much too young, of course.' He eyed Muus suspiciously. 'Who are you, exactly?'

'My memory is still misty,' said Muus. 'I know I'm Terrel from Owwich, son of Slade. I was stolen from my village by a Viking raider called Largassen. Broken bits of memory float around in my head. I remember pieces of the journey overseas and of the place where they sold me. After that, I was Muus, body slave to the Lord Holderling.'

'Owwich.' The druid made a sign, at the same time a blessing and a warding off against evil. 'I heard what happened there ten years ago. I knew Slade; we studied together. He married Aeylla, a girl of the Un-a-Dach, the rune people of Alben. They had a son called Terrel; that is truth. Their village was pillaged and burned. No one survived and Owwich ceased to exist.' His pale eyes bored into Muus. 'You say you are that Terrel? You have much of the Un-a-Dach in you, young man. Not as much as your friend here, but still a great deal. Give me your hand; show me you speak the truth.'

Without hesitation, Muus held out his hand and the other gripped it. As with the Völva Asgisla, he felt a faint tingling. The druid's face strained and sweat stood out on his forehead. Finally, he sighed.

'No.' He let go of Muus's hand and stared at his own fingers. 'I can't read you. The *geis* blocking your memory is strong. It will take years for it to dissolve fully.'

'I don't have years,' said Muus. He squared his shoulders. 'But I do speak the truth.'

The druid stared at him. 'Un-a-Dach don't lie, so I must accept your word.' He touched Muus's forehead with his fingertips. 'You are young; let the *geis* run its course.'

'I can't.'

'Why not?' asked the druid softly.

Muus looked around. 'I can't tell you here.'

Ewynn's brows rose. 'Come with me then.' He unfolded his long legs and went outside with Muus and Hraab, leaving Ottil snoring on the bench. As they walked through the village, big-eyed children followed in their path like ducklings. The druid's house was small, almost bare of furniture and scrupulously clean. Ewynn closed the door, shutting the children out. 'Sit down,' he said, waving to a low bench, and sat himself down on the edge of his cot. 'Now tell me.'

Instead of speaking, Muus took out the shard. Its blue light filled every corner of the hut.

Ewynn's face had gone white. 'The skyshard?' He stared at Muus. 'Are you the one?'

Hraab looked at the druid, his dark eyes still, his young face strangely intent. 'Muus is the Shardheld. He has to be made ready.'

Druid Ewynn swallowed. 'Not by me.'

Hraab smiled gently. 'Don't worry, Master Ewynn, your assistance will not be required. Who of your order would be advanced enough to help?'

'That would be Fardoragh,' said the druid without hesitation. 'He's an Archdruid and as old as the earth. If he can't assist you, nobody can.' He sighed in regret or relief as Muus put the stone away and dimness returned with double strength.

'Where will we find this Fardoragh?' asked Hraab.

'He is living to the west of here, past the marshes. I'm not sure he will consent to see you, though. Fardoragh is a recluse.' Ewynn thought for a moment. 'You need a guide. I know just the one: Moirra. She's a girl of your mother's people, Shardheld. She studied under Fardoragh and she's about the only one with access to him. She lives alone in the Bloodbogs not far from here. It will take some time to contact her and ask her if she will receive you. I suggest you, eh, rest, sleep and eat in the meantime.'

It took a sevenday and three for Moirra's answer to return. It sounded, barely, positive. She agreed to see the strangers and discuss their problem, but she wouldn't promise anything until she had spoken them. The message, written in runic letters on a writing slate, sounded slightly peevish, echoing the face of Ewynn's servant, whom Moirra had kept waiting for nearly two full days before consenting to see him.

'She isn't an easy one,' said the druid apologetic. 'Besides, she is in retreat, searching for her *uwa'th*, her self-awareness. That is never an easy road.' With a look at the closed face of his servant, he added, 'The chief will give you a guide to her house.'

Two days later, they took their leave of the hospitable Windiss folk, riding double with Gillach and his two friends. The Windiss riders didn't mind their assignment at all. The weather was dry, and they were in good cheer as they rode through the fields.

'That's one big tree,' said Ottil suddenly, pointing at an enormous ash in the middle of a stubble-field.

'Our holy tree,' said Gillach proudly. 'It's the biggest one in the world. We hold our feasts and ceremonies right between its feet.'

On impulse, Muus pulled at the rider's sleeve. 'Stop for a moment, will you,' As Gillach reined in, Muus sprang down and walked over to the tree. It was the biggest ash he'd ever seen. Its gnarled roots were thick as a man's body and in summer, the circle of its shade would be at least six manlengths.

Muus touched his heart. Ritual words sprang to his mind. 'I would beg a gift, great ash.' He stooped and carefully dug a small seedling from between the tree's feet. 'Thank you for your seed, ash tree. May you grow ever stronger.' He put the seedling with a bit of earth into the pouch with the skyshard and climbed back onto Gillach's horse. Nobody said anything, although Hraab smiled slightly.

Muus felt he had to explain. 'It just came to me; the ash helps me to grow in understanding and keeps me rooted to the ground at the same time. I think I can use such guidance.' Then he looked at Hraab. 'Where did I get this idea? I never thought of the wisdom of the trees before.'

'Your understanding is already growing,' grinned the boy. 'Hold on to that little one for a while.'

'Wasn't your father a druid, Runemaster?' said Gillach carefully. 'Perhaps his teachings return to you, now you're back on sacred soil.'

'You could well be right,' said Muus. 'But it's damned unsettling to have memories jump at you from nowhere.'

'I'd say that's better than getting them back all at once.' Hraab wriggled on the horse's broad back. 'If you're finished, can we get on? This isn't the most comfortable seat for someone of my size -- my crotch is feeling a bit stretched, you know.'

The others laughed and they rode away.

CHAPTER 2 - KJELLE

'Look!' Birthe's joyful exclamation made Kjelle turn swiftly away from the empty expanse of sea. Ajkell was waving from farther down the beach, and Kjelle bit back a groan of disappointment. With their friend was the paladin, but no Muus. Automatically he looked back towards the water.

'Come on,' said Birthe urgently and Kjelle nodded. Gripping the girl's hand, he forced his stiff body into an awkward, squelching run.

'You're safe!' Ajkell clasped Kjelle's arm in an unaccustomed display of emotion that made the Holderling ashamed. Then he caught Birthe and the baby on her back in a bear hug. 'The little man came through all right? He's a tough guy, that son of yours.'

Birthe smiled. 'He's fine, slept most of the time.'

'Have you seen the Prince?' Paladin Valiantrude looked angry, and curiously different without her armor. Her always neatly braided hair had come undone and hung wetly down, almost touching her buttocks. 'He must be dead, then, because he couldn't swim. Damn, triple damn; I lost him. What am I to tell the Queen?' For a moment, her eyes misted over. 'He often angered me, but he was a good lad and a fine fighter, young as he was. He will have died bravely.' She shook her head and walked a few steps away, staring at the sea.

'She takes Ottil's loss hard,' said Ajkell. 'I've never seen a woman so angry as when she realized her pupil was gone.'

Kjelle sighed. 'How did you get here?'

The bear warrior pointed to the ship's boat lying half on the beach. 'When the *Madgund* struck those reefs, the ropes that held the boat down snapped. A wave lifted up the boat and transported it into the sea. A sailor jumped into it, and I followed. We managed to fasten the boat's line to the railing of the ship and went for the others. The *Madgund* lay wedged on the rocks, moving only slightly without her mast. With the paladin, the captain, the last five of his men and me, the boat was a bit crowded, but the sea carried us straight to the beach as if she wanted to get rid of us. Once on land, we found our saviors waiting.' He gestured toward the rocks, and only now did Kjelle see the strangers, three men in sober robes, standing with Captain Gunthchramn.

'Who are those people?'

Ajkell smiled. 'They're the merchant Theodgard of Harflot and his assistants. Come and greet them.' They walked over the wet sand to where the men waited.

Kjelle clasped Gunthchramn's arm, but the captain didn't look at him. His eyes stared out over the sea, searching.

'The good captain is in shock,' said one of the merchants. 'The loss of his ship hit him hard.' The speaker was an older man, with a careful mustache and incongruous gray stubble on his chin.

'Master Theodgard,' said Ajkell. 'This is Holderling Kjelle of Eidungruve. The girl with him is the Völva Birthe with her baby son Búi.'

Theodgard offered his hand in a hard grip. 'Glad to see you three safe,' he said in almost fluent Nordish. 'I've seen many a storm at sea, but this was a nasty one. I'm glad we found a place to ride out his wrath.'

Kjelle stared at the trim merchant ship at anchor in the cove. 'Where are we, Master Theodgard?'

'We're on the coast of Brytanna; on the other side of the Narrow Sea is Frisia. It's not a safe place for men of the Norden, Holderling. Your Viking countrymen have stirred up an enormous amount of ill will against Nords.'

'Bearjaw Largassen again, the cursed dog,' said Kjelle.

'I know of that one.' Theodgard stroked his unshaven chin. 'He has an ugly reputation.'

Kjelle growled. 'He's a murderous dog.'

'Quite. Well, I'm about to sail for Harflot. I can offer you transport, for a modest sum of gold.'

'I have to discuss this with the Völva; she holds the purse-strings.'

'These things are a woman's business,' said the merchant gravely. 'A real Nord won't demean himself with money.'

Kjelle eyed him suspiciously. 'Well, it is her money, after all.' He led Birthe away. 'What do you think?'

Birthe raised her eyebrows. 'You're asking me?'

The Holderling clenched his fists. 'Yes! I want to go and search for Muus,' he said. 'But I realize I can't. This is hostile country. I don't speak their babble, so I wouldn't get very far. I can't risk that; I have my oath of revenge to think of. There is no alternative now; I must go to Rhemes, to Jarl Dettrich, if he's indeed there.' He swallowed, not bothering to hide his despair.

Birthe stared at him. 'Muus and Hraab will be all right. The magic protecting those two is very strong. I don't know about the Prince, but I think Hraab will look after him.' She closed her eyes for a moment. 'Everything around Muus is misty, broken, and unclear. It's giving me a headache. Let's go to Gaul.'

'Do you have the money?'

'Don't be a fool, of course I have. It's securely wrapped in with Búi. Now, let me bargain with this master merchant. I'm sure I won't agree to his price.'

'You're a sharp dealer, girl,' said Master Theodgard when they finished. 'You negotiate like an old hand.'

Birthe shrugged. 'I learned from my father. He was Bearjaw's accomplice for years, the fool.'

The old man looked at her sharply. 'Who was your father?'

'Gude,' she almost spat the name. 'Gude the Viking, from Helmshaven.'

'You should show him more respect. Gude was Skid Largassen's conscience. Bearjaw's rampaging began only the year your father stayed at home. Why did he do that?'

Birthe clenched her jaws. 'My mother was seriously ill and he wanted to be with her.'

'So that was it. A pity; without your father's restraining presence, Largassen ran wild. Largassen was a knave, but not Gude. You should honor his name.'

'I can't!' she said. 'He abandoned me.' With an angry twist of her head, she turned and hurried away.

'Your pardon,' said Kjelle to Master Theodgard and followed her. He caught up with her on the wet sands. 'Hey,' he said, gripping her shoulders. 'It's all right.'

'No!' She shook her head. 'It won't ever be all right again. My father left me, Barn left me, I'm all alone.'

'You're not. I am here and...'

She twisted out of his hands. 'You!' she spat. 'You're a coward, a nothing.' Then she walked back, leaving Kjelle standing on the beach.

The Gaullish merchant ship sailed on the tide. Kjelle leaned against the railing and stared out over sea at the disappearing coast of Brytanna. Darkness hung over his soul, a feeling of betrayal for leaving Muus, and for breaking his promise to go with him to Falrom.

'Kjelle?' Slowly the voice at his shoulder penetrated through his somberness. 'Are you still mad at me?'

He turned around and looked at Birthe. 'No.' A little of his darkness lifted.

Birthe grabbed his arm. 'It was a stupid thing to say. You saved my life, pulling me onto that hatch door and keeping me close. You were very brave and I... I'm sorry.'

Kjelle smiled a bit. 'It's all right, really. I've been a coward all my life. Muus made that very clear to me. I never wanted to admit it, even to myself. Now I do, and guess what? I'm running away again. I know I'm failing him.'

'You're not.' Birthe wiped her tears away. 'Muus isn't in any danger. He had to go to Brytanna. Asgisla told him; his magic is there.' For a moment, she was silent. 'I think it was fore-ordained.'

Kjelle found himself staring at her. 'The whole storm?'

'Where the Shardheld goes, there are mighty powers at work.'

'You don't say Muus caused that storm?'

Birthe's face was serious. 'Not he. The shard could have done it, or the Gods, or even the Kalmanir. Muus will be fine; don't worry.'

The weather stayed calm and after three days, they sailed into the Senne estuary, towards Harflot harbor. Sun had driven most of the clouds away. Her rays touched the houses, the quays and the many ships, making the old town look nearly cheerful. They took their leave of Master Theodgard and stepped from the ship onto the soil of Gaul.

'Well, finally we're here,' said Kjelle, as he stared around at the busy port. 'It's bigger than Helmshaven.'

Ajkell laughed. 'Compared with Harflot, Helmshaven is a hole.'

'But we come without the Prince.' Lady Valiantrude's face was stern, with lines that had not been there before.

'It wasn't your fault,' said Kjelle. 'The Queen can't blame you for a God-made storm.'

The paladin pressed her lips together. 'I've known Leocastre for twenty years, and believe me, she can.'

Kjelle thought of Jarl Dettrich and wondered about his own reception. To lose Eidungruve was as bad as losing Prince Ottil. He rubbed his forehead as if to wipe away his worries. 'We're here, so what do we do now?'

Valiantrude sighed. 'We need a river boat.' She led them through the throng of longshoremen, sailors, merchants and passengers to a separate quay. She pointed to a long, low barge with a roofed section amidships. 'I've sailed in that one before. The skipper is a reasonable man and not overly grasping.'

Birthe nodded firmly. 'Fine, let's talk with him first.'

The captain of the good ship *Belamie* was a potbellied Gaul from Armorica. After some haggling, Birthe booked passage for them to the small island settlement of the Parisi.

'How long till we're there?' asked Kjelle.

The captain tugged his drooping mustache, stared at the sky and said slowly, 'If the weather holds, five days, Lord.'

The five days seemed endless to Kjelle. He had nothing to do but eat, sleep and watch the scenery. The food the *Belamie* provided was a portion of soup, bread, fish, some sour cheese and thin wine -- not an adequate meal for a person of his size. Besides, he was tired. Sleeping was difficult on the *Belamie*. They never shared the cramped boat with fewer than twenty other passengers. On the second day he tried to walk around the deck, in order to move at least a bit, but the other passengers resisted him strenuously and only the presence of stern Ajkell at his back prevented trouble.

On the fifth day, the wooded riverfronts gave way to marshlands, high reeds with here and there a solitary tree. The winter had been mild this year, with an early thaw, and there was an abundance of wildlife. Herons posted as one-legged sentinels, guarding ducks and swans. Images of stuffed goose filled his food-starved mind.

'We're almost there, Lord,' said the captain, stooping to look at his passengers under the low roof. 'Another hour and we'll be at the Parisi Isles landing.'

'Good.' Kjelle stretched in the narrow, curtained off piece of the deck that was theirs. 'I'm getting stiff.' He walked to the railing and stared at the approaching town. There, in the middle of the river, lay the two islands that together formed the land of the Parisi. Both were rocky, filled to the edges with wooden houses. There was a solitary red mill, its vanes turning slowly, and above all rose the large stone castle, gloomy against the grey clouds. At its foot was a jetty where the *Belamie* moored.

'Wait,' said Birthe, holding Kjelle back.

After the rowdy passengers had disembarked, the four took their leave of the captain and stumbled ashore.

'Phew,' said Kjelle. 'I was turning into stone there.'

'Oh, it wasn't that bad,' said Ajkell, yawning.

Kjelle grinned. 'No, I think you slept all the way.'

'What else was there to do? Pray, like our Lady Valiantrude?'

'I wasn't praying,' said the paladin stiffly. 'I was communing with Odin.'

'Communing with Odin?' said Kjelle, suppressing a vision of the one-eyed old God Muus and he'd met. 'That sounds rather, eh, intimate.'

Lady Valiantrude gave him a withering glance. 'Don't be vulgar.'

'Now we are here,' said Birthe, disregarding their banter, 'how do we get to Rhemes?'

'We need horses.' The paladin opened her pack and took out an iron neck chain of intertwined oak leaves. 'My uniform lies at the bottom of the sea, but I've still my Palatine order.' Proudly she hung the chain around her neck. 'It identifies me as a paladin of the Royal court. Come, let's see the garrison commander.'

At the castle entrance, the guards threw Valiantrude a stiff salute. 'The Captain? You'll find him in the Great Hall, Lady.'

With a curt nod, the paladin led them inside the walls. Across the courtyard was the keep, built from rough-hewn blocks of stone. In a small room beside the entrance, they found the garrison commander, studying a map. As they entered, he looked up, frowning at being disturbed. His face cleared when he saw his visitors. 'Paladin,' he said, saluting. 'I'm Captain Vectitos. How may I serve you?'

'I'm Paladin De Vergy, in Queen Leocastre's service,' said Valiantrude. 'I just arrived from the Norden with urgent news for her Grace. Could you supply me and my companions with mounts?'

Captain Vectitos pursed his lips. 'Who are your companions?'

'The Holderling Kjelle of Eidungruve, the bear warrior Ajkell Gudrofsen and the Völva Birthe from Belisheim.'

'A Völva?' Captain Vectitos regarded the girl with some doubt. 'Are you able to defend yourself, Lady?'

Birthe scowled. 'I have my chants, Captain,' said she coldly. 'Besides, I'm an archer, hunter trained. Do you expect trouble?'

Captain Vectitos looked at her gravely. 'Pardon the question, Lady. There are outlaws in the forest. I've my men out searching for them, thus I'm unable to come to your assistance should you get into trouble.'

'Don't worry,' said Birthe, 'We'll manage.' At that moment, Búi started to cry. Captain Vectitos lifted an eyebrow while she soothed the babe.

'It's all right, Captain,' said Kjelle hastily. 'Just the horses will be fine.'

Captain Vectitos shouted some orders and while they waited, they talked about the two islands amidst the sea of forest.

'In the days of Rom this used to be an important city,' said the Captain wistfully. 'Sometimes we find bits of old ruins way out in the woods. But that was long ago and somehow the Parisi fell behind.' He grimaced. 'They're a backwards, suspicious lot, which may have helped. Ah well, another two years and I can draw my pension. I'll go home then. Back south, after so many years. I'm from Aquitania, the land of wine, women and poetry.' He sighed. 'There's a lack of all three in these forests.'

The arrival of a stableboy with their horses spared them the need to answer. Captain Vectitos rose. 'Leave the mounts at the Royal stables; I'll get them back, Gods willing.'

They crossed the wooden bridge into the forest north of the Parisi Isles. It was raining slightly, a thin, unhappy drizzle that soaked one slowly instead of at once. The pinewoods on both sides of the highway were filled with the sound of dripping branches and their gloom infected them all.

Kjelle, riding in front, was thinking of Eidungruve, with its rows of gruesome heads staked along the entrance, and of his own need for revenge. Would the Jarl help him? Would he even believe him? What should I do if he didn't? His hands clenched on the reins.

'Jarl Dettrich will be glad to have you,' said Birthe. 'You've proven a good fighter and he'll need every man he can get.'

'He won't believe me.' Kjelle looked into the rain, afraid of Birthe's clear gaze. 'I'll never get Eidungruve back.'

'Of course you will. My lady knew you were the Holderling and I know it.'

Now he looked at her. 'Will they believe you?'

She stiffened. 'Because I'm a girl?'

'No, because you're young.'

'Idiot,' she said icily. 'I'm a Völva. Of course they'll believe me. But if you'd rather I kept silent...'

'No, please don't.' He wiped his face on his sleeve. 'I'm sorry. It worries me. And...'

'You're missing Muus.'

He lifted his hands helplessly. 'Yes.'

Birthe sniffed. 'You'll have to get used to the idea he's no longer here to lean on. Stand on your own legs.'

'I know that. It's just...' Something farther down the highway caught his attention. 'Wait.'

Without a word, Ajkell dismounted and threw his reins to the paladin. Through the edge of the forest he moved, until all of a sudden he disappeared.

Not much later, he was back. 'Outlaws. They're attacking a lone traveler. Ten men, seven left.' He jumped in the saddle and broke into a gallop. Kjelle went after him with the paladin on his heels. Birthe followed slower, riding with her knees while she readied her short bow.

Six ragged outlaws, armed with nothing more than clubs and knives, cautiously circled one small, baldheaded young man, who fended them off with a stout stick. The four limp and bloody bodies on the ground proved the victim wasn't harmless, but he was tiring and the bandits started to close in.

'For Eidun!' Kjelle's battle cry startled the outlaws and for a moment, they gaped in confusion.

Ajkell silently set his horse at the nearest one, his little ax swinging. The man went down, blood spilling from the sudden crevasse in his head. Lady Valiantrude rode into the middle of the group, swinging her sword about in deadly arcs. A burly outlaw in dirty skins, his arms scarred by countless blade cuts, knocked the bald man in a heap and turned around to meet Kjelle's ax head on. His face split as he tumbled backwards into the mud. The last bandit made a desperate effort to run, but Kjelle set his horse after him and rode him down before he'd gone far. The man's scream broke off abruptly as the mount's hooves trampled him into the ground. Kjelle felt the vomit rise at the sight of the bloody pulp on the path. He turned his horse around and rode slowly back.

Without a word, Valiantrude handed him her wine sack and he took a deep swill.

'Thanks,' he said. 'Somehow, that got me.'

The paladin shrugged. 'Dead is dead. You get used to it.'

Ajkell crouched beside the baldheaded victim. 'It's but a boy,' said he surprised. 'A hairless lad with an iron hand. Strange, he didn't seem a cripple.'

'He looks like Muus,' said Birthe. 'Only without the wild hair.' She knelt opposite Ajkell and felt the young fellow's breast. 'His heart beats strongly.'

'He's faking,' said Ajkell. 'See how his eyelids quiver.' He poked the other in the shoulder. 'Open your eyes, you're safe.'

'Am I?' said the young man. 'Who might you be then?' His eyes, large and bright yellow, like an owl's, studied them one by one.

'We're the ones who saved your ass,' said Ajkell. 'Servants of Norden's Queen, on our way to Rhemes. I'm Ajkell Gudrofsen; what's your name?'

The young man's eyes fastened onto Birthe's face. 'You're a girl,' he said, surprised. 'You're not an outlaw.'

Birthe smiled. 'No, I'm not. I'm a Völva. You're among friends, Niflung.'

At this, the yellow owl's eyes opened wide. 'You know.'

'Only your people have both eyes like yours and bald heads. You are far from home, friend. How are you called?'

The face of the bald young man relaxed. 'I'm Elbrich of the Silver Mountain, son of Bruuhl, grandson of Aayse.'

'Well met, Elbrich of the Silver Mountain,' said Ajkell. 'The Völva is named Birthe. He on the horse is the Holderling Kjelle of Eidungruve and the second lady is the Paladin Valiantrude of the Norden Queen's court. We are on our way to Rhemes with messages for Her Grace.'

'I too am underway to Rhemes. I...' Then a spasm of panic crossed the other's hairless face. 'I must see if they're still there.'

Effortlessly, Ajkell put the lad back on his feet. Elbrich whistled sharply, and a small black horse appeared from between the trees. 'Good girl,' said the lad, while he opened a saddlebag. With great care, he took out something wrapped in blue cloth. 'Weland be blessed,' said he with a deep sigh, 'they're still there.' He looked at the others. 'Can I trust you?'

Birthe smiled. 'Would it help if we said yes?'

'I'm a Paladin of the Court,' said Valiantrude, stiff-faced. 'My honor is my life.'

The young man's face was serious. 'You saved me; in return I will trust you. Come over here.' They gathered round him while he unwrapped a pair of golden upper arm bracelets. On them, graceful deer pranced through a wood, under a sunny sky.

'Oh,' said Birthe, with a strange longing in her voice. 'They're beautiful.'

The young man glowed. 'You like them?'

'They're perfect! Did you make them?'

Shyly Elbrich nodded. 'They're my masterpieces. I'm a journeyman smith, you know. These are a gift from King Leodowric to his sister Leocastre. Will the Queen like them?'

'Yes.' Lady Valiantrude smiled. 'I am certain she will. You have golden hands, young man.'

With great care, he rewrapped the bracelets. 'Should the Queen accept them, I'll be a Mastersmith.'

The bear warrior nodded. 'You will have earned it. What's wrong with your hand?'

Elbrich lifted an iron fist. 'This? It's a workhand. Every metal- or stoneworker gets one as soon as we pass our journeyman's test. It's like a glove, but much more. A mystical tool, only now its power runes are far depleted.' He smiled ruefully. 'Ten enemies were too much. After the fourth, my energies were gone. If you hadn't come to my aid, I wouldn't have killed a fifth. Thank you all, I'm in your debt.'

'You're welcome,' said Birthe. 'Are you fit to ride?'

'Sure.' The young smith climbed in the saddle. He swayed a little. 'Oops, I'm wobbling like I've been at the autumn beer with my brothers. Hold still, damned horse.' He raised his iron fist and for the time of a heartbeat a faint light surrounded him. His shoulders straightened and his strange eyes shone. 'This'll keep me going for a while.'

Birthe rode her horse next to him. 'What did you do?'

'My workhand has the power to give me new energy. That's very practical when working on a big project. I made my masterpiece in three days and three nights, without eating or sleeping. After that, I passed out for four, but the work was done.'

'Ah, that's handy, but dangerous. How long can you keep it up?'

'Eight days,' said Elbrich.

They were interrupted by little Búi, who started to scream his hunger. Routinely, Birthe plucked her son from her back and opened her tunic. At the sight of her breast, the little smith made a strained sound and hurried to the front, where Kjelle and Ajkell rode.

'Does she... does she always do that?' said he in a shocked whisper.

Kjelle looked around. 'Yes, several times a day. Why?'

Elbrich shook his head violently. 'Such things are private; you can't have everyone looking. It's like... like copulating in public.'

Kjelle looked at Ajkell and thought of the cramped conditions in a longhouse. Breast-feeding, having sex, giving birth, dying, it was all done with lots of people watching.

'You're in for a shock then,' said Ajkell calmly.

It was dark when they reached the first military rest house along the route to Rhemes. A soldier with a torch inspected them closely. When the light fell on Elbrich, he nearly dropped it. 'What's this?' he said sharply.

'A citizen,' said Lady Valiantrude, maneuvering her horse so that the torch reflected on her neck chain.

The soldier blanched. 'Of course, paladin,' he said, saluting stiffly. 'I was just surprised. I never saw someone like this... person before.'

'He is a subject of the king, soldier, just like you and me.'

'Yes, paladin. You may enter, if you please.'

It was quiet that night and they had the whole dormitory to themselves. Two rows of wooden cots, each with a straw mattress and a chamber pot, was all the comfort it offered.

'Far better than sleeping out in the rain,' said Ajkell, rubbing his hands.

Elbrich cast a doubtful eye at the dented pot under his bed and nodded.

CHAPTER 3 - NEVER LOVE ANYTHING

Eidungruve was an obscenity. The rows of rotting heads had served as meals for the ravens, but there were too many of them for the ravens to eat all.

'Ullr aid me,' said Tuuri softly. He fixed his eyes on the clear sky and marched inside. Here, it was even worse. To the right lay a heap of bodies, mostly female. Some of them had been dead for quite some time. Inside the longhouse, the men were drunk and in various states of unreadiness. Only the Warchief, Tarkynn Vulf, sat in the high chair, looking as fresh as ever.

'You again?' said he, with a sardonic grin at Tuuri's sick face.

'Orders.' Tuuri handed him the written scroll and stepped back.

'Is your tummy bothering you, little Fynnikin? You'll never be a man, I fear.'

Tuuri didn't answer and Vulf chuckled. His eyes skimmed the document. 'South!' He stared at Tuuri, a wolfish look on his face. 'And you're to go with me? Why? You're Rannar's lapdog.'

Tuuri shrugged. 'My lord didn't see fit to tell me.'

'So now I'm saddled with a raw, weak-minded child? Tell me, why shouldn't I kill you here and now?'

Tuuri froze. 'Because we serve the same master?'

'Do we, Fynnikin? Do we really?' Vulf laughed soundlessly. 'Poor Fynnikin. You're so clueless. I think I will take you along. It might be amusing.' Then he rose and kicked the nearest snoring body. 'Get up! We're off, you beasts. Wake the others, we're going south.'

Tuuri hadn't thought the Fynni in a condition to travel, but an hour later the whole horde was up and packed for the march.

Vulf looked back at the longhouse. 'Torch it all. We're leaving with the smoke to our backs.'

Eidungruve burned greedily, sending thick clouds to the sky. Vulf looked at them and turned to Tuuri. 'We are ready, but you're not.'

Tuuri had fetched his horse back from the open spot in the woods were he'd left her and now patted her fondly on the neck. 'Of course I'm ready.'

A hint of a grin touched Vulf's lips. 'If I have to take you along, at least I'll teach you our ways.' He stretched out his hand and something black spat from his fingers. The little horse caught the blackness head-on, kicked once and dropped down dead.

'No!' screamed Tuuri, as the loss tore at his heart. He crouched, ready to spring at the Tarkynn, but Vulf laughed. 'Lesson one, never love anything. Take what baggage you can carry and be quick about it.'

Ten minutes later they marched out, Tuuri last, his face stiff and his heart filled with murder. Behind him, the flames consumed the despoiled holding, burning the agony out of the soil, and the gaping heads.

CHAPTER 4 - MOIRRA

The second day out from Windiss they reached the Bloodbogs, an endless world of soggy peat, covered with purple and blood-red mosses. Small, snakelike lakes mirrored the drifting clouds. Here and there grew clumps of skeletal beeches, and tufts of orange grasses.

'From now on we'll walk,' said Gillach. 'No need for the horse and you both to drown in the mire if you misstep.'

His mates laughed at that and Prince Ottil sniffed. 'Very funny.'

The narrow trail their guides followed was only recognizable for those who knew the way.

'You'd get lost here easily,' said Gillach, without taking his eyes from the ground.

Ottil stared at the eerie mosses. 'It is creepy.'

'After nightfall, when the souls of the dead drift over the treacherous parts and the dargadul wings his way among the trees looking to suck your blood, then it's creepy.' Gillach pulled a mock-fearful face and his friends laughed.

'You're making fun of me,' said Ottil disdainfully. 'But you won't scare me.'

'Just you wait,' said Gillach. 'It's nearly dark already.'

'Where do you halt for the night? Or were you planning to walk on?' asked Muus.

The young rider shook his head. 'No, that would be too dangerous. We don't want to stray from the trail. Further on is Grimtower Hill. We can stop there.'

'How do you know which way to go?' asked Ottil. 'Everything looks the same to me.'

Gillach looked a bit uncomfortable. 'I can't tell you. It's Moirra's secret. I don't want any trouble with that girl, she's a feisty one.'

Muus smiled. He had seen the stones along their way, their position pointing the way. It was a Un-a-Dach trick. He remembered making trails like that when he was a boy playing with his friends in Owwich. How long ago that was.

The hill was firm and dry. On the top, they saw overgrown stones, showing that a building had stood here once.

'Grimtower,' said Gillach. 'It was a place of the Grim Doubh, razed nearly a century ago by the men of Yarroin.'

'Grim Doubh?' said Ottil. 'More of your spooky stories?'

But the chief's son was serious enough. 'The Grim Doubh are very real. They're fateful people, who go about naked and painted. They want to call back the Old Ones, the Gods that lived here before us. Some even used to be druids, they say.' He shivered. They sacrifice people.'

'Best not speak of it here,' said one of the other riders, his voice uneasy.

Gillach looked around quickly. 'You're right. How's that fire coming on?'

'Nearly ready,' said the third. 'It's all a bit wet, y'see.'

'Like you then,' said the second and all three riders laughed nervously.

Muus's thoughts wandered again. He'd had friends like these; guys he'd fished with, and with whom he'd played their endless games of hide and seek. No other boys had been captured, only him and a few girls. Where were the rest? Where they dead? Or had they managed to flee the village, before Bearjaw burned it all? *Largassen! You murderer of innocent people.* He knew he had to rid the earth of that poxhound. A vision of burning lands filled his mind. *Yes, I know,* he thought, irritated by the intrusion of the shard's images. *But first I must do something about Bearjaw.* The burning grew hotter till he gasped for breath, then vanished, leaving him bathing in sweat.

That night, Ottil woke abruptly. It was pitch black and several stony lumps pricked into his back. A voice called his name, stepping from his dream into reality. 'Ottil, come to me. Come, your mother awaits you. Come.' He sat up and saw, vaguely, a white clad shape moving at the foot of the hillock, as if searching. Mother? Looking for him? Noiselessly, he rose and walked down to the bogs. 'Mother?' he whispered. The white shape didn't hear him and wandered away. 'Ottil? I am here, son. Come to me, Ottil.' Without any further thought, he followed the white figure. 'I'm coming, Mother. Wait for me. Wait!' Through the low mists he stepped, oblivious to the sopping, clutching surface of the bogs, his eyes focused on the white shade and his mind empty.

'Help!' The distant cry pulled Muus from a restless dream. He raised himself on an elbow and looked around at his companions. Hraab was there. and the three riders, but no Ottil. Muus sprang to his feet. Slow daylight was spreading over the wild lands, making the patches of mist gleam.

'Help!' The sound came from somewhere in the bogs. He set his hands to his mouth and shouted. 'Ottil?' His cry roused the others from their sleep.

'Here!'

The sound came from the northeast.

'It's not far, or the wind would have blown the sound away,' said Gillach, wide-awake. 'We'll go and get him. Cut me three stakes, mates,' he said to his friends.

'Ottil?' shouted Muus. 'Where are you?'

'Here!'

'Stay where you are, we're coming.'

Each armed with a long stake, the three Windiss lads took the lead. 'Stay right behind me,' said Gillach. 'We'll test the ground for firmness, so don't stray. The bog can be deep in places.' Pricking and prodding with their sticks, the three made their way through the moss-covered land. Now and then they halted for a rest at a clump of trees or a large rock. Muus shouted Ottil's name, and his 'here' sounded closer and closer. Then they saw him, a small person standing in the middle of a deadly emptiness. He waved, and Muus waved back.

When they came nearer, Ottil stepped forward.

'Stay where you are,' shouted Gillach, but he was too late. The treacherous bottom gave way and the boy sank into the muck past his knees.

The three from Windiss increased their pace till they were at the spot of firm ground where Ottil had first stood. By now, the mire had swallowed the Prince up to his middle.

'Keep quiet,' warned Gillach. 'Don't move and don't panic.'

'I'm not panicking.' Ottil's voice sounded hoarse, but calm.

'All right, then, lean backwards.'

Obediently, Ottil leaned as far back as he could. Gillach and the second rider reached out and grabbed him under the armpits. Together they pulled and, with a sucking sound, the boy came free of the mud.

'Thanks,' said Ottil, holding out his hand. 'I'm in your debt.'

Gillach smiled. 'No matter, I'm glad you're safe.'

Muus felt his anger rise and he gripped the boy's shoulders. 'What are you doing here? What made you go walking the bogs in the dark?'

The Prince looked nonplussed. 'Someone called my name. It woke me up and I went to see who it was. But every time I neared, it wandered off and I followed.'

'Bog dreams,' said Gillach. 'I should've warned you three. Sometimes at night, the Bloodbogs get at you. Especially when you wake up. Then things happen. Strange things. Like you said, shapes that call your name, beckon to you.'

'It seemed so real,' said Ottil ashamedly. 'I thought it was...' he swallowed, 'my mother. There wasn't anything? It was all my imagination?'

'Oh, there was something,' said Gillach seriously. 'Those lights are real. Pixies bear them, and pixies have a mighty unpleasant sense of humor. You're lucky to be alive, lad.'

'I know. And I'm very grateful to you all.' Ottil bowed his head. 'I'm feeling very stupid now.'

Hraab crowed. 'Good! Remember that feeling for when you're stuck-up and proud.'

'I'm not!' said Ottil indignantly.

'Not yet.' Hraab grinned. 'I'm kidding ya, mate.'

Back at the hillock and the horses, Ottil sat down and tried to scrape the caked mud from his body. It didn't work very well, though, and Hraab smiled.

'Wait till the next river. You'll need lots and lots of water.'

Ottil gave him a dirty look but wisely kept his mouth shut.

They ate some bread the chief's wife had baked for them and shared a jar of the local sour smallbeer. When they were done, they untied the horses and resumed their journey. As they neared the center of the Bloodbogs, the sky darkened and the gray drizzle turned into sleet.

Muus shivered. 'I'd forgotten this, too. Heavy snow and freezing cold are better than this slushy wetness.'

'Was it very cold in the Norden?' asked one of the Windiss riders.

'Yes. The snow reached to above your knees and it was so cold that your breath froze into a mask of ice on your face.'

'And you liked that?'

Muus smiled. 'There wasn't much to like in the Norden.'

'Were they very cruel there? You hear terrible stories about the Viking that pillages our coastal towns.'

'Largassen? He's a beast. He was the one who stole me and some of my friends, ten years ago. Not all Norden are like him. Most are just as honest and hardworking folk as you.'

'Yeah, right,' scoffed the rider. 'And of course your master was kind and didn't beat you.'

Muus thought of Kjelle. 'The lord's son who owned me did beat me at first, but later we got to understand each other. He drowned in the shipwreck and I'm sorry.'

'I can't imagine any Bryt liking a Nord,' said Gillach slowly. 'It's very strange.'

'Ten years among them is a long time.' Muus looked at the chief's son. 'I always thought I hated them, but then they were murdered and I found I didn't really.' He balled his fists. 'Largassen is the one to hate. Don't judge the rest of them by his behavior. He's rotten.'

Later that day they reached a wooded hill, an island in a sea of red moss. At a crude wooden sign tied to a tree, Gillach halted.

'Here begins Moirra's land,' he said. 'We can't go any further; she invited you, not us. You'll have to go the last mile on your own, Runemaster.'

Muus shook their hands. 'I'm grateful for your help; we'd never have made it without you. May the Gods speed your way home.'

'May they bless you, too, Runemaster. And you, lads. I don't know what roads you walk, but let it end in glory.'

'Yes!' cried Ottil eagerly and they all laughed.

Then, with a last wave, the three riders went back to Windiss.

'Let's go,' said Muus. In single file, they followed a path uphill through the woods, until they came to a hut beside a small lake.

As they neared, a shriek came from inside and a small girl in a short dress appeared, yelling curses and waving a wicker broom. 'That boy! He's a Nord. Take him away, before I kill him' She took a swipe with her broom at Ottil's head and the boy ducked hastily.

'I'm only half a Nord,' he said in protest. 'My mother is from Gaul.'

'I still hate you. Get away. Now! Leave me.'

Hraab said something Muus couldn't follow, but his piping voice silenced the girl abruptly.

She turned to him. 'Who are you to command me?'

'I am one who has the right,' said Hraab.

The girl frowned and threw the broom into a corner. 'You are, too.' She sighed.

'Don't take it to heart, girl,' said Hraab, with a grin. 'The lad is a fairy; he can fulfill some of your wishes.'

The girl stared at Ottil, disgust clear on her face. 'The big lump is a fairy?' she said. 'Who is he then?'

Ottil, unaccustomed to being called a big lump, blinked. 'I am Ottil Vidmersen, Prince of the Norden. What is it you would ask of me?'

The girl eyed him greedily. 'You're the one who will be King? Listen then, Prince. To make our peace, I demand two things of you. One: no more Viking raids to the isle of Brytanna ever again.'

'I don't know if I can promise that,' Ottil said anxiously.

'Of course you can. The time of the Viking is over. Tell them you've made peace with Brytanna and send every restless soul to the new lands across the great sea.'

The young prince brightened. 'That's a good idea. What is your second demand?'

'I want my people to be able to return freely to our ancestral mountains, the ones you call Alfheim. Without being killed.'

'Granted,' said Ottil. 'We'll discuss mining rights later.'

'Drat it, I forgot about that. You're a clever one, Prince. For a Nord.'

Muus looked at the girl. She was of his age and small enough to fit nicely into the crook of his arm. Her hair was as black as his, and like his, haphazardly cut. What he could see of her skin was nicely pale and she had the most beautiful eyes ever.

'Well,' she said tartly, 'do you like what you see?'

Muss smiled. 'Very much.'

'Huh? Idiot. Now, come on in.' She dove back into the hut as fast as she'd left it.

Inside, it was remarkably clean. Rush lights spread a welcoming glow and a small hearth burned merrily.

'Sit down,' she said, pointing at the simple stools in front of the fire. 'You, Nord, on the floor. You're too dirty for a chair.'

Ottil plucked at his muddy clothes and sighed. 'How did you know I am a Nord?'

'Do you think I'm blind? Your whole aura shouts 'Nord'. Your Gaullish half is terribly underdeveloped. Have you ever been there?'

Ottil shook his head. 'As Prince, I wasn't allowed out of the Norden. What I know of Gaul is what my tutor taught me.'

'And that's not much. Well, I'll try not to be too bothered by your Norden aura.' Then she looked sideways at Hraab. 'I know... him. Dreamed of him often enough.' Hurriedly, she turned to Muus. 'And you. The secret one. The unreadable rune. Who are you?'

Muus said the one thing uppermost in his mind. 'I'm the Shardheld.'

'By the Three!' Moirra's voice rose again. 'Don't make jokes like that, boy.'

Muus took the shard and the little ash seedling from their pouch. Blue light filled the hut and the girl stared at the skyshard in his hand.

'It's true,' she whispered. 'And I didn't even feel it when you arrived. Oh, Mawgan...' She looked at Hraab, who winked at her. Her eyes went to Muus's face and desperation sounded in her voice. 'Why do you come to me? You must know I can't help you. I'm still searching for a new balance.'

'I know,' said Muus gently. 'There is a thing you can do for me, though. Take me to Fardoragh.' He held out his hand with the little ash seedling. 'Here, I brought you something. It's from the holy ash at Windiss.'

'Ohh,' she said and her eyes grew big. 'And you kept it with the shard? Don't you know what you have done?'

Muus looked puzzled. 'What I have done?'

'The skyshard infused the seedling with some of its powers. And you give it to me? This is a... costly gift.'

Hraab looked from the girl to Muus's face and doubled down with laughter. 'Now you've done it, my friend. And so innocently, too. Among the Un-a-Dach, a present this powerful is a bridal gift.'

Muus grew beet red. 'I didn't know that. I apologize for offending you.'

'I'm not offended, only I shouldn't keep it; you gave it in ignorance. Here, take it back.'

Muus shook his head. 'No. A gift once given cannot be taken back.'

'I must... think about this,' said Moirra. 'Meanwhile, this tiny seedling needs a bit of care.' With the little green treelet carefully sheltered in her hands, she hurried outside.

'You certainly know how to do things in style,' said Hraab. 'That seedling will grow into a mighty tree, a magical tree, through both the influence of the skyshard and the innocence of the gesture, Shardheld.'

'I don't know what you're talking about.' Muus stared stiffly at his hands. 'I feel I've made a fool of myself.'

'You haven't,' said Moirra as she came back. 'It's a very precious gift for a girl.' She'd put the ash seedling in a small bowl filled with earth and placed it on a spot next to the hearth. 'There is a leak in the roof right above it. Every time it rains, this beautiful ash will get its water.' She kicked a fourth stool towards the hearth and plopped down. 'Now, what is it Fardoragh must do for you?'

Muus told her of the spell in his head that prevented his memory from returning, of his inability to control the power of the rune and his fear of the skyshard's influence. 'It is getting stronger,' he said. 'It is trying to push me and getting emphatic about it. I need ways to control it, before it controls me.'

The girl nodded. 'Old Fardoragh must be about the only one who can help you. He's a fool, but very, very wise and runes are slippery things to master.' She hesitated and then held out her hand. 'Here, one gift should be balanced by another.' On her palm lay a finger-bone like the ones Muus already had. 'It is the Uwa'th rune, called Expansion. They say it broadens your mind. I'm not really good at it. You can take it; perhaps it will aid you.'

'A great gift, thank you,' said Muus gravely.

'It's a fair way to Fardoragh's dwelling,' said Moirra. 'We'll need horses. That means going to the Royal garrison of Ad-Cadol first. Do you have any money?'

Muus shook his head. 'Fate brought us home as flotsam in a storm. All our possessions are at the bottom of the sea.'

'No matter.' The girl went to where Ottil sat. 'Shove over, half-Nord.'

Obediently, Ottil moved aside.

Moirra stooped and pried loose a floorboard. 'How much do we need?'

Muus heard Ottil's gulp and saw him growing red. 'It's a dragon's hoard,' the boy said.

Moirra looked up at him. 'We're not getting personal, are we?'

Ottil shook his head.

'That's all right then. Be nice and bring me that cloth from the table.'

Hastily the Prince did what she asked.

'Fold it open.' She grabbed two full hands of gold and silver coins from the hole and put them on the cloth. 'There you are, Muus. Now you've started your own druid's stash.'

Muus accepted the coins. 'Is this all yours?'

'Not only mine,' said Moirra. 'It goes with the house. Generations of druids have added to it. Some of these coins are over six hundred years old. Don't worry about taking it; hardly anyone uses this hut nowadays and there's plenty left. A dragon's hoard, indeed. Only I'm no dragon!' she added, poking Ottil in the chest.

'Don't do that,' said the Prince stiffly. 'It's a liberty.'

The girl laughed. 'Don't worry, I was only joking. At least you're not scared.'

'I'm never scared.' Ottil looked at the others. 'Well, hardly ever.'

CHAPTER 5 - REUNIONS

The Royal capital of Rhemes was a large city, bordering the Vesel River and dominated by a massive castle in the center.

'Captain Gunthchramn was right,' said Kjelle. 'It looks like the king's castle at Nidros, only larger.'

Valiantrude gave him a lofty glance. 'Nidros is but a poor imitation. Its builder was a pupil of the man who designed this. Rhemes Castle is the strongest keep in the world.' She straightened her palatine neck chain and without another word, led them across the Vesel Bridge into town. She returned the salute of the guards at the gate distantly. Her face was drawn, now that the dreaded confrontation with her Queen neared, but she rode straight and proud. Kjelle looked at her squared shoulders and tried not to fidget. Fear had gripped his heart and it lay cold in his breast. A sideways glance told him that the little smith was nervous, too. Only Birthe and Ajkell seemed imperturbable. They followed a broad street paved with stones big and round as a child's head. It let them directly from the bridge to the castle, past brick houses as large as the Viking's one in Helmshaven, with painted doors and shutters.

'Rich folk here,' said Ajkell nonchalantly. He looked at Lady Valiantrude. 'You must have felt you were living in a wilderness, all those years in Nidros.'

The paladin colored red. 'At first, yes,' she said stiffly. 'But you get used to it. The court will find me changed.'

The castle gates earned her another pair of salutes. Then she led the way across a busy courtyard to a stable, where boys came to take their horses. Valiantrude looked the others over, rearranged the collar of Kjelle's tunic, straightened Ajkell's cloak, and closed her eyes for a second. With a sigh of resignation, she took them into the main building. They marched through a waiting room crowded with supplicants, gathering dark looks left and right, and entered the main hall.

The thrones were empty and Lady Valiantrude beckoned to a servant.

'The King and Her Grace of the Norden are in the Royal Parlor,' said the man. 'You wish me to announce you?'

The paladin gave a short nod.

Behind the dais with the thrones was a room, separated from the main hall by a heavy cloth.

'The Paladin de Vergy and company,' said the man, as he held open the curtains

'Valiantrude!' A tall woman with dark hair rose. The resemblance to Ottil was striking; the eyes, the chin, the same straight carriage. 'Where is my son?'

The paladin bowed her head. 'I bring bad news, Your Grace.'

The Queen blanched. 'He's dead? Don't tell me he's dead! How? Was he murdered, too? Why didn't you protect him? Oh, Ottil my son...' She rocked softly to and fro, her face anguished.

'Let the paladin make her report, dear,' said the man with her. He sat at ease, while his sharp eyes studied the visitors one by one. Seeing the little smith, his eyes widened for a heartbeat, before his gaze went back to Lady Valiantrude.

'He was not murdered, Your Grace, although he came close once or twice. After the king's death, Landesregent Brundal sought to confine the Prince, awaiting Jarl Rannar's coming. Thanks to Lord Logmar and others still loyal, he and I managed to elude the guards. With the help of our friends here, we escaped from Nidros safely. We set sail to Agdir, hoping to find Your Grace still at your estate. There, we received information that you had removed your Person to Rhemes. Therefore, we followed you; the Prince and I, the Holderling Kjelle, the Völva Birthe with her little one, the bear warrior Ajkell and several other brave souls who were instrumental in your son's rescue. Then Fate turned her other face and a violent storm arose as we were crossing the Narrow Sea to Harflot. The winds blew us onto some rocks and only the ones you see here were thrown upon the beach. There was no trace to be found of Prince Ottil or our other companions.'

The Queen's wail rang through the room as she tore at her hair and cried. 'My son is dead!'

'I don't think the Prince drowned, Your Grace,' said Birthe seriously. 'I would have felt it had we lost any of our company. They must have landed farther south and made their way inland. Searching for them would have been impossible. The local populace sees us as enemies. To let the paladin go alone, without money or possessions, would have been unthinkable. What purpose would it serve to have her end up dead or enslaved?'

'That would have been her duty,' snapped the Queen. Her voice rose. 'You have failed me, Paladin De Vestry. Get out of my sight; I have no more need of your services.'

Lady Valiantrude, her face pale but composed, bowed.

'Come with me,' said the King. 'We will leave my sister alone with her grief.' Back in the main hall, he sat down on his throne, waving away the courtiers. 'Later; let us speak in private, my lords.'

'I am sorry to bring such a message to Her Grace,' said Birthe.

'Who exactly are you, girl?' asked King Leodowric, while he ran his fingers through his black beard.

Birthe lifted her chin. 'I am the Völva Birthe Gudesdotter,' she said proudly. 'I was the pupil of the Völva Asgisla, who was brutally killed by the Fynni murderer Vulf.'

The king sat up, clearly shocked at her words. 'Asgisla is dead? That is dire news indeed. And are you a true Völva?'

Birthe showed her wand, the short iron rod that was proof of her profession. 'My lady tested and passed me herself.'

'I hope your strength will prove sufficient,' said the king. 'The future is full of strife.'

'Strife and treason,' said Kjelle. 'By your leave, Your Highness, where can I find my lord, Jarl Dettrich?'

'You are of his men? You will find Dalland some twenty miles east from here, on this side of the river. He is preparing to go back north, to oust that traitor Rannar of Westhal. Before you go, I would hear your whole story. Not just what you told my sister, but all of it.'

Kjelle bowed and told him the whole of what had passed. When he came to the Shardheld, he looked at Birthe. She nodded. 'It is better His Highness knows that, too.'

The king listened without moving. 'The Shardheld returns,' he said softly, when Kjelle had finished. 'Would my nephew be in his company?'

Birthe thought for a moment. 'That could well be, Your Highness. The Shardheld is protected; neither the Gods nor the skyshard itself will let him come to harm. If Prince Ottil is with him, he will be safe.

Though perhaps his mother's eyes will see it differently, the Prince is a capable young man. And this should take away some of the blame Her Grace laid on Lady Valiantrude's shoulders – he declared himself a man in front of witnesses, and free from her tutelage. He had his father's death to revenge, he said, and his throne to recapture.'

The king smiled. 'The rascal. I can just hear him say that. He's right; when the declaration is accepted by the witnesses, it's binding both by Nordish law and by our own. I will tell his mother. Later, when she's calmed down a bit.' He looked at Valiantrude. 'You know my sister well enough, paladin. She is upset by her flight from the Norden as well as by her changed status as a king's widow. Stay out of her way and her mood will blow over.'

The paladin bowed. 'Thank you, Your Highness. I think, by your leave, I'll go with the Holderling to Jarl Dettrich. My heart craves for action; I was a tutor overlong.'

'Go with my good will, paladin. Dettrich is a noble lord with a just cause. Do you have need of anything before you depart?'

Kjelle shook his head. 'No, Highness. All our needs are met.'

'Then I wish you all a safe journey.'

Kjelle bowed. As he turned, his glance fell on the little smith. Elbrich stood there, with his gift in his hands and tears in his eyes. The Holderling turned back. 'Your Highness, I nearly forgot our new friend here, who came a long way, bringing a great gift for Her Grace your Sister.' He shoved the lad forward. 'Here, find your tongue, smith. Your offering is grand enough.'

'Are you of the Niflunger?' said the king graciously.

The young smith looked up. 'Yes, Highness. Elbrich is my name, of the Silver Mountain I come. I bring a gift Your Highness had ordered of us some time ago.' He offered King Leodowric the wrapped parcel and stood back.

The king pulled the cloth away and stared at the two golden bracelets. 'Exquisite,' he said after a while. 'Is this your work, smith Elbrich?'

'Yes, Highness. It is my masterpiece, if you would deign to accept it.'

'Accept it? Of course I will. My sister will be delighted. I'll wait a few days before I give it to her, though. It will ease her distress. Tell your people your mastery has the king's approval, Mastersmith. What is your price?'

'No price, Your Highness. It is a gift to Her Grace.'

The king stood. 'That is very gracious of you, Master Elbrich. It will greatly enhance your reputation. I am sure the ladies of the Court will deluge you with orders. Are you going back home now?'

'I am uncertain, Highness.' Elbrich lifted his eyes to the king's face. 'This is the first time I've been out of my mountain. The world appears far larger than I had thought and I would like to see a bit more of it before I return.'

Kjelle stared at the little smith. 'Do you make weapons, too?'

'Of course. All of us do. Weapons, armor, shields.' Elbrich smiled a little. 'I can make plowshares, too, if I must. Or shoe horses.'

Kjelle felt his heart beat faster. 'Would you join us? A good weaponsmith would be invaluable.'

The smith stared into the distance. 'You're fighting Fynni?'

'Yes, them most of all.'

Elbrich's face was grim now. 'They are our enemies of long standing. In the olden days, they sought to rob us, and to enslave us for our crafts. We fled them, fought them, and hid from them. Since we came south, we haven't seen them until lately, but our hatred is still strong. Yes, I think I will join you. It would be nice to hit back at them.'

'You just made a fabulous deal, Holderling,' said the king. 'I'm chagrined at not having thought of it.' Then he smiled. 'But if I were to approach your kin, Mastersmith, would there be more who think like you?'

'Several, Highness,' said Elbrich. 'I have at least three cousins who would jump at the chance to serve away from home.'

'Excellent. I'll send an envoy at once. Now I must return to my sister. She will have need of me. Let me bid you a good journey.'

'A noble king,' said Ajkell as they stood outside. 'I see a lot of young Ottil in him.'

'Well, Mastersmith; this calls for a drink.' Kjelle slapped Elbrich on the shoulder. They walked to the tavern across the square and called to the landlord. 'Bring us wine, a bottle of your best.' And with a nod to Birthe, 'I order, she pays.'

'That's a trick my wife never learned,' said the landlord with a grin.

'Wife!' said Birthe and her eyes spat fire at Kjelle. 'I'm not your wife.'

Kjelle lifted his hands. 'Ho, that's what he said. I only meant that you're our brave Völva, who keeps good care of the money.'

The girl gave him a chill look. 'Of my money, you mean.'

Then, when the man came back with the wine, she ordered a piece of soft bread and a saucer of warm milk.

'Warm milk?' said the man surprised, but he brought her order without further ado.

'It's getting time to wean him,' said the girl as she cradled Búi in her arm. 'When we're in the field, I can't breastfeed him all the time.' She dipped a piece of bread in the milk and offered it to Búi. Obedient as a baby bird he opened his mouth and sucked the bread down.

'He's a quick learner,' said Kjelle.

Birthe gave him a dark look. 'Greedy, just like his father was.'

'Actually, I'm just as hungry as your son,' said Ajkell. 'Does your hoard stretch to a bit of soup and bread for us?'

The girl sniffed. Again, she summoned the landlord, and ordered food.

Finally, Kjelle laid his hands on the table. 'Let's go and find Dettrich.'

As they rode out of town, it started to rain. Ajkell went to ride beside the paladin, who hadn't spoken since they left the Queen's presence. 'How're you?'

'I'll live,' said Lady Valiantrude. 'You know, I find I'm not sorry to be freed from her service. I'm a warrior, not a courtier; I hope your Jarl will accept my sword, I'd be glad to be back in the field.'

A half-day later, they came to a wooden settlement, built like the stronghold at Helmshaven with a round palisade and longhouses inside the walls.

A bearded guard in the colors of Dalland barred their way. 'Identify yourselves.'

'I am Kjelle Almansen, Holderling of Eidungruve.'

The soldier's face became wooden. 'Eidungruve? I hoped we'd seen all of them by now. You're the Holderling? As far as I know he's dead. Follow me to the Jarl, and no funny moves.'

He led them to a small hut next to the main longhouse. 'Lord Jarl, here's someone who says he's the Holderling of them buggers from Eidungruve.'

'Send him in.'

The guard motioned for them to enter.

Kjelle walked forward. At a desk sat a sparse man with pepper-and-salt hair and a nearly white beard. Two small earthenware oil lamps produced just enough light for the two men to see each other's faces. 'Kjelle Almansen, Lord, Holderling of Eidungruve.' He saluted, not flinching under Jarl Dettrich's scrutiny.

'You are Alman's son? All reports say you're dead in an avalanche.'

'I am not, Lord, though we had a narrow escape.'

'Then you will tell me all. Who are your companions?'

Kjelle presented them and the Jarl greeted each of them gravely.

'You I know, Paladin. How is Prince Ottil?'

Valiantrude bowed her head. 'I lost him, Lord. There was a shipwreck. He is probably somewhere in Brytanna. It is part of Holderling Kjelle's report.'

Dettrich pointed to a crude bench. 'Sit down, all of you.' He placed his elbows on the table and laced his fingers. 'Tell me about Eidungruve. How large was last year's silver output?'

Kjelle frowned, surprised at the question. He had heard numbers, of course, but he'd never paid much attention to the business side of their holding. Still, what he managed to dredge up seemed to satisfy the Jarl, and he relaxed slightly.

'Tell me more,' said Dettrich. 'Tell me of your parents, and of the minehold.'

Kjelle spoke of his home. He told of the mother he barely remembered and of his father's wound. Dettrich glanced sharply at him when Kjelle told of his father's failing health, as if this part was new to him. Then he nodded slowly.

'And what about the avalanche?' the Jarl asked finally.

For the second time that day, Kjelle recounted the story, including the Shardheld business.

Dettrich sat up straight, his hands flat on the table. 'So your own body slave is the Shardheld? Remarkable. Did you free him?'

'Yes, Lord. As the Völva Birthe reminded me, the Shardheld can't be a slave. Besides, we were almost... friends, in the end.'

Jarl Dettrich lifted an eyebrow. 'You surprise me.'

Quickly Kjelle told of their journey to Belisheim and Swinne's attack.

The Jarl cursed. 'He did that? He should be hanged a thousandfold.'

'Yes,' said Birthe loudly.

'You were her pupil? She was a grand old lady; her death is a loss to us all.'

Kjelle went on with Ajkell's story and Jarl Dettrich's face darkened. 'What kind of people are these men of Rannar's?'

'Fynni ulvhednar, Lord,' said Ajkell.

The Jarl looked incredulous. 'Rannar hired *Fynni* to win his crown?' He shook his head. 'Go on. Your story is getting more and more grim.'

In a low voice, Kjelle told of their return to Eidungruve. Jarl Dettrich stared at him. 'So they weren't men from Herigel after all. Your fugitive clansmen thought they were.'

Kjelle's heart skipped a beat. 'Clansmen, Lord?'

'Yes, some thirty of them arrived here a sevendays ago. Harald Enske leads them, with the Wisewoman Siga. More about them later; finish your story first.'

Kjelle obeyed. 'From Herigel we went to Harkoy, to report to you, but you had already gone to the King. We spoke with the Lady Radgundis and she sent us after you. I was to present you with this brooch as proof of my words, Lord.' He took the lady's jewel from his pouch and handed it to Jarl Dettrich. The Jarl sat looking at it, turning it around in his hands. Then he sighed and carefully put the brooch away. 'Thank you. It's difficult for me, with her there. Luckily, my castle is strong and I left her enough men to defend it. What happened then?'

'We sailed to Nidros, as the lady told us. In our innocence, we asked for you, Lord. Our reception was less than cordial.'

Dettrich gave a curt laugh. 'I can well believe that. My men and I left the castle just in time. An hour later, and you'd have found my head over the gate when you arrived. But they didn't kill you, obviously.'

Kjelle grinned. 'No, they thought to keep us for Rannar. He was on his way and they were certain he'd love to offer us to the Gods. So Landesregent Brundal had us arrested.'

The Jarl made a rude sound. 'Brundal. Witless pig.'

'He had us locked up, till Councilor Logmar and his men freed us. The Councilor escorted us back to our ship on the condition that we accept two extra passengers. I'm sorry I have to report there was a fight at the quay; we don't know how it went with Logmar. We sailed from Nidros with king's ships on our heels and the artillery shooting at us. A harrowing experience.'

'I'd thought it was impossible to escape the fjord. How did you manage?'

'The Shardheld, Lord. Muus wasn't only that. He was a Brytannic Runemaster, with his memory returning. He had this little fingerbone that made terrible lightning. It sank the ships, destroyed the artillery and nearly killed Muus himself. But we escaped.'

Dettrich's eyes rested on Birthe. 'What kinds of tricks were those, Völva?'

'Male tricks, Jarl Dettrich. Very powerful ones I can't do, nor any Völva or Wisewoman in the Norden. Not since we chased away the Un-a-Dach.'

Elbrich coughed.

'And your folk,' Birthe added. 'We lost a great deal through the fear of ignorant peasants.'

Dettrich frowned. 'I never heard a Völva say that before.'

'You probably never asked her.'

Hurriedly, Kjelle went on with his story. 'And so, after reporting to the Queen and King Leodowric, we came to you, Lord.'

Dettrich's face was stern now. 'And what is your purpose with me, Kjelle Almansen?'

Kjelle stared at him. 'My father was your man, Lord, and so am I. I have sworn revenge on my kin's killers, I want the land of my fathers back and the enemies of the Norden defeated. I am here to serve and to fulfill my oath.'

'And your companions?' said Dettrich, closely watching them.

'I have nowhere else to go, no purpose with Asgisla dead,' said Birthe. 'So I'd rather stay as Kjelle's advisor, Lord.'

'I have my own oath.' Ajkell looked calmly at the Jarl. 'I failed my master once, and now I have to kill his enemies to get my honor back. I'll serve Kjelle, but I will swear no oaths as long as my old one hasn't been absolved.'

Lady Valiantrude stared straight ahead. 'My Queen loathes my face for the absence of her son. I cannot stay at court, and I want to fight again. So, like Ajkell, I can serve Kjelle, but not swear.'

'I'm no great warrior or wise priest,' said Elbrich earnestly. 'I want to see a bit of the world. I am willing to assist Kjelle as Mastersmith.'

The Jarl gave a short laugh. 'You're bringing your own staff already.' Then his face grew bleak. 'I must be honest with you, Kjelle. Your men have a bad name here. Their leader, Harald, is a good man, but he's a farmer, not a soldier, and he's old. Your people are an undisciplined rabble, not worthy to be called a fighting hird. They cause me more trouble than I care for. I was about to break them up as a clan force and use them as common workers. Now you are here, I give you the chance to shape them into something useful. I'm not sure you can do it. You are young and your own reputation is not stellar, but you're making a good impression. I'll retain you as Holderling of Eidungruve. You get one chance. Use it well.'

Kjelle saluted. 'Thank you, Lord. I'll not betray your trust.' As in a dream, he walked outside. *What's been going on here?* He stood there, with the rain gushing down his cloak, and looked at the faces of his companions. 'Thank you all for your trust. Valiantrude, it's below your rank and status, but will you act as my second in command?'

The paladin smiled. 'My rank and status... they're mud at court, with the Queen angry at me. But even if it were not so – of course I will.'

'Thank you. Ajkell, you're my bodyguard, all right?'

The bear warrior nodded.

'Birthe is my advisor. And I'm lucky to have you.'

The girl threw him a sharp look. 'Do you want something from me?'

'Of course I do. I want a lot from all of you, and from myself. Elbrich, I've no idea how we are situated for smithing. You need equipment, of course.'

The Niflung smiled. 'I'll walk around and see what's to be found here. A lot of stuff I can make myself. Don't worry; this isn't half as scary as talking with kings.'

Kjelle stared after him as he left. Then he turned to Ajkell. 'Will you go and find Harald Enske. Say the Jarl wants him. No one must know I'm here; I want to know what's going on first.'

'Wise,' said Birthe. 'Put your hood up, then. You never know who's walking around here.'

Hurriedly, Kjelle covered his head. 'I wonder what's gone wrong. My father never had problems with discipline.'

'We'll see. Let's hear first what this Harald has to say. What kind of man is he?'

'He was the foreman. Capable, with a lot of authority.'

'But he wasn't a fighter?'

'No. Never had been one, either. He's a freedman who worked himself up. With my father and the senior warriors dead, it's logical he took over.' Kjelle's face clouded over. 'It can't have been an easy task, maintaining discipline under those circumstances.'

Birthe looked him in the eye. 'Don't worry, you'll manage all right.'

It didn't take long for Ajkell to return. Kjelle was shocked to see Harald's face. The foreman had been a grizzled, ruddy man, broad-shouldered and strong. Now his hair was thin and white, his face gray and his gait uncertain. 'The Jarl asked for me?' he said. His voice had lost the assurance Kjelle remembered so well. He sounded like a man exhausted by too many woes.

'No, Harald, I did.' He pulled back his hood and watched the other's reaction. The foreman's eyes grew large and his mouth fell open. Something between hope, fear and shame passed over his face.

'Holderling?' he whispered. 'I thought you dead. That avalanche... how did you escape?'

'Muus and I went through Old Garn's tunnel.'

'So it really did pass through the mountain?'

'It certainly did.'

'And the others? Muus, Hagen and...'

'Muus and I survived. The two karls must have been swept away by the avalanche, because we never saw them again. Hagen was badly hurt. We...' He hesitated for a heartbeat. 'We gave him a Warrior's Death.'

'That's good. He was a proper fighting Nord, Hagen was. He should've been here in my place.' He looked up. 'Where's Muus? Is he with you?'

Kjelle shook his head. 'He's in Brytanna somewhere. He's a powerful Runemaster and working on a quest Fate didn't want us to share. I'll tell you more about it later. First, I want you to tell me who's with you and how things stand. The Lord Jarl confirmed me as Holderling, but he wasn't pleased with the men of Eidungruve.'

Harald sagged. 'He is right. All's not well, Holderling.'

'Let's walk a bit, while you tell me,' said Kjelle, covering his head again. 'We'll go outside; I don't want the men to know I'm back yet.'

'That's wise, Lord,' said Harald as they walked towards the gate. He stared in the distance. 'I have failed, Lord. Failed you and your father, may Odin feast him well. You knew he died?'

'I've been to Eidungruve, Harald. I've seen the dead. I'm sworn to avenge them.'

The old man nodded. 'He died bravely, fighting too many at once, ill as he was. When all was lost, I gathered the survivors and fled. Siga brought us through the Ghestland.'

'So that was you,' said Birthe. 'We went the same way and I felt the song of your passing in the air.'

'It was a terrible thought, our own ancestors hating us so. Siga sang us past them, but in the end a ghest attacked her and it sapped her strength.' He looked at Birthe. 'You're a Völva? Could you perhaps see her then, Lady?

Birthe nodded. 'Of course I will. Though I'm more a hunter than a healer, I'll see what I can do.'

'Thank you. Forty souls got out, Lord. We're all that survived, Lord.' He paused for a moment. 'We reached a fishing village on the coast and worked our way south till we came here. And all the way the hopelessness grew. The men, even the soldiers, they're no longer proud Norden warriors, Lord. They're fugitives. They hang around the barracks, drink too much, fight too often and there's no discipline. I... I am too old, Lord. I can't lead them as I ought. All my life I learned how to run the Hold, but never the ways of the warrior. And that's what I needed most, with all the leaders killed. Had Hagen lived...' He sighed. 'Fate.'

Kjelle nodded. 'That's what I gathered from Jarl Dettrich's words. He wanted to disband the force of Eidungruve and use you as common workmen. He gave me a free hand, but only one chance. So let's tell them. Harald, go and bring them here. Tell them the Jarl wants to see them. Men and women, sick, old or drunk, I want them here. Go now and let us stuff pride back into our people.'

The foreman straightened. 'Yes, Lord. I will get them and bring them to you.'

It took an hour for Harald to collect everyone and return to the field beside the fort. Kjelle, angry and impatient, seethed as he walked to and fro along the edge of the forest.

'Calm down,' said Birthe after a while. 'It takes time for them to stop with what they were doing, especially the women. You can't just leave bread in the oven or a roast over a hot fire.'

Kjelle paused. 'I hadn't thought of that.' There was more, but he didn't have to speak of his own uncertainty, his fear of failing like old Harald, of not being accepted. She probably knew all that. He stood still, facing the field, his face hidden in his hood.

Finally the foreman appeared, with his people in a ragged line behind him. Even if Harald hadn't told of their dispiritedness, it was quite clear from their shuffling feet and sloping shoulders. They stopped in the middle of the field and Harald came forward. 'They're all here, Lord.'

'Thank you.' Kjelle walked towards his people, with Ajkell at his shoulder and the two young women left and right of him. For three heartbeats, he stood there looking at them. Then he pushed back his hood.

Cries of surprise, some curses, and one or two mumbled blessings greeted him. Then he saw Siga, leaning on Harald's arm, looking pale and withered, as if she were dying where she stood. With quick steps he was with her and put his arms around her. 'Wisewoman! I'm glad to see you.' He smiled a little. 'Muus said me to tell you your dream was true, that last day. He and I in the snow, and the old one-eyed man who was Odin himself. And the raven over Eidungruve... Those things were all too true. It got worse since that day, and we have lost much, but now it will get better.'

Siga's thin hands clasped his arms. 'Holderling! I've never dreamt since that night. I don't sleep much anymore, either. Every day has been a nightmare. My powers are spent, Lord. But your return must be given to us by the Gods.'

'We'll speak again, Siga. I must address the others.'

Kjelle stepped backwards and faced his folks. Their faces were a mixture of conflicting emotions. Hope, shame, suspicion. 'People of Eidungruve,' he said. 'I've seen the Hold. Seen what they did to our home. To our dead. I have sworn an oath there, of revenge on the beasts that did it, an oath that we will return and rebuild. I believed no one had escaped and I've never been so happy to be proven wrong. You've gone through hard times, but together we're going to make it better.'

'You!' cried a bearded young man from among the people. 'You smooth-talking bastard! You're a coward! Everyone knows you're afraid of your own shadow. You're not a leader, coward. You're a joke. A Gods damned, sick joke.'

'Come here,' said Kjelle calmly. He seethed, but his face didn't show it.

The man swaggered out of the waiting mass and a deep silence fell. Kjelle handed his long cloak and his weapon belt to Ajkell and flexed his muscles. The man topped him by half a hand, he saw. But a lot of his strength had turned to flab and the smell of stale beer on his breath told him how. 'I know you, Jarrol,' said Kjelle and the man's eyes narrowed at the sound of his name. 'You're all mouth. Put up your fists, and I'll show you how much of a coward I am.' Then the Holderling proceeded to punch the bearded warrior all over the field. The sum of his anger and frustration lay behind his blows and Jarrol didn't stand a chance. When he thought the man had had enough, Kjelle knocked him down in front of everyone. 'You're an overweight fool, Jarrol,' he said. 'You're no longer a fighter.'

He stepped back and all at once, his anger overflowed. 'Smooth talking bastard? Then I'll give it to you straight. You're no Nords! You're not the tall men and women my father Holder Alman was so proud of. You're shades, almost as gray as our forebear ghests. But that's over. I swore a holy oath to revenge myself on those bastards who took Eidungruve. For that, I need warriors. Valiant men and women. So I'm going to turn you back into those Nords you were.'

He paused and glared at his people. 'Listen closely! I'm Holderling. The Jarl himself confirmed me. Here is the Lady Paladin Valiantrude de Vergy. She's my second in command. My personal guard Ajkell is a bear warrior of the Gudrofsen clan. The Völva Birthe is both my advisor and the leader of the hunt. And for weapons and armor, I have a Niflung Mastersmith. Harald, you are thanked for your services as leader. Will you serve again as foreman?'

The old man saluted. 'Yes, Lord, if you want to have me.'

'Right, then that is settled.' He looked at the crowd before him. 'Show hands. How many of you are slaves?'

Some seven hands went up.

'Eidungruve won't keep slaves. Muus taught me it isn't right. You're all freedmen, although I can't pay any one of you. All men and fighting women will report to the paladin. I want a list of names, ages, available weapons and capabilities. All those too old, too ill or too young report to the foreman. I need a list from you, too, Harald. Afterwards, those who are ill or infirm see the völva. But wait till she's finished with Wisewoman Siga. Tonight I'll inspect your barracks and the soldiers. We're going to work together and, when necessary, to fight together.' He raised his fist. 'And you all know why. For Alman and Eidungruve!'

His people repeated his shout, even Jarrol, who'd groggily rejoined the men.

'It worked,' said the paladin, after the Eidungruvers had left. 'You had the right tone, and beating that big fellow was masterly.'

Kjelle balled his fists. 'I'm glad my father can't see them like this. He never said so, but he always was proud of his warriors.'

'He will be again when you've finished with them,' said Lady Valiantrude. 'Hold up your hands, I've got a soothing salve that will quicken healing.'

'We must think up some exercises,' said Kjelle, while she spread something cool that stank of long dead meat over his knuckles.

'I'll make you a list from my training days.' Valiantrude put the salve away and wiped her hands on her cloak. 'The men won't like them, but they'll see results quickly.'

A sevendays later, he met with his staff in the small local inn as they did every evening.

'We're making progress,' said Valiantrude. 'Our people are harder and faster than they were.'

'They shoot better, too,' added Birthe.

Kjelle nodded, only half listening. 'This isn't the right place for us,' he said suddenly. 'Too cramped, too many outsiders, and I can't forbid them going to the inn forever. Harald, could you build a small stronghold from scratch?'

The old man smiled. 'Given the right tools, yes. I've led enough repairs on Eidungruve's walls not to know how it all fits together. Why? Do you plan to start your own place?'

Kjelle nodded. 'Just a longhouse, a barn, a smithy. I'll talk it over with the Jarl first.'

'You want your own fort?' Dettrich grinned. 'You're not ambitious, are you?' Then he grew serious. 'Kjelle, I'm gathering as many as I can of the people who come to join the Queen and hammer them into a fighting force. Then I'll go back to hang all those stinking Fynni, Rannar's traitors and others that raised their hand against my King. So everything we do here is temporary.' He unrolled a map and stared at it for a moment, tapping the table with his fingers. 'Go northeast. There's a river there, the Ajsne or some such. You're pretty close to the border with the Teutonic kingdom of Lotharn. The map says there's an old hill fort there. Take that one.' He lifted his head. 'Are you sure you have enough control over your folk?'

Kjelle looked his lord in the eye. 'Yes. They've always been good people and inside they haven't changed. Only their losses, the lack of leaders and the shock were eating away their spirits. I -- we gave them a new purpose.'

'Here speaks Alman's son. Have you need of anything?'

'The loan of a carpenter would be welcome, Lord.'

Jarl Dettrich thought for a moment. 'I have this barbarian. He's a Rus and one way or another he doesn't fit in very well. He's great with all things wooden, though. You can have him; I don't really need two carpenters.'

'That would be great. Harald is handy with his hands, but he can't do everything.'

'Be ready all the time,' said the Jarl. 'As soon as I'm about to go north, I'll summon you and your men.'

Kjelle's face was grim. He thought of Eidungruve and he, too, wanted nothing better than to go home. 'That's something to look forward to, Lord.'

And so, two days later, a long line of Eidungruvers left the Jarl's fort, carrying what little they possessed. Siga rode in an old cart Birthe had arranged for her. The old Wisewoman looked slightly better after her daily sessions with the young Völva.

'Craft secrets,' Siga had said when Kjelle had teased her with those sessions. 'Your Birthe is young, but she's a real Völva. I feel so small beside her knowledge. Only you must be careful with her, Holderling. She's strong, but more vulnerable than you may think.' Carefully she shifted little Búi in her lap. 'And she has such a beautiful son, too.'

CHAPTER 6 – GRIM DOUBH

The next morning they left early. Moirra doused the fire in the hearth and packed what foodstuffs she had available. Then, after a last look at the ash seedling, she led them into the wildlands.

'We'll cross the bogs,' she said. 'I know every foot of this land, far better than those boys from Windiss. I'll bring you to Ad-Cadol without secret signs.'

'They weren't all that secret,' said Muus with a slight smile.

Moirra pulled a long face. 'Spoilsport. Of course you knew, every Un-a-Dach does. Only that big lump over there wouldn't.'

'Why do you keep calling me that? I'm not big and no lump,' said Ottil.

'You're bigger than me,' said Moirra. 'Bigger than Muus and bigger than Hraab. And everyone not a Un-a-Dach is a lump.'

'Am I really?' said the Prince, surprised. 'I don't feel that tall.'

'Don't worry,' said the girl. 'I'm just teasing you. You're a well-grown lad, that's all. My people are smaller, because we used to live inside the mountains of Alfheim, digging corridors and halls, mining for metals and precious stones, which is easier if you're not too large. Nords need bulk to stay warm in the snow.'

'And to fight,' said Ottil. He had picked up a stout stick and swung it around, looking fierce.

'Yeah, that, too. If you want it the simple, uncomplicated, menial way.'

'You mean like bang, slash, you die? I'd like that.'

Moirra sighed. 'Barbarian.'

The little druidess wove them a twisted path across the dangerous Bloodbogs, all the while pointing out items of interest. She showed them edible plants, animal trails, the flight of birds that could be used in prophecies; she knew them all.

It was heavy going across the soggy lands and as dusk crept over the bogs, even Ottil had lost much of his zest. 'Where shall we sleep? Is there another hill nearby?'

'A cave,' said Moirra without looking. 'It's not far from here.'

The boy peered in the distance. 'What is that light? Not another lantern-bearing pixie?'

'Pixies don't exist.'

'They don't? Damn,' muttered Ottil. 'Those guys got me there.'

'There is a light,' said the girl after a while. 'You have sharp eyes. It's a bonfire.'

'Fine, then we can get warm.'

'Too warm, perhaps. The only people braving the bogs by night are hunters and Grim Doubh.'

Ottil stared at her. 'What is there to hunt here? I haven't seen even a rabbit yet.'

'Deer, mostly. But you're right; I haven't found signs of any animals, either. And that's bad.'

'Why?'

'It means they have all fled. No hunter is careless enough to chase his prey away, so I'm afraid there are Grim Doubh staying at the cave.'

Ottil shrugged. 'What does that mean?'

'Trouble, boy.' This time Moirra looked at the young Prince. 'They are mad people, idolaters who want the return of the cruel Old Ones, the displaced Gods.'

Ottil frowned. 'I don't know them. Who were the Gods Before?'

'The primitive powers of Earth, Sea and Sky, that got born when the world was created. Just remember -- the Gods Before are very dangerous, very cruel, and they hate us new peoples.'

'Listen.' Muus stared at the fire in the distance. Now they all heard a peculiar chanting. 'I want to see what they are doing.'

'Whatever it is, it's bad,' said Moirra. 'Those idiots chew types of fungus and herbs that bring frenzy and visitations of spirits you don't want to meet. They're very evil. Come, but be careful, I'll show you.'

They followed her till they came to a narrow, rocky dike cutting through the bogs towards the cave. When they came near the singing, the girl whispered, 'Keep your head down. With luck they are too far gone to notice us.'

Bowed low, they crept towards the camp. The fire was high and so seemed the Grim Doubh. They danced in wild abandon, their naked bodies covered in red markings. At the cave's entrance, a tall, muscled man with hair long enough to hide in leapt and jumped. He wore a large bear pelt hanging down from his shoulders and a snarling bear skull on his head. The staff in his hand was crowned with strings of dried seeds that rattled with his capering. He sang with a powerful voice and gut-wrenching intensity.

Muus felt his fingers itch. In his mind an image formed, of lighting crashing from the sky, killing the ecstatic Grim Doubh and setting their priest on fire. *No!* His denial was firm and the vision went away. Something moving behind the priest made him look closer at the cave. In the dark he saw, huddled together, bound shapes. Prisoners, he thought. What will they do with them? Then he saw Moirra's face, and the revulsion in her eyes told him. Those people were sacrifices to the Gods Before. He had seen enough, and backed away from the dancing Grim Doubh. Without a sound, the others followed.

'We've got to hurry,' said Muus. 'We must get help. That garrison of yours, they must stamp this out, free those poor folk.'

'Animals.' Moirra spat in the direction of the dancers. 'They aren't human anymore.' She froze. 'There's a rider leaving the camp! Oh Mawgan, he will certainly see us!'

The rider followed the dike faster than a sane man would, his whole posture betraying a maniacal urgency.

'Out of my way, scum,' he shouted as he came near. 'I'm the messenger of the High Priest.'

Ottil laughed, a high, boyish sound, as he sprang to the head of the horse, spread his arms wide. 'Scuuum!' The poor beast took fright from his yelling figure with its flapping cloak. The horse reared and its rider struggled to stay in the saddle. Hraab, joining in the spirit of the fight, grabbed the man by his leg and pulled him down.

'Get the horse,' said Ottil, as he raised his stout stick and cracked the man's head. The messenger tumbled down the dike, while Muus and Moirra jumped at the horse's reins. The druidess sang a few notes that seemed to calm the animal enough to stop him from running away.

'Man's down!' shouted Ottil.

'He's dead,' said Muus, checking over the body. 'You broke his head.'

Ottil didn't bat an eyelid. 'Fine. They're crazy people, aren't they?'

'Maybe, but dead men can't give information.'

Hraab sank next to the body and started to search its clothes. 'Pilfering again?' said Muus.

Hraab threw him a beatific smile. Then he held up a square of baked clay. 'You wanted information?'

It was a tablet, scribbled over with peculiar rune signs. They seemed to form a message, but none of the signs looked like anything Muus had ever seen. 'I can't read it,' he said, disappointed.

'Let me see.' Moirra almost snatched the tablet out of his hands. 'It's an old druidic code. It tells someone there will be a grand ceremony with human sacrifices when Moon is fully eaten.' She stared at the stone message. 'That's in two moons time.'

'What shall we do with him?' said Ottil, nodding at the dead man.

Moirra looked around. 'Over here,' she said, pointing at a stone sticking out of the moss covered soil. 'Dump him like he cracked his head on that rock. He fell from his horse, the animal bolted and he died.'

'Like this?' said Ottil, as he dumped the dead man into a crumpled position by the rock. 'Looks very, eh, accidental.'

The druidess laughed. 'Excellent. Now, let's get away from here.'

Leading the horse, they left the camp behind them. A sense of haste drove them on and the distance seemed to fly beneath their feet. Daybreak saw them out of the marshes, into a wooded land of birches and rowan trees.

'Caradann land,' said Moirra. 'But we won't see the village; it's to the east.'

After half a hour she reined in. 'There it is, Ad-Cadol Garrison.' Beyond them was a broad hill, bearing a wooden fort as its crown.

Muus felt a pang; the high palisade reminded him of Eidungruve. They rode towards the gate, which was guarded by a grizzled warrior. Suddenly the man's face creased into a smile. 'Druidess Moirra! It's been too long since we saw you last.'

'May the Gods be with you, my friend. Is the Warleader in?'

'Certain he is, grumpy as always. 'E's spoiling for a fight.'

'Isn't he ever? Well, we're bringing good news, then.'

The guard rubbed his hands. 'Hurry on, druidess, we can use something to kill the tedium.'

Inside, Muus saw that the stronghold was like the fort at Helmshaven, a stout palisade circling the hilltop. Only here the buildings were round, instead of the familiar longhouses. Moirra let them to a large hut in the center. Inside, a large man, bare-chested, with copper bracers on both arms, sat polishing his sword. When he saw them enter, he jumped up and spread his arms. 'Moirra! Bless the Gods for luring you out of that soggy hole of yours.'

'I was sent, Warleader Orlach. Mawgan told me to cure your boredom.'

'Double blessed is she then. Who are your friends? Rather young to be wandering the wide world, aren't they?'

'Terrel here is a full-grown Un-a-Dach, Warleader. He's a Runemaster, growing into his powers. The small one is Hraab, his cunning is far greater than his stature. The third is Ottil, a fledgling warrior from Gaul. He is of noble birth; he is not very familiar with our language, so sometimes we converse in Nordish. They escaped from the Norden and their tale is heroic.'

'Welcome, then, though there's little scope for heroics in this forsaken outpost.'

Ottil nudged Moirra. 'Have you told him about the Grim Doubh?'

The Warleader looked at the young prince. 'What did he say? Grim Doubh?'

Moirra nodded. 'We found a camp of them occupying the cave on the bogs. We killed a rider just leaving. He had a message with him. They're waiting for Eaten Moon to start their sacrifices.'

'That's tomorrow night. Time enough to surprise the foul beasts. I'll send messengers out to the local villages. If it's a full nest of them, we'll need a lot of warriors.' The Warleader gave a shout and a young girl entered. 'Bring food and drinks for our guests, daughter. They are heralds of good news.'

'You look pleased. Anyone who kicks you out of your sulks is my hero,' said the girl tartly. 'They'll get the best we can offer.'

And that they did. Bread and beer, mead, cheese, cold venison and small, sour apples appeared, and Ottil's face got greedy. 'My, I am hungry,' he said, before stuffing his mouth full of meat. Hraab followed his example. Only Muus ate sparingly.

'You're not eating much, young Runemaster,' said Warleader Orlach.

Muus sighed. 'I'd like to, but this terrible headache prevents me.'

'It's his growing runepower,' said Moirra. 'I know the feeling. Pain fills both your head and your belly. We're under way to Fardoragh's place. The Archdruid will help him find his balance.'

Muus said nothing. He knew it was the skyshard, sapping his willpower. He buried his nose in his mead horn and drank deeply, hoping it would still the shard.

That evening Orlach held his council of war. Muus repeated their report of the dancing, naked people. 'Men and women, in a state of frenzy, calling out something like *Urus Comes*.' A ripple of unease went through the attending warriors.

'Don't say that,' one of them shouted, looking angrily at Muus. 'It brings bad luck.'

'Sorry,' said Muus. 'I just tell you what I heard; I don't know what it means.'

Moirra patted his hand. 'Urus is the Old God of Earth. He created the trees and plants of bygone ages.'

'He's also called the Destroyer,' piped up Hraab. 'He creates life and uncreates it.'

'Enough!' The angry warrior slammed the table with his ax and sprang to his feet.

'There's nothing to be afraid of,' said Hraab softly and the man halted in his stride.

'I'm... not afraid.' The warrior sat down again and stared with a puzzled look at the small boy.

'You're a brave man,' said Moirra and her smile for the warrior nearly broke Muus's heart. 'You were just confused for a moment.'

Orlach coughed. 'If we're all agreed, then. We'll ride at daybreak. Remember, we rescue the prisoners and I want no Grim Doubh survivors.'

The confused warrior shouted his agreement loudest of all.

The morning came bright and clear. Young boys brought the horses and prepared to ride behind the warriors. They would care for the mounts during the fight. Some of the older lads looked with jealousy at Ottil and Hraab, who wore the accolade of adulthood and would join in the fighting. Hraab didn't appear to notice it, but Ottil's indifferent glance at their glowering faces seemed enough to set their souls on fire. The biggest of them tried to trip the Prince, but to no avail. Ottil simply lashed out with his fist and sent the other sprawling. Holding his bleeding nose, the boy went back to work. Muus suppressed a smile. The young prince had fought for too many years to stay on top in the harsh world of noble boys at the Norden's royal court to be impressed by local lads.

Shortly after, the whole warband left the fort. Muus hadn't ridden a horse since his arrival in Eidungruve, over ten years ago, but his body remembered the pony rides in his youth and his natural agility helped him to stay in the saddle. His horse followed the others and Muus looked with some jealousy at Hraab, who rode as if he'd been born on horseback, and at Ottil's princely carriage. Still, they arrived at the spot where they'd killed the messenger the day before without him falling.

'The body is there,' said Ottil. 'Just as I left him.'

'Those guys are too busy orgying.' Hraab jumped in a fair imitation of the dancing Grim Doubh and everybody laughed.

'Watch those horses,' said the Warchief sternly to the garrison lads. 'No loafing, this is a serious fight. Understood?'

The boy with the bloody nose nodded. 'I'll make sure nobody is going to play.'

'You had better. And clean your face, son. You look like you've lost the fight already.'

His peers laughed as the glowering boy rubbed his nose on his sleeve.

'Son?' said Ottil innocently.

The Warchief gave Ottil a hard stare in return. 'That no-good lazybones is my son, yes. The only one I have.' Then his face relaxed. 'That was a nice one you gave him. He earned it, too. It was no way to treat a guest, and I felt ashamed for him. But you handled it well, so no harm was done. I'm in your debt.'

His son hung his head and blushed.

Ottil opened his mouth to reply, but at that moment they all heard a terrible cry coming from the direction of the camp.

'Damn, have they seen us? At them, quick!' The Warleader started to run towards the camp, with the whole band on his heels.

'Whoop!' cried the Prince, his face flushed in anticipation of a fight.

Before Muus could react, Ottil and Hraab were gone, too. Muus looked at Moirra, who was inserting a poisoned pellet into her favorite blowpipe.

'A real Nord, that prince,' said the druidess sourly. 'They've all got brawn in their heads instead of brains.' Together, she and Muus hurried towards the camp.

They hadn't been seen. It was clear to Muus that the dancing Grim Doubh were completely surprised by the arrival of the warband. Still, they fought like beasts, biting and clawing. A painted girl with a pretty face and firm breasts danced past him, her eyes mad and her mouth dripping blood. In a flash, she sprang at Muus, snarling like an animal.

Silently, Moirra put the blowpipe to her lips. A red stain appeared between the wild girl's breasts. She screamed and doubled over in pain. A warrior hacked her down with his ax, his eyes coldly merciless. 'Die, hag!' he spat, before running on.

To Muus's horror, the pretty girl changed in death into a wrinkled old woman.

'Surprised?' said Moirra. 'They're bewitched. Some of these imbeciles are over a century old.'

A shouting drew their attention. The large high priest had raised his staff to the sky, and clouds were gathering -- black, with angry purple lining.

Moirra stared at the sky. 'That one must be a fallen Druid,' she said, and Muus was surprised at the naked horror in her face. 'He's calling a tempest.' She raised her blowpipe, but her next pellet bounced harmlessly off the priest's broad chest. The man didn't react.

'I was afraid of that.' Moirra shivered. 'He has made himself impervious to bodily harm. He must be killed by magic.' She pointed at the priest and started to chant. A soft glow spread out over the man's muscled torso and now the priest answered. He made a curt move with his hand and Moirra crumpled to the ground. Hot fire exploded in Muus. The skyshard moved the muscles in his right arm. Muus gritted his teeth. 'No!' he shouted and wrenched the control over his body back. He took the runes from his neck and lifted them to the sky. 'F'lach!' he shouted and the dark clouds were rent away. A bolt of lightning came down and hit the high priest. Many-colored light engulfed the Grim Doubh, and Muus saw his eyes open wide. His mouth tried to shout, but no sound came. Slowly, his magnificent body caved inward and withered until a husk tottered and dropped to the ground. Muus felt torn, as if mighty powers warred inside him. He cried out and dropped down, down...

CHAPTER 7 - ARCHDRUID

Ottil fondled the small club on his belt, and he was pleased. He gazed at Hraab, riding next to him, and smiled.

'Nice smasher,' said his friend. 'Where did you get it?'

'That silly son of the Warleader's gave it to me just before we left. It was his own, he said, and he'd carved the holy symbols himself.'

Hraab looked at the Prince, his eyes unreadable. 'And he gave it to you? Just like that? Why?'

Ottil shrugged. 'Perhaps he was sorry for trying to trip me. But I'd bloodied his nose already, so we were quits.' He didn't really care, either. He saw the gift as a tribute to his superior strength, and that gratified him. He straightened in the saddle and looked around. For the first time since their flight from Nidros he felt like a Prince again, mounted on a great horse, followed by the six men the Warlord had lent them. He tried to think they escorted him, instead of the small wagon carrying the unconscious Runemaster to the Archdruid.

'Feeling the great man, aren't you?' said Hraab with a sly smile. 'Quite the Royal Prince.'

Ottil sighed. 'Now you've spoiled it.' Then he laughed. 'You know, I haven't been so happy for years. At last I'm free of that silly paladin with her dos and don'ts, and of all those slimy traitors at court who saluted and honored me, all the while keeping their hand near the knife they wanted to kill me with. Hella take the lot of them, the bastards. No, I'm glad to be here.'

'They did kill your father.'

Ottil felt a rush of hot anger. 'Look, my father and I weren't close. He wasn't a good king. Most of the noblemen found him ignorant and big-headed. They were right. He hated my mother because she was much smarter than him. And he hated me because... well, because I am like my mother. I don't mind he's dead. If it had been Jarl Dettrich who had killed him, I would have pardoned and rewarded him. And if Jarl Rannar did it, I'll hang him on a tree with a golden chain to show my thanks. I can't even pretend I am sad.' Angrily he spat in the side of the road and took a deep breath. 'How's Muus?'

Hraab glanced at the cart. 'Still the same, out like a blown candle.'

'It was the strangest thing,' said Ottil. 'I never fought naked people before. They weren't hard to kill, but it was... different. Not really fun, you know. Still, Muus's exhibition was neat. He burned that creepy high priest in a good way. Pity those runes take him out so.'

He glanced at Moirra, riding next to the cart. 'She's looking peaked. Must've been a hard slap that crazy priest gave her.'

'The druidess got her own chant thrown back at her. People can die from that.'

'She's a strong one.'

'She's Un-a-Dach,' said Hraab. 'One of high degree. And she's a high druidess.'

Ottil hesitated. 'What ís a druidess? I supposed them to be Wisewomen, but Moirra seems more.'

'Druidesses and druids are much like a Völva, but they're also priests, healers and judges,' said Hraab. 'They're welcomed everywhere and their word is law. That's why a fallen Druid like that Grim Doubh priest is an abomination. They're traitors of the worst kind, betraying a holy trust.'

'You're serious,' said Ottil surprised.

'On the subject of Grim Doubh I'm deadly serious. All followers of the Gods Before are beasts, to be killed on sight. Grim Doubh, Fynni, whatever they call themselves, are enemies to the whole world.' Then Hraab's face relaxed. 'Moirra is a puissant lady, boy. I'm not sure she doesn't outrank you.' He gave Ottil a poke. 'Don't gape; we Un-a-Dach have our ranks, too. Going back for thousands of winters.'

'What's your rank?' said Ottil, on impulse.

Hraab grinned broadly. 'Is that important?'

'Not really.'

'Ask me again when all this is over,' said Hraab. 'Perhaps I'll answer.'

Around noon the fourth day, they entered a dark wood of large trees, many of them oak, bizarre trees with twisting branches that swayed without wind. In between the trees, large patches of bracken, looking dead and brownish, waited for the sun of spring. Muus was still unconscious, but his friends trusted Moirra's assurance that the Archdruid would be able to help him, so they didn't worry too much.

'Through the bend is a path to the right,' said Moirra. 'It should be wide enough for the cart. Try to hurt the trees as little as you can.'

The leader of the warriors nodded. 'Understood, druidess.'

'Nervous?'

The man laughed a bit sheepishly. 'They say the archdruid is a strange man, and unpredictable.'

Moirra laughed. 'He is. But he won't hurt you, don't worry. As long as you are very careful with his trees.'

'We'll do our utmost, druidess.'

After a while, they came to a clearing with a large white tree.

'Wait here,' said Moirra to the others. Quick as a deer, she disappeared between the oaks.

Ottil glanced at Hraab and sighed. 'We wait. I hate waiting.'

'That's because you don't use your time properly. Waiting time is thinking time. Use it to think out some problem.'

The Prince pulled at his face. 'That's the last thing I want. I'll go thinking about my mother and I'll get all unhappy inside. Or I think of Rannar putting his flea-eaten behind on my throne, and I get so mad I could scream. I don't know what to do.'

'Do you want to go to your mother?'

'Yes, and no.' He grinned but there was no mirth in his face. 'Here I'm a man. Should I go to Rhemes now, I would become a boy again. My mother would keep me by her and Valiantrude would watch me twice as close. And I can't go home and handle Rannar on my own, for the same stupid reason. No nobleman of the Norden would accept me as commander. They'd say I'm too young.'

'And they would be right.'

Ottil's eyes bored into Hraab's. 'I know that. I'm better off here, getting experience.'

'You're not stupid,' said Hraab.

'No. I told you that's why my father hated me. I'm not stupid and he was.' He gripped the reins of his horse.

'You see how easy that was? Think and your problem is gone.'

Ottil laughed, relaxing. 'You twisty little beggar.'

Then Moirra came back, accompanied by a bent man in checkered trews and a greenish cloak. He had a staff of the same twisted oak that grew around here, and he looked as old. He walked to the wagon and studied first Hraab and then Ottil. What a strange eyes he has, thought the Prince. Like pools of molten ice with the light of the sun in them. Laughter light. He smiled and the old man smiled back.

'Welcome,' said he in nearly flawless Nordish. 'Warrior Prince.'

'The blessing of the Gods and the non-Gods upon you,' said Ottil, giving a traditional greeting he had picked up during their stay at Windiss.

Archdruid Fardoragh chuckled. 'Polite, too.' Then he turned to Hraab. 'A welcome to you, child of mischief.'

'Me?' The innocent glance Hraab gave the Archdruid would have deceived the most suspicious onlooker, but Ottil knew him by now. He wasn't surprised by anything his friend did. Nor, apparently, was the Archdruid, for he laughed softly. Then he turned to the leader of their escort. 'You are thanked for your vigilance, soldier of the High King. You can take back the wagon, but leave them their horses.'

'Leave the horses?' said the man. 'But they are the garrison's; I'm supposed to take them with us.'

'The Runemaster and his companions need them. Thank the Warleader for his assistance.' He turned to the boys. 'Please carry the Runemaster to my cave, will you?' With a dismissive nod to the warrior, the Archdruid led the boys via a small path to a dark entrance into the mountain.

Inside, the cave was large and surprisingly well furnished. 'Put him on the bed,' said Fardoragh.

Ottil knew his face was red and sweaty. 'By Thor, he's heavier than he looks.' With a heave, they dropped the unconscious Runemaster onto the cover. Then he wiped his brow with his sleeve. 'Can you make him better?'

The Archdruid glanced at him. 'Can I? If you mean this shock he's in, yes. If you mean, better with his power, no. He has to walk his own road, just as Moirra must. I can teach him some tricks to help him along the way, but first I must wake him up.' He pointed at a large kettle. 'Get me some water from the fall outside.'

Sighing, Ottil picked up the copper kettle and stepped out of the cave. Looking around, he heard the sound of rushing. Then he spied a clear little waterfall, hidden behind a spray of golden flowers. It was only when he had filled the kettle and was halfway back to the cave that it dawned on him that all the plants in this small spot were flowering, and all the trees had a full head of leaves, as if it were summer already.

Once inside, he hung the kettle over the fire. Immediately, the flames burned higher. Ottil gave the flames a cold stare. Then he looked at the Archdruid. 'Are you finished speaking secrets, or is there more for me to do that your powers could do faster?'

The old man chuckled. 'He is indeed smart. You are right, young friend; forgive me for the subterfuge. How did you guess?'

'Your forecourt is blooming in winter, your fire takes care of its own heat and I'm sure your kettle can fetch its own water.'

'True, it usually does. We three had to exchange some secret information of concern to the Druid Circle. We are a rather secretive bunch, I'm afraid.'

Ottil looked pointedly at Hraab. 'You are not a druid, are you?'

Hraab managed to look a bit shamefaced. 'My father was.'

'Your father? A druid in the Norden? You were spies!'

The red in Hraab's face deepened. 'Not spies. Agents of the Un-a-Dach. Your Gods knew we were there, as did the Völva Asgisla. Your father didn't, of course. We were just watching and waiting for a chance to arrange a return to the Alfheim Mountains. Your father wouldn't hear of it, or your grandfather before him. They were fearful kings. I'm glad you are not, Prince of the Norden. My people want to go home.' He studied Ottil's face. 'Are you mad at me now?'

Ottil snorted. 'Of course not. Are you certain you're not a druid yourself?'

'I can honestly swear I am not a druid,' said Hraab solemnly. 'May the raven of my name steal my tongue if I lie.'

Ottil gave him a suspicious look. 'Yes,' he said. 'All right then. Now what are we going to do?'

The Archdruid looked up. 'Is the water boiling?'

The Prince glanced at the kettle. 'It is. That's one fast-boiling fire, Master Archdruid.'

Fardoragh winked at him, before turning back to the matter at hand. 'Moirra, m'dear, show me how far you've come.'

The girl sniffed. 'Me? Then at least, it will be potable. I remember most of your potions taste awful. Let's see what you have in stock.' She rummaged through the chests and cupboard drawers and sniffed again. 'What a mess. Can't you clean up once in a while?'

'I'm missing your clever hands, dear. My things have never really learned to stack and stash themselves.'

With a deep sigh, Moirra started mixing a potion. Ottil soon lost interest and wandered outside. Hraab followed.

'What's going on?' asked Ottil bluntly. 'There are all kinds of things happening and I don't understand a bit of it.'

'Then I'll let you in on a secret, neither do we.'

'We?'

'Moirra and I, and I suspect old Fardoragh doesn't either. Don't break your head over it. There is only one important thing; the Shardheld must reach the Kalmanir. If we are the ones to help him, then we'll do so.'

'You never told me what's so important about that stone and the skyshard.'

'Muus doesn't like talking about it. The Kalmanir holds all the magic in the world. It's nearly empty and the Shardheld is the one who has to fill it.'

'That's all? Go there, refill it and go home? Where is that Kalmanir?'

'In Falrom.'

'Oh.' Ottil was silent. Falrom he knew about. A whole country, the most powerful empire in the world, wiped out by volcanoes, lava streams and terrible earthquakes. 'We must go there?'

'Yes.'

He sighed. 'Then we'll do so. We'll die, of course, but it'll make for a great song.'

'Not so somber, young Prince.' The Archdruid stepped from the cave and smiled at the two boys. His strange eyed warmed up and Ottil felt the gloom in his heart lift. 'No one has to die. Falrom is dangerous, but the task is not impossible, merely difficult. The Shardheld is asleep now, but tomorrow he will be well enough to begin his training. For you two and Moirra I have another task.'

'More water fetching,' said Ottil with dismay.

'My kettle won't work well without supervision, so yes, I need your hands to hunt, fetch wood and water, boil and toil.'

'At least we won't die from that,' said Hraab.

Ottil pulled a face. 'Die of boredom, probably.'

Muus awoke on a bed in a strange room. A shadow fell over him and he stared in two eyes of blue so pale that they would look like pure frost, were it not for the golden specks in them. Laugh lines took the cold from them, as did the red cheeks and the round, old face. Who?

'Ah, the Shardheld is awake. Welcome to my home, Terrel of Owwich. Or do you prefer Muus of the Norden?'

'Muus. And who are you?'

'Fardoragh am I. Archdruid they call me, but the title is not of my choosing. I'm but a student of Nature's wonders, and she has given me knowledge. Nothing like the vast powers of the skyshard you bear or of the stone you seek. Those are mighty enough to rock the stars.'

'Fardoragh. You are the one I sought.' He remembered seeing Moirra fall under the spell of the Grim Doubh priest. 'How is she?'

'Moirra is a tower of strength. She will go far, that young lady.' The old man's eyes laughed at Muus. 'You are a sly one, giving her an ash bough with a whisper of the skyshard. No surer way to bind a Un-a-Dach druidess to you, my friend. They adore trees.'

'I didn't know that,' said Muus.

'Perhaps you only thought you didn't. No matter, it is done now. She will go with you to the end of the world and further, if you ask her.' He cocked his head. 'How do you feel?'

Muus thought. 'All right, I guess. Confused, but I've been that since I picked up that piece of sky.'

'You are not the only one. I assure you it caused great dismay in the druids' Inner Circle. My learned brethren were walking around tearing their hair out.'

'Why?'

Fardoragh grinned, showing strong white teeth. 'The skyshard didn't land where it was supposed to. Through their arts, the Circle can predict Shardfall. That gives them time to prepare someone for the task. They've been doing it for ages, every half-millennium.'

Muus didn't know the word. 'How long is that?'

'Five hundred years. The Shardheld Saga is thousands of years old.. Only this time my brethren were wrong. The skyshard landed where it wasn't supposed to and was picked up by one unprepared for it.'

'Me?'

'You. An ignorant slave, living in the most backward place imaginable.'

'Thank you.'

The Archdruid chuckled. 'Lad, the Norden are not the center of civilization. Dalland is a snowy waste, and with all respect, your knowledge of the mystic world could drown in a blob of spittle. But all that is no longer important. You are the Shardheld and we must prepare you as best as we can. Fortuitously - or perhaps not, with the shard you cannot tell – you have a curious background. You're half an untrained druid and half a Un-a-Dach. An uncommon combination, my friend. The Un-a-Dach don't mingle easily with folk not of their kind. Your father was an Archdruid and your mother - she was a bit like Moirra. Eager, able and headstrong. It is her geis we have to undo.'

'Can you do that?'

'Not all at once, no; that would shatter your mind. We'll be careful and spread it out over a few sevendays.'

'Those damned runes!' said Muus, looking at the vague burn scars on the back of his hand. 'How can I use them without setting myself on fire? I'm getting pretty tired of that.'

'That's the easiest thing of all. You have three of them. F'lach the Lightning, U'th the Expander and A'yin the Protector.'

'That's the one my mother gave me. It never did anything.'

'You probably never noticed what it did. A'yin's power is to protect you against mystic harm.'

'But F'lach still burned me.'

The Archdruid sighed. 'Muus, the Lightning Rune obeyed your commands because you gave them aided by the skyshard. It was forced to obey and it didn't like that. So it lashed back at you and you got hurt. Had you not worn A'yin, the lightning would have fried you the first time you used it. You should never command a great rune directly. Instead, you ask A'yin to do it for you.'

Muus stared at him. 'That's all?'

'That, my friend, is all.' Fardoragh stood. 'Go outside and practice.' Then he looked at Muus. 'There are fourteen of these little fingerbones. Fjinge's Knucks they are called, and they are very old. Fjinge was a servant of Kalman himself, at the beginning of time. His Knucks are nigh on indestructible, so do not be afraid you might damage one. Now go, I must meditate.'

For the next month, Muus worked. Usually a session started with him and the Archdruid holding hands, while Fardoragh chipped away at the barrier in Muus's mind. Each time, Muus felt a piece give way and images came out. Memories, names, lessons -- things that needed a place in his head, that needed to be recognized, categorized and digested. Some of the memories were painful, such as the images of his parents' death at the Vikings' hands and the murder of Owwich's villagers. Those made him cry, and for two days the sessions stopped.

'I never could see their faces,' said Muus, as he and Moirra walked down the path to the woods. 'But I didn't forget them either. They kept coming to me; shapes in my dreams, faceless and unknown. They gave me nightmares, those strange faces. I knew they wanted to tell me something terrible had happened, but I didn't know what.'

'Perhaps your mother never fully realized what the Protection Rune did,' said Moirra. 'It couldn't undo her geis, but it weakened it. And so bits of memory remained, floating like dust motes in your brain.'

Muus halted so suddenly that Moirra nearly stumbled. 'A'yin was given her by a God. That's what she told me, not long before it all happened. Iowynh, God of Magic, had appeared one day shortly after I was born and gave it her. As soon as I could walk and leave the hut mother gave me the rune to wear.'

Moirra gave him a sidelong glance. 'Iowynh? *The Trickster God* gave it for you to wear?' Somehow, she had to laugh a bit at this, but she refused to say why.

Muus accepted her silence. 'It was terrible to see the smoke pouring from the houses and the barns. After that, we sailed away, straight into a storm. For days and nights it went on, raging and blinding us. I stood at the mast, the whole time. I wasn't scared, couldn't cry or scream. I had no emotions at all; there was emptiness inside me even the storm couldn't fill. Was I alive, these days? I hardly ate, hardly slept. Only when I arrived at Eidungruve, sitting in front of Hagen on his high horse, I started life again as a slave.'

After that day, his recovery went faster. Now that his walls had been breached, the present took possession of the remnants of his memories, until after a while Fardoragh stopped holding his hands.

'We're finished. You are yourself again, so far as I can help you. The last bits will break loose by themselves. Now you'll have to make plans.'

'What plans?' said Muus, as he dragged his mind away from his memories.

'You must find the other runes. As many as you can. I have been meditating on this and I have a few suggestions. First of all, pay a visit to Cucharann in King's Lud. Ah, your blank looks betray all. You've never heard of Cucharann. Well, many of us wish that they hadn't either. He is the High King, and useless. The one to meet in King's Lud is the Royal Druid, Tyllas. He's not very important either, a courtier more than a druid. But there is a story about a Wiseman using an amulet somewhere near the capital that sounds like it could've been a Knuck. Tyllas ought to know all about it.

'After that, you go to the Great Temple and see Arraw, the High Druid. He's all right; he's the head of all the druids. I'm sure Arraw has one of the fingerbones. And he should know where some of the others might be. Next, if at either place you run into the Oaken Bard, Vyvain, speak with him as well. He's the Circle's Masterbard and he sees and hears everything. If you chance on any more Grim Doubh, kill their priest. I'm almost certain one of them has a Knuck.'

Muus nodded.

Fardoragh's smile grew bigger. 'Some of the Knucks went to the mainland. Those will be difficult to trace, but one thing works to your advantage. The more Knucks you have, the easier it will be to find others. They call each other, you now. They want to be reunited.'

'Join the Shardheld and see the wooorld,' sang Hraab.

Muus was not amused. 'I really have to do all this? Can't I just go to Falrom directly?'

'No,' said Fardoragh. 'All the legends point to the same condition for success: You need a certain level of proficiency in order to enter the caves under Falrom. You haven't reached that level yet.'

The next morning they saddled their horses, ready to leave.

Moirra stood looking at them, her arms folded and an unreadable expression on her face.

'What is it?' asked Muus. 'Don't you have to pack?'

'Why?'

Muus felt the color drain from his face. 'We're leaving.'

'You're leaving, yes.'

'But... but... aren't you coming with us?'

'Did you want me to?'

'Of course, I...' Suddenly he remembered what Fardoragh had said, talking about Moirra and the ash bough – 'She will go with you to the end of the world and further, *if you ask her.*' He let the bag in his hands drop to the ground and hurried to her. 'I took it for granted you would come with us. Please, Moirra, I am going away. It will be a long, hard and dangerous journey. Please, will you come with me?'

'Long, hard and dangerous? Strange arguments you use to invite a girl.' Then she smiled and the lump of ice in Muus's stomach melted. 'Of course I'll come with you.' She looked at his horse. 'Haven't you started packing yet? We're going today, boy, not next sevenday. Why don't you go and saddle up?' Muus gaped at her while she laughed. She whistled and her horse trotted from between the trees, all packed and ready. 'I'm always prepared.'

Half an hour later, they took their leave from Archdruid Fardoragh. 'Here,' said the old man. 'I wrote you an introduction to the Royal Druid. Perhaps my name is still worth something at court after all these years in seclusion.'

Muus thanked him and put the wrapped tablet in his saddlebag. They shook hands in the curious, reserved way of druids and left through the trees, down the path.

CHAPTER 8 – ALMANSFORD

Kjelle's scouts found the river easily enough. Swift and clear it ran over a stony bottom. It was too deep and strong to cross, yet not deep enough for a riverboat. Following its banks eastward, they reached a low, grass-grown hill that must have been built to guard the nearby ford in the river.

'That must be it,' said Kjelle, staring with some dismay and the ruined walls and dilapidated buildings. 'It looks a hundred years old.'

Harald rubbed his hands. 'Not to worry, Lord. There's wood a-plenty. Let's have look.' He beckoned to his mate, a handy fellow he'd chosen to do much of the legwork, and went to inspect the palisades.

Kjelle stepped inside the walls. Looking around, he sighed. 'What a ruin.'

'It was a proper stronghold,' said Lady Valiantrude. She stuck her knife into one of the posts of the main building. 'This wood seems solid enough.'

'It doesn't have a roof.'

'We can make another one.' They entered what had been the communal area. 'It is plenty large enough. There are several fire pits, too.' Something creaked ominously and Kjelle jumped backwards.

The paladin grinned.

Harald returned, rubbing his hands. 'This place doesn't look very promising right now, but give me a tenday and it will be as good as new. Most of the walls are fine and there's forest to replace what's rotten.'

Kjelle sighed deeply. 'All right. Give your orders, foreman.'

The old man saluted. He turned to the Eidungruvers outside. 'We've a new temporary home to restore, so listen well for what your task's goin' to be.' He called out names. A team to clean out the rubbish, another to start cutting new poles, a third to remove the rotten parts of the palisade. Every man and woman named put away personal belongings and went to work.

Kjelle saw Jarrol digging a hole for a new pole. 'It's good to be doing something, Lord,' said the man. 'Those empty days were killin' me.'

'I promise you no more empty days, friend,' said Kjelle.

Siga was overseeing the cleaning-out of the cooking place. 'If you're looking for Birthe, she's gone out hunting. There's deer in the neighborhood; I'd fancy a nice bit of venison.' She cackled, and Kjelle, remembering her as she had been before the avalanche, cringed.

He turned to Ajkell. 'Let's go explore a bit.' He signaled the paladin his intentions and went to get his horse.

The wood on both sides of the stronghold ran almost into the water, forming a nearly impassable barrier. It was a wild, green wall, stretching out as far as they could see. The path they had followed crossed the river at the ford, and thus they rode through the swift waters towards the other side.

It was quiet among the trees. There was hardly any wind and only an occasional bird called a greeting. The path was narrow, overgrown with brambles and low-hanging branches; no one had come this way in a long time. There were plenty of hares, though, running out from the bushes and Kjelle made a note to tell Birthe about them. After a half hour, they came to a fallen tree blocking the path.

'End of the way,' said Kjelle. 'No getting the horses past it. We'd better go back.'

'Wait,' said Ajkell. 'I see grass. There' must be an open spot further on. Let's check that out first.'

They tied the horses to a tree and climbed over the overgrown trunk. Kjelle wore trousers, protecting him against the intertwined brambles, but Ajkell's legs were bare in the old Nordish way. Red patterns appeared on his skin and trickles of blood ran down into his boots. The bear warrior took no notice of the scratches. Something had caught his attention and he seemed to have forgotten Kjelle as he moved forward along the forest edge. The Holderling hurried after him, curious as to what had alerted the bear warrior. Ajkell jumped him and pushed him down in the prickly vines. A hard hand covered his mouth to stifle Kjelle's pained yell. Ajkell pointed with his head. In the center of the clearing stood a wooden stronghold, a copy of their own. Only this one was in good repair, and the most alarming was the detail of men practicing archery nearby. Fynni! They wore the same leather uniforms as the men they'd killed in Eidungruve, they had the same cruel markings on their faces and they spoke in the same harsh, foreign tongue.

What were Fynni doing here, so far from the Norden? Kjelle bit on his knuckles to still the rage trying to blind him. A glance at Ajkell found the warrior watching him. 'Later,' his bodyguard mouthed and Kjelle nodded. It took an hour, a painful, cold hour, before the archers finished their exercises and Ajkell and Kjelle could escape. Hurrying back to the horses, both were careful not to leave any signs of their passing. After they'd climbed over the fallen tree, Ajkell rearranged the trailing brambles before they left.

'Well done,' he whispered. 'Mastering rage is never easy for a warrior.'

Kjelle nodded, pleased with the compliment.

Back at their stronghold, Kjelle called his staff to him.

Birthe had just returned with her hunting party. 'You stayed on this side of the river?' asked Kjelle.

The girl nodded, wiping her bloody hands on an old cloth. 'Why?'

'Problems,' he said, looking from her to the others. 'Ajkell and I did some scouting across the river. The path goes northwest. Half an hour's walk away is a roadblock, a fallen tree. Past that is a large clearing with a stronghold just like ours.' He took a deep breath and his hands shook in anger. 'Fynni!' His voice was a snarl and in a reflex Birthe gripped his arm.

'Did they see you?' said the girl anxiously, but Ajkell shook his head.

'We were very careful. Our horses' footsteps end at the barricade and turn back from there.'

Kjelle raised his fists to his shoulders. 'Still, they will find us, so much is certain. Well, we're Nords and no Nord will avoid a battle. But we're ill prepared, undertrained and badly armed. We must hurry the palisade at least. We must prepare weapons: clubs for those who are without arms, bows, if there is proper wood available and arrows; spears.'

'I can start on making bows,' said Birthe.

'If you'll excuse me for a moment,' said Lady Valiantrude. 'I'm going to post a lookout across the river.'

Kjelle looked at her. 'Wise idea.' He looked around. 'One more thing: do we tell the people?'

'Yes,' said Harald. 'They deserve to know. We've gone through a bad patch together, but we're struggling back.'

'Agreed,' said the paladin over her shoulder, and the others nodded.

'All right, I'll tell them after the evening meal.'

Birthe stared at him. 'What did you do to your face? It's full of scratches.'

'Brambles,' said Kjelle. 'We had to hide in a hurry.'

'Aren't they itching?'

'Yes.'

'Why didn't you say so?' She pulled him with her to the cooking space. From her satchel, she took a small pot of salve and started to rub it into the scratches.

Kjelle hissed. 'It stings!'

''Course it does.' Then she stepped back. 'There you are, Lord, all nice and shiny.'

'You have my thanks, wench,' said Kjelle with a straight face.

Birthe grew red. 'Wench! Not yours, man.'

Kjelle smiled. 'I know. You're Búi's wench.'

The girl relaxed. 'Yes. It's time for his dinner. I'm not making milk for nothing.'

The palisade grew rapidly. With the threat of an enemy attack hanging over their heads, the Eidungruvers worked harder than before. On the third day, most of the stockade, except for the gate, was finished. The great door stood against its post, but by now Sun had gone and Harald thought it too dark to hang the door properly. 'First thing tomorrow,' he said. 'We need daylight for that last bit of work.'

'Tomorrow, then,' said Kjelle. 'But as early as you can.'

The next morning, Kjelle awoke with the screamed warnings of the lookout at the ford in his ears. He saw the man splashing though the water, only to tumble down on the bank with an arrow in his back.

'To arms!' he shouted, running around and kicking his people awake. 'To arms!' Sleeping out in the open had helped, because they were still clothed and Kjelle's urgency was plain to see.

'Damn,' said Birthe, while she was stringing her bow. 'We should've placed a second man at the entrance.'

Kjelle didn't answer, but he knew she was right. He hurried to the door-less gate and watched the enemy coming. To his surprise he counted no more than twenty of them. But they were all big men, hardened and dangerous, led by one who wore a wolf's head, like Rannar's man Swinne at Belisheim. On impulse he said, 'Pass the word, archers to kill that guy in the wolf skin first.'

'Step aside,' said Birthe. She'd readied her bow, and looked both angry and intent. Obediently, Kjelle moved.

The wolf-skin halted and called out something. Then he raised his right arm and yelled, pointing at the stronghold. At the same moment, Birthe let her arrow fly and got the man in the throat. Three other arrows, launched almost at the same time as hers, sprouted from his chest. His yell died away as he arched backward and thudded to the ground. For a second, the Fynni gaped at their dead leader, then Birthe shot the man nearest to him. The enemy broke into a forward run.

'At them!' shouted Kjelle and led his people out. Only the archers stayed behind.

Just like those hunters at Eidungruve, the Fynni lost their confidence. Each fought, but the fire had left them and one by one they died. The last few attempted to escape.

'Now, archers,' Birthe yelled from the palisade. 'They shall not escape.'

After a few moments, all the Fynni were dead.

'Well done! Oh, well done,' cried Kjelle, embracing the nearest of his warriors. He ran back to the stronghold and looked around. 'Birthe! Your archers were great.' Then he saw her, at the cooking-fire outside the unfinished longhouse. She sat on her knees beside

Siga, crying and cradling little Búi. He sank down beside her. 'What happened?'

Birthe's face was a mask of tear-streaked agony. 'They shot at me, and killed him. Oh Gods, they killed my son.'

'Siga was cuddling the baby like she often did,' said one of the women. 'Then the arrow came. It happened so fast.'

'Old Siga wasn't hurt, yet she died too,' said another woman. 'Her heart must've stopped.'

Kjelle knelt down next to the girl and held her and the dead child close. 'I'm sorry,' he said awkwardly. 'I'm so terribly sorry.'

Birthe turned her head, her eyes wild. 'Don't be sorry. Go! Go and slay all of them. All, for my Búi.'

'We will, I promise. But we must plan first, lest we all end up dead.'

The girl snarled. 'Don't be a coward now, Kjelle Almansen. Go and kill them.'

He shook his head stubbornly. 'That place of theirs is strong. We need a way to breach their defenses. How will we get in?'

'Fire?' said the bear warrior from behind him. 'They have a thatched roof and it's been dry for a sevenday now.'

'Can we make fire arrows?'

Birthe nodded, her eyes big and cruel. 'Easily.'

Kjelle grew pensive. 'How will we light them?'

'We need tinder.'

'That's too slow. How can we transport live coals?' Kjelle's glance fell to the drinking horn at Ajkell's belt. He grabbed it. 'In these. A horn won't burn. We can carry coals in them to light the arrows with. We'll attack tonight, after dark. Warn everyone; collect some horns and set people to making arrows.'

'What about the dead?' asked Lady Valiantrude.

'How many did we lose?

The paladin bit her lip. 'Three men. That's including the lookout.'

Five dead, of their small clan. He gritted his teeth. 'We'll burn our own when we've finished. The Fynni we'll bury.'

'Leave them to rot!' said Birthe through clenched teeth.

'We don't want to attract wolves.'

The girl growled. She shrugged off Kjelle's arms and rose. 'Leave me alone.' She went to the back of the settlement and sat down against the wall, rocking the dead baby in her arms.

The rest of the day passed in furious action. New lookouts were posted, scouts were sent out, the doors were hung in their posts, more arrows were prepared and drinking horns tested with glowing coals. When darkness finally fell, all the able-bodied Eidungruvers collected at the ford.

'They will not expect a night attack,' said Kjelle. 'Certainly not right after their attempt. Archers, you are our greatest hope today. Aim for the straw roofs and let every flaming arrow count. Let's go in silence, my brothers and sisters, and kill those treacherous beasts. For Alman and Eidungruve!' He saw Birthe, bow in hand, her face pale and determined. His eyes went to Buí's backpack and she stared stonily back. 'You're taking him with you?'

She clenched her teeth. 'I want him to see how we burn his murderers. I want him to know we avenged him.'

Kjelle nodded. 'Good.' Then he walked into the cold waters and waded to the other side.

At the fallen tree, they met their two scouts. 'They had two lookouts,' whispered the eldest. 'Now no longer.'

'Well done,' said Kjelle.

'That leaves only the man on the watchtower,' said the younger one. 'Neither of us shoots well enough to bring him down.'

'I will.' Birthe fingered her bow.

'Your hands are steady?' said Kjelle.

'My hands are always steady.'

Kjelle touched her cheek and she didn't even flinch. 'Do it then, Huntmaster.'

She slipped away in the darkness and moments later they heard her bowstring sing, within two heartbeats followed by the soft thud of a body hitting the ground. A door opened in the enemy barracks and the light of many lamps shone into the dark. Kjelle cursed softly and covered his eyes. But apparently, the one who looked outside was satisfied, for the light disappeared again. The Holderling sighed inaudibly. 'Archers, light your arrows. Arrow handlers, prepare the second shaft. You others, look another way, lest you lose your night sight.'

Most coals still glowed and twice ten arrows bore flames. Ten glowing trails sped through the night air and bit into the thatched roof. The handlers gave over their shafts and lighted the next. Flames played over the roof like dancing lightalves in an open field. More and more joined them, until suddenly with a roar, the flames bit through the roof. Burning straw rained down and in his mind Kjelle saw the panic -- hangings and clothing catching flame, torches on the walls adding their heat, and he thought he could hear the yells of pain and shock. He shook his head to clear it, but the screams were real. The wooden walls burned quickly and changed the safe stronghold into a trap. Then the door burst open and men stumbled out.

'Archers, shoot!' The archers changed to ordinary arrows and loosed them at the enemy. Kjelle started to run forward, followed by his people. The battle was quickly over, and soon only the crackling of the fires was heard.

'You're avenged, my son,' said Birthe, tears streaming down her face. She stared at the flames. Kjelle stood besides her, feeling the heat of the burning stronghold on his skin. He touched Birthe's shoulder and she clung to his arm without turning her head. 'Now I've lost all of them. Only I am left. Why, Gods?'

Kjelle knew he didn't have an answer, and that she wouldn't listen if he had. He just held her as she cried.

'It's done here,' said Lady Valiantrude in his ear. 'We can inspect what is left by daylight.' She looked at Birthe, and said softly, 'It was a great victory. No new losses at all. You caught them completely by surprise.'

Kjelle grimaced. 'They underestimated us. They thought us demoralized. By the Gods, we're not.' Clasping Birthe close he shouted, 'We are Nords and we will fight.' His people cheered as he guided Birthe back to the road and their place across the river.

The next day they built a huge funeral pyre for the three men who had been killed in the first attack, for Siga and for blue-eyed little Búi. Kjelle praised the warriors, recited as many of their ancestors as they knew and told the Gods of their glorious deaths. Of Siga he recounted her wisdom, the way she had run the house at Eidungruve, her singing of the ghests. And last, the little bundle of furs on top. 'This is little Búi,' he said. 'The bravest of babes. Never a cry at the wrong moment. He survived snowstorms, drowning seas and months of traveling, only to be slain by a wicked arrow. If infants had a place in Valhalla, then Odin himself would come and fetch him. May he forever be happy in Hel's house.' As Birthe sang a dirge that set their hairs on end, Kjelle put the burning torch deep into the pile. Flames bit in the layer of tinder and soon roared their hunger for more. The girl sang till all was consumed and when the last tongues of fire died, fell into an exhausted sleep.

They finished the rebuilding of their stronghold in another sevenday. Almansford, Kjelle called it, in tribute to his father. That same day a messenger arrived from the Jarl, in answer to his report of their victory against the Fynni. To everyone's satisfaction he confirmed Kjelle as Holder of Eidungruve. He also issued a warning, Vulf was coming south. He had been seen crossing the Ardens Mountains and was heading more or less in a southwestern direction. *The idea of Vulf heading for Rhemes was too outrageous to be believable, but keep your guard up,* wrote Dettrich.

'He's coming here,' said Birthe. Her face was pale, and her whole body tense as her own bow string. From under unkempt hair, her eyes looked both angry and hopeless. Kjelle wanted to take her in his arms, hold her and protect her, a feeling he'd never had for a girl before.

'Why here?' said Valiantrude.

Birthe shrugged. 'I just know,' she said harshly.

'Maybe he comes for the men we killed?' Elbrich pushed his helm back to peer up at them. It was a strange thing, that helm, like an upturned plate. He had made it himself and worn it ever since the first attack.

Kjelle blinked. 'You could well be right,' he said. 'If he's gathering forces for something...'

'He won't be pleased to find his men dead.' The little smith shivered. 'I need more iron to make weapons and arrow points.'

'Where will we get it from?'

'Search the Fynni's burned-out ruin. I can re-use most of the iron.'

'Tomorrow,' said Kjelle.

CHAPTER 9 – HOLDER

Tuuri looked at the burning farmhouse. 'Was it worth it?'

Tarkynn Vulf turned on him, his thin face livid with anger. 'Of course! We've got food, the men have their plunder and...'

'You lost another three warriors.'

'So?' Vulf spat into the fire. 'I still have thirty-five left. That's plenty to catch one man, even if he is the Shardheld.' He glanced at his men. 'They don't give a damn who dies. They're animals, unused to thinking. When this task is done, and Rev allows us to go home, I'll have to kill them anyhow. They're spoiled; I can't take them back with me, they'd run wild.'

'And that's the Fynni way?'

Vulf gave a barking laugh. 'You're learning.'

By Ullr, thought Tuuri. I'm learning. How mad you all are. You're vermin. Like diseased rats, spoiling everything you touch. 'Tell me about Rev.' It was five sevendays after their departure from Eidungruve. Five sevendays of forced marches, of hunger, terror and the insatiable bloodlust of the Fynni. Behind them lay a trail of killings, of plundered villages and burned farms like this latest one. Days in which Vulf talked to him of the glory of being Fynni, of their civilization, of the four Gods they worshiped. Now, for the first time, the Tarkynn had mentioned a name.

'Rev? He is the mightiest of us all. The Sa'amaniman, the speaker for the Gods. He's Rannar's advisor.' Unexpectedly, Vulf laughed, as if he found something comical in his words. 'Your poor master doesn't know what he let himself in for. Rev doesn't serve, boy. He leads, in secret, cunningly. That's his greatest strength, Fynnikin.' He turned around to his men. 'Up, up, lazy pigs. We go on.'

The next day they left the fertile farmlands to climb the treacherous route through the Ardens, the wooded mountains that gave entry to Gaul. This was different land than what Tuuri had been used to. The mountains of the Norden were high and for the most inaccessible. These, however, were much lower, but steep and the paths were very precarious.

'Where are we going now?' he asked, following Vulf through a swift brook. Behind them plodded the thirty-five men, never complaining, like a long row of cows.

For a moment Vulf didn't speak. 'Ildr's stronghold,' he said after a few moments. He stopped and looked at Tuuri. 'You see, I took your advice to heart. I need more men. Ildr is a small chief, though his force is larger than he needs. He was sent to Gaul to spy on Rhemes, and to act as a safe house for agents going south. He can do that with half his present strength. That should give us another twenty fodder. Satisfied, Fynnikin?'

Tuuri grunted. He didn't give a damn about the men or this whole idiotic expedition. He wished he were home, in Westhal, or anywhere else but here. Vulf must have understood his reaction, for he laughed softly. 'Brave Fynnikin,' he said mockingly.

'We still need more iron,' said Elbrich. He glanced at Kjelle. 'I know where we can get more arms. Very good arms. But it's going to cost you.'

'I don't have much coin,' said Kjelle.

Elbrich smiled. 'Gold is of no interest to a Niflung. We know where to mine it if we need more.'

'Then what would be the price?'

'My people want to go home. Arrange that, and I can get you weapons.'

Kjelle thought. 'Prince Ottil would be agreeable, I'm sure,' he said. 'And if not, I'm Holder of Eidungruve, a mining Hold. We operate a silver mine. I will offer hospitality, if your kin can run the mine.'

'Sounds fair,' said Elbrich. 'Let's see what Arkenhapt says about it. She's the Mistress of Wederer Mountain. The clan leader,' he explained.

'A woman as clan leader?' said Ajkell.

The young smith smiled. 'You'll find it strange, but we Niflunger see no difference between women and men – as workers.'

'How will we contact this Mistress Arkenhapt?'

'Just use the name,' said Elbrich. 'Mistress is a job, not a title. There's only one way -- you have to go to her mountain. She will want to see you, hear what you offer out of your own mouth and judge your trustworthiness.'

'I can't stay away for long,' said Kjelle. 'I must be here when Vulf comes.'

'It's about six days by horse and cart. Two sevendays to and fro.'

Kjelle looked at his staff.

'We need weapons,' said Lady Valiantrude. 'Vulf won't be here for another month. If you hurry, you'll be back in time to beat the crap out of him.'

Kjelle blinked at her language. Being back in a military position was slowly eroding the paladin's primness. He smiled.

'Of course we're going,' said Birthe, glowering. 'You, I, Elbrich and ten men. I've an archer to take my place, Göll Haldisdottr. She's ready for promotion. Arrange it, we're leaving tomorrow.'

No one laughed at her words. Her moods were brittle, with alternating fits of rage and despair. Kjelle saw the hurt behind her tempers and nodded. 'You're right. Ten men, mounted, the cart, we leave at sunrise.' He turned to Ajkell. 'Will you support Valiantrude?'

The bear warrior hesitated. It was clear he wanted to go with Kjelle, but then he looked at the paladin. 'Of course. We'll make sure you have a stronghold to return to.'

'I'd appreciate that,' said Kjelle.

The first night on the road, in the little tent he shared with Birthe, he was awakened by her crying. He stretched out his arm and felt her tremble.

'I'm scared,' said she through her tears. 'They're all gone. Even Búi. I'm alone now, all alone. What must I do?'

'You're not alone,' said Kjelle, gripping her shoulder. 'You've got Almansford, all of us. You've got me.'

With a snarl, she rolled on top of him. 'You're with me? Prove to me you are.' She put her arms around Kjelle and turned around, dragging him on top of her. 'Take me,' she said hoarsely. 'Prove to me you're here with me. Take me, quick.'

'But...' Kjelle, who once considered himself a great lover, hesitated. Birthe wasn't just any girl; she was a trusted friend. Then she bared her breasts, still large with milk, while her yearning mouth found his, and he surrendered. She received him moaning and crying, with an urgency none of his earlier conquests had shown. Later, spent, she lay in his arms and slept. As he held her, softly caressing her hair, he stared at the stars peeping though the tent flaps and tried to think. He didn't understand what just happened. Birthe had needed him. No one ever had before.

Next morning Kjelle woke in an empty tent. Quickly he pulled on his boots and went outside. It was still early, and a low fog hung over the land. He nodded to the woman who'd had the last watch.

'It was a quiet night," she reported.

'All the better,' said Kjelle. 'You can turn in for another hour, I'll stay here.' He checked the ashes of last night's fire. It was cold and he began to collect wood to relight it. Half an hour later it burned, spreading welcome warmth to his fingers. The sound of breaking twigs alerted him and his hand went to his knife, but it was Birthe, with a half dozen partridges. She didn't look at him or say anything, but hung the dead birds head down from the side of the cart.

'You were up early?' said Kjelle.

She only nodded.

'They're nice partridges. Where did you find them?'

The girl stiffened. 'I... I...' She turned around, beet red. 'I'm sorry about last night. I feel I raped you. Don't know what happened. Felt so damned lonely and... and....'

Kjelle grabbed her arm and pulled her down next to him. 'Listen, don't blame yourself. Nothing happened that I couldn't handle. Just remember you're not alone. And you know what? I liked it last night. You were damned good.' Then he kissed her. For a moment, she tried to push him away, but then she relaxed.

'Damn,' she said. 'I'm crying again.' She slipped out of his grasp and rose. 'We need food.' And with a look at the sky, 'It's past five already.'

Kjelle chuckled. 'Time aplenty, wench.'

She turned to him, stiffening. But then she grinned. 'I got that one coming, I guess.'

By day, they rode; by night Kjelle and Birthe made love till even the dullest of the warriors knew what was going on between their Holder and the Völva. Apart from some sly smiles, all were discreet and kept their mouths shut.

As the days passed, the mountains in the distance grew nearer and the land higher. On the sixth day they rode through a broad, grass-grown canyon.

Elbrich pulled up to ride next to Kjelle. 'Do you see the path going up the mountain? It begins next to that large boulder.'

Kjelle examined the mountainside. 'Yes, I see something that looks like a trail.'

The young smith nodded. 'It leads straight to the main gates.' He looked at Kjelle, his gaze intent. 'Remember, no fondling and kissing inside the clanhold; that would ruin your chances.'

Wederer's gates were tall and heavy, made of some dark metal Elbrich refused to identify. 'It's almost indestructible,' he said. 'Once the doors are closed, you won't get them open by any man-made means.'

As they came near, an armed warden came forward, and they halted.

'What is your business, please?'

Elbrich bowed from the saddle. 'I'm Mastersmith Elbrich of Silver Mountain. With me are Holder Kjelle of Eidungruve and the Völva Birthe. We have a proposal for Mistress Arkenhapt.'

The warden looked dubious. 'The Mistress isn't very interested in anything at the moment. Some of our fighters were ambushed and killed by Fynni yesterday. One of them was her daughter.'

'Fynni?' said Kjelle sharply. 'Here in the neighborhood?'

'There's a small group of them holed up on the other side of the bridge to the next mountain. We think they're scouts. The Guardmaster is forming a counterattack just now. He's trying to find enough archers; they're in a spot difficult to reach. Problem is, our archers use shortbows; their arrows won't reach across the gap. That makes the bridge a death trap.'

Kjelle looked at Birthe. 'I...'

'Of course,' said Birthe. 'We've got six longbow archers available, and me.'

'You would fight with us?' The warden stared up at them. 'Well, that's uncommon civil of you. Follow me.'

They dismounted and handed their horses to another warden.

The Guardmaster was one of those fiery types, broad-chested and fierce.

'You offer your services?' said he, frowning. 'We don't have much to do with other peoples, so why would you help us?'

'We hate Fynni,' said Kjelle. 'They're overrunning the north; they murdered my Hold, and killed my Völva's baby son. That's not all, but it's enough to get us started. I've got six archers and the Völva is a Huntmaster.'

The Guardmaster turned to Elbrich. 'You're one of us. Do you vouch for these Nords?'

'Yes,' said the young Mastersmith soberly. 'They saved my life and my honor. I work and live among them, and they are worthy of trust.'

'Well, I need longbow archers, so this offer is too good to let pass. On the Mastermith's word, you're welcome.' The Guardmaster offered his hand. 'I'm Welddich, responsible for the defense of Wederer minehold. Funny idea to be helped by a bunch of Nords.' He turned and shouted to another warrior, 'It's on; let the assaulters collect at the high passage.' To Kjelle, 'Follow me. It's a bit of a climb.'

The corridor led them to a narrow staircase that went on and on past well-lit halls. Up they went, as if to the very peak of the mountain. The Eidungruvers were in good condition, but climbing these stairs was difficult and breathing became more difficult. Only thin little Elbrich walked as if it were a stroll in the park.

Finally, they reached a second, smaller gate, which opened to a panorama of snowy mountains and deep gorges. Here, they were met by Welddich's force of some twenty warriors, male and female. They were clad in heavy-looking armor, with helmets just like Elbrich's covering their hairless heads, and armed with a variety of weapons.

'Who are those?' said one massive warrior. 'Nords? Are you crazy, Guardmaster?'

'They have the long reach we lack, Kremmendor. Now, shut yer gobs, all, and let's go.' Aside, he said to Kjelle, 'Don't mind that fellow, he's always been a cantankerous bastard. He's the nephew of the Mistress and that's swollen his head. He's good in a fight, though.'

They followed the path that led them to a narrow bridge over a jagged, snow-covered chasm. Here, some discarded weaponry and bloodstained rock showed where warriors had died.

Welddich pointed to the other side. 'Behind that purplish outcrop is their camp.' The words hadn't left his mouth, or Birthe's arrow crossed the gorge and a dark figure fell screaming into the deep.

'You won't kill any more babies!' she cried. 'Archers, you saw what I did. Fire at will.'

The Niflung warriors ran across the narrow bridge. A Fynni arrow caught one of them and slammed him over the side. Two, three bows sang and the enemy archer followed the Niflung down to his death on the rocks.

Kjelle saw the bow pointing at them across the abyss. 'Watch out!' he cried, instinctively pushing Birthe aside. The world exploded in his head and he felt himself collapsing into nothingness.

'He's been extremely lucky,' said the Niflung healer. 'The Fates must really like him.'

'And you've wonderful reflexes, Huntmaster,' said Welddich. 'If you hadn't dragged him back he'd be at the bottom of the gorge.'

'When will he be able to travel?' Birthe's nerves were taut as she looked down on Kjelle's unconscious body. She tried the calming words Asgisla had taught her and they helped a little. 'We expect a Fynni attack on our stronghold and he must be back by then.'

The healer placed his fingers on Kjelle's temples and seemed to listen for a moment. 'The damage from that arrow is negligible. After ricocheting off the rock wall, it had lost a lot of force. The wound over his ear will leave a nice scar, but that's all. His problem is concussion. He hit the rock with the back of his head before falling forward. Do you practice sympathetic restoration, Völva?'

Birthe forced herself to look at him. 'I'm not really a healer,' she admitted. 'I liked prophecies and singing magic, but I was too impatient to study much healing.'

The Niflung smiled. 'I'll send one of my assistants with you. She's a young girl, just finished her basic training, and it would be good for her to spend some time elsewhere to practice.'

'We would be grateful,' said Birthe. 'She and I could exchange our knowledge and grow.'

'You would do that?' The healer watched her face. 'That's unusual; not many Völva would agree to share the secrets of their craft.'

A warden entered. 'Beg pardon, but the Mistress would like to see you, Lady Völva. Mastersmith Elbrich is already with her. I'm to bring you to her.'

Birthe turned to the healer. 'I must go. Could we depart on the morrow, do you think?'

'Yes. I'll tell Annlith to get her things together. She'll take care of transport. Now go, the Mistress is in no mood for delay.'

Birthe followed the warden through a warren of large metal-clad halls, linked by broad corridors, well lit and remarkably similar in their dull yellow paint and grayish crystal patterns.

'How do you know which tunnel goes where? They all seem the same to me.'

The warden gave her a hard look. 'Believe me, Lady, they aren't.' Then she relented and smiled. 'Our eyes see many more colors than yours. I lack the words to describe them, but each corridor is different and the crystals flash in the prettiest hues. Other folks call us drab, but it's they who are blind.'

Mistress Arkenhapt received her in a small room, with a big desk, some chairs and a map filling nearly a whole wall. Arkenhapt was a thin woman of indeterminable age, her skin taut around her face bones and her eyes lacked the light that characterized her people. Elbrich was with her, looking strangely different among his own people.

'Welcome to Wederer Mountain,' said the Mistress. 'You have my personal thanks for helping us kill those who murdered my daughter and her weapon mates.'

'We'll kill Fynni wherever we meet them. We too have lost many to their bloodlust. My baby son...' For a moment, the anguish threatened to overwhelm her and she couldn't speak.

'I'm sorry,' said the Mistress finally. 'So we have both suffered. Sit down, Völva. You must have come here for a purpose. Please, tell me what I can do for you.'

'I will speak for our Holder, Kjelle of Eidungruve, as he lies hurt. We came here with an offer, Mistress. Seeing that we have a mutual enemy in the Fynni, we would trade with you. A Fynni army is on its way to our stronghold, some six days to the east of here. We have need of both weapons and ore, and Mastersmith Elbrich advised us to make you an offer for them.'

Mistress Arkenhapt straightened in her chair. 'You are from the Norden,' she said softly. 'Normally I wouldn't want to do business with you. Since you helped us and we have a common enemy, I am willing to listen. What is it you offer?'

'You know of the trouble we have in the Norden? A rebellious Jarl had King Vidmer killed, while the Queen fled to Rhemes. This false Jarl is the one who hired all the Fynni and sends them rampaging.'

The Mistress' face grew taut. 'I had heard of the rebellion, but not of the connection with our arch-enemies. It makes me like Nords even less.'

'We want to bring this Jarl to justice and put an end to the Fynni problem. During our escape from the north, we saved the life of Prince Ottil, the Royal heir. He is now with friends of ours in Brytanna, but he will return to claim his throne. Our offer is this: We arrange with the Prince the restoration of your ancient rights to the mountains you once possessed. We think Prince Ottil will agree to this. He is in no way like his father, and can be reasoned with.' Birthe paused for a moment. 'Even if the Prince can't agree, our Holder promises your people a safe place in his own domain of Eidungruve, a silvermine hold. All his own miners were murdered and he offers you the exploitation of his mountain.'

'He sticks his neck out for us?' said the Mistress with a shadow of surprise in her tone. 'That's mighty generous of him.' She reached for a large bell and rang once

A soberly dressed Niflung came in, ready to take any orders, and waited till the Mistress had finished speaking.

'This offer is too good to let pass,' said the clan leader. 'I'll have a contract made out. Stay and listen.' She dictated a deal based on Kjelle's promises. 'Weapons and ore, some rough gold and a little bag of gems, the services of a junior healer, and finally,' she added, 'a unit of ten warriors, fully armed and armored, to be deployed at the Holder's discretion.' She winked at Birthe. 'We must help keep you safe. With you all dead this contract isn't worth a sliver of ore.'

'We'll discuss the stipulations with our own Jarl, Dettrich of Dalland. He is an honorable man and he'll see this agreement carried out even if all of us have joined the Gods.'

'I can't ask more of you,' said Mistress Arkenhapt. 'You and your Holder have restored some of my trust in your people, Lady Völva. For that, I thank you.'

Early the next morning they were ready to return to Almansford. The generous Niflunger had added a horse and cart to the deal, both for the weapons, and for Kjelle, who was still unconscious. Healer Annlith rode with him, sitting uncomfortably on a sack of supplies.

'Don't mind me,' she said happily. 'This is all very exciting!'

The ten warriors, thin, young and fit, were clearly of the same mind. They marched behind the last cart, cheerful and joking and saw no problem with walking for days.

'We're not used to horses,' said Bemm, their leader. 'Of course, for such an exalted person as a Mastersmith it's different. They have a position to maintain.'

'That's it.' Elbrich grinned at the good-natured joke. 'I'm an important man now.'

The first night of their homeward journey, Birthe lay on her back in the tent, listening to Kjelle's heavy breathing. He was there, next to her, and yet so far away in his unconsciousness. She wanted, needed to touch him, to hold him. She'd been lonely for so long. Her father had always been away on raids, while her mother had the household and her many social duties. When her mother fell ill, her father came home, but his thoughts were all for his wife, with nothing left for his daughter. After her mother's death, he was broke and they went to live in the woods, collecting pelts for local merchants.

Her father hadn't been pleasant company; his moods were brittle and sometimes he drank too much. That's why he'd let the bear surprise him. Birthe stared at a small hole in the roof of the tent without seeing the star peeping through. She'd never told anyone. Killed while crapping was bad enough, but being blind drunk as well was too much. She growled softly in the dark. *Bastard!* She was ten, then, and all alone, till her flight brought her to Belisheim.

There, she had served Asgisla and studied her craft. But that yearning void inside her remained. Until Barn came, he of the blue eyes. Handsome, strong Barn, who jumped into the emptiness and her bed like he'd been born for it. They married in secret, because his family certainly wouldn't agree. She was happy then, blissfully happy. Oh, Barn was still a boy, seventeen and thinking like an overenthusiastic ten-year-old. She'd realized that only after his death. His stupid, useless death, hunting a bear while he could hardly point a bow. To impress her. *Gods!* She cried softly, thinking of his strong arms, his blue eyes, his blond curls around her finger, the big stupid child. How she missed being held, being loved. Even little Búi hadn't stilled her longing.

Kjelle's snoring stopped and her heart with it. But then he snorted and started breathing again.

She rolled over to his side and touched his forehead. It felt cool and healthy. With her fingertips to his breast, she checked the beating of his heart. Its rhythm was strong and regular. She pressed her lips to his skin, drew her fingers across the muscles on his chest, and trembled with longing. Softly, she kissed him again, and once more. 'Oh Kjelle,' she said. Suddenly his arm moved and his hand went to her hair. 'Where...?'

'You're awake?' said she, almost breathless. 'O Gods, speak to me.'

'Birthe? Where are we?'

'On the way back. All is well. How do you feel?'

His hand gripped her shoulder. 'The way back? Did we...?'

'Yes. We've got weapons and ore. The Mistress gave us gold and gems, a healer and ten warriors. Everything you wanted, love.'

The hand on her shoulder stiffened. 'Love?'

'Sorry,' she said, 'I shouldn't....'

'Love.' He pulled her to his breast and held her close. 'My head hurts. What happened?'

'You missed death by a finger's width,' said she. 'That arrow you saved me from hit the rock wall first and then your head. You'll have a nice scar over your ear to show for it. Apart from that, you have concussion from hitting the mountain.'

His hand touched her face. 'You're crying?'

'I'm happy you're awake,' she lied.

'Why are you crying?'

She opened her mouth but no words came.

'I know,' said Kjelle. 'Come.' His lips found hers and he kissed her, hard.

'Enough,' she said, while a warm flood of happiness spread through her. 'You must recover first.' She sighed and cuddled up to him. 'Sleep, love.' With one arm across his breast, she obeyed her own command.

CHAPTER 10 – BEARJAW

Muus was more at peace with the world than he'd been for a long time. He had plenty of sleep, good food and a horse to ride. And best of all, he had been given a clear purpose. He looked at the girl beside him. She had donned a white tunic that almost covered her knees, with a thin yellow band along the hem. A bunch of oak leaves around her neck was all the adornment she wore.

'You're looking very official,' said Muus. 'How did you become a druidess? Isn't that a lifelong study?'

Moirra colored slightly. 'Yes. Only one out of a hundred students of the Circle ever earns the right to wear oak leaves. But I am a Un-a-Dach, as your mother was. Not many of us choose the Path of the Circle, but some of us are Druidborn. We are druids from the moment we start dreaming. That is usually before birth. Now I may not study any more. Instead, I must go out in the world and act. Only by using what I've learned will I develop and grow. I would have gone with you anyhow. You're the Shardheld, and a chance to study such a one is a once-in–a-half-millennium opportunity. That I wanted you to ask me is... well, that is personal. Between us. Do you see?'

Muus nodded. 'It's what I want, too.'

'Yes!' Her eyes bored into his. 'You can lean on me, Muus. Always remember that. When things should get rough, lean on me. I am not as frail as I look.'

Behind them, Hraab let out a crackling laugh. 'Frail? You? You're the toughest animal on earth, druidess. You could wrestle bears with one hand tied behind your back and win.'

Now Moirra blushed deeply. 'Don't be silly.'

'Silly?' The boy looked hurt. 'Me?'

'What about you, youngster?' said Muus. 'You started out hunting for Vulf. Aren't you sorry you are here now?'

'Of course not. This is high adventure. And Vulf... we will get him in the end. That's as sure as daybreak.'

Muus turned around in the saddle and stared at him. 'Vulf is in the Norden and we are going south.'

'Vulf is going south, too.'

'Are you sure?' Muus sighed. 'Of course, you're a Un-a-Dach, too. And you're certain you are not a druid?'

Moirra laughed at that. 'Him, a druid? No, he isn't that. Do you have the Sight, Hraab?'

'I can't see the future,' said Hraab seriously. 'But when Muus mentioned Vulf, I saw him riding over wooded mountains. Not a Nordish land, less gloomy. The trees were different. And there wasn't any snow.'

'One of the Teutonic lands perhaps? Or the north of Gaul? They won't have any snow there now.'

Hraab shrugged. 'Could be. It's not Brytanna. He and his ulvhednar wouldn't last a sevenday here; they'd all be slaughtered by the locals.'

'You told me about Vulf, but who is he exactly?' asked Moirra.

'Vulf is a Fynni Tarkynn,' said Hraab.

Moirra hissed and her eyes spat fire. 'Fynni! Why didn't you kill him?'

'I couldn't.'

'What is a Tarkynn?' said Ottil. 'I accept Vulf's men are rabid wolves, but nobody told me they're Fynni.'

Hraab shook his head. 'They're followers of the Gods Before. All Fynni are, like the Grim Doubh, but much cleverer. Their Tarkynni are war chiefs with mystical powers. They hold absolute authority over their people and they are killers.'

'We know they are killers,' said Muus. 'But I didn't know Vulf was more than just a war leader. Besides, they weren't naked.'

Hraab grinned mirthlessly. 'Of course they weren't. Grim Doubh aren't running around like nekkid rats all the time, either. That's only when they dance. They look just like ordinary people, most of the time.'

Just like ordinary people, thought Muus. So everyone could be an enemy, not only in the Norden, but in Brytanna as well.

The fourth day they came to the hill fort of Denar Byn, near the coast. It was the spitting image of that earlier garrison near Windiss. Even the warrior at the gate looked the same. Only when they came near, they did they see that this guard was much younger and in a high state of nervousness.

He glanced at Moirra and his eyes grew big. 'Druidess,' he said. 'Your arrival is a gift from the Gods. Go quickly to the Warchief, he has great need of you.' In his nervousness, he seemed to forget the entrance was closed. Moirra clad herself in an air of authority. 'Open the gate so that I may enter,' she said quietly. 'Then lead me to him.'

The young man jumped and threw open the wooden gate. 'I... I may not leave my post, druidess. Enemies are nearby. But you will find Warleader Uthar in the great hall.'

Muus frowned as he looked around. 'What enemies do you speak of?'

The watchman's face twitched. 'Please go to the Warchief. He will explain all.'

In the great hall they found Uthar amid a group of young, wounded soldiers. At their entrance, he turned and his face lit up. 'A druidess,' he said. 'By the Gods, a bit of fortune at last. Please look to my men, Wisdom. I'm goin' to need them shortly.'

Most of the young warriors were dripping blood from several cuts; they seemed dazed and shocked. One man's leg was twisted in a cruel way. He was unconscious and uncommonly pallid, but he breathed. Moirra didn't hesitate. She pointed at three men. 'You and you, hold his shoulders, you the good leg. The damaged limb will have to come off.' She took a slender iron saw from her bag. 'Listen, you men, your friend is out now, but he will awake when I start. You must hold him down for me to save him. Understood?' The men nodded. She raised her arms to the ceiling. 'Aid me, Annawn of the Healing Light.' She started to sing, while at the same time she began to saw off the now useless part of the man's leg.

As she had said, he reacted violently. His screams filled the hall and the three warriors needed all their strength to hold him. Muus saw the man's face, purple and wet with sweat. *A'yin,* he thought, laying his hand on the knuckles on his breast. *Is there a way to let him sleep till Moirra is finished?* He felt power coursing through his body. Not the fierce current of the lightning, but something soft. A white light sprang from his fingers to the struggling warrior and

101

immediately the man relaxed. 'Is he dead?' said one of the man's friends in a shocked voice.

His mate shook his head. 'No, I see his chest moving.'

'He sleeps,' said Muus. 'When the druidess is ready, he will wake again.' Then he turned to the Warchief. The fearful respect in the man's eye irritated him. 'Whom did you fight?'

Uthar rubbed his nose. 'Viking raiders,' he said. 'They were goin' to attack Luddagh, the town on the coast. We fought them, but...' He sighed. 'This is a new batch of soldiers, Wisdom. They are young and raw. We pulled back to the stronghold, but I'm certain that dreadful Bear will come after us. I've too few men left to man the palisades.'

'A bear?' said Muus sharply. 'A sail with a red bear standing, about to attack?'

'Yes, holy one.' Uthar looked at Muus. 'You've seem 'im before?'

Muus stared. 'How many men does he have?'

'About a hundred,' said Uthar. 'There were two boats on the beach. They looked battered, as if they'd been in a storm. Still, they are five times as strong as my force.'

'Doesn't the High King have ships, troops to root him out?'

'Cucharann?' The Warchief spat in the rushes on the ground. 'The High King is a lazy no-good. He doesn't give a damn as long as he's safe in his fastness in King's Lud. Got a whole fleet on his doorstep, but the fool is too scared to use it.'

'I must see Bearjaw Largassen's face,' Muus said.

'Let's go and look then,' said Hraab at his shoulder.

Muus looked at him and nodded. 'I'll get my horse.'

'Ottil and I are coming too. We're getting used to spying.'

The three of them left the stronghold. 'He can't be far.' Muus's hands gripped the reins. His breath seemed too large for his chest and he felt tense. He urged his horse into a gallop.

The sun shone and the weather was mild. Overhead, a bird sang. Its warble followed Muus to the top of the next hill. There they halted. In the distance was the sea, a blue-gray expanse, stretching towards a cloud-covered horizon. Closer by on the beach rested two longboats. The Warchief had been right; they were battered. Muus saw the repairs to the mast of the second boat and the patch in

Bearjaw's sail. A hasty patch, cutting the terrible bear neatly in two. Muus smiled grimly. *A bad omen, Largassen.*

To the right was the town that must be Luddagh -- a wooden palisade surrounding a group of houses, much like Windiss. The Viking army had lit fires on the large meadow between the town and the beach, while from the palisades the townsfolk watched the enemy slaughtering their cattle.

'So that is the famous Viking,' said Ottil. 'I've always thought going a-viking was a glorious adventure. But it isn't. I don't think I have a need for murderers like Bearjaw Largassen.'

Hraab grinned. 'I never liked it, but then, it's my folks they're killing.'

'They're going to feed,' said Muus.

Ottil grimaced. 'Damn, seeing all that meat roasting makes me hungry too.'

'Watch those archers,' said Hraab.

Several raiders put flaming arrows to their bows and shot them off into the town. Puffs of smoke rose up from thatched roofs and the wind carried the sound of cries.

'They're going to have some sport while they eat.' Ottil sounded indignant.

Muus felt his growing anger explode. 'I'm going to stop them.'

The two boys looked at him.

'You can't fight them,' said Ottil. 'There's only the three of us.'

Hraab's eyes narrowed as he stared at Muus. 'Are you sure? Really, really sure?'

Muus nodded. A cry from the raider army told him that their approach was seen. Several arrows sped their way, but with a wave of his hand, Muus burned them from the sky. A second hand wave showered angry sparks over the raiders, who scattered hurriedly. Bearjaw stood his ground and now Muus really saw him for the first time. The Viking was big, even for a Nord. He had blond hair, cropped close to his skull, and a sevendays' beard. His powerful chest was bare, showing muscles that would have made a real bear jealous. His hands held a heavy battle hammer, too massive for most men to lift. He stood, legs slightly apart, and stared at the young man on the horse.

'Largassen!' screamed Muus as he rode forward. A shock ran through the big man at the sound of his name. He stared at the boy on the horse and then recognition appeared on his face.

'You!' he said. 'The crazy boy who didn't cry.'

Muus clenched his fists. 'I was that boy. I, Terrel of Owwich. Remember Owwich, Largassen? The day you feared has finally arrived, Largassen. I am their revenge.'

'You're a fool, boy,' said the Viking. 'I've a hundred men at my back. Submit and I'll let you live. I can always sell you a second time.'

'Your hundred men are nothing, Largassen. You made a fatal mistake in stealing me. I am a Runemaster.'

At that, the Viking threw his great hammer at Muus, but the weapon stopped in mid-air, halted by a hail of sparks. Bearjaw's eyes bulged at the sight, and he drew his knife.

With a wide sweep of his arm, Muus created a circle of flames around the Viking. 'You killed my parents, Largassen.'

Bearjaw started to sweat profusely. 'I'll pay! I'll pay you compensation! I swear it!'

With a contemptuous gesture, Muus sent a small flash of lighting in front of Bearjaw's feet.

The Viking screamed and jumped. 'Please don't! I'll pay you anything, but don't do this.'

'This is for Slade, my father,' said Muus. Lightning burned the Viking's left hand, and again he screamed, the sound strangely high for so large a man.

'And this one is for my mother, Aeylla.' Now Bearjaw's right hand started to smoke. Babbling wildly, the man fell to his knees. He lifted his ruined hands, as if in supplication, but Muus felt no mercy. 'You murdered and raped, burned villages and stole the children. You cheated Birthe Gudessen's father, so this is for her, too. You will not misuse any more of the children your wife procured for you, Largassen.' A shower of tiny sparks engulfed the Viking. Largassen arched back, screaming and twitching spasmodically. While he lay there, Muus looked aside at the raiders, watching in motionless horror. He gathered new energy and hurled a searing bolt of fire at them. One after another burned and fell smoking in the grass. Muus lifted his hands again, but through the fog in his mind, he felt someone tugging at his sleeve. It was Moirra. The Gods knew where she came from, but she stood next to him. Then she hit him full in the face and his magic faltered. 'Stop this,' screamed Moirra, and she slapped him a second time, hard. 'Stop misusing your powers, idiot.'

Her voice made the fog in his head waver. 'Aaah, damn you, Bearjaw!' he yelled. A massive flash came from the sky and burned the suffering Viking to cinders. Then Muus half turned toward Moirra and sagged. Crying bitter tears, he buried his head in the girl's shoulder.

'How did you come here so fast?' asked Ottil, after things had calmed down a bit.

Moirra, holding Muus in her arms, looked up from where they sat. 'I felt him collecting his power. It was so strong; every druid in the area must have noticed it. I knew he was going to do something awful, so I ordered Uthar and his men to follow me. My horse will be angry with me, because I urged her to run faster than she should, but I arrived in time.'

'What's wrong with him? He didn't faint this time, but why is he crying? It was a great victory.'

'Muus isn't a Nordish warrior, Prince. He feels very sorry for what he did.' She stared into the distance. 'Be glad he does. With the skyshard to aid him, he has great power. If he never suffered remorse, he'd be very, very dangerous.'

'That's why you are here,' said Hraab. 'You're his conscience.'

Moirra nodded. 'I know.'

CHAPTER 11 - GEIR

The Warchief came over. 'I have collected all those Norden scum, druidess. Would you like to see them before they're executed?'

Muus sat up straight. 'Just kill them,' he said bitterly. 'They don't deserve our attention.'

Uthar nodded. 'I will have my men handle their execution. Most of my soldiers are young and they're still unused to this. But it is a part of war and they need to know it.' Without more ado, he set his men to digging a large hole at the crossroads between the town and the stronghold.

When it was finished, the raiders were brought thither, naked and shivering. They knew what was awaiting them. They had trusted Largassen to protect them from this fate and he had failed. The knowledge was visible in their faces, in the set of their shoulders. Suddenly one of them, a young fellow, started to scream. 'No! No!' One of his mates, a burly man with old markings buried among the hair on his chest, cuffed him. 'Silent, cur. Don't die like a girl.'

'Take him first,' said Uthar. 'Before he panics the rest of the dogs.'

The executioner, about the same age as the young raider, gripped his ax in both hands. His eyes met those of his victim, and he swallowed. Two soldiers pushed the raider to his knees, with his neck on the wooden block. As they stepped back, the executioner swung his ax. His nervous stroke lacked force and the naked young man fell, twitching like a landed fish. Captors and captures alike began to murmur. The two soldiers manhandled the half-dead raider back into position.

'Keep quiet there! And you, soldier, steel yourself,' snapped Uthar.

Beads of sweat appeared on the executioner's brow. His second stroke carried so much force that the young raider's head rolled over the grass towards the waiting captives. The burly Nord with the markings folded his arms across his chest. He looked down at the head and then at the sweating soldier. 'Get on with it, you sniveling buttercup,' he growled.

The soldier reddened. 'You're next,' he said, lifting his ax.

Calmly, the raider knelt at the block and a moment later his head joined his mate's.

The killing went on until the grass became red and slippery. Though the executioners got better at it, they rarely managed to end a life in one stroke.

Ottil looked at his countrymen. Their fear clung to him like a wolverine's scent. They looked so ordinary, not like rapists and killers of children at all. Bearded and unkempt, many with badly healed scars, but not any different from the farmers and fishermen he knew around Nidros. One of them was a boy, he saw. A thin boy of his own age, too young for this work. He looked terrified, too; his eyes wide in his face and his nose running. Curly red hair ran down to his shoulders. It was clean, so he must be proud of its length. Between two burly raiders he looked so small. Ottil turned to Muus. 'That boy,' he said. 'They can't kill him. He's only a child.'

Muus seemed to come from far away. 'What?' Then he saw the lad. With a curse, he rose and walked towards the waiting raiders. They made way for him in silence, until he and the redhead were at the center of a circle.

'You, what is your name?' he said, but the boy only stared at him with a dazed look in his eyes.

'He has no name, Lord,' said the big raider man next to him. 'We took him and his brother from a shipwreck in the last storm. The brother was half-dead already and died soon after. The boy hasn't spoken a word; must be dumb, I guess. Bear planned to sell him as a prize.'

Muus stared at the raider till the man lowered his eyes. 'I became one of Largassen's victims when I was younger than this one. He sold me, too. Now I'm back to show you how I liked that. Remember it when your head rolls, pirate,' he said. 'Come with me, lad.' Muus took the boy's arm and pulled him out of the circle.

'Here he is,' said Muus, as they returned to the others. 'Ottil, you wanted him. Here you have him; he hasn't spoken yet. I make him your responsibility. He's your bondsman, not a slave. I've been one too long to force slavery upon another.'

'My bondsman?' Ottil looked at the boy, naked as the day he was born. 'He needs clothes.'

Muus nodded. He beckoned one of the watching townspeople, a stout lady who had eagerly followed every execution. 'Good woman, will you arrange for some clothes for this boy?'

The townswoman looked as if he'd made an indecent proposal. 'He's one of *them*. He should be killed. Let him die from cold.'

'It wasn't a request, mistress,' said Muus darkly.

His anger must have reached her, for the woman blanched. 'Of course, Runemaster.'

Moirra smiled at the woman. 'You will be compensated, mistress. The Runemaster requires some new clothes for himself and our companions. If you happen to know some able seamstresses who could oblige us with their work, they will be amply rewarded.'

The town woman's eyes got greedy. 'Certainly, druidess. It would be an honor.'

'We'll speak of this shortly. First some clothes for the boy, please.'

The stout woman hurried away, no doubt thinking about which ones of her cronies she would ask to assist her with this unexpected windfall.

The executions went on. Some raiders fought the soldiers with their bare hands, collecting cuts and broken bones, others were brought to the block screaming or resigned, but all were killed. The boy had a wild look on his face. Suddenly he turned and sprinted for the nearby wood. Archers aimed for the fugitive, but Muus cried, 'Don't shoot!'

Ottil and Hraab ran after him, swift as hounds, and Ottil tackled his barefoot prey halfway across the hill. The boy fought silently, biting and clawing, but to no avail. Finally, he had to submit and he started to cry. Ottil helped him to a sitting position. As he saw how the boy shivered, blue with cold, he wrapped his own cloak around the heaving shoulders. 'Are you finished with this silliness? Running away is foolish, you don't have any clothes or weapons, and even the rabbits could kill and eat you.' He gave the boy a stern stare. 'You're better off with us. What is your name again?'

For a moment, there was a silence. 'Geir Gormsen,' said the boy then.

'So you can speak,' said Ottil, satisfied. 'Where are you from?'

The boy wiped his nose. 'Walfell. When me eldest brother's babe was born, there wasn't any place left for me at the farm, so me brother Olf took me with him to sea.'

'Walfell. That's in the south. Whose man are you? Rannar's or the king's?'

'Me father is Rannar's sworn man. Olf didn't care for either one.'

'And you?'

The boy shrugged. 'Rannar would think me too young, I'm not big enough for a sailor, and they say the king is a fool. I don't know. Don't care, either. I only wanted to be with me brother, but then the storm came and now Olf's dead.'

'We were in that storm,' said Ottil. 'It wrecked us too, and we landed here instead of in Harflot. I am sorry about your brother, but now you are here and I want to know what you're going to do. If you want to run, I'll turn my back and let you go. Else, you'll become a king's man and swear to serve me. Now choose.'

The boy looked torn between fear and a wish to escape. 'You didn't tell me your name. Who are you?'

Ottil's face was ferocious. 'I'm not going to tell you unless you swear.'

The boy slumped. 'Choose between death and serving the enemy. What choice is that?'

'Are you my enemy?'

'You say you're the King's man. Vidmer is no friend of the Jarl.'

'But you're not the Jarl. Now, I'm getting fed up with this. Choose.'

The boy looked at the dark wood and shivered. 'I'll swear.'

'Great. I haven't got a sword, so my club will have to suffice.' Ottil sat up straight, his legs crossed, with the weapon over his knees. 'Kneel.'

The Prince knew the oath of loyalty by heart; his tutor had made sure of that. Geir didn't, but repeated obediently what was said to him, and so it was done.

'On your honor, you're a true king's man now, Geir Gormsen.' Ottil smiled grimly. 'I will let you in on our secret. King Vidmer is dead. One of Rannar's men had him murdered, two months ago.'

At this, the boy looked up. 'The King is dead?'

'My father is as dead as Largassen. He was a fool and he won't be missed, but I wish they had waited till I was older. Now you know. I'm your Prince, I'm Ottil Vidmersen.'

Geir gaped at his words. 'How can this be? The Prince wouldn't be here! He lives in Nidros in his castle, not on a beach in this land of barbarians.'

'But in Nidros I would have been killed. Rannar would have seen to that. I escaped their clutches, thanks to the Runemaster. We were on our way to Rhemes, where my mother has gone, when that storm ruined all. Now I'm on a quest with the Runemaster and Druidess Moirra. When that is done, I'll be older and I'll go home to retake my kingdom.' His voice sounded so serious, that Geir stared at him in silence.

'Close your mouth,' said Hraab, 'before a bird steals your tongue.' He laughed, clapping his hands in glee. 'Come; let's go back. You need clothes.'

The townswoman had managed to scrape something together for the boy, an old and faded tunic with some often-patched trousers. There were no shoes, but Geir didn't care. He seemed mostly surprised they had given him things at all.

The boys wandered over to the longships on the beach. An armed townsman had been posted there to keep curious folk away. 'These ships are the town's property. Nobody is allowed on board.'

Ottil looked the man in the eye. 'What do you mean the town's property? Did the town kill those raiders? When we arrived, we saw the people of Luddagh cower behind their thin walls. Our Runemaster killed the Viking and captured his men. These ships and all that's in them are his to depose of. Or were you going to tell him your town takes what he rightfully won? He's over there. His mood isn't too good, but he is approachable. Go tell him.'

The man swallowed. 'No, that's all right. Your arguments convince me, youngster. The rest is for the headman to worry about. You, eh, you don't mind my staying on post here? I don't want no trouble.'

'Post to your heart's content. Admit no one, not even the headman himself, without the Runemaster's permission.'

They jumped into Largassen's boat, the one with the bear sail.

'It's a big one,' said Ottil, looking around. 'Thirty benches, and room for seventy men at least. Must have cost them a lot of gold.'

They walked to the red-and-white striped awning that covered everything amidships.

'That's where it is,' said Hraab.

'Where what is?'

'The loot.' With a dreamy look in his eyes, the boy walked forward. 'Bales and chests,' he said. 'Let's see what's in them.'

'Don't touch anything!'

Ottil looked at Geir's frightened face. 'Why not?'

'He had his treasure cursed, so that only he could touch it. It's death for all others.'

Hraab laughed. 'The dirty old fraud. There isn't a curse in the neighborhood.' He bent over a large chest and tried to open it. With a loud crack, an arrow came from somewhere and smashed into his right shoulder. 'Dammit, ' Hraab said, pivoting. 'I didn't see it.' Then his eyes turned away and he fell down.

'Quick! Get the druidess,' said Ottil. Without a word, Geir sped away.

It didn't take long for him to come back with Moirra and Muus.

'What's this about an arrow?' began Moirra as she ducked under the awning. '*Hraab* is hit?' She knelt next to the motionless body and touched the arrow with her fingers.

Ottil stared at the wooden shaft and the small trickle of blood that stained Hraab's tunic. 'We wanted to look at the loot. Geir warned us about a curse and Hraab laughed. Then he... he touched that chest and the arrow came from nowhere.'

'Not from nowhere,' said Muus. 'It's a trap, a dirty, cruel Largassen-type of trap.' He pointed at a contraption of wood and ropes hidden among the chests.

'The arrow went right through the muscle,' said Moirra, while she ripped open the neck of the dirty tunic. She took her little saw from her pouch and started to remove the arrow's point. Then she tugged slightly at the wooden shaft. 'You boys, press his body to the deck while I pull out the arrow. Ready? One, two...' At three, the slender shaft slid easily from the wound. Moirra produced two wads she had held concealed in her left sleeve and pressed them to both the entry and the exit wound. 'Ottil, Geir, turn around please. You too, Muus. Please. Ah, secrets of my craft.' Obediently, the others did as she asked. Moirra lifted Hraab's tunic. While the wads stayed miraculously in place, she wound a long strip of linen around the shoulder and across Hraab's chest. She pulled the tunic down again. 'There, that should keep him quiet for some days.' She stopped over the supine boy. 'You can open your eyes now, poseur.'

Hraab gave her a bitter look. 'I'm dangerously wounded.'

'You're a fool.'

'I know.' Hraab gritted his teeth as he sat up. 'I didn't feel the trap. It was so stupidly *human* I didn't expect it.'

'How do you feel?' said Ottil anxiously.

'I feel fine.' He frowned. 'Damned cross, but otherwise fine. This scratch will be healed in a few days; the damage to my pride will take much longer.' He held out his left hand. 'Sorry I laughed at you, Geir. You were right; it was a curse. Only of another type than I expected.' He fingered the bandage gingerly. 'It itches already.' Then his eyes searched Moirra's face. 'I'm in your debt. Twice over.'

The girl winked at him. 'Write it down somewhere. In case I need something in return.'

'So this is Bearjaw's loot.' Muus eyed the chests with a feeling of distaste. Ill-gotten loot. It felt like plundering Owwich. 'He'd been quite busy.'

'It's all yours.' Ottil grinned. 'The guard outside said the headman claimed everything, but I told him you won the battle singlehanded and so the loot is yours, too.'

Muus shrugged. 'I'm not interested.'

'I am,' said Hraab swiftly.

Ottil stared at Muus. 'Not interested? They're riches. I could buy an army with this to beat Rannar and recover my throne.'

'Don't bother your head about it, Muus,' said Moirra, smiling up at his troubled face. 'I'll arrange things with the headman and the Warleader. They both have suffered losses that need compensation. Those bales of cloth will go to our new clothes the town women will make. We'll divide the loot in three parts. One for the town, one for the garrison and one for us.'

'I need some weapons and armor,' said Ottil. 'Geir too.' He saw the boy's surprised face. 'I can polish my own boots, mate. I want you to fight beside me.'

'I'm not a warrior,' said the boy.

Ottil clapped him on the shoulder. 'Then I'll make you one. We have some time till Hraab is recovered enough for travelling. I think the garrison took everything Largassen's men owned. We'll see the Warleader about it.'

'That's the way to go,' said Hraab with one of his broad grins. 'Stick with the man; you're going to make it in the world.'

Geir looked confused. 'I'm only a farm boy.'

'Some of our greatest heroes were farm boys,' said Hraab. 'Now, where was I?' With his left hand, he pulled open the large chest that had triggered the arrow and rummaged through the leather-wrapped items inside. Suddenly he whistled. He held up a beautiful casket of gold, inlaid with precious stones. With his thumb, he opened the lid and there, on a cushion of purple velvet, lay a small knuckle bone. He smiled slightly and closed the lid. 'Muus, look at this. Here, it's very valuable.'

'Very, very,' said Ottil. 'My mother had a box like that, a gift from my Royal uncle. It was worth an army, she always said.'

'Then perhaps Muus will let you keep the box. Don't buy any Fynni with it. They play false.'

'It is beautiful,' said Moirra. 'What is inside?'

'Present for the Runemaster,' said Hraab.

Quickly Muus flipped the lid open and looked at the bone inside. 'It's one of them,' he whispered. 'I feel the others shake, as if they're glad.' He picked up the bone and added them to the three he already wore. 'It really is one of them. One of the great runes.' He heard a vague whisper in his head. *L'aj*. 'The Rune of Tongues.' He had no idea what this rune would do. Tongues? Lick his enemies to death perhaps.

Moirra had to laugh at that. 'No, silly. It's about *strange* tongues. Understanding languages. We'll meet plenty of these once we go to the mainland.'

Muus's head shot up. 'The mainland. Why did the Gods choose me for this task?'

'You wouldn't want to know the answer,' said Hraab. 'Just be glad you weren't killed at Owwich.'

'Sometimes I wonder,' said Muus, staring at him. 'Funny, you're not exactly the little boy we met with Ajkell, all those months ago.'

'Ajkell,' said Hraab. 'I often think of him. He was so steady, so unflappable. And Kjelle. Don't you ever think of Kjelle?'

Muus was surprised at the question. He hadn't thought of Kjelle for a long time. 'Funny, I hardly have, there is so much going on. But now you ask, sometimes I miss him. We shared our lives for ten years; that's a long time. I wonder how it is with him, Birthe and little Búi. Shall I ever see them again?'

At that, Moirra frowned. 'You wouldn't want a girl with a baby.'

Muus took her hand. 'What are you saying? I wouldn't want Birthe without a baby either. She's a Nord, far too big and capable. I like them small. And capable. Birthe was a friend; she accepted my powers although she hated men who had them, but would I want her? No.'

Moirra smiled sweetly. 'It's all right, I'm not jealous.'

'There's nothing to be jealous about,' said Muus in a firm voice.

The next morning the women of the town started on suitable clothing for Muus and the boys. Largassen's loot contained many fine fabrics, from which they wrought a long, darkly red robe for the Runemaster, with a thick woolen cloak. For the boys the ladies made fine tunics and plaid trousers. The local cobbler provided them with new boots, for most of their shoes had been ruined by seawater. Ottil looked at his handsome clothes with approval. The mail coat he'd chosen from the garrison's booty fitted well enough over the tunic. With the belted sword at his side and an iron cap with eye guard to wear on his head he felt fully the warrior. Geir accepted everything they handed him with astonishment, as if he couldn't imagine why they gave him things. Hraab, on the other hand, eyed his fine tunic with something like revulsion. 'It's far too clean,' he said. 'I hate feeling respectable.'

'Would you rather look like my servant boy?' asked Ottil haughtily.

Hraab threw him a dirty look.

'And while you're at it,' said the Prince, 'ask Moirra to wash your hair, before some cuckoo thinks you're a nest.' He was polite enough to wait till his friend was out of earshot, before he started to crow. 'I got him! This time I got him!'

When Hraab returned, he positively shone. His hair was neatly combed, his skin sparkling white, and in his new clothes, he looked like a young prince himself. Jewels shone on his fingers and round his neck. A beautiful smallsword hung from a copper belt at his waist and his feet were shod in fine leather boots.

'Damn,' muttered Ottil. 'Where did you get all the sparklies?'

'Oh,' said Hraab offhand, 'I found them. Not here,' he said earnestly, looking at Muus. 'Most of them I picked up in Nidros. People are so careless with their valuables.' He grinned at Ottil. 'Am I fine enough for your exalted company, Prince?'

Ottil sighed. 'Why do you always get the better of me?'

'Are you mad at me?'

The Prince sighed. 'Of course not.' Then he laughed. 'Just watch out for robbers, you glitter-cat.'

CHAPTER 12 – A VENGEFUL VILLAGE

Two days later, they left. Hraab's shoulder had healed so fast that young Geir stared at him in disbelief when the dressing was removed and only white scars showed where the arrow had gone in and out. Several times, Ottil saw Geir looking at Hraab and shaking his head, but he never said anything. The boy wasn't very voluble anyway. Whether he was still mourning his brother or naturally untalkative, Ottil couldn't say. Finally, he decided his new hirdman was a taciturn, gloomy farmer. The lad was handy with an ax, though, and soon Hraab was teaching him all manners of tricks that could be useful for those who weren't overly big and brawny.

One evening when they had stopped for the night, Muus was watching their training. 'You didn't really need Kjelle's teachings, that time on board the *Madgund?* he said after a while.

Hraab smiled. 'No.'

'Why all the acting then?'

'Because Kjelle needed something to feel good about.'

'That was nice of you.'

Hraab shrugged. 'It was necessary. Kjelle has things to do. Besides, I felt sorry for him. He needed help much more than you did.'

'You're deep, for a kid.'

Hraab started to grin. 'I am, ain't I?' Then he shouted at Geir. 'Not like that, you cack-handed lout! Or do you carry spare body-parts somewhere?'

A very fleeting smile passed the farm boy's face. He pushed his red curls from his eyes and tried the overhand throw again. As his ax stood quivering in the tree, Hraab clapped his shoulder. 'Better. Much better.'

Nearly a sevenday later, from the top of a bald hill, they saw a river in the distance, flowing sedately westward.

'The Temysis,' said Moirra. 'We must go upriver to reach King's Lud.'

'Can't we get any closer?' asked Ottil.

The girl shook her head. 'Between here and there it's one great wetland, full of reed swamp and mudflats. We'd never get through it.'

'I smell the sea,' said Geir suddenly.

Moirra smiled at him. 'The marshes and the river are very salty here. I've heard it said the tide reaches past King's Lud.'

'I like the fjords better,' the boy said softly. 'They're cleaner.'

Ottil stared at him. 'You're not homesick, are you?'

'Ever since we left the farm,' said Geir simply. 'Having Olf near helped, but now...' He wiped his nose. 'I wanna go home.'

'Well, you can't,' said the Prince bluntly.

Geir rubbed his eyes. 'I know.'

They rode on, past isolated farms and small settlements, until they saw ships on the river. Rows upon rows of ships, in shape like the boats Bearjaw had used, but many of them larger. A sea of masts, with flocks of seagulls soaring and diving around them.

'What's that!' said Ottil, amazement clear in his voice. 'A war party?'

Muus stared at the ships. No sail raised, no crew on board. 'It must be that Royal fleet the Denar Byn Warleader told us about.'

'There are hundreds of ships,' said Ottil. 'Even ten of them could have finished that Viking easily. What sort of king is this Cucharann?' He scratched his nose. 'I can't see any guards.'

Hraab pointed. 'Only in those two towers.'

The Prince sighed. 'Stupid. With fifty men I'd have burned the whole fleet.'

He was more impressed by the first sight of King's Lud itself. 'Stone walls,' he said. 'What are they afraid of?'

'You and your fifty men perhaps?' said Moirra.

Ottil's eyes started to gleam. 'There must be ways to get into the town. Where there's a will...'

Geir coughed softly. 'Highness, what's that hole in the wall for, halfway under water?'

'Possibly a river outlet,' said Muus.

Red locks danced as the boy shook his head. 'It looks like an open door to me.'

'Brilliant,' said Ottil. 'A door indeed. We could swim right through the walls.'

'You don't mind if we less warlike folk use that bridge?' said Moirra.

Ottil sniffed. 'If you must. I think our plan much grander, though.'

'Have you learned how to swim, then?' said Hraab.

'Hush, don't bother me with details.'

Their horses' hoofbeats echoed loudly over the planking of the bridge. Halfway was an open gate, with a guard lounging as if he was the king of boredom. He opened one eye at them and waved them through.

'With guards like that we could come in ship's boats, waving flags and blowing trumpets, for all he'd care,' said Ottil sourly.

Once inside the town he looked around. 'I don't think I'll bother, though. The walls are fine, but this is just like any other old place.'

Muus could only agree with him. Brytanna's capital was a disappointment. The streets in King's Lud were muddy, the wooden houses small and dark, and there were more pigs in the road than people. The largest building in town was the king's hall, so they went there, to be greeted by the yapping of a kennel full of guard dogs. They left the horses at the large drinking trough outside and made to enter. At the door, they were stopped by an armed guard.

'The High King is seeing no one,' he said. 'You'd better come back another time, druidess.'

Moirra smiled in the way that always wrenched Muus's gut. 'I don't seek the king; I want to see royal druid Tyllas.'

'Of course.' The guard looked relieved. 'Tyllas. That's no problem, druidess.' He stuck his head around the door and shouted something. To the servant that answered, he said, 'Take the druidess and her followers to Master Tyllas. And be quick about it.' Then he turned to Moirra. 'Follow the slave, druidess. He'll bring you to His Wisdom.'

For his help he got a second smile, which nearly made him drop his spear.

'Don't do that,' whispered Muus. 'You're breaking my heart.'

Moirra merely laughed; a sound so pretty it turned many heads in their direction. The slave was impervious to her laughter, however.

He led them through the busy hall to a shadowed alcove. 'Visitors for you, Master Tyllas.' With a short bow, he left.

The Royal Druid was a small, thin man with a nose like the beak of the raven on his shoulder.

'Druidess Moirra? Oh, Fardoragh's student. Yes, yes, I remember now. What can I do for you, m'dear?'

'Your Wisdom, I am guide to the Runemaster Terrel here. We are on a quest of the utmost urgency. It would be a great service if you could provide us with some information.'

Tyllas looked doubtful. 'What kind of information?'

'There have been stories about a wise man who could read minds. He died some forty winters ago. Can you tell us where this took place?'

Tyllas' face grew longer. 'I can't tell that to an outsider. Your Runemaster, whoever he may be, is not a druid, no member of the circle. He is just a nobody.'

Muus took a deep breath, forcing his anger down. Outwardly relaxed, he stepped forward. 'Wisdom, I am the Runemaster Terrel from Owwich, not *a nobody*. I am on a very important journey and I request any help you can give me.'

Master Tyllas straightened. 'Runemaster, I can't tell you.'

'Oh stop being fussy, Tyllas,' croaked the raven on the druid's shoulder. 'Give him the information, his business is vital.'

Tyllas had paled and he stared at the raven with horror on his face. 'You... you can talk?'

'Of course I can talk, fool. When it is necessary. Now hurry up, will you?'

Muus glanced at Hraab, who shone with innocence. Then he looked up and met Moirra's eyes, shining with some inner glee.

'I wouldn't tarry when Mawgan's Envoy speaks,' she said, her voice almost mocking.

'Come with me,' said the Royal Druid hurriedly.

He led them to a small room at the back of the hall. A bed, a chair and a writing desk were the only pieces of furniture. *At least Tyllas lives soberly*, thought Muus.

From a chest, the druid took a small book. He flipped the pages till he came to the place he sought. 'Yarras,' he said. 'It's a village somewhere to the north of here. It must be on or near the river. Reports speak of a Wiseman who could look inside people's heads. He read what they were thinking. His power seemed to rest in an amulet of sorts he wore around his neck. It must have been buried with him, for nothing was heard of anything strange after his death.'

With an attempt at graciousness, the Royal Druid handed the little book to Moirra. 'Here you are. Could you tell me what the importance is?'

'I'm afraid not, Wisdom,' said Muus as formal as he could. 'It's the Gods' business and I am not free to speak of it.'

Tyllas nodded. 'A pity. I understand, though. May I wish you a safe journey?'

On their way back through the hall, a loud voice made them halt.

'You, boy! Come here.' The command came from a fat man on a gilded stool at the head of the hall.

'The High King,' whispered Moirra. 'Be careful.'

Muus walked towards the Royal seat and bowed slightly, in the Brytannic fashion. 'You wish to see me, Highness?'

'That child, the redheaded one. He's a Nord.' The High King's face was swollen and flushed and his eyes were bloodshot. His enormous body overflowed the stool and there was a faint, unhealthy sound to his breath.

'He is only a servant, Highness.'

'He's a Nord. I don't want Nords at my court.' The king's voice sounded petulant. 'Hand him over, then, and I'll have him killed.'

Behind his back, Muus heard Ottil gasp. 'I can't do that, Highness,' said he firmly. 'He is only a child. There is no need to kill him.'

'You cannot refuse me,' snapped the king. 'Or I'll have you all hanged.'

Muus pulled himself up. 'I am a Runemaster, Highness. It would not be a wise idea to threaten me.'

'Guards!' shouted the king. 'To me!'

Moirra stepped forward and the candlelight made her white robe shimmer. 'Highness, I am of the Un-a-Dach, as is the Runemaster. If you harm any one of us, the Un-a-Dach will pull their protection away from you.'

The fat High King hesitated.

'I will not threaten the person of the High King, Highness,' said Muus pointedly. 'But I can burn down this hall around Your Highness' ears. I can burn your soldiers as I did the Viking Largassen. He is dead, by the way, and so are his men.'

'What!' The High King's face had gone pale, but now a bit of color returned as he saw the face-saving straw and grasped it. 'That monster is dead? How did it happen? When? Where?'

'Let me tell the tale,' said Moirra. In a light voice, she began with their arrival at the garrison at Denar Byn. She stressed the bravery and loyalty of its soldiers and the High King smiled.

'I like that,' he said. 'I like brave men to guard me – my borders'.

Then she told of the ships on the beach, the raiders starting to flame the town. She described in detail the Runemaster's dealing with Largassen, and the way he cowed the raiders into surrender. The High King laughed at that and clapped his hands. 'They're all dead?' he said eagerly. 'Dead and buried?'

'All, Highness.'

'Well done. And where did you get that nasty raider boy?'

'He is not a raider, Highness. He survived the wrecking of the merchant ship he served in. We took him on as a servant, because he is too young to have done anything wrong.'

The High King's breast swelled. 'They are never too young! Those damned Nords are born wicked. Take him away! The next time you come to tell me of your victories on my behalf, leave him in the kennel outside.'

'Your Highness is too gracious,' said Muus and bowed again. They left the hall, while the High King yelled for more wine.

'Let's get away from here,' said Moirra, 'before he changes his mind.'

They hurried to their horses and within minutes rode through the town to the western gate.

'What a joke,' said Ottil. 'I thought my father was a fool, but this one beats all.'

'His subject kings keep him here, well provided with money, food and drink,' said Moirra. 'He never leaves the hall.'

'It would kill him,' said Muus. 'He won't have many years to live.'

Moirra looked at him. 'You're probably right.'

A choked sound had them looking over their shoulders.

'Why are you crying?' asked Ottil.

'I was scared,' said Geir through his tears. 'W-would you really have fought for me?'

Muus smiled at him. 'Of course I would. You're one of us now and I won't let some fat fool lay a finger on you.'

'Nor would I,' said Ottil. 'Dammit, I'd declare war on him.'

Muus winked at Moirra, knowing better than to laugh at the Prince's bold promise.

'Anyhow, we have what we came for,' said the girl. 'Thanks to that raven.'

'I didn't know they could talk,' said Ottil.

Hraab raised his eyebrows, and the Prince colored. 'Damn, of course they can't. It was you, with your clever tricks.'

'Ravens can't talk, you silly boy,' said Ottil's horse. 'Only we stout Brytannic mounts are clever enough.'

As they passed the west gate at that moment, the guard looked open-mouthed at the brown mare. 'Don't stare at me, young man,' said the horse in passing. 'It's rude.' The soldier jumped and fled.

Laughing wildly, they hurried away from King's Lud.

North they went, through a thick forest, till on the fourth day they came to a small river.

Muus halted. 'This will be the tributary from the Temysis that Tyllas mentioned. Yarras must be near.'

They followed a small path along the smaller river, until they saw some buildings. At the first house, a dour-looking man watched their coming from inside the door. As they drew near, he turned his back to them.

'Good day,' said Muus. 'Is this the village of Yarras?'

'It might be,' said the man over his shoulder. 'Dependin' on yer business.'

'Druids' business,' said Moirra sharply. 'Could you point us to the headman's house?'

The man turned to face them. 'Follow the path along the river. The house at the mill.'

'Thank you,' said Muus and they rode on through the village.

Yarras didn't look like much. The houses were uncared-for, with overgrown home gardens and broken windows. Sullen people hung about, doing nothing and eying them with suspicion.

At the silent mill house they found the miller, a surly old man who admitted to being the village headman. 'Welcome to my house,' he said, clearly meaning little of it. 'Sit ye down. How can I be of service to yer honors?'

'This is the village of Yarras?' asked Muus.

The old headman nodded. 'It is.'

'Then I want to speak with you about something that happened some fifty years ago.'

As Muus spoke, the headman's face seemed to turn into stone.

'Don't know what you're talkin' about,' he said when Muus had finished. 'We're a simple village; no Wismen were buried here.'

'We have a book,' said Muus and he held up the slim volume that druid Tyllas hadn't wanted to give him. 'It's all in here, written down by a druid in the holy tongue. The Wiseman lived in a nearby cabin and the stories tell us he could read peoples' minds. After some years, he died, said the witnesses. According to the book, he could have possessed an amulet we need, so we want to find his body.'

'He wasn't buried here,' said the old man again.'

Moirra cocked her head at him. 'Not buried,' she repeated. 'But his body is here somewhere?'

'No,' said the headman after a while and Moirra frowned.

'Watch what you are saying; it is unwise to lie to a Druidess.'

The old man paled. 'I...'

'Where is he?' said Muus.

'We left him in his cabin and barred the door,' said the headman finally. And fiercely he added, 'He was a terrible man. He read our minds and then he tattled about it in the village. Nobody was safe from his malicious tongue. He had to die, but in dying he cursed the village!'

'You killed him?' said Moirra dispassionately.

The headman's face worked. 'We executed him, yes. It was unlawful, but we were desperate. He cursed us when he sentenced him to death, so we cut out his tongue before we hanged him to a tree. After a tenday we took him down, laid him in his house and locked the door. But his curse lived on and gnaws at us still, making us fearful and suspicious of outsiders. Before, we traded furs with the merchants in King's Lud, but we daren't any longer. His magic stops us.'

Moirra rose and it was as if her white robe shimmered in the dim-lit room. 'Will you show us this house?'

The headman nodded. 'It's not far from here.'

The cave lay on a slope just outside the village. Once there had been a path, but fifty years of disuse had almost obliterated it. The old man, however, followed it unerringly. After a while they came to a desolate hut, surrounded by soft winds and whispers. Muus shivered. 'What an awful place. Those voices...'

'You hear them too?' said Moirra surprised. 'That must be your Un-a-Dach blood.'

'My Knucks are shaking,' said Muus. 'I think we've found another one. How do we get inside?'

'We threw away the key,' said the old headman. 'Into the river it went.'

Ottil placed a hand on the wooden door and pushed. 'The planks are still strong. I could break it open, or would you rather...?' He wiggled his fingers.

Muus shook his head. 'That would cost me too much energy just for a door.'

Ottil looked at Geir. 'You do it; you have an ax.'

Without a word, his hirdman unhooked his weapon. He measured the door for a moment and started to chop. Shortly, the lock gave way and the door swung open.

'Thank you,' said Muus and Geir nodded.

Inside, the air was musty and dry. Muus stepped forward and felt the amulet around his neck tug. Following its lead, he walked on until he came to a wooden cot. On it lay the wrinkled husk of a dried-out old man. His body was clad in a soiled long tunic and the rope they'd hanged him with was still around his neck. With a shudder of distaste, Muus searched for the Knuck he sought and there it was. Easily it came away into his hand. *G'hez.* 'The Rune of Sharp Hearing,' Muus said. 'The man was no mind reader.'

'He wasn't?' The headman stepped back in shock. 'But he knew all our secrets.'

'He was just a nasty old man,' said Hraab. 'Not a Wiseman at all. I think of him creeping around the village, listening. A nosy, mean old gossip, that's all he was.'

'Don't worry about it,' said Moirra to the headman. 'It happened long ago. You can bury him now. He had no magic.'

'The curse!' There was a deep pain on the headman's face. 'The fear he punished us with?'

'You did that to yourself.' Moirra's face was stern. 'It was your guilt that made you afraid. Now it's gone. There is no more need for either guilt or fear. Go; tell your people the merchants in King's Lud still need furs.'

'He must have had magic,' said Muus later, as they rode away from Yarras. 'The Knuck wouldn't have worked if he hadn't.'

Moirra glanced at him. 'Of course. But the powers he had dissipated long ago and the curse with it. The villagers' fear had become self-imposed -- a habit I had to break.'

'Will it work?' asked Ottil.

Moirra shrugged. 'That depends on how deeply ingrained their despondency is. Perhaps.' She sighed. 'I'll mention it to the Circle; the High Druid will send someone to help them.'

CHAPTER 13 – BATTLE AT THE FORD

Tuuri walked at the head of the thirty-two men, next to Vulf. It was two months since they had left Eidungruve and his hatred for the cruel Fynni leader had only grown. Tuuri wanted to know all about his father's people, though. What drove them, who were those Gods they worshiped. So he kept asking questions, and Vulf, with that sly smile of his, kept answering.

'Sky is the Bashing Wind,' said the Tarkynn, as they walked through the endless forests of northern Gaul. 'He created the clouds and the storm, the killing from above by the claws and the toothed beaks of the leathery birds. Mighty is Sky and a tempestuous God.'

Tuuri looked askance at the Fynni, whose face was palely ecstatic, and nodded without speaking. His nose caught a smoky air, like the smell from all those farmsteads Vulf had burned. Surreptitiously, Tuuri checked his weapons.

The path passed underneath the branches of an immense beech, whose branches overhung the path and intertwined with the trees on the other side. As they came out of this tunnel of leaves, they found themselves at the edge of a clearing. The stink came from the blackened remnants of a wooden stronghold in the middle of the field. Vulf made a strange sound in the back of his throat. Tuuri saw him stare at the ruins, saw the red of his fury rising in the Tarkynn's thin cheeks, and he kept very still.

'Damn you, Ildr!' screamed the Tarkynn. 'Curse and damn you for failing.' For a moment, Vulf's shape wavered and then a large wolf howled its rage to the sky.

So that's why he could see through my bear shape, that day at Eidungruve, thought Tuuri with a shock. *I should have known. Ulvhednar, wolf berserker. Of course their leader is a shape changer.*

A figure left the shadows of the forest and moved on all fours across the grass towards them. It was their scout, a revolting, crablike young female, grown from birth into her present form of speed and stealth. 'There's enemies ahead,' said she in a high voice. 'A while further, a fordable river. Other side a field like this and a ruined stronghold, barely habitable. I saw rabble, men and women, poorly armed. Twenty, twenty-five, no more.'

Vulf changed back into his human self. He made a yapping sound that sounded curiously dog-like, and Tuuri froze. It was Vulf's hunting call, and his men answered with a baying that sent shivers down Tuuri's spine. It didn't bode well for those poor folk across the river, he thought.

Vulf broke into a run, his Fynni following with the loping gait of a wolf pack smelling their prey. Tuuri knew he could never match their speed, so he followed them at his own pace, jumping over a tree trunk blocking the path towards whatever lay in wait.

At the river, the Fynni sat hidden in the forest's edge as Vulf stared at the stronghold on a low hill. Tuuri slipped past the waiting men and crouched next to him. 'Is this wise?' he said. 'Their walls seem stout and your force isn't overlarge.'

Vulf turned his face towards him. 'You're always the coward, aren't you? A disgusting mongrel Fynnikin. I spit on you, bastard boy. And now forward, we'll attack and I want to see you fight, or by the Four, I'll rip your throat out.'

A warrior said something and pointed towards the stronghold. Slowly, a large banner rose on its staff.

'Hah!' Vulf rose and turned to his men. 'They just challenged me. Attack!'

'They've arrived,' said Kjelle to his staff. A feeling of anticipation gripped him. *Vulf! I'll have you, murderer.* His eyes met Ajkell's and he saw his excitement mirrored in them.

'Both Birthe and Göll are in position with their archers,' said Valiantrude. 'So are Bemm's warriors. The fighters are armed and Annlith has pre-empted part of the longhouse for any wounded. Let the buggers come, we'll never get readier than this.'

And ready they were. In the time since their return from Wederer Mountain, they'd worked towards this moment. Training the men with their new weapons, strengthening the walls and the house without losing that dilapidated air, exercising their plan again and again till every man and woman knew their place and their job with their eyes closed.

'Holder, the enemy's at the ford.' The lad running messages grinned.

'All right,' said Kjelle, rising from his chair. There was no trace of his old fears, and he was sure the plan would work. 'Hoist our banner.'

The youngster saluted and hurried back.

Kjelle listened, but no sound came. That was part of the plan, act cowed. He rubbed his hands. 'Let's go, I want to see the bastard's face.'

The Fynni came splashing through the river, screaming like demented beasts. They were a fearsome sight, with their painted faces and their muscled bodies. Behind them ran their leader, a young man with a sharp face contorted in a snarl.

So that's Vulf, thought Kjelle. A rabid wolf. His companion, a black-haired boy, appeared to hesitate. He hung back and his sword was still undrawn. Was he afraid?

Birthe's fourteen archers loosed their first volley from their concealment in the forest edge. Some Fynni fell, tripping up their brothers, and in the confusion, a second volley followed. Then the gate opened and Bemm's ten warriors poured out, waving their weapons and yelling.

Kjelle turned to his men. 'Come on, for Alman and Eidungruve!' He stormed through the gate with his fighting men and women, wild with the taste of revenge in his mouth.

Ajkell ran past him, setting a straight line for Vulf. He roared and there was something bear-like about him. Kjelle froze, halting to look. The bear warrior plowed through the fighting men till he reached the Fynni leader. As they confronted each other, all fighting stopped as everybody paused to watch.

The Fynni howled and his sword glittered in his hand. A lightning-swift thrust at Ajkell's head made Kjelle's heart run cold, but the bear warrior parried the blow, countering with one of his own. Vulf jumped back and Ajkell followed, raining blows that were stopped one by one. It went quick, in a tempo Kjelle knew he'd never match. Ajkell hewed at Vulf. The Fynni somersaulted away, turned on the ground and tried to kick Ajkell's legs from under him. The bear warrior wasn't caught and dove on top of Vulf, gripping him by the throat. He started banging the other's head against the ground, and blood covered the Fynni's face. Vulf howled and began to change. Fur sprang up and his face changed into a wolf's head. Ajkell's grip weakened and the wolf turned around, missing Ajkell's face by a finger's breath. Ajkell put his arms around the beast and squeezed.

The wolf wrestled and tried to bite Ajkell's face, but the bear warrior strengthened his grip. The beast's howling was panicked. Vulf no longer fought to win, but only to escape. The nails on his hind paws drew deep scratches in Ajkell's bare legs. The bear warrior gave one last hug and Kjelle saw the wolf go limp. Ajkell let go and stood up, panting. The dead wolf shimmered and turned back into Vulf, a bloodied, dead Vulf.

Around them, the fighting resumed, but not for long. The leaderless Fynni fought badly and died one by one, until none were left.

Kjelle walked to where Ajkell stood. 'You did it,' he said. 'By Thor, you did it.'

Ajkell lifted his head. 'I avenged Meili and his lady. My honor is restored.' Then he grabbed Vulf's sword from the rocks and cut off the Fynni's head. Holding the dripping trophy up, he yelled, 'Hraab, do you see? I killed him, little one. I killed Vulf!' Then he looked around. 'I need a stake.'

Tuuri had seen Vulf die, squeezed to death by a massive warrior. He couldn't help but chuckle and once he started, he couldn't stop anymore. Sobbing and chuckling he fled back the way they'd come. 'Vulf, stupid animal,' he cried aloud. 'I warned you. But you called me a coward, didn't you? And now you're dead, with your men. Wasn't I right, Vulf? Wasn't I?' He ran till his breath gave out and his chest threatened to burst, and then he stopped. There was the ruin of Ildr's stronghold. He could stop here for a while; he had to sleep. They wouldn't search for him, they wouldn't know he was here. Where should he go? He thought of Jarl Rannar, and of his duty. 'I'll go south. To that place where the Shardheld was going. I don't know what I can do, but I'm not a Fynni. I won't fail my master.' He closed his eyes and slept.

CHAPTER 14 - RECOGNITION

Kjelle sent a messenger to Jarl Dettrich with a report of his victory. The next day they were busy laying out the dead and cutting logs for a large funeral pile, when the lookout at the Rhemes road came running.

'The Jarl's here,' he said breathlessly.

Kjelle, working side by side with his men in stacking the logs, paused and wiped his brow. 'Jarl Dettrich? Damn, what an awkward time. Warn the kitchen before you go back to your post.'

The Jarl came accompanied by all the other clan leaders and their followers, some twenty men in total. As they neared the stronghold, they halted and stared at the rows of dead Fynni and the seven men Kjelle had lost.

Slowly, Dettrich rode forward, while Kjelle walked to meet him. 'Welcome, Lord,' said he, saluting.

'Your report wasn't overlong, so we come to see your victory for ourselves. How many did you kill?'

'Thirty-five, including their chieftain, Vulf. Oaths were fulfilled with these deaths, Lord.'

Jarl Dettrich looked at him. 'They were the ones?'

'The ones who murdered my father and my people at Eidungruve. It was Ajkell Gudrofsen who killed Vulf in single combat for the death of his master and mistress.'

Dettrich looked at a tall man with blond braids. 'Thus he redeemed himself.'

'I am pleased to hear it, Lord,' said the man. 'I will tell him so myself.' He turned to Kjelle, 'Well met. I'm Barulf, Holder of Leidwald since old Brandr died. His spirit will be rejoicing in Valhalla tonight. Where can I find young Ajkell?'

'He's logging trees for the funeral pyre,' said Kjelle. 'Vulf was a shapechanger and turned into a giant wolf. But Ajkell just crushed him against his breast and the monster died in fear.'

'A pleasant thought,' said Barulf grimly. 'I'll wait till he returns then.'

'Are they Niflunger?' said Jarl Dettrich, nodding towards Bemm's men. 'Not only do they smith for you, but they fight for you as well?'

'They are from Wederer Mountain. It's a bit of a tale, Lord. Shall we go inside? It's primitive, but well enough for our own needs.'

In the longhouse, they sat round the fire and Kjelle started his tale of their doings since they left Dalland's fort.

'Well done,' said Dettrich, after Kjelle had finished his account of yesterday's battle. 'Alman was a great warrior and he must have left you more of his cunning than we thought. You've amply justified my trust in you, Lord Kjelle.'

Servants brought them ale and wine, with cheese and sausages. 'Imported from Rhemes,' said Kjelle proudly.

Jarl Dettrich smiled. 'Your people eat well.'

'We did our friends of Wederer some service,' said Kjelle. 'They paid us enough to buy food.'

'I am surprised. I always thought Niflunger were ugly monsters, but they're not. They look like proper warriors to me.'

'They are,' said Kjelle. 'Small, but you don't want to face them on the field of war.' He looked squarely at Dettrich. 'They want to return to the Norden. I promised to speak to Prince Ottil about it. Would you do the same, Lord? They'd be very useful friends.'

'I'm not sure. They seem capable, and I know King Leodowric sent emissaries to Silver Mountain,' said the Jarl slowly.

'For Mastersmiths that could have served us,' said Birthe. She had just entered and sat down next to Kjelle. 'If we stay suspicious of them, then all our neighbors will have better arms than us. Is that what we want?'

'They are dvergar,' said a thin warrior quickly. 'We kicked them out because they were bewitching us.'

'Our Elbrich is no sorcerer,' snapped Birthe. 'All his power goes to smithing the best weapons and armor in the world.

'Next you want them svartalves back as well, woman,' said the thin warrior angrily.

'Calm down, Asger,' said Jarl Dettrich. 'The lady is a Völva.'

Birthe didn't wait for the thin man's answer. 'Svartalves don't exist, Lord Asger, nor do dvergar. The Niflunger are people, just like you and me. Not as big as Nords, but then, you're not that tall yourself either.'

'Enough!' shouted the Holder, deadly pale. 'I didn't come here to be insulted. You will repent your words, woman.'

Birthe opened her mouth and sang a few lines. Asher sat down on the bench with a crash, staring glassy-eyed at the girl opposite him.

'I am a Völva,' said Birthe in a deadly voice. 'I won't be threatened by anyone. Remember that, *Lord* Asger.'

Kjelle took her shoulders and turned her so she faced him. 'No, love,' said he softly. 'Not that way. I will defend your honor with my sword, but don't use your power on friends.'

'A friend?' said Birthe, shaking off his grip. 'I have other ideas of my friends, Lord Holder.' Then she ran from the longhouse.

'Your pardon, Lord Asger,' said Kjelle heavily. 'The Völva played a large part in yesterday's battle. She's also my Leader of the Hunt, you see. Her shots are deadly and she killed many. Yet the strain tells.'

'Is she really that good?' asked Barulf of Leidwald, bending forward.

Kjelle smiled. 'I've not yet seen her miss. She killed a bear when she was fourteen.'

Barulf gave Asger a contemptuous look. 'It seems you fell afoul of the wrong person this time, Asger.'

'It's time to return,' said Dettrich. 'My compliments on your victory and give my apologies to the Lady Birthe.'

Barulf was the last to leave the longhouse. 'Don't mind Asger. He's a fool and most of us hate his guts.' Stepping outside, he nearly bumped into Ajkell.

The young bear warrior froze. 'Barulf.'

'Ajkell.' For a moment, there was silence. 'Old Brandr died, you know. His son's death was too much for his heart.'

Ajkell didn't relax. 'And you took over?'

'We held a Thing to discuss the succession. Several names passed round, and mine the most. So I got chosen. After that, the Fynni came and we had to... pull back. Our forces weren't over large and they came in the night, when all slept. We warriors managed to hold them off while the others left by the back gate. Then we let the enemy within, torched the buildings and joined the rest. We left precious little to plunder for the buggers. We went south then, and joined Dettrich.' He gave Ajkell a hard stare. 'You avenged Meili?'

Ajkell waved towards Vulf's on a stake near the gate. 'That's the dog.' He shrugged. 'Wasn't all that much of a fighter, even if he was a shape-changer.'

Barulf clasped Ajkell's hand. 'Welcome back, brother.' Then he grinned. 'But you won't return with me.'

Ajkell shook his head. 'No, I serve Kjelle now.'

Barulf looked at the young Holder. 'You're a lucky man, Kjelle. Ajkell's the most loyal guy alive.'

Kjelle looked stared at the two faces. 'I didn't realize you were family.'

Barulf laughed. 'We don't look alike. He's the youngest, and I the eldest-but-one.' He looked proudly at Ajkell. 'He may be my little brother, but I wouldn't want to face him in battle. He's like our father, and old Gudrof is the strongest creature this side of Godsdammer. Well, the Jarl is leaving. Gods bless you both.' With that, he hurried after his lord.

Ajkell's face showed the biggest grin Kjelle had ever seen on him. 'My brother, a Holder. Pa must be proud.'

'Of you both,' said Kjelle, and he clapped his bodyguard on the shoulder. 'Now I must go and look for Birthe.'

'She went upriver,' said Ajkell. 'She didn't look too happy.'

'I'll go and find her.' Kjelle hurried towards the river. As he waded against the current towards the rapids beyond the bend, he heard a scream. 'Birthe!' he shouted, trying to go faster. But the racing waters were strong and his progress was agonizingly slow. As he rounded the bend, he saw Birthe fighting with a weird, crablike creature.

'Hold on, I'm coming.'

The creature was jumping about on all fours, slashing at the girl with a clawed hand, crying 'Kill! Kill! in a high voice. It was fast, circling around her, while Birthe parried its attacks with her long hunting knife, cursing and swearing incessantly.

Then, when Kjelle as almost there, the creature sprang at Birthe.

'No you don't,' shouted the girl and her knife bit deep into its neck. Blood spurted and the creature slumped down, gashing Birthe's arm with its sharp nails in a last convulsive swipe. The girl crouched, knife in hand, snarling like a wild animal.

Kjelle, who had wanted to put his arms around her, stopped at the look in her eyes. 'Well done,' he said, keeping his voice calm.

All at once, the tension left her and she sagged. 'I... What was it? I sat here, thinking, when suddenly it hopped from the trees like some overgrown frog and attacked me. It... Is it human?'

Kjelle studied the dead creature. It had spindly limbs, a thin body and a stubble-covered but unmistakably human head. It was naked, and covered in many-colored symbols that had glowed when it lived, but were now dull and lifeless. 'It's Fynni; some of those markings are the same as Vulf's. And it is female.'

Birthe rubbed her eyes, as if to clear them. 'You're right,' she said. 'I should've seen it. I'm dizzy.'

Quickly, Kjelle looked at her. 'Your arm. Those gashes must be cleaned.'

Birthe sat down on her knees and put her arm in the swift, clear water. 'I'm still dizzy,' she said after a while. Then she pitched forward.

Kjelle caught her and took her in his arms. 'Annlith should look at it.' Birthe didn't answer. Her heavy breathing frightened him, and walking fast now with the current, he bore her back to Almansford.

'Those gashes are not why she fainted; I've cleaned them and they will heal,' said Annlith, after she'd examined Birthe. 'The problem is, her life energies are very low; she needs a great deal of sleep.'

'I don't understand,' said Kjelle. 'She's always so energetic.'

'That's just it.' The girl peered up at him, her large yellow eyes shining. 'She does too much. Fighting her emotions and worrying, leading the archers, all her singing and chanting. She's using far too much energy in her condition.'

Kjelle's heart skipped a beat. 'What's wrong with her?'

Annlith smiled gently. 'She's expecting.'

Kjelle stared at her. 'Expecting what?' Then it dawned on him what the healer meant. 'She's with child?' He reeled, steadying himself against the wall. Birthe was with child? His child?

'Are you all right?' Annlith's tiny face had grown anxious. 'Yes, she's at least six sevendays pregnant.'

He counted quickly. That was the sevenday they went to Wederer Mountain. The familiar, paralyzing fear clutched at him, but he gritted his teeth and willed it away. *Keep calm,* he thought, *it's only a babe, you can handle that.* He stared down at Birthe's face, pale and motionless on the wooden cot. Her breathing was easier now, he saw, but she looked so unlike herself.

Annlith, seeing the play of emotions in his face, went to a chest and took out a jug and a stone beaker. A darkish fluid gurgled and a heady smell filled her tiny room. 'Drink this,' she said.

Kjelle took a deep swig and gasped. Tears sprang into his eyes as the drink boiled down his gullet to explode in his stomach. 'Thor!' he said hoarsely. 'What's that?'

The healer grinned. 'It's brannevin,' she said. 'An old Gaullish recipe.' She studied his face. 'Feeling better now?'

Kjelle nodded. 'Gods, it was a shock. Does she know?'

'Birthe? I think so. It's not her first, so she should recognize the signs. Besides, as a Völva she'd know her body inside out.'

'This changes a lot of things,' said Kjelle. 'I must think about it.' He emptied the beaker and wiped the tears from his eyes. 'Thanks.'

He walked outside, his mind in a whirl, and ended up on the riverbank. There, he sat down and stared at the water.

'How is she?' A voice behind him made him look up. It was Lady Valiantrude, so unlike the stiff paladin she used to be. With her hair loose and unkempt over a man's tunic, and checkered trousers with the legs stuffed in her boots, she looked more like a Gaullish warrior than a lady paladin of the Court.

'She's overtired,' said Kjelle carefully. 'She needs lots of sleep.'

Lady Valiantrude frowned. 'Did Annlith tell you about her condition?'

'How did you know?'

'I'm not blind, Kjelle. She kept the signs to herself, the morning sickness, the pains and the other symptoms, but I'm from a large family; I recognized them. What are you going to do about it?'

Kjelle blinked. 'What do you mean?'

'Do you want her as your wife, or not?'

He froze, he hadn't thought of that. But he had known the answer already. 'I do,' he said.

The paladin relaxed. 'Good. She'll balk, so you'll have to convince her.' She rose and turned to walk away. Over her shoulder she asked, 'Who killed that weird beastie at the rapids, you or she?'

'She did.' Kjelle smiled suddenly. 'She doesn't need me to kill things.'

Valiantrude grinned. 'That's the Gods' truth.' Then she got serious again. 'She needs a purpose, Kjelle. She's a fighter; give her something to fight for.'

Kjelle stared up at her. 'She doesn't want another man; she said so often enough. She wants to be free.'

'You'll have to let her be free. Accept her as an equal. Is that difficult for you?'

Kjelle shook his head. 'No.' He knew he meant it.

'Good. Go and find a way to sell her the idea, Holder.'

He smiled and rose. 'Thanks, Lady Paladin.'

She sniffed. 'Not too much lady left.' Then she marched off to inspect the guards.

Tuuri had seen Vulf's scout scuttle by. She knew him and he wasn't in command, and therefore unimportant. He smiled grimly. All for the best -- he wouldn't want to be saddled with a monster like that. His curiosity awakened, he followed her across the grassy hill towards the trees. She disappeared into the forest and he followed her. He hadn't any scout training, so his passing was clearly audible.

'Silly Fynnikin walk more quietly,' piped the scout's voice from between the trees. 'No Fynni scout; is blundering around like blind pig.'

Silently, Tuuri fumed. That misshapen *thing* called itself a Fynni? He tried to watch where he put his feet down, till they reached the river.

He saw a series of rapids, passing through huge boulders strewn across the river. On one of them sat a girl. Openmouthed, he stared at her. She was one of the ones he had seen at Brundal's court in Nidros. The ones who had stolen away Prince Ottil. That changed things. He must stay and get more information. Would the Prince be here? And the one they called the Shardheld?

The scout scuttled forward. Stay here, thought Tuuri, but the scout leaped onto the first rock on all fours, like some hideous beetle. The girl was deep in thought and didn't immediately notice the scout. With a screech, the creature attacked. The girl sprang up, pulling out a long hunting knife.

Breathlessly, Tuuri watched the duel, and when the Fynni creature died without killing the girl, he sighed in relief. Then he moved back through the woods to the burned ruin.

Birthe was awake when Kjelle re-entered her room. The look with which she greeted him was a mixture of chagrin and defiance.

'Feeling better?' He sat down on the edge of her cot. 'Why did you keep it a secret?'

'So you know,' she said, and her eyes narrowed.

Kjelle nodded straight-faced. 'Annlith told me. Six sevendays.' Then he relaxed. 'Our child.'

She frowned at him. 'Our?'

He had to laugh now. 'Did you think I wouldn't acknowledge it? Ever since we returned from Wederer I was trying to think of a way to convince you to marry me and here it is. Love, will you marry me?'

Birthe had grown pale. 'You can't ask that! I'm a Völva. I swore not to marry again.'

'Would you be less a Völva if we married? You don't think I would try and make a tame housewife of you? That's not what I want from the girl I love.'

'Love?'

'Yes, I know it's indecent; we Nords don't marry for love. Still, there it is; I want to marry you. We can be equals. Being the wife of a Holder adds to your reputation as a Völva and being the husband of a Völva gives me an aura of wisdom.'

A little color had crept back into Birthe's face. 'I won't decide now. Give me time to think, Kjelle.'

He kissed her softly. 'All the time you need, love.' He rose. 'Rest now, you must recover your strength, said Annlith.'

'Don't coddle me,' she growled.

'I'm not coddling you. I need my Huntmaster fit and able, not fainting after the first kill of the day. Sleep, my love; the little one and I rely on your strength.'

'Get out, you smooth-talking... No, don't! Oh Gods, Kjelle, come here!'

As he bowed over her, she pulled his head down and kissed him hard, just like that night he had lain in the tent, weak as a newborn snow rabbit. 'I'll marry you. Don't you betray me, Kjelle Almansen.' The intensity of her longing was almost painful.

'I won't,' he said hoarsely. 'I swear by my clan's honor.'

She relaxed and closed her eyes. 'Then I'll sleep now, I need to be well to entertain my Holder.'

Kjelle wiped the sweat from his forehead and staggered as he straightened up. *She'll marry me,* he thought. *I'll be married and a father.* A hint of panic reared its head, but he stamped on it and walked outside, looking for Valiantrude.

He found the paladin at the back of the barn, with Annlith the healer, examining the carcass of the strange being Birthe had killed.

'Well?' asked Lady Valiantrude, wiping her hands on an old piece of cloth.

'She said yes.' Kjelle breathed deeply.

The paladin gripped his hand. 'Well done! What now?'

'Would you act as her sponsor, Valiantrude?'

'Of course, she has no kin to speak for her and you are the head of your clan. We must agree on a bride-price. What can you offer her?'

Kjelle thought of all his worldly possessions and grimaced. 'A pound of silver, a horse and cart and her own receiving room, as soon as we've got Eidungruve back. She's a völva and she needs all the trappings necessary to her state.'

'Make that two pounds of silver, she's been educated by the best, the Lady Asgisla.'

'Agreed,' said Kjelle. Then he smiled. 'Birthe hasn't got a dowry, so instead I'll set aside a yearly amount of silver from the mine for her use.'

Lady Valiantrude gave him a straight stare. 'That's more than fair. I'll take your proposal to her and see what she thinks. I won't give her much chance to say no, though.'

'It's nice to marry a rich husband,' said little Annlith with a sigh.

Tuuri sat down against part of the palisade and let pale Sun play over his face. 'Ullr give me strength,' he sighed, feeling the tiredness steal over him. Those forced marches with Vulf's men had taken more from him than he'd cared to admit. He closed his eyes for a moment.

For the second time someone woke him up with a kick in the side. He sat up in the moonlit darkness, staring at the leveled weapons of two very angry men.

'We got us a live one!' said the one, a small, unshaven fellow. 'A real, live Fynni. Holder will be pleased.'

'I'm not a Fynni,' protested Tuuri. 'I'm...' A blow from the large second man slammed his head against the palisade and he felt a tooth come loose.

'Shut up, lying beast,' said the big man savagely. 'I know a Fynni when I sees one.' Again, his fist lashed out and Tuuri cried out. He wanted to call Sha'akaii, but the big man's fists broke off the ancient bonding and his totem bear didn't hear him. He felt the blood spurt from his nose and he yelled.

'The Holder wants him alive, Jarrol,' said the small man. 'Don' beat him too hard.'

'Don't you worry, Art, he'll be alive. Only a bit damaged.' He dragged Tuuri to his feet. 'You're murderous scum, Fynni. Not human.' A third blow started the blood flow from Tuuri's nose and he brought his hands up to stop it.

'You wan' to fight?' said Jarrol with a grin and slapped Tuuri's face repeatedly.

'Enough,' said Art. 'You know the Holder; he won't be pleased if the prisoner's too damaged. Let's get him back.'

Between them, they half dragged Tuuri the whole way back across the river to the stronghold on the other side.

At the gate they were halted by a tall, tough-looking woman. 'What have you got there?'

'We caught us a spy, Lady Paladin,' said Art eagerly. 'He was creeping about the burned fort.'

Tuuri stared at with his one good eye. The other was swollen and hurt. The woman looked him up and down with an expression of disgust on her face. 'You beat him up?'

'He resisted, Lady. We had to calm him down somewhat, he was terribly berserk, you see.'

'No, I don't,' said the woman bluntly. 'Neither of you has so much as a scratch. Beating a Fynni up is one thing, lying to me is a deadly sin, Jarrol. Give him other clothes and bring what he wears to me. Then bind him up and throw him in the shed. Lord Kjelle will want to see this beast tomorrow - tonight he's with the völva.'

'Lady,' began Tuuri through swollen lips.

'Shut up. Spare your words for the lord holder, beast. If it were left to me, I'd hang your carcass on our wall. Take him away.'

The two men marched him through the gates and every one they met spat at him, with so much hate in their faces that Tuuri expected them to wrest him out of the two men's hands and tear him to shreds. He was actually glad when they hauled him into a small building, where he would be safe.

'Undress,' said Jarrol. 'And hurry up, I'm getting cold.'

Without a word, Tuuri started to strip.

The big man took an old blanket from a peg on the wall. 'Here, take this, we wouldn't want you gettin' ill.' He grinned. 'Not before we hang you.' He produced some leather strips and bound Tuuri's arms and feet. Then he kicked the messenger's legs from under him and the two men left, locking the door behind them.

There he lay in the dark, bleeding and battered, bereft of everything. He mumbled the words of his bonding song, but he couldn't properly pronounce the words and Sha'akaii remained silent. Tuuri tried to stop his tears, but he was frightened, cold and filled with pain. 'Ullr, aid me!' Alone in the dark, he sobbed softly.

CHAPTER 15 – DREAMS

The next morning Kjelle awoke on the chest next to Birthe's cot. He remembered sitting there, looking at her sleeping face, so calm and unworried in repose. *I must have fallen asleep,* he thought, stretching his stiff back. Outside, the grey of dawn greeted him as he walked to the outhouse. The women in the bakery were already at work and their jovial good-mornings cheered him.

'Have you seen him, Lord?' asked the younger of the two, looking up from the dough she was kneading. 'Terribly wicked-looking is he.'

Kjelle blinked. 'Have I seen whom?'

'That awful Fynni the scouts caught yesterday evening. I'm glad they locked him up safe.'

'A Fynni? Where do they keep him?'

'In the shed, Lord,' said the woman. 'Have a care, he's very dangerous.'

Without another word, Kjelle marched to the shed, stiffness and full bladder forgotten. There was a guard seated at the door. 'What's this about a captured Fynni?' said Kjelle, furious that no one had seen fit to inform him.

The guard, an old man who was no longer able to work, rose and gave a sketchy salute. 'Yea, Lord. He's inside. I haven't seen him, but I heard him whimper all night, so he can't be dangerous as Jarrol said.'

Impatiently, Kjelle remover the bar from the door and stepped inside. The early morning light was dim and his eyes had to adjust. He stared down at the prisoner, who looked back at him with one red-rimmed eye. The other eye was puffy and purpled as if he'd been in a fight. He was the same young fellow he had seen walking with Vulf, the one who'd held back during the Fynni attack. 'Who are you?' said Kjelle, disgust making his tone sharp.

The young man flinched. 'I'm Tuuri Little Knife, from the Ostmark,' he said painfully.

'You're a Fynni.'

'No! By Ullr, I'm not.'

Kjelle was surprised at the lad's vehemence. 'But that's a Fynni mark on your cheek.'

Tuuri struggled to sit up; he probably was stiff with cold. 'My father gave it me. He was a Fynni; my mother came from the Ostmark. I... I hate those murdering animals. But the mark will betray me forever.'

Kjelle saw him shiver. 'Where are your clothes?'

'The men who captured me took them, on a woman's orders.'

Kjelle stuck his head around the door and beckoned the guard. 'Get the Lady Valiantrude, quick as you can.' He turned back to the prisoner. 'So your father's a Fynni.'

'I can't remember him, Lord,' said Tuuri quickly. 'He left us ten years ago and I haven't seen him since. My mother never spoke of him.'

Lady Valiantrude entered, fully uniformed. She smiled at Kjelle. 'You're up early. I was just about to do morning rounds.'

Kjelle wasn't in the mood for pleasantries. 'Who captured him?'

The paladin stiffened at the tone in his voice. 'Jarrol and Art the Archer. Last evening they found him lurking around the burned fort.'

'I wasn't lurking,' said Tuuri with some difficulty. 'I was sleeping.'

Lady Valiantrude ignored him. 'The men said he resisted when they wanted to bring him here. He went berserk and they had to fight him.'

'Berserk? Look at him,' said Kjelle grimly. 'Does he seem a fighter to you?'

Valiantrude stared hard at the shivering lad. 'Not really,' said she finally. 'He looks like a runaway boy.'

'I'm not a boy,' snapped Tuuri. 'And that big one just wanted to beat me up. He too said I was a Fynni.' He laughed bitterly. 'Gods, the irony. The Fynni hate me because I'm not one of them and the other folks hate me because I'm a Fynni.'

'It doesn't matter whether you're a Fynni or not,' said Kjelle. 'You must be Rannar's man.'

'I can't tell you,' said Tuuri. 'Hang me if you want to, but I'll not betray my oath.'

'You betrayed your oath already,' said Lady Valiantrude shortly. 'No one ever told you not to carry written orders?'

The young man slumped back on the ground. 'Oh Gods,' he said. 'I never thought of that.'

'What documents?' said Kjelle, and his anger showed in his voice.

'I am sorry,' said the paladin, pulling a rolled paper from inside her tunic. 'Here, I would have told you after breakfast. Last evening you were sitting with Birthe and I didn't want to disturb you. He is Rannar's messenger, with orders to join Vulf and go south.'

'Is he.' Kjelle's accusing finger pointed at Tuuri. 'You may be no Fynni, but you are a damned traitor.'

'I'm not,' said Tuuri, again struggling with his bound hands to sit up. 'I am loyal to my lord, Jarl Rannar of Westhal. I swore him an oath, not King Vidmer or anyone else. I am not a traitor.'

Kjelle let his arm drop to his side. 'Perhaps not a traitor, but you are an enemy. I'll send you to Jarl Dettrich to be judged.' He turned to Lady Valiantrude. 'Give him back his clothes and feed him. Ask Annlith to check his eye and his bruises.' He stared at his second-in-command. 'No more beatings. We're honorable folk here.'

The paladin flinched at that and nodded stiffly.

Having relieved himself and washed, Kjelle went to see Birthe. She was awake and at her morning meal. 'Join me,' said she with her mouth full. 'There's plenty.'

Kjelle sat down on the chest and broke off a crust of the still warm bread. 'We have got ourselves a prisoner,' said he casually.

Birthe paused with a piece of cheese halfway her mouth and stared at him. 'We have what?'

'That blustering fool Jarrol and one of your archers were scouting the area last evening. They caught a young fellow sleeping at the burned fort. The guy wears a Fynni mark on his cheek, so of course Jarrol had to rough him up.'

Birthe hissed. 'Fynni! Why didn't you kill him?'

'Because Dettrich will want to see him. He bore documents identifying him as Rannar's messenger and he was sent with Vulf to capture someone. I think he's telling the truth, but I can't be sure. '

'I can help you there,' said Birthe, starting to get up.

'No, love, you must regain your strength first. The lad will stay where he is, there's no hurry.'

'I'm fit enough,' said Birthe, and her eyes flashed.

'You're not. In a few days' time, if Annlith agrees, you can have a try.'

With a curse, she sank down on the bed again. 'I hate lying still and doing nothing.'

Kjelle bent down and kissed her. 'I know, love.' Suddenly he thought of something. He brought out the rolled orders. 'Here are Rannar's orders. See what you can make of them.'

Birthe took the papers and gasped. 'Rannar handled these himself?' she said, with a queer look on her face.

'I suppose so. Why?'

'Blow out that candle.'

Obediently, Kjelle snuffed out the flame with his fingers and near dark filled the small room. Softly, Birthe began to sing. Kjelle opened his mouth to protest, but his instincts told him it was already too late.

'Rannar,' she whispered. And, surprised, 'Ottil was right, his hair is really white! There's a ship's cabin, another man. A Fynni with a terribly marked face, full of cruelty and power. They're talking. Oh no, not Muus! And there's something in the background. A shadow of badness. It's not cast by Rannar, nor entirely by the Fynni. It's...' She screamed, 'No!'

Kjelle sought for her in the dark. 'Birthe!'

'It's all right,' said she hoarsely. 'I just had a shock. Light the candle, will you?'

Fumbling with his tinder box, Kjelle managed to relight the candle. As he turned back to Birthe, she gave him a shaky smile. 'Don't be angry, it was but a divination. That's not tiring at all.'

'Why did you cry out then?' said he furiously.

She held up her hand. 'I was shocked. We must act, Kjelle. Please call Valiantrude and Ajkell; there are things we should discuss.'

Kjelle gave her a hard stare and nodded. 'Valiantrude, Ajkell - and Annlith to keep an eye on your health.'

Stepping out he almost walked into Annlith. 'Sorry,' said he. 'Go in and check her up, will you? She's been at her tricks again.' Then he hurried on to get the others.

Shortly the three of them squeezed into the small space around the cot. Kjelle looked at Annlith and the healer smiled. 'No harm done, she's fine.'

'As I told him already,' snapped Birthe. 'Men!'

'I'm careful of your health, love,' said Kjelle calmly. 'Well, we're here.'

Birthe held up the papers. 'Kjelle handed me these documents that Tuuri carried.' She paused to sip a bit of wine. 'The moment I touched those documents, some terrible purpose shouted at me, so I tried a divination. I saw Rannar, on board a ship, with the foulest Fynni alive. A powerful, mean sorcerer of sorts. But even worse, I saw the shade of something I never expected to see in my lifetime.' She paused, her face strained. 'The Gods Before.'

Lady Valiantrude jumped up, kicking into Ajkell and Kjelle. 'Impossible!'

'Their shades were really there, all four of them, hanging like a black shroud around that Fynni's body. He may be a powerful sa'aman, but they played him as the wind does a fallen leaf.'

Kjelle shook his head in stupefaction. 'Rannar in league with the Gods Before? His people would rip him to pieces.'

'Perhaps he doesn't know it?' said Ajkell. 'Say he thinks he has hired the Fynni to do his bidding, and he's now their unwitting tool?'

'Trice-damned fool!' growled Lady Valiantrude.

'It's not all,' said Birthe. 'I know where Vulf was going. They're after the Shardheld, Kjelle. They're hunting Muus.'

The Holder stiffened, and turned to Birthe. 'They dare...'

'The Fynni pointed out to Rannar how powerful he'd be with the skyshard in his hands.'

'It's the Gods Before,' said Lady Valiantrude. 'They want the shard. With all that power, they'd be supreme. They would return, kick out the New Gods, and we'd become slaves to their Svartalves and such.'

'This changes everything,' said Kjelle. 'I must go south, warn Muus.'

'We'll all go,' said Valiantrude.

'No, I can't lead an army through the length of Gaul. That would take ages. Besides, Jarl Dettrich's counting on our men to help defeat Rannar in the north. I'm sorry, Valiantrude, I must leave you here. Birthe, Ajkell and I go south.'

The paladin looked hard at him. 'I'm not a Nord, Kjelle. I agreed to serve with you, not with Dettrich. Let Göll Haldisdottr lead the men, she's got more balls than most of them.'

Kjelle looked at Birthe, who nodded. 'She can do it.'

He sighed. 'All right then.'

'I still need to speak with this Tuuri,' said Birthe. 'He may know more.'

'We can beat it out of him,' said the paladin grimly.

'We could, but that would make us not much better than the Fynni,' said Ajkell softly.

Valiantrude growled something and colored.

'My way is much surer,' said Birthe. 'I can read him, like Asgisla did with Muus, and all his secrets will be an open book.'

'Tomorrow,' said Annlith firmly. 'You've done enough for today. If you think of traveling south, you need to rest first. Or do you want Kjelle to carry you all the way?'

Birthe sighed. 'No, you're right. I'll see that half-breed tomorrow and then I'll be good and sleep a few more days.' She gave Kjelle a hard stare. 'Days, I said. Not sevendays.'

'I'll have to speak with Jarl Dettrich first,' said Kjelle. 'I can't just pack up and walk away. But we'll depart at the end of this sevenday at the latest.'

The next morning Birthe rose quietly. She took a blue under-dress from her chest, as well as a dark red robe -- her Völva robe, that she had never worn before. From the stone bottle of mead Kjelle had brought her, she filled a small flask, added a prepared powder and shook it heartily. It's too cold to be effective, she thought, and slipped the bottle and two thimbles into her bodice to warm. Lastly, she bound a white cloth over her hair and gripped her wand. Dressed for war, the Völva left her tiny room.

As she entered the common hall, everybody fell silent and looked at her. Her color rose as she stepped forward. Kjelle stood and smiled broadly, 'My love, will you marry me now?'

'Speak with my sponsor,' she said haughtily. Then she relaxed. 'Asgisla had the dress made for me after I passed my test, but there never was an occasion to wear it.'

And now you don it to impress another young man,' said Kjelle sadly. 'An enemy.'

'Such are the ways of the Völva. Well, where is my hapless victim?'

'Come with me, we'll face him together.' Kjelle beckoned a worker. 'Bring a chair for the Völva, will you.'

The young messenger was sitting dejectedly on the ground when they entered the shed. He jumped up and stared openmouthed at Birthe.

'I'm the Völva Birthe of Belisheim,' said the girl icily. 'I come to speak with you. With me is the Holder Kjelle Almansen, of Eidungruve Hold.'

All color drained from the young man's face. 'Eidungruve...' He tottered, and without another sound, crashed down on the hard packed floor.

'Get the healer,' said Kjelle to the guard at the door.

'His heart beats,' said Birthe. 'I think he just fainted.'

Tuuri's eyes opened with a fear in them that shocked Birthe. 'What's wrong?' said she.

The lad covered his face in his hands. 'I can't, I just can't.'

Annlith hurried in with her large bag of medicines. 'What happened?'

'He swooned,' said Kjelle, keeping his voice neutral.

The healer placed her fingertips on Tuuri's temples. 'He's all right,' she said after a while. She took a bottle that Kjelle recognized from her bag. The rich smell of brannevin filled his nose as the healer poured two fingers in a glass. 'Drink this,' she said, handing the brannevin to Tuuri.

With his eyes closed, the lad emptied the glass in one gulp. Then he gasped as Kjelle had done and tears sprang to his eyes.

'Whoo,' he said, blinking mightily.

Birthe sat down on the chair the worker had brought. 'What made you faint?'

Tuuri's face was tight, as if he expected death to embrace him for his words. 'Your connection with Belisheim and Eidungruve, Lady. I was at those places, after the bad things had happened. They're gone.'

Kjelle was staggered. 'Eidungruve gone? What happened?'

The messenger's voice was quivering with strain. 'My orders were to join the Tarkynn Vulf at a place called Eidungruve, Lord. When I arrived, the place was a shambles. Ullr! Dead women dumped like...' He gagged and put his hand to his mouth. 'Pardon, Lady. Rows of staked heads, blood everywhere, Vulf's men beastly drunk as ever. No sane men live like that, I'll tell you! I handed Vulf his orders and he started to laugh at me joining him. He threatened to kill me, but then he seemed to find it more amusing to take me along. He killed my horse instead.' Birthe guessed by the spasm of emotion that crossed the lad's face that the death of his mount had hurt him deeply.

Tuuri looked squarely at Kjelle. 'Then, before we left, he ordered his men to torch Eidungruve. It... burned swiftly, Lord.'

Birthe saw the pain on Kjelle's face and she put her arm around him. 'We'll rebuild it. Just as it was. You'll see.'

Kjelle nodded, wooden-faced. He squared his shoulders. 'You will tell me your tale, messenger Tuuri. Your life depends on the honesty of your words.'

Without hesitation, Tuuri started to recount all that had happened since he first set foot ashore in Helmshaven.

Birthe sat back in her chair and listened, with her eyes closed. She couldn't hear any falsehood. Tuuri's story sounded true and his emotions sincere. Still, there was that shadow she had seen in Rannar's orders. She looked at Kjelle. 'He sounds all right,' she said hesitantly. 'But...'

'If you're not sure, love, I must kill him.'

Birthe half-heard Tuuri's gasp. 'There's only one way to make certain.' She took the little flask from her bodice and quickly filled the two thimbles. 'Here,' said she, handing one thumb-sized beaker to Tuuri. 'Drink this.'

The young man looked suspiciously at the wine. 'It smells... funny.'

'I'm not going to poison you, boy,' said Birthe testily. 'Drink it. Your life depends on it.'

'What are you doing?' asked Annlith, but too late. Birthe had tossed back the prepared wine and the healer's words were but dim whispers. Around the Völva was darkness, endless and without form, of which she was the center. The power within her grew into a majestic Light, as she sat enthroned on a rock in the middle of a raging ocean. Before her were three hooded crones. One with distaff and spindle spun glittering threads that a second crone wove into the foaming waters, while the third stared blindly in the distance, like the very old do. Sometimes she cackled, as if she saw something that amused her, but mostly she just sat, snipping at the nothingness around the gleaming life threads with a pair of scissors. None of the old women paid attention to the Völva, but she knew them. They were the Fates, the three Goddesses who controlled all life.

At the Völva's feet, the white crested waves tossed a tiny flickering life to and fro, bound by the thin threads of the spinning Norns.

'Help me,' the spark fluted, wrestling with the waves of Chance. 'Save me.'

'Show me who you are,' said the Völva, wrapped in her Light of Wisdom. 'Show me everything.' At her command, row upon row of images flowed from the spark. Tuuri's birth, his first steps, his childhood. The branding his shadowy father figure gave his cheek. The proud, white-haired man that was Rannar. Finally, his arrival in Helmshaven and everything he had told. She saw Vulf – alive and arrogant – exuding an awful darkness. And behind Vulf the man with the cruelest face of them all. The man who was Rannar's advisor, Rev. Rev looked directly at her and smiled. The waves disappeared, taking the spark with them. The Norns changed into swans and fled away. Only Rev's smiling face remained, hanging in the sky like Whole Moon. His gaze turned away from the Völva, looking to the right, towards a lone steeple in the center of a town. All around were snow-topped mountains, against a backdrop of flaming skies. On the top of the tower she saw Muus. He stared at the mountains and said something to a young woman beside him. Then he was gone and the day turned to starry night. Now another man leaned on the tower's balustrade. Rannar, too, looked at the mountains. At the foot of the tower, soldiers waited -- a Fynni horde, cruel and hungry. Fire-specked clouds covered the stars, while dark winds from beyond the Norns' weavings blew in and swept the Völva away into nothingness.

When she opened her eyes again, she lay on her cot in her room. It was dim in the room, and no candle burned. She saw the yellow orbs of Annlith's eyes upon her.

'Awake?' said the little healer. 'How do you feel?'

Birthe's tongue refused service and she pointed to the glass on the little bed stand.

Annlith poured some wine and held it to Birthe's mouth. She drank greedily, and it loosened her tongue. 'How long?' she said hoarsely.

The healer understood her question. 'You've been out for two days. Kjelle is very worried, but I knew you were all right. I don't know if I can say the same of your child, though. It was a very foolish thing to do; the Gods may know what your Dreaming did to it.'

'I had to,' said Birthe. 'I simply had to.' A sense of urgency filled her and she tried to get up. But her vision blurred and the room swayed.

'Stay in bed,' said the healer firmly. 'No getting up today.'

Birthe nodded. 'Call Kjelle for me, please.'

Annlith gave her a hard stare. 'You will stay in bed, won't you?'

'I'm too dizzy to even think of getting up,' said Birthe wearily.

'Then I'll go get the Lord Holder for you. I'll be right back.'

Alone in the dark, Birthe closed her eyes. It hadn't been an ordinary Dreaming. Of course, she had done it only once before, with Asgisla, but nothing her old patroness had taught her spoke of Dreams a völva couldn't fully control. And indeed, her Dreaming had gone as it should. Until Rev came. Who or what was Rev that gave him the power to appear in a Völva's Dreaming?

Kjelle was in the smithy with Elbrich when Annlith brought him Birthe's call. Without a word, he turned and ran to her room. He entered with a bang of the door, breathing hard. 'How are you? What happened? I...' He took a deep breath and steadied. 'I must stay calm.' He grimaced. 'You had me worried.'

'I'm sorry.' She patted the edge of her cot. 'Come sit beside me. Try to hold on to that calm while I tell you.'

'Is it that terrible? That damned half-Fynni lied? I'll have the miserable coward flogged to death.'

'Tuuri's tale was true.' She took Kjelle's hand and told him of her Dreaming. All the while, Kjelle remained silent, but she felt the muscles of his hand straining in her grip. When she had finished, he sat without speaking, staring at her hand, his thoughts far away.

'So you saw Muus, on a tower near mountains, against a flaming sky. Then Rannar, on the same spot, but later. Does he mean to capture Muus himself? And that Rev, he sounds powerful. We must learn more of him.' He looked Birthe in the eye. 'I understand the necessity of what you did, but next time talk it over first. Remember you're expecting a child, love.'

'The child will have to get used to it. It has happened before.'

Kjelle knew what she meant; she had carried little Búi throughout her training and the child had been none the worse for it. He sighed, she was right. As Völva, she had her duties.

'How is Tuuri?' asked Birthe.

Kjelle cursed. 'The fool just slept it off and woke up next morning without remembering anything.'

'So that part worked all right. For Freya's Love, I must know more about this Rev. Who knows anything about Fynni priests?'

Elbrich coughed from the doorway. 'Outside the Ostmark, not many. I know of one. If he still lives, he must be very old. Dryskell he was called, Dryskell the Lithan. He knows everything that a man may know about the Gods Before.'

'Who is he?' said Kjelle. 'Where could I find him?'

'He is the Lithan, the one who leads by suffering, the eldest of our cousins still in this world. He remembers the exile of our two peoples from the Norden, and through remembering, he suffers. He is the Son of Dach, the brother of Rhan.'

Kjelle took a deep breath. 'I am sorry,' he said. 'We Nords have short memories and we have forgotten those names. Who are these people?'

Elbrich's glance was unreadable. 'Dach was the Father of the Un-a-Dach, the magic people. His brother Rhan was the Father of the Un-a-Rhan, the smithing people. That's us. We answer to Niflunger, People of the Misty Mountains, but it is not our real name. Don't call us dvergar either; that is more of an insult than you will ever understand. We are just as much dvergar as you are draugar.'

'Dvergar don't exist,' said Kjelle. 'Nor do svartalves.'

'They no longer exist,' corrected Elbrich him, his yellow eyes round and serious. 'Once they did, as creatures of the Gods Before. They were our forebears, but vastly different.'

'Asgisla would have known,' said Birthe with anguish in her voice. 'She would have taught me but she always said the time wasn't right.' Then her hands went to her mouth. 'She knew she was going to die. That means she didn't tell me on purpose. Why?'

'She didn't want you to know about the Gods Before?' said Kjelle. Seeing she was about to protest, he added, 'She must have had her reasons. Perhaps you need to find it out for yourself.'

'Gods,' said Birthe. 'I hate all that mysticism.'

'So we'll have to go and see this Lithan,' Kjelle said. He wanted to pat her hand, but he didn't, afraid to appear patronizing. Instead, he looked at the smith. 'Do you know where we can find him?'

Elbrich nodded. 'South. I'll have to go with you, I'm not sure he'd consent to see you otherwise.'

'Right then,' said Kjelle. 'You must come, then, with Birthe, Ajkell and me.' He rose. 'I'll ride and see the Jarl. We leave at the end of this sevendays.'

Tuuri lay on a pile of straw, staring into the darkness. He ached all over and his head hurt from his meeting with that völva. Ullr's Mighty Bow, what happened there? He didn't remember a thing past that thimble of wine she gave him. It was morning then, and now it was the middle of the night. *At least they gave me back my clothes,* he thought. *And they didn't discover the gold coins sewn into the hem of the cloak.* He cursed softly. *That's about all they haven't found. I must get out of here.*

He rose and walked stiffly to the back of the shed. They had left him unbound, trusting in the stoutness of the wooden walls that locked him in. By touch, he tested each of the planks for a weakness, a loose pin, a knot, anything. Nothing. The building was new and well built. He dragged a small tree trunk aside and there was what he sought. Bless the ones who dumped that trunk there, he thought. They were careless and now two planks were loose. Without thought, he fell on his knees and pushed.

The planks moved and he tried with his hands to measure the size of the hole. Rolling up his cloak, he lay flat on the earth and stuck his head out. No one in sight. For once he was glad of his slender body, because he wriggled through the hole, to stand in the small space between the shed and the palisade. He donned his cloak and pulled the hood far over his head.

With a show of confidence, he walked towards the gate. 'Going out?' said the watcher surprised.

Tuuri made his voice as gruff as possible. 'Orders,' he growled.

'Mind the rabbit holes,' said the man. 'It's pitch dark outside.'

Tuuri lifted a hand and hurried out. It was indeed dark, but his vision was a lot better than that of the Nords, one of the few good things he had inherited from his father. He hurried towards the ford and the freedom of the forest on the other side.

As he stepped from the water, a voice greeted him. 'Where are you going?' A small candle shone on his face. 'You!'

It was Jarrol, guarding the crossing. Before Tuuri could react, two hands gripped his throat. 'This time I'll squeeze the life out of you, damned Fynni.'

Tuuri kicked and threw himself backwards, dragging the heavy Nord on top of him. Jarrol's grip was strong and cut off Tuuri's breathing. The pain of Jarrol's hard fingers on his tender throat was unbearable. His mind started to spin from lack of air and Tuuri felt panic threatening to overwhelm him. He squirmed and wriggled, flailing around with his arms. 'I'll kill ya, murdering beast,' muttered Jarrol, panting heavily. *No!* Tuuri forced himself to concentrate, to keep the pain at bay. For a moment he tried to push the Nord away, but the other was too heavy. Then his fingers touched the handle of Jarrol's knife. Fighting for breath, with his blood roaring in his eyes, he yanked the blade from its sheath and stuck it deep in Jarrol's side. The other grunted and loosed his grip. Again, Tuuri struck, under Jarrol's collarbone, towards the throat. Arterial blood spurted as the Nord reared up and flopped down again. Tuuri wriggled from under the limp body. Gasping for air he stood, and wrestled to suppress the coughing that would have betrayed him. Then he unbound the knife belt from Jarrol's body, sheathed the blade and ran off as fast as he could.

When Sun came up, he was far away from the Nord settlement and from the path. 'They won't find me,' he said aloud. 'Not even dogs could follow my trail through these woods.' He stopped at a majestic oak, climbed high between its branches, and fell asleep.

'Jarrol is dead?' Kjelle sat up on his cot.

'Yes,' said Lady Valiantrude tersely. 'And that damned prisoner escaped.'

'What time is it?'

'Still another two hours to Sun's rise.'

'No use sending out search parties in the dark.' He put on his boots. 'How did he escape?'

'There were two planks loose in the back wall,' said the paladin with some embarrassment. 'The damage was camouflaged by spare tree trunks, and that was why we didn't see it. It's but a small hole, but it was large enough for him, the rat.'

'And the gate?' Kjelle grabbed his sword and stepped out, with Valiantrude behind him.

'The guard didn't recognize him in the dark. He just walked past.'

Kjelle cursed. No use blaming the watchman. His orders were to keep enemies outside, not the other way round. The guard was pale-faced and sweating as Kjelle approached. 'Was it you who passed the prisoner through?'

'Yes, Lord,' said the man, standing straight. 'He had his hood up and I couldn't see his face. I said something about going out late and he said 'orders'. I didn't think anything was amiss. I'm sorry, Lord.'

Kjelle stared at him till the man squirmed. 'No, you didn't think. Well, it's too late now. Have you been relieved yet?'

The guard nodded to a second warrior. 'She's taking over, Lord.'

'When Sun's up you can help searching the area.'

The man gave a relieved salute and hurried off.

'Oaf,' muttered Kjelle as he hurried towards the ford. 'He's supposed to know who goes in and out.'

The paladin stiffened. 'You're right, that's my fault. I'll add it to the standing orders.'

Across the river a lamp burned where Jarrol had been killed. Next to it, a warrior waited, sword in hand.

'You found him?' said Kjelle.

'I did, Lord. I crossed the river to relieve Jarrol, but I couldn't see. So I called softly and then I stumbled over him.'

She seemed nervous, but not particularly shocked. Jarrol wasn't popular, thought Kjelle. A bully, more wind than work. And he had hated that Fynnikin. 'He's been knifed,' Kjelle said aloud, looking at the tracks. 'Have you been trampling around here?'

'No Lord,' said the warrior. 'I knelt to check if he still lived, and then I went to alert the man at the gate.'

'There was a struggle. Jarrol was a lot stronger than that Fynnikin; the lad could never have bested him. And he'd beaten the lad up before.' He looked sharply at Lady Valiantrude, who nodded.

'Jarrol had sworn he would kill that painted bastard,' said the warrior. 'He really hated his guts.'

Kjelle stared at the body. There was something wrong here. Did he often go on duty unarmed?'

Both the warrior and Lady Valiantrude looked surprised. 'No,' said the paladin. Every guard is supposed to carry a weapon.'

The warrior nodded. 'He had this big hunting knife he was proud of, Lord. He never went anywhere without it.'

'Well, the knife is gone now.' Kjelle sighed. 'Tuuri escapes from the shed, bluffs himself past the gate watch, crosses the river and runs straight into the hands of the one man who won't hesitate to kill him. A man who is far stronger than that undersized half-breed. There is a struggle, during which the Fynnikin gets his hand on

Jarrol's knife and stabs him twice. Then he pockets the blade and runs off.'

Lady Valiantrude stood still. 'I can't see anything else. The rat would never have attacked Jarrol by himself.'

'Quite possible he didn't know there was a guard at the ford.' Kjelle turned to the warrior. 'I'll send someone to remove the body. Keep your eyes open, but the fugitive will be gone by now. He knows I will hang him if we catch him a second time. Even if it was self-defense, I'll have no choice.'

'You don't want to hang him,' said Valiantrude as they walked back to the stronghold.

'No. The lad is true to his oath. That his master is a knave isn't his fault. I like him better for sticking to Rannar than if he had abandoned him. Jarrol got what he asked for.'

'The people won't accept that.'

'I'm not going to tell the people what I think. As soon as it's daylight, we'll have a search. That finishes this business and then we'll go south as planned.'

'Right.' Valiantrude glanced at Kjelle. 'You're getting pretty devious. That's good.'

Kjelle smiled. 'I'm Alman's son, after all. They didn't get sneakier that him.'

CHAPTER 16 – ENVOY

Two days after the Runemaster and his party left Yarras, as they passed through one of the many pine forests, they were alerted by the sound of fighting nearby.

'I'll scout ahead,' said Ottil, as he dismounted. 'Geir, come with me.'

Hraab had opened his mouth, but now he said, 'Go, lads, and keep your head down. Well down.'

Ottil waved

Along the edge of the path they went, until the sounds were close by. Then the Prince dragged the other boy into the shadow of the forest.

'What do you see?' he whispered.

Geir paused and looked past the bushes at the scene before them. 'Soldiers fighting painted men. A merchant's caravan? The painted men are going to win.'

'Very good,' said Ottil. 'Run back to the others. Tell them to polish up their fightin' spirit and come here. Say this: Grim Doubh.'

The boy smiled slightly and hurried away. Ottil nodded approvingly and turned his mind to the fighting.

Geir slipped to a halt in the sand. 'It's a fight,' he said, panting slightly. 'Painted men against merchant's soldiers. The Prince says come, ready to fight. Grim Doubh.'

Muus swore. 'We'll have to hurry.'

'Good work,' said Hraab. 'Mount up and take Prince Ottil's horse with you.'

The boy obeyed, and they all galloped towards the fight. There was a lull in the action, with thirty or more painted idolaters dancing around a smaller group of soldiers protecting a well-dressed man. The dancers brandished long spears and wicked knives. The soldiers looked exhausted.

When they were spotted, the Grim Doubh uttered a wailing cry.

Muus stopped and the others followed his example. Moirra had her blowpipe readied. She raised it to her lips and puffed. Almost immediately, an idolater started to scream and claw at his breast.

Muus raised his hands and short lightning beams felled the painted men one by one. One of the Grim Doubh tried to flee, but Ottil appeared from among the trees and crushed the man's skull with the new sword he wore. 'First blood!' he shouted, and grinned. Geir crept round the fighting till he saw his chance, and then jumped an idolater. With one hand, he pulled the woman's head back, and with his knife in the other he slit her throat. Then he jumped back and watched in visible horror as she changed into an old woman.

'They're bewitched,' shouted Ottil, dodging a tall man with a spear. Geir nodded and, with his face screwed up, brained the overbalancing enemy with his ax. In the meantime, the soldiers had rejoined the fight, and soon it was all over. The last of the Grim Doubh took to his legs.

'No, you don't,' shouted Ottil. He ran after the fleeing man with Geir on his heels. The Grim Doubh had to swerve around a fallen tree and lost speed. Shouting a battle cry, Ottil dove for the man's legs and the two of them went down in the trunk's branches. Geir raised his ax and slashed at the man. He missed the head and the Grim Doubh screamed when the ax bit into his collarbone. Again, Geir hit out and this time opened the man's skull at the same moment as Ottil planted his knife in the Grim Doubh's side. The man flopped once and then the magic left him. With a shout of disgust Ottil crept from under the wrinkled carcass and stared at Geir. 'Do you see now that you're a warrior?' he panted.

Geir said nothing. His face was screwed up as if in pain and his hands shook.

Ottil threw his arm around the other boy's shoulder and together they walked back to the road.

The well-dressed man came forward, hands outstretched. 'Thank you,' he said in slightly accented Brytan. 'Without your help we wouldn't have survived.'

'It was a pleasure, Segnor Euthon,' said Ottil.

The man gave him a startled look. 'You know my name?'

The Prince took off his helmet and smiled at the man. 'We met at my father's court, last year.'

Euthon threw up his hands in surprise. 'Prince Ottil! Freya's Mercy, I am extremely happy to see you.'

Ottil's eyes danced. 'Muus, this is the Segnor Euthon, envoy of King Leodowric, my uncle. Segnor, this is the Runemaster Terrel.

De envoy bowed to Muus. 'The light of your power still dazzles my eyes, master Terrel.'

After Ottil had presented the others, they sat down at the roadside, while the soldiers cleared up the area by dumping the dead Grim Doubh behind a large bush.

Euthon stared in wonder at the Prince. 'Your mother thought you dead. Yet you live, and in fighting trim, too.'

'It is a long story, Segnor. My mother is at Rhemes?'

'Yes. She arrived five sevendays ago, with her whole retinue, her horses, transport, jewels and even her cat. She was prepared for this, she said. Her Highness knew it would only be a matter of time before someone would do the fool in and...' He paused, shocked. 'Your pardon, I shouldn't speak so of your father.'

'Why not?' said Ottil nonchalantly. 'He was a fool. Are there more of my people at Rhemes?'

'Yes, Jarl Dettrich arrived shortly after the Queen. He had a sizable force with him, but he is troubled, because his wife is still in Harkoy. More fugitives, mostly from Dalland, have drifted to Rhemes.'

Ottil threw Muus a quick glance. 'Was the Holderling of Eidungruve among them?'

'A stout young fellow, Kjelle? He arrived with a Völva and her baby, along with another warrior and one of the Queen's paladins.'

'They're safe!' said Ottil. 'Even Valiantrude.'

Muus nodded, and a rare, big smile made him look younger. 'Thank the Gods!'

'You must have had wondrous stories to tell,' said the envoy. 'Would you care to share them?'

Leaving out everything about the skyshard and the Shardheld, Muus told of their adventures in the Norden, the shipwreck where they had parted from Kjelle, his search for the rune stones and their journeys in Brytanna. At his description of the High King, Euthon nodded. 'I agree with your view, master Terrel. I have had many a discourse with His Highness and they asked the utmost of both my tact and my patience.'

One of the soldiers came and saluted. 'I'm happy to report that we are ready to proceed, Segnor. We have buried poor Dagi and packed his belongings to return to his widow.'

Euthon rose. 'Very good. Don't you send his things off; I want to add a note. And some compensation must be arranged.' He turned to Ottil. 'Prince, I am desolate to leave you, but I am expected at court. I will inform your mother of our happy meeting. She will be overjoyed.'

'Tell her I cannot join her at the moment, because my duties call me elsewhere. She shouldn't worry; I am a man now, Segnor.'

The envoy bowed in the Frankish fashion. 'I understand, Prince Ottil. Duty calls us all. I will give the Queen your message. I hope the Gods bless your way and that of your companions.' He turned to Muus. 'I saw those damned Grim Doubh coming from an abandoned hill fort some miles down the road. Should you want to make sure you got them all.' He looked Muus in the eye. 'You have my King's thanks for saving the life of his envoy, Runemaster. Leodowric is not one to forget. You will find a welcome at his court.' Then he mounted up and, with his guards around him, galloped away.

'I'm glad my mother is well,' said Ottil happily. 'What luck, meeting Euthon here. He's always been a good friend. A great lord, too, although you'd not say so seeing him ride with only some soldiers.'

'And all your friends are safe, too,' said Moirra, gripping Muus's shoulder. 'Even your girl with the baby.'

'I tell you she's not my girl,' began Muus. Then he saw her laugh. 'Yes, it is a relief. I would have missed those wonderful blue eyes.'

Moirra's face fell. 'Are her eyes really beautiful?'

'Not hers,' said Muus, and he grinned. 'The baby's. He got them from his father. Amazingly beautiful.'

'You beast.' The druidess shook him. 'I always wanted blue eyes.'

'They wouldn't suit you.' Muus took her chin. 'Your eyes are black as a stormy night; tempestuous eyes.'

Ottil coughed. 'Are you going to kiss her, or shall we go on? There's an empty stronghold waiting.'

Guiltily, the two stepped apart. 'No kissing with you eager children watching,' said Muus. 'We'll go.'

Hraab crowed, and Moirra blushed furiously.

It wasn't very far till they came to an overgrown hill, on whose top the walls of a fort were still standing.

'It must be old,' said Ottil, gazing at the rowan trees growing through the palisades.

'Two centuries,' said Hraab nonchalantly. 'All those petty kingdoms fought for dominion, in the days before Cucharann's great-grandfather was made the first High King.'

'How do you know?' asked Ottil. 'Or are you making it up?'

Hraab sniffed. 'Am I a teller of tales? There's a sign inside naming King Adwalla, who was the first High King's father. It's in two languages, runic and Old Rom.'

Ottil looked at Muus. 'Are we going to look inside? Perhaps there are more Grim Doubh.'

Muus sighed. 'We had better.' They tethered the horses and went up the hill. There was a small path, proving that the fort was visited regularly.

At the entrance, they halted. 'It's quiet,' said Muus softly. 'But let's be careful.'

They stepped inside over the remnants of wooden doors, into a stony field. Most of the buildings were ruined, but in the center, the original mead hall was still standing.

'Someone did some repairs,' said Muus. Only there's nothing moving.'

The words hadn't left his mouth before the door to the hall swung open. A tall woman confronted them, beautiful like a sculpted Goddess, her naked body covered in glowing symbols. She shook her head and a wealth of blonde hair waved around her like a cloak. 'Supplicants?' she said. Her voice was wonderfully deep, both resonant and compelling. 'Give yourself to the mercy of the Old Ones. You will be blessed, my children.'

'Hollow words, Grim Doubh,' said Muus, his voice stern. 'Your Gods Before are powerless shades. They're past, as are you. Begone, untrue one.'

He raised his arms and thought *A'yin...* But then a beam of purple light shot from the woman's hand and splashed all over his body. Pain too great to allow him to scream gripped him and he stiffened.

Around him, the others scattered, but the woman in the door had no eyes for them. 'A pity, my son. You would have made a strong high priest.' Again, she pointed her hand, but now a blue light enveloped Muus. 'Enough,' said a voice that wasn't his. 'I'll not be stopped by some petty priestess.' The blue light shot out towards the woman and in an intolerable flash of lightning, she withered. The blue around Muus went out, and he screamed and screamed.

'What is wrong with him?' said Ottil. Why doesn't he speak?

Moirra had Muus's hands in hers and was staring in his eyes. 'It must be the shard. It protected him from that priestess's magic, but now it won't go away.'

'We must get to the High Druid,' said Hraab. 'He will know a way to push its force back into the stone.'

Ottil stared at Muus, who stood stiff and unresponsive. 'Can he ride?'

'I think so.'

'Well, what are we waiting for? Let's go.'

Visions of fire - molten rock flowing past - smoke rising from fissures in the ground. Mountains exploding, rocks raining from the air. Ash falling, covering buildings three stories high. Poisonous gases drifting in yellowish clouds, killing men and animals with equal disregard. Ground shaking, toppling centuries old monuments, mansions, palaces. Falrom.

A ruined castle on a burning mountain - a tunnel, leading downward. Shaking, shaking. Suffocating air. A cave, boiling hot, with lava dripping down the walls like water. A black monolith, a voice. 'Come.'

'Not yet.' he thought. 'I come, but not yet. Don't push me. DON'T PUSH ME! I – am – not – ready.'

Two equal powers trying to move each other. Stasis.

CHAPTER 17 – THE GREAT TEMPLE

From a distance, the Great Temple was awe-inspiring, an immense circle of standing stones topped with horizontal slabs.

'Thor's Beard,' said Ottil. 'Those stones are huge.'

At the entrance to the holy circle, they were stopped by a young druid bearing the rank of ovate, or senior student. 'Welcome, druidess,' he said in a soft voice. 'May the Gods bless and guide your path. Did you come seeking wisdom?'

'I'm the druidess Moirra,' she said. 'Have I been gone so long that you have forgotten me? I must see the High Druid; our business is most urgent.' The ovate studied her from top to toe and suddenly his face changed. 'Druidborn! Of course,' he said.

Unhurriedly, he led them over grassy lanes into the circle. 'You are on the most holy ground,' he told the others. 'For thousand upon thousand passings of winter, people have prayed here and their faith has permeated the very soil.'

'What are those five... doorways?' said Ottil.

'You name them rightly, young man. Doorways to the elements of Fire, Earth, Sea, Sky and Death.'

The Prince looked at him. 'Death is an element?'

'Death and Life are elements as much as Fire or Air.'

'What would happen if I stepped through such a door?'

The ovate laughed softly. 'You are not of the Circle; you would not go anywhere or even notice something different. Perhaps...' He looked at Moirra.

'I have been there,' said the girl. 'Through all of them. I will not speak of it.'

The ovate bowed. 'You are five times hallowed, Druidborn. I respect your reticence and ask no more.'

At a small building, he stopped. Inside, a stairway went down into the earth. 'I may not go any further,' said the ovate. 'You will find the High Druid downstairs. May your days be filled with rightness.'

Without another word, the young man left. Firmly gripping Muus' arm, Moirra walked him down the stairs, with the others following her in single file. They came to a large, circular room, torch-lit. Large racks filled with rows of bound scrolls filled the walls. Several persons stood or sat, studying written books. One of them, a sparse man with a graying beard, looked up. His face lit up in a smile. 'Moirra,' he said. 'You came back.'

'I had to come, Your Wisdom. I seek your help and your insight, for our need is great.'

High Druid Arraw studied Moirra's face. 'Follow me to my room.'

Past the round room was a private study, furnished with a large table and several stools. 'Sit down. What troubles you so much that you return here against your will?'

'It is not me, Wisdom. It is him.' She laid her hand on Muus's arm.

'A Un-a-Dach,' said the High Druid, staring at Muus. 'Who is he?'

'Terrel of Owwich, son of Slade and Aeylla. He was sold as a slave and managed to escape.'

'Oh my,' sighed the High Druid. 'Is he that boy? His parents had such great hopes of him. A pity, a terrible pity. The boy will never become a druid now.'

'He became something else, Wisdom. But now he can't function. We must help him.'

Arraw rose and put his hands on Muus's temples. He tutted. 'Something inside him is blocking him. Is that your problem? Why is he important to you?'

'Wisdom, he is the Shardheld.'

Slowly, the High Druid's eyes turned from Muus's face to Moirra's. 'What proof do you have?'

Moirra pulled open Muus's robe. On his chest, the leather pouch hung next to the runes.

'He is a Runemaster?' asked the High Druid in surprise.

'They are supposed to be his defense against the skyshard,' said Moirra. 'Only he has too few of them.' Very carefully, so as not to come into contact with the shard inside, she opened the pouch. Blue light shone out and transformed Muus's face into a gargoyle's mask.

The High Druid took an audible breath. 'I see. So this is the one who...' He snapped his mouth shut. 'What brought him to this condition?'

Moirra told about the Grim Doubh priestess in the old hill fort and the way the shard had taken over Muus to prevent his death. When she had finished, Arraw was silent for a moment. Then he took

Muus' hands. Everything became quiet. The sound of voices from the book room, the buzzing of a fly, the hissing of the torches on the walls, all died away. It seemed an endless moment before the world came to life again.

'He is fighting the shard,' said the High Druid. 'His whole being is resisting being taken over. He is strong; I give you that. A lesser man would have given in long ago. Now the shard cannot exert more power on him, for fear of killing him, so they are locked. Could he but reach his runes, he would break free. But the shard is blocking that way. I must try to strengthen the runes, so that they can reach him.' He sat back and rubbed the joints of his left hand while he thought. 'I need herbs: trefoil, mandrake, ragwort, avens, salverum oil...' his voice drifted off. 'We must see what we can do, Moirra, you and I. Your companions...'

'This is Prince Ottil of the Norden,' said Moirra. 'He is a very broadminded young man, so you won't shock him with unfamiliar rituals.'

The High Druid smiled slightly. 'Welcome, Prince. You are in a place no Nord has ever been, in the heart of the druidic Inner Circle. The wards have accepted you, so you must be a Power for Good. Still, I would ask a vow of silence from you. And you, young one with the hair of Brann?'

'He is Geir,' said Ottil stoutly. 'He is of my hird.'

'The same vow goes for you as well, hirdman Geir. On your solemn honor is it.'

Geir had taken a step back at being addressed, and tried to hide behind Ottil's back. But he nodded anxiously.

The High Druid and Hraab exchanged glances, as if a message passed between them. Then Arraw nodded. 'I bid you welcome, son of Kainnos.'

Hraab was completely serious. 'I may not assist you in this, Arraw.' Then his impish smile returned. 'But I'll do you a favor. We'll leave you alone with Moirra and the Shardheld. Let no wrongly timed curiosities hinder your efforts.'

'You are too good,' said the High Druid with a straight face.

'Who is Brann?' whispered Geir, once the three of them were outside. 'Did he have red hair too?'

'He still has,' said Hraab. 'Heaps of it. Brann is the God of Strength and Martial Prowess, Master of the Battlefield.'

A slow smile spread over Geir's face. 'We share only the red hair, then. I'll never make a great warrior.'

'Don't sell yourself short,' said Hraab. 'On a battlefield, a keen mind and a sharp eye are as important as brawn. If you're not born for the hew, focus on the how.'

Both Geir and Ottil had to laugh at that.

'Clever fellow,' said the prince. 'Was Kainnos your father?'

Hraab looked at him. 'Kainnos is the Master of Wisdom, the Skyfather of whom the Gods were born. Could he be my father?' He didn't give them time to answer. 'Come, let's look around a bit. I must see if everything is as I remember it.'

'Have you been here before?' said Ottil, once they were outside.

'Long ago.' Hraab cocked his head. 'With my parents.'

'Why are those stones here?' said Geir. 'There's a standing stone near our farm that has all kinds of signs on it. These stones are much bigger, but they're empty.'

'That's because these are not remembrance stones,' said Hraab. 'The one near your farm probably tells of someone's brave deeds or some other important fact. This temple was originally a burial place.'

Ottil's jaw dropped. 'For whom? Who was mighty enough for a place like this?'

'It wasn't for one man, but for a whole people. Thousands upon thousands lay buried here.'

'What people was that? They must've been a race of giants.'

'No, many of them were actually very small. They were the forefathers of the Un-a-Dach, the original people who lived here before the Bryts came.'

'How old is this temple?'

'Muus is the eighth Shardheld to come to this place.'

Ottil was still for a moment. 'I heard there's only one Shardheld every five hundred years,' he said, almost timidly.

Hraab smiled. 'That's right. We're talking about four thousand years.'

'Why did they raise those stones? It must have been an impossible job.'

'Ask the High Druid,' said Hraab. 'It's his secret, not mine.'

In silence they wandered, but watching druids at their prayers wasn't all that exciting, so they left the temple proper and entered the fields beyond. Nearby, a village beckoned, and that was where they ended up.

'All stone houses,' said Ottil. 'Must be rich folk here.'

'Most of them serve the Circle,' said Hraab. 'The druids are generous in paying.'

In the center of the town stood the mead hall, from which the sound of singing came.

'A skald?' said Ottil eagerly. 'Let's go inside.'

'It's a singing class.' Hraab looked around the hall at the rows of young musicians sitting on the floor and listening intently to a giant of a man in a green tunic and trousers. All their mouths opened and closed in the same tempo and the result was so comical, that Ottil couldn't help but giggle.

The tall man broke off in the middle of a verse. 'We are disturbed, my children. Go off and study what I showed you, while I chastise these intruders.' A hairy hand shot out at Hraab. 'Not a singing class, triple nuisances, a master class. Know that you silenced the voice of Vyvain with your disrespectful giggles.'

'Your ears are sharp, good Vyvain,' said Hraab.

'Of course my ears are good. I am the Oaken Bard, the Mastersinger of the Inner Circle.' He relaxed and smiled. 'No matter, I was tired of those gaping frog mouths. Tell me, oddly composed trio, whom you might be.'

'Call me Hraab, good Masterbard. That suffices. Archdruid Fardoragh told us to seek your wisdom, so I will tell you all. My companion is the rightful Prince of the Norden, Ottil Vidmersen; shining offshoot of a dull branch. The one with the flaming head is Geir Gormsen, who has been a farmer, a mariner, a Viking raider and is now a Royal hirdman.'

'Well, Hraab, bird of battle, a famous company you three are. Let us go and drink a glass of wine while you tell me of your glorious adventures.' He signaled a serving girl, who must have known him well, for she brought horns of wine for each of them. The bard's was a giant aurochs horn three times the size of the others.

Vyvain sat down in the only chair, in front of the fire, and lifted his drink. 'May your life stories be long,' said he, and put his nose in his horn.

The boys followed suit, sipping cautiously, for the wine was hot, spicy and stiff.

'Well, now,' said the bard, wiping red droplets from his mustache. 'Tell me all, and don't omit a thing.'

Hraab plopped down on the ground, folded his legs under him and relaxed. He started his story at the moment Vulf's men entered his home. His voice took on a nearly magical quality, so mesmerizing, that even Ottil, who'd heard the story before, listened spellbound. He spoke of everything but the Shardheld. Finally, he ended with their arrival at the Great Temple, and lifted his drinking horn. 'So that's how it all happened,' he said, and drank.

Slowly, the Oaken Bard returned to the here and now. 'You!' he said, and his face was shocked. 'Who are you? No one can tell stories like that.'

Hraab shrugged. 'It's just a gift,'

Vyvain shook his head. 'I'm feeling humbled. Here am I, claiming mastership. But you out-tell us all.' He let out a long sigh.

'You're a well-traveled man, master Vyvain," said Ottil carefully. 'Have you heard of Fjinge's Knucks?'

The Oaken Bard smiled a bit. 'I've traveled, yes. Fjinge, Kalman's dvergar? I know of him and his fingers.'

'He was a dvergar?' Ottil stared at the bard. 'I didn't know they were real.'

'They have died out.' The bard yelled for a girl to refill his horn. 'There weren't all that many to begin with. Some cousins of the Un-a-Dach, long ago. They were a technical people, making weapons and, supposedly, enormous metal halls in the mountains. Their magic was mainly of iron and fire, stone and gold. One of them, Fjinge, was an assistant to the great Kalman. His left hand was made of iron, his right hand filled with magic. When he died, Kalman used the right hand's fingerbones to make a powerful runic necklace, to go with a standing stone he was creating.'

'The Kalmanir,' said Ottil.

Vyvain peered at the Prince. 'Yes, but how did you know?' Then he straightened himself abruptly, splashing wine over his green tunic. 'So that's it!' he said in a great voice. 'The...' His eyes met Hraab's and immediately he lowered his voice. 'The one who shouldn't be is here. The Shardheld.' He shook a finger at the boys. 'I said, tell me all. But you didn't. That's no way to treat the Oaken Bard.'

Hraab spread his hands. 'That part of the story wasn't mine to tell.' He looked at Ottil, who frowned anxiously. 'Don't worry, your point had to be made. That Master Vyvain guessed the rest isn't your fault.'

'Who is the druidess accompanying the Shardheld?'

Hraab smiled. 'Moirra of the Un-a-Dach.'

It was silent for a while, but then the Oaken Bard began to laugh. His mirth filled the hall to the top of the rafters and shook the spiders from their holes. 'Moirra! That, by the Gods in their Might, is the best jest I've heard for a long time.'

Ottil bristled. 'She is a good friend and a powerful druidess.'

Vyvain calmed down. 'That's just it,' he said. 'She is and much more.'

'Prince Ottil's original question is still unasked.'

Ottil looked confused for a moment. Then he said, 'Runemaster Terrel looks to collect all of the Knucks. Would you, in your wide travels, know where we might find one?'

'Reassemble the Hand of Fjinge... Yes, I can imagine the need. Let me think awhile.' The bard leaned back in his chair and closed his eyes. 'The Imperial City, Kartakos. Three centuries ago, an astrologer, Kalech of the Mountains, slew a bunch of fanatic unbelievers with a quake of the earth, toppling their temple near the harbor. Kalech was killed by one of the falling rocks while exulting over his victory. The Magic Bone was taken back to Kartakos by one Euchanistos, of the Imperial Guard. The bone disappeared with him.' He relapsed into silence for a moment. 'Baian, Gaul. The Legend of Sarrias the Thief, who was invisible to his enemies. After he was caught, he was walled up in, the only room he couldn't break out of.

There were some whispers of a magic item that he used. If true, it must have been incarcerated with him.'

He opened his eyes and took a deep draught. 'Those are two possibilities. Thirdly, a druid got a mission to a sacred place somewhere in the south of the mainland. He was said to carry a magic bone. It was not all that long ago, so perhaps one of the scribes can find out.' He emptied his horn and belched. 'Now you must excuse me, it's time for my nap.' He closed his eyes and started to snore.

The boys looked at each other and managed to leave the hall before bursting into laughter.

'So Euchanistos of the Imperial Guard, and a thief in Gaul,' said Ottil, standing. 'And an unknown druid in Southern Gaul.'

'Gaul isn't far,' said Geir unexpectedly. 'Where is Kartakos?'

Ottil stirred. 'That's the Imperial City of Baljaren,' he said. 'They possess some islands and the southern coastlands of the Sea of Rom, which is a long, long way from here.' He looked at Geir and smiled. 'Don't worry, we'll get there. I have kin in that city.'

'You have?' said Hraab. 'How come?'

'Some of my cousins on my father's mother's side have been members of the Varanten, the Imperial Guard, for ages. The present one is Hernald Arnsen of Swalen. Perhaps he knows of this Euchanistos.'

'Something that happened three centuries ago? He'd need a mighty long memory for that.' Hraab scratched his head and smiled. 'But still, it's handy to have someone who knows the city.'

Slowly the boys wandered back to the Great Temple.

Halfway, they were met by a young girl in the green robe of an ovate. 'Your presence is required,' she said, frowning heavily. 'Don't ask me what the High Druid wants with some boys.'

'I wouldn't dream of asking you,' said Hraab. 'But I do suggest you take some extra lessons in Neutral Humility. Your ignorance is showing.'

The girl colored deeply. 'Why, you...' Then she took a deep breath. 'You are right. Thank you for your correction.' She bowed stiffly and walked away.

Ottil couldn't suppress a giggle.

'Don't,' said Hraab. 'For her this is no laughing matter. Moirra the Druidborn can afford to let her tongue run wild, but for an ovate it is a deadly sin.'

'I don't think I would like to be a druid,' said Ottil.

Hraab grinned. 'Don't worry, they don't want you either. You're far too unruly.'

They hurried down the stairs to the High Druid's room.

'What kept you?' snapped Moirra. 'You weren't supposed to run off.'

'That's what I meant,' said Hraab to Ottil. 'Moirra's status is high enough to use that tone.'

Moirra glared at them. 'What are you talking about?'

'Nothing,' said Ottil with a grin. 'Hraab just told us about, what did you say? Neutral humility?'

The girl sniffed. 'I've no time for that, I'm worried.'

'There you are,' said High Druid Arraw, looking up from his thoughts. 'Our preparations are finished, but they are not strong enough. We believe an ingredient is lacking, something I would like to name the 'call of friendship'. Moirra alone can't add this; her call is tainted, if you pardon me the expression, by other emotions.'

'Yeah,' said Ottil with a knowing face. 'That kissin' stuff.'

Moirra blushed as they laughed, but she kept silent.

The High Druid nodded. 'You will learn that call in time, young Prince. For this, friendship is what we need. Please, if you will join hands and form a circle around the Shardheld? I'll pour him the potion we concocted, while you all think friendly things at him. Not shout, please, just thinking is sufficient.' He held the glass, with a thick, greenish fluid inside, up against the light.

Ottil looked at Muus, who had saved him from Nidros, who had stopped his pursuers and had done so many other brave things.

The object of his thoughts suddenly slammed forward, and it was only the High Druid's arm that kept him from hitting the table.

'N-n-noooo!' Muus cried, his hands clawing at nothing. 'You won't... possess me!'

Then, he sat up straight. 'It's gone?'

Moirra drew her arms around him. 'We helped the A'yin rune to drive the skyshard's force back into its stone. How do you feel?'

Muus thought. 'Confused,' he said finally. 'How long has it been?'

'Six days since that awful priestess almost killed you.' Moirra clung so hard to Muus that he flinched.

'I don't remember much,' said he. 'Only that she was faster than I. Did she have a fingerbone?'

Moirra paled. 'I didn't think to look.'

'I did,' said Hraab. 'She hadn't. The power was her own, a corrupted Growth spell.'

'Oh, dear,' sighed the High Druid. 'She must have been one of us. How terrible. I must have known her.'

'She was very old, Wisdom. Over a hundred winters,' said Muus.

'So am I, boy, so am I.' Arraw shook his head. 'If only we knew why she, and those others, defected. Something must have corrupted them.'

'That girl you sent after us,' said Hraab slowly. 'She tried to snub us. Her control was really insufficient.'

Arraw's face went gray. 'Is that so? She's an ovate. I would have sworn she was ready. Am I amiss?'

'Why do you blab about her? Now she'll get into trouble,' said Ottil indignantly.

'Because I must, Prince.' Hraab's face was unusually stern. 'An ovate cannot allow emotion to overcome her judgment, which is what she did. Just like Kings can't. Remember your father?'

Slowly, Ottil nodded. 'But it was such a small thing.'

'It wasn't. She wears green; she should be able to preside over a court of justice, over life and death. She must remain neutral, always in control. That's what she has been trained for, the last ten years. And she wasn't.'

'Somehow, we have missed that. Have we grown complacent?' The High Druid looked troubled. 'I must think on this.'

Moirra unwillingly let go of Muus. 'Are you really feeling all right?'

'I'm feeling fine. The shard knows it must keep me alive, so it took good care of me. What are we going to do?'

'We met with the Oaken Bard,' said Ottil, and proceeded to tell all about their meeting.

Muus rubbed his face when the Prince had finished. 'Still further to go. Baljaren... A colorful name, reeking of riches, corruption and decay. They worship Sol there, but not the gentle Goddess we know. Sol Invictus is a stern master.'

'The Masterbard spoke of a druid with a fingerbone, who got send to a place in the southern mainland. He didn't know his name. Perhaps Your Wisdom...' Ottil's voice petered out; the High Druid was clearly elsewhere with his thoughts.

'Your Wisdom?'

'Ah?' The old man coughed. 'Your pardon, I was thinking.'

Ottil repeated his question, and Arraw nodded slowly. 'I remember only one druid who possessed an original Knuck, and that was Dallyw. My predecessor sent him to Fois, in Southern Gaul, but Dallyw never reported back.'

Muus rubbed his temples. 'What is this whispering I hear? It's all around me, a far-away sound of countless voices.'

The High Druid smiled. 'I should have warned you. Only here can you catch those voices. It is the sound of magic.'

'Magic makes a sound?'

'Not of itself. You hear the magic wielders. One or two, or perhaps ten persons practicing their art at the same time makes no audible sound. But here you hear thousands of druids, priests, wisemen and women at work at the same time.' Arraw put his hands on the table. 'The Great Temple is more than a place of study. It is the center of the mystic power in the world. This is the place where every skyshard has landed, to be picked up by our prepared candidate. This year we were ready, but the shard didn't come. Our candidate waited, but left when Shardfall didn't occur. We weren't happy with that and there was a dispute... however, no druid can be forced, and in the end we had to accept it. We did not realize yet how deeply Fate mocked us. Not only did the skyshard fall somewhere else, it chose its own Shardheld instead of ours. For the first time, the shard was picked up by someone eminently unsuitable for his role.'

'Me,' said Muus. He knew by now that he was second choice.

'You.' The High Druid smiled. 'Don't take offense, but when word arrived that the shard was in the hands of an unknown slave in the polar regions of the Norden, we despaired. But slowly we gathered that this nameless slave was a curious person. A Bryt, born from a union between a Un-a-Dach woman of high degree and an Archdruid of the Inner Circle, taken as a child by raiders. We knew you had disappeared after taking the shard, and our agent in the north was searching for you.'

Muus' eyes went to Hraab, who was listening with an expressionless face. 'My father,' said the boy. 'I had nothing to do with his work for the Circle.'

'Indeed, Hraab was completely unknown to us.' said the High Druid. 'Then all went wrong. Our agent died, and with him our eyes and ears. We didn't know what was going on until you showed up here. I can't describe the relief I felt at your coming.'

'Only I am not your trained puppet,' said Muus softly, clenching his fists on the table. 'I'm not a druid, nor do I want to be one.'

'You don't have to be. And we are not going to tell you to do anything. That is against our tenets.'

Moirra growled softly and the High Druid waved his hands. 'That was in our panic. You know I apologized afterwards. Anyhow, Muus is a Runemaster from his mother's side. That may serve just as well. Especially if you collect all or most of the fingerbones.' He rose and walked over to a chest. 'I have got one. It is a priceless possession and we will sorely miss it, but your need is the greater.' He returned with a small, brown box and flipped the lid open. 'Behold the Rune of Truth. You must take it; it will tell you if anyone is lying to you.'

'Truth,' said Muus slowly. 'For one as confused as I, this is vital.'

'There are several kinds of untruth, Shardheld, and the malicious lie is the rarest. Most people speak untruths without realizing, for many reasons: from ignorance, because their memory is at fault, or because they don't want to realize the truth. You must learn to recognize the difference.'

Muus understood. He was terribly tired all at once, and his fingers fumbled with the Knuck. Then, as if impatient, it snapped into place. *D'vyn.*

Moirra's look at his clumsiness was worried. 'You're done up. You should sleep.'

'Take him to the guesthouse,' said the High Druid. 'There is no one else here from outside, so you'll be undisturbed. Sleep well, Shardheld.'

CHAPTER 18 – FALSE DRUIDESS

Three days later they left the Great Temple as inconspicuously as they had come. Apart from the High Druid and Vyvain the Oaken Bard, no one knew the Shardheld had been here.

Muus rode stiffly, his whole body ached. He was conscious of Moirra, riding at his side. Something bothered her, but he had no idea what. His eyes caught hers and she looked swiftly away. 'What's wrong?' said he softly.

She shook her head. 'Nothing. Just let me be, will you?' It sounded strained, not like the bouncy girl he knew.

Muus stretched out his hand and touched hers. 'You can tell me if you want.'

She looked straight at him. 'No, I can't. This is one thing I cannot tell you. Let it go, Muus, please.'

He sighed. 'All right.'

They passed some low hills, strangely round and grassy.

'Funny hills,' said Ottil.

'Those are barrows,' said Hraab. And in a sepulchral voice: 'Graves.'

Geir laughed. 'Who lies buried there?'

'People who wanted to be important enough to be buried inside the Great Temple, but weren't.' Hraab grinned. 'So they found a spot nearby, long ago. They came from another people. Not a drop of Un-a-Dach blood among them.'

'There is no shame in that!' said Ottil. 'I don't have either.'

'No, but you don't pretend you have.'

'Why would I? I am a proud Nord, not a...' Hastily he shut up.

Hraab gave him a mocking glance. 'A svartalf?'

'I didn't mean that.'

'No, it is your Nordish prejudice showing. As Prince you shouldn't.' Then Hraab laughed. 'Don't worry; just remember the Un-a-Dach are your people too.'

'I will,' said Ottil earnestly. 'I promised Moirra.'

Riding slowly past the barrows, they came to a wood. Tall oaks mingled with birches, giving off an aura of age. After a short while, they came to a spot where the path ran around an immense oak tree.

'Wait!' said Muus. 'Something is wrong.'

From the shadows stepped a green-cloaked shape. 'Ha, so we meet, False One.'

'I know that voice,' said Ottil, surprised.

'You do? No matter, heathen. Your intrusion into our secrets ends here.' The green-cloaked figure lifted her hands and started to sing.

'Don't do that, foolish girl,' said Moirra sharply. 'It is dangerous.'

A patch of smoke appeared between the trees. It grew thicker, and coalesced into an enormous white dog with red ears and glowing eyes.

'Harvester!' cried the green-cloaked girl. 'Behold what was sown.'

'Damn!' cried Hraab. 'May the Mawgan take you!'

The dog walked from between the trees, its tongue lolling. It gave off a vague glow. Then it barked, once. Slowly it turned its head to the girl and its terrible mouth opened in a fearful grin. It took one step toward the one who had summoned it.

'No,' the girl gasped, her hands gripping the sides of her cloak. 'You're an illusion.'

'This isn't an illusion, you stupid bitch!' yelled Hraab. Never had his friends seen him this angry. His small face was red and pinched, his eyes wide open and his lips were drawn back so he looked like a small caricature of the monster dog. 'You ignorant fool! You summoned the real Harvester. Now I must do something forbidden.' He lifted his fists. 'I should let him get you, but that isn't allowed.' He looked at the Shardheld. 'No, Muus, you can't do anything. It's a God's dog. Damn this.' He shouted: 'Arawan! Come get that fool beast of yours!'

A voice, youthful and vibrant, came from all around. 'Who is that calling my name?'

'No games today, Arawan, I'm not in the mood for jokes.'

A young man appeared underneath the tree. 'You? *You* are not in the mood for a joke? The end of the world has come.'

'It will come, if you don't take that mongrel away. Should it kill the Shardheld...'

'That wouldn't be a good idea. Harvester, here, boy.' The dog barked and went to the young man, ready to be caressed. 'But why did you summon my pet? You don't even like dogs.'

'I wouldn't call him if my life depended on it. That stupid girl did it. Just wait till I finish with her.'

'Well, I don't want her, so behave yourself. Nice having seen you!' The young man waved and disappeared with the dog.

'Who was that?' said Ottil pale-faced.

'Arawan, the Death God,' said Hraab curtly. 'Now! You!' He pointed at the terrified girl. 'Why?'

'I only wanted to frighten you.'

'Me? Because I said you lacked Neutral Humility?'

'Y-yes. *She* thought it fitting. I thought it was an illusion. She *said* it was an illusion.'

'Who said it was an illusion?'

'My instructor. She knows a lot of things like that.'

Hraab looked at Muus. 'We must speak with this instructor.'

Muus nodded, puzzled. 'What's going on?'

'Later. We go back now. Moirra, kindly take that girl up with you. I don't trust myself enough to touch her. Might do her harm. Muus, from here you handle it.' Hraab clamped his mouth shut, and rode on with his thoughts clearly somewhere else.

Back at the Great Temple, Muus said to the girl: 'Where is your instructor?'

'Over there, at the Gate of Air,' said the girl. 'She is the tall one in the blue robe.'

'Come with me.' Muus jumped from his horse and walked towards the instructor. She was indeed tall, more Nordish than Bryt, with long hair wound around her head in a braid like a crown.

'You there,' said Muus, staring evenly up at the young woman. 'Who are you?'

The instructor looked down on him. 'I'm Mabain. But why...'

The rune around Muus' neck started to murmur. *False.*

'Why did you teach this girl how to summon Arawan's dog?'

'I... I didn't!'

'You are not Mabain and you did teach her. You are lying,' said Muus. 'Follow me to the High Druid.'

'Miserable worm!' yelled the woman, moving her hands. 'You don't know who I am.'

Now Muus understood. 'You are a Grim Doubh.'

With a scream of rage, the instructor threw a bolt of blackness at Muus, but this time his Protection rune was ready and the power ran crackling into the ground.

'That won't work a second time,' said Muus. His mind sought contact with the runes around his neck. *Knock her out.* A tiny flash of lightning shocked the woman and she crumbled. Muus pointed to two nearby druids, who stood looking openmouthed. 'Pick her up and bring her to the High Druid. He and I'll want to talk to her.' He turned to Hraab, his face stiff and angry. 'And to you too.'

The boy nodded.

In his workroom, the High Druid looked up in surprise as they filed in. 'Back already? And what...' He didn't finish, as the two druids dumped the unconscious instructor on the floor and left in a hurry.

The girl in the green robe rushed forward, her face distorted and tear-streaked. 'It's my fault,' she cried, tearing at her clothes. 'I failed my oath. Unworthy, I can't wear this. I...'

'Be still,' said Moirra sternly and she pushed the girl down on a stool.

'She,' Muus said, prodding the senseless woman with his foot, 'is the - or at least a - source of corruption in your temple, High Druid. This woman, whose name is not Mabain, corrupted at least your young ovate here. She taught a spell that called Arawan's dog into the world and fooled the girl into thinking it was an illusion. Your ovate cast the spell at us. When tasked with it, Mabain tried to kill me with the same spell the earlier Grim Doubh priestess had used. She lives yet, in case you want to speak with her.'

The High Druid looked at the girl in green. 'Is this what happened, daughter?'

'Yes, yes,' the girl sobbed. 'I see now how stupid I was, but I believed her. All she taught about the Gods and the Old Ones, the spells, they were all false. Why did I believe it? Why I stray? I was always so sure about my purity.'

''None of us are pure,' said Moirra softly. 'The Gods know I'm not.'

The girl lowered her head. 'I was vain, I felt so superior, and all the while I wasn't... I wasn't.'

'At least you're speaking the truth, girl,' said Muus. 'I leave you to the wisdom of the Circle.'

The girl stretched a hand out to Hraab. 'I was angry at you, for your earlier harsh words. I told Mabain and she thought up this plan to frighten you. I am sorry.'

'Change into the brown of penance, retire to one of the cells and wait until you're summoned,' said the High Druid. 'In the meantime, reflect on what you think you know and what of it is true. We will speak later.'

Squaring her shoulders, the girl left.

'In a few months' time I'll have her summoned and we'll see how far she has progressed,' said the old man. 'You have done us a great service, Shardheld. Now I must examine all of us, to see if there are more strays from our druidic fold.' He stared at the woman on the ground. 'What shall I do with Mabain? How far is she gone?'

'Ask her,' said Muus. 'She's awake.'

The woman opened her eyes. 'Blind fools,' she said, staring up at them. 'So easily you sheep are fooled. So weak you are. It was not that gullible lamb who strayed - but you did, druid.' She nearly spat the last word out. 'You strayed when you left the path of the real Gods, Those That Were Before. You degenerated, became as children. Not for long though. They will return, I bid them to return. Darh, come to aid your servant. Orwang, come and help me. Uuuu...' A dark shadow seemed to form over her.

'Stop her!' cried the High Druid, and there was panic in his voice. 'She's calling them!'

Without wanting to, Muus kicked the woman. Words came unbidden from his lips. 'You will not fool around with forgotten powers, woman. I have some questions and you will answer them.'

The woman stared at him, blood running from her nose over her rage-twisted face. 'I will not, worm. You can't make me, the Four protect me.'

'Tell me who leads the Grim Doubh.'

The woman laughed scornfully. 'The Caller of Earth is too mighty for you, pitiful man. He walks in and out of the Great Temple at will and no one can stop him. You will not find him; he will find you and end your useless existence.'

'Answer my question.'

Instead, the woman spat a blob of bloody saliva over his feet.

Muus' face contorted in pain as the runepower pulled at him. *A'yin, make her talk.* He felt how a wave of U'th's self-awareness shocked the woman, broke open the core of her being, dug up her well-hidden delusions and magnified them a thousand-fold. She started to scream. 'No! Take it away! Please...' Her words changed into babbling and the naked horror on her face tore at Muus' heart.

'Answer my question.'

'The Caller leads us. He's the mighty one, the child of the Four! More I can't... Aaahh, take it away! He... he is at Granwen, the Earthgate!' Her eyes started to turn in her head and her voice became insane gibbering. Muus looked at the High Druid, who shook his head.

'She isn't repairable,' he said. 'Better kill her, before her insanity poisons us all.'

Muus snarled. The woman on the floor looked hardly human and the dark shadow hovering over her writhed and pulsed on the rhythm of her screams.

A flash of light from his hand stilled the Grim Doubh's voice. The darkness behind her contorted and Muus raised his hands. 'Begone!' Immediately the black dissolved. Only the dead false priestess, now a fat old woman with a face blackened and scorched, remained on the floor.

Moirra stared at Muus, her mouth half open. 'How did you do that?'

'What?' said Muus, angry beyond measure with all these fools who kept him from his goal.

Moirra shook her head. 'No matter,' she muttered.

With a growl, Muus turned to Hraab. 'Now you, master little-boy Hraab. Who are you?'

CHAPTER 19 – HRAAB

Gravely the boy looked at Muus. 'I can explain,' he said. Then the figure of a small man appeared next to him. He was bigger than the Un-a-Dach, but smaller than the other people. His face was thin, his nose pointed, and his mouth wide. It was a rogue's face, a jester or juggler's, and the gravity seemed somehow unfitting on it.

'I wasn't planning on showing myself. In fact, I am expressly forbidden this. But I must and the others agreed. Shardheld, I am Iowynh.' His name met with blankness and an ironic smile pulled at his lips. 'Such is fame,' he sighted. 'I forgot you were away for so long. I happen to be a God, friend. Magic is my strength, and some say Trickery.'

Muus' eyes were hard. 'And Hraab? Are you separate from him?'

The boy laughed. 'I am myself and he is, well, hisself.' Somehow he sounded different now, more the original Hraab.

The God stepped forward. 'See? Quite apart we are. Let me assure you that friend Hraab - what a terrible name you chose, little one – really is a child. His entire story is true, ne'er a lie was spoken, and only a thing omitted. A piece of me is inside the infant, sometimes using his mouth. Not I myself, that would be... awkward, but a tiny piece to keep me aware of what's happening. There is a purpose, of course. Gods always have a purpose, after all, that is their p... that is what they are here for.' He smiled at Muus, but the Shardheld didn't respond. Looking slightly disappointed, the God continued. 'You must understand the importance of your task, Shardheld. Not only the druids, prophets, Völva and other priests will suffer if the Kalmanir runs dry, but we too.'

Muus heard the High Druid's slight gasp, but he just looked at the God.

'Your task must succeed, Shardheld. The world as we know it would cease to exist if you failed. Therefore, seeing your, eh, inexperience, the collective pantheons decided to send an observer with you. And with you being a Un-a-Dach and my school of magic closest to yours, this task fell to me. Be glad it was, for else you'd have Odin with you, and I can assure you he'd get wearisome after a while.'

'All the Gods decided this?' said Muus, for the first time less grim.

'Well, except for Sol Invictus. That old fool has an overly high opinion of himself and he refused to join us. So be careful when you're in Baljaren, my friend.'

'And you're an observer? You can't help us?'

'That is absolutely forbidden. Not every one of the supreme deities was convinced of my helping you with that fool dog Harvester, but I'm pretty good at cajoling and finally they all agreed. I can't pull that card again. You're on your own. Even my being here is troublesome.'

'I accept what you're saying, Iowynh. I have to, probably.' Muus looked at Hraab. 'You're still welcome, of course.' He laughed softly. 'I can't have you trailing us like you did Vulf.'

Hraab crowed at that. 'Vulf, Vulf, Vulf! May his afterlife be all I dreamed of.'

'Who are the Gods Before?' Muus watched the Tricky God closely. 'Are they real?

'Oh, yes, they are, all Four of them. They were here before us. Creators of the mountains and the pebbles on the beach, the clouds and the rivers, the fiery mountains. They made strange trees and barbed grass, animals that only kill, and twisted beings to worship them. Then we came and vanquished the old Gods. They were banned from the world, to wander the spheres past the sky, ever trying to get back in. We shouldn't let them, Shardheld. There would be bloodshed like no one ever saw. For with them, their followers would return as well, and they are rather different. So kill those Grim Doubh, Fynni and whatever they are named wherever you can.'

'Muus commanded the Four to leave just now, you know,' said Hraab and the God frowned.

'He did? Open your mind, child. By my Father, you're right.' The God gave Muus a hard stare. 'How did you do that?'

Muus shrugged. 'They irritated me, so I told them to go. That's all.'

'Be careful with that,' said Iowynh. 'It could be coincidence, so don't count on it. I must think on this. Nice speaking with you, Shardheld. You're not as hopeless as I feared. Moirra, you're as lovely as ever. Prince, be a man and you'll win. That goes for you as well, young hirdman Geir. Your servant, High Druid.' With that, the God of Magic disappeared.

'He spoke to me,' whispered Geir. 'He knew my name. While I... I don't even believe in him.'

'Better believe in all Gods everywhere, boy,' said the High Priest dryly. 'For they all exist. You don't have to worship all of them, of course.'

Muus sat down at the table and buried his face in his hands. Moirra put her hands on his shoulders. Her face was sad.

'I hate it,' said Muus, his voice muffled. 'I hate this power and everything with it. I wish I could get rid of it. I hated being slave to Kjelle, but this is worse. They're fighting over me, the runes and the shard. Both of them want to possess me. How can I escape?'

'You can't,' said Hraab, completely serious. 'You will have to overcome them yourself. I can't do it for you, nor can the Gods.'

'I will help you as best as I can,' said Moirra fiercely. 'I so wish I could take it all away from you, but I can't either.'

The High Druid looked at her and his voice was full of compassion. 'No, dear, you won't ever be able to take his place.'

Muus lifted his head. 'Don't cry, girl,' he said. 'We'll manage somehow.'

He banged his fists on the table. 'Damn those Grim Doubh. What or where is Granwen, and what is an Earthgate?'

The High Druid looked worried. 'The Earthgate is outside. It's the leftmost of the five portals connecting to the Elemental Realms.'

'Granwen is the underground warren you enter through the Earthgate.' Moirra's voice sounded almost desperate. 'We can't go there!'

Muus gripped her hands. 'Why not?'

'It's... awful. Filled with *things* that used to live in the open, but were rejected by Time. It's a place of strange powers. I've been there once, at the end of my training. I don't want to go there again.'

'Not to worry,' said Muus. 'I go in alone.'

'No!' Moirra nearly shouted. 'If you go, I'm coming with you.'

'And I,' said Ottil firmly.

Geir blanched, but he nodded.

'You know you won't be so easily rid of me,' said Hraab. 'Although Iowynh won't be pleased to be cut off from me.' He shrugged. 'The Gods should've cleaned out those places ages ago.'

'They can't,' said the High Druid. 'The Gods Before have too many followers still to be done away with.'

'Followers?' said Muus. 'Are there that many Grim Doubh?'

'Blessed be, no! I'm talking about the rocks and stones, the air, the water. They all follow the Gods Before as well as our new ones. As long as the world exists, the Old Ones will be found lurking somewhere. And that is all right, as long as that somewhere is not here.'

The five portals were much smaller than the surrounding stones, but now they loomed over Muus as the gates to the Underworld.

'You're still sure?' said Muus to the others.

'Just hurry up, will you,' said Ottil testily.

Moirra stepped forward, looking pale and worried. She raised her hands and started to sing. Slowly the air within the portal stones became opaque, at which point she stopped. 'Ready.'

Muus took her hand in his and felt her shaking. Then he smiled at her and together they walked through the portal into a gloomy tunnel.

'This is it?'

Moirra nodded. 'Tunnels longer than the whole of Brytanna, spreading out in all directions like the roots of an old tree.'

'How shall we find the way back?'

The girl's mouth worked. She held up a large piece of white stone. 'Chalk,' she said. 'We make markings on the walls to show where we're going.'

'Clever.'

She shrugged. 'It's just druid training.'

They started walking. Ottil had his sword in his hand, with behind him Geir and Hraab, each carrying a small ax.

'Back to basics,' said the latter.

Muus stared hard at him. The boy looked and sounded younger, more like when they first met.

'I'm myself now,' said Hraab. 'It is strange, to be without Iowynh, after so many months together.'

'Must be funny, having someone else in your head,' said Ottil.

'He wasn't really there. It's more like being in a dark room with somebody else. You can't see him but you know he's there.' He was silent for a moment. 'He saved my life, you know.'

'Oh?'

'I was dying, that day. Vulf's Fynni had broken my skull and I was slowly bleeding to death. Iowynh stopped the hole in my head and put life back into me. That's why I serve him, not always gladly, but because it's his right.'

'Listen,' said Geir. He spoke so seldom that everybody fell silent. From somewhere came the sound of many feet, and voices singing a dolorous song, accompanied by the sound of chains.

'It's coming our way.' Ottil sounded calm.

'In here,' said Muus, and quickly they slipped into a deep alcove.

Peering around the corner, hidden by the gloom, they saw a long row of small men and women of extreme pallor, with large shocks of black hair and pinched faces full of malice. They were chained together, each carrying a small pickax and singing their dirge-like song.

They couldn't be anything else: svartalves. Muus felt Moirra's hand squeezing his and when he turned to look at her, he saw the horror in her eyes.

When the long row had passed, they hurried on.

'Those were svartalves? They do look like us,' said Muus softly.

'In a twisted way. They're mad,' said Moirra with a mixture of pity and revulsion. 'They are our progenitors, the ones that built the first Great Temple and many other wonders. But these were completely mad, no longer human.'

A flapping of wings alerted them just in time, before a leathery beast screeched and dove low over their heads.

'Watch out!' cried Moirra. The animal, a cross between a lizard and a bird, turned sharply and screeched again.

Can you kill it? thought Muus.

The runes seemed to hesitate. The monster started to smoke and its movements became slower.

Ottil slashed at it, his face fierce. Under other circumstances, it would've been a comical sight, for he had to jump high in the air every time he struck at the passing monster. Most of his strikes connected, though, and the animal began to bleed. On its next passage, it went for Ottil, who dropped to the ground and rolled away. Geir swung his ax at the beast's head. With a squawk it crashed into the ground, to be hacked to death by the three boys.

'You got him,' said Ottil proudly, clapping Geir on the shoulder.

The boy looked confused. 'I did?'

'You did,' said Hraab. 'It was your kill, mate.'

'It's a big one too,' said Ottil, eyeing the strange animal. 'Look, from tip to wingtip it's taller than me.'

'Those flew in the world long ago, before the New Gods came,' said Moirra. 'Well done!'

After a while, the walls began to change. At first they were made of stone, but now they looked like entrails, as if they were inside an enormous being. Red veins ran criss-crossed through the walls, pulsing like living things. Further on, Muus and his companions heard singing. Not a dirge this time, but something more like the demented songs of the Grim Doubh in their bog camp.

They came to a brightly lit hall, with a giant fire in the middle, around which a heaving mass of Grim Doubh were dancing.

Muus directed his thought at both the runes around his neck and at the skyshard. *Now, runes, work with the shard because I command you to. Skyshard, I know where you want me to go. Don't worry, I will go there. But not yet. If you help me, we'll get there faster than when you try to work against me.* The Runestones just sighed, but the skyshard wasn't exactly happy with the idea.

Aloud, Muus said, 'Step backwards, all of you. Stay behind me.' Then he raised his arms and felt an enormous surge of power run through his body. Lightning cascaded from the floors and the walls, jumping onto the screaming Grim Doubh and killing them in droves. It took only minutes before the area was empty, except for one man. He was a giant, twice as tall as an ordinary man, with muscles like slabs of stone. His hair was blond, braided into strands that nearly touched his buttocks. He, too, was clothed in nothing, with only a familiar fingerbone on a cord around his neck.

'Who are you?' Muus remembered the priestess who had nearly killed him and his nerves were stretched taut.

'I am the Caller of Earth,' said the man and his voice echoed off the walls. 'I'm the Servant of the God of Earth. But you! Who are you to kill my children?'

'I'm Terrel of Owwich,' said Muus. 'Runemaster and the Shardheld.'

Pure madness crossed the man's face. 'You're the one who's keeping our Gods from returning. You must die.' He sent a wave of shimmering fire towards Muus, but the combined powers of runes and shard countered it with a strong wind full of moisture, and, spluttering, the fire died. The world began to tremble and shake. Rocks rained down from the ceiling and cracks appeared in the floor. Vaguely, Muus heard the others behind him cry out as they were thrown about like a handful of dice, but he kept to his feet and his will commanding both runes and shard didn't falter.

The Caller shouted a word and a wave of pure black sprang from his hands.

Now! The blackness halted a few feet from Muus. It hesitated, then melted together into the shadow of its master and stalked back to the Caller.

The giant priest stepped backwards, gaping in shock. 'Impossible!' In desperation, the Caller began the same chant his minion at the Great Temple had tried. 'Darh, come to aid your servant. Orwang...' but he was too slow. The figure of blackness lifted him from the floor and smashed his head against the wall with a sickening crunch. His body shrank from a giant to a sticklike creature barely recognizable as a svartalf.

The shadow looked at Muus and flickered out. *Nicely done, friends. Now we can go back and on with the journey.* The world around him shifted and with a rush of wind, they stood in the Great Temple.

Not so hasty! Where's that damned fingerbone?

Something in his mind coughed and when he took the runes out, there was a new one. *T'oyt, the Rune of Illusion.*

'You're hurt!' Moirra hurried to Ottil, who had a large bruise over his left eye.

'I got a rock in my face,' said the boy through clenched teeth.

Moirra placed her fingertips on his temples. 'Do you have a headache? Dizzy?'

'No.'

She nodded. 'Luckily, you've got a hard head.'

They hurried down to the High Druid's rooms.

'So their head priest is dead,' said the High Druid, after Muus had told of their doings in the Earth sphere. 'Then the power of the Grim Doubh must surely wither. He was the fount their priests drew their strength from. You have done a great thing for Brytanna today, Shardheld.'

'The Caller was a svartalf,' said Moirra, her face strained.

'They were an ancient people,' said the High Druid. 'Created by the Gods Before at the beginning of time. After the New Gods came and Rom was founded, they disappeared and their descendants became the Un-a-Dach. It is not strange that svartalves still live within the plane of the Gods Before and serve them.'

CHAPTER 20 – GOING SOUTH

'There's a village,' said Kjelle.

Birthe didn't look up. The first signs of civilization in two days didn't lighten her bleak mood. She rode tail, alone, just aware enough to follow the others before her, but too lost in her inner self to show any interest in what happened around her. The thought of that awful Rev filled her mind almost to the exclusion of everything else.

Running past the village was a small river with a fordable crossing to the Kingdom of Lotharn on the other side. Here, an old man and a child of perhaps nine years were fishing, both serious-faced, as if the day's meal depended on their efforts.

'G'day,' said Kjelle. 'Are they biting?'

The old man looked up. 'Fairly. Me partner's doing best, today.'

Next to him, the boy grinned. 'It is me lucky hook that does it.'

'That's a hook I gave him,' said the old man with a smile. 'I never caught anything with it.' He spat into the water. 'You're passing through?'

'Southward, yes,' said Kjelle.

'You picked a bad time.' The old man raised his fishing rod and inspected his bait before casting again.

'What is bad about it?' said Birthe, suddenly alerted by a look on the old man's face.

There's trouble in Lotharn.' The fisherman cast a quick glance at the boy beside him and lowered his voice. 'There are bandits on the loose over there, raiding villages and farms. The King of Lotharn doesn't seem too concerned; at least he hasn't done anything yet to protect his people. Only last sevenday, the bandits raided Malbeck town, that's less'n two days from here. My son's wife's family lives in Malbeck county. They sent the wives and children this way for safety. The bandits are armed like soldiers and it's said they're using forbidden powers. I sure hope they all stays on their side of the river, it's coming mighty close.'

Birthe looked sharply at the old man. 'What kind of powers?'

Again, the old man looked worriedly at the boy next to him, but his grandson wasn't listening. 'My son's wife's sister wasn't very clear.

She said the bandits couldn't be harmed by sword or arrow. She was rather upset about it all, quite hysterical, actually. But there it is; our fish have a lot of mouths to feed today.'

Birthe nodded. 'We won't keep you then.' She raised her wand and chanted a blessing. 'May the Gods protect you all.'

The old man made a sign over his heart. 'Thankee, holy one. We can sure use all the aid we can get.'

That evening, they all heard the sound of thunder in the distance.

'Thor is angry,' said Ajkell. 'We're in for some rain, I'd say.'

His words became truth before long, when the dark clouds overhead opened and a downpour soaked them. Bluish flashes lit up the forest with an eerie glow.

'Over there,' shouted Elbrich over the sound of thunder. 'I saw the light of a fire or something; perhaps there's a place we can find shelter.'

Kjelle looked at him. 'Where? I didn't see anything.'

'My night sight is a lot better than yours,' said the smith. 'Come, follow me.'

Through the rain they went down a small path that ended at a brook. Now they saw what the light was.

'Oh, Gods,' said Birthe. On the other side of the brook lay a small village of some five or six houses, all burning fiercely in spite of the rain. 'This can't have been Thor's lightning.'

'No,' said Ajkell tersely. He pointed -- and now they saw the trees, each with a naked, headless body tied to the trunk.

They heard a yell, and six soldiers dressed in red-painted leather armor blocked their way. A seventh man, in a long robe trimmed with red fur, passed through their line to halt a few steps in front of them. Sodden with rain, his hair plastered against his hollow face, he looked more like some walking draug than a living man. He spread his arms in awful ecstasy. 'Behold the revenge of the Blodward against those who have sinned and them who aided them. What seek you here?'

'It was you who killed those villagers?' said Kjelle, fighting against rage.

Birthe saw his face and freed her strung bow from the folds of her cloak. 'Kjelle...'

The man lowered his arms. 'I freed them from their sins, stranger. Such is my duty as Voice of the Four.' The man's eyes started to glow. 'How is it with you? Do you follow the Four, strangers?'

Birthe laid her hand on Kjelle's sleeve, but he shook it off. 'I spit on your Four,' he said, the revulsion clear in his face. 'Bury them in the deepest depths of the planes and piss on them.'

The man hissed. 'Saaaaah! This will mean your end, blasphemer.' A shimmering appeared around him. He raised his hands to the sky and started to chant. A cold wind rose, blowing the rain away. Four shadows appeared, brooding and silent. Waiting.

Birthe loosed an arrow, only to see it bounce off the Voice without touching him. Her cry of frustration rent the sky. 'He's protected!' Ajkell ran past her and swung his ax at the priest. His weapon didn't harm the other, but the force of his stroke made the man break off his chant.

A soldier came at Birthe, and by reflex she shot him point blank, straight through the throat. 'Damn,' she said, surprised. She saw Kjelle engage another enemy, but the soldier, empty-faced under his helm, somehow evaded his stroke. He slapped Kjelle's face hard with his leather-clad hand and raised his sword. Again, Birthe's bow sang. An arrow appeared in the soldier's forehead and he stumbled, clutching at the feathered shaft. Kjelle spat out some blood from a split lip and ran the soldier through with his sword.

A bright flame hit one of the soldiers full in the face. The man dropped his weapon and his screaming mouth was a hole in a black and crackling face. Elbrich held up his smith's hand, blowing off the smoke from his middle finger. He tipped his helm backward and said something the others couldn't hear. The sight of his nonchalance was irrepressibly comical and Kjelle laughed like a maniac as he thrust his sword deep in the next soldier's midriff. The man's eyes glazed over as he slit from the long blade to the ground.

On the path, Ajkell was still battering the priest, forcing him back. The shadows hovered around the gaunt man, evil yet impotent. His robe caught around a low branch. With a cry, the man fell backwards and there was an audible crack as his head struck the tree behind him. The shimmering disappeared for a moment, and with a swift stroke Ajkell split the priest's skull. A peal of thunder sounded as if in Godly triumph. The hovering shadows winked out silently.

The last soldier fled, with Kjelle in pursuit. After a few moments, screams coming from among the burning houses told Birthe the fugitive hadn't got far.

Kjelle returned, looking satisfied. 'Got him. Nicely done, all.'

Around them, the rain fell, washing the blood off their armor.

Tuuri heard the first peal of thunder and he cursed. He was in for a manifestation of Thor's wrath. Immediately, a mighty crash straight overhead made him jump. Then the downpour started. Lightning killed his night vision, but not before he spied the remnants of a stone building beside the path. He ran towards the gaping doorway and came in a small room. It had the feel of a temple. The walls were covered with faint, much-damaged murals, showing a large city. Here and there were added bits of text written in Old Rom, a language he recognized but couldn't read. A doorway opened into a tiled corridor. Strange to find a ruin like this in the middle of a forest, he thought, peering into the dark opening. He stood listening, all his Fynni senses alert. There was something inside. With hesitation, he stepped over the threshold and listened again. It sounded like sobbing. He had heard of monsters who lured their prey that way, but he sensed no evil. Slowly he walked down the corridor.

The darkness would have been impenetrable to ordinary folk, but to him the dim light was enough to see where he placed his feet. The building was remarkably solid, though its walls of chiseled stone blocks gave off an impression of great age. Only here and there had a branch wormed its way through a crack, brushing the tops of Tuuri's head as he moved forward. He passed several side rooms, all bare of anything but dust. It must be an old Rom place, he thought. Then he stopped. The sound of crying was straight ahead.

Carefully he walked forward, his hand at his long knife. He must have kicked a stone, for it shot away and hit the wall with a loud crack.

'Who's t-there?' said a voice, sounding young and fearful. 'D.don't come any nearer, or I'll k-kill you!'

Tuuri rounded the corner and came into a circular space that had clearly been a temple sanctum of sorts. Against the back wall stood a stone image of a bearded, stern-faced man, his armored hands resting on a large sword held point down before him. Kneeling at his feet was a young girl with a tear-stained face, pressing a sharp knife to her breast. On her cheek she bore a mark like his, the symbol of the God of Sky Before. He couldn't suppress a gasp of surprise. 'Ullr's Peace be with you,' he said in his own Ostmark dialect. Haltingly, she answered, 'May He guide your feet.' For a moment, they just stared at each other.

She wasn't much more than a child, he thought, thirteen or fourteen years at most. 'What's your name?'

The girl fastened her weeping eyes on his face. 'Why do you want to know my name? For the power it gives you over me?'

'I don't crave power, girl. But I can't call you "hey you" all the time.'

The girl giggled through her tears. 'My name sounds just like that. I'm Hilja.' Then her hands went to her mouth in shock. 'Oh!'

'Don't worry,' said Tuuri. 'Your name is safe with me.' He sat down opposite her, carefully keeping some distance between them. 'Are you hiding here?'

After a heartbeat's hesitation, the girl nodded.

'Who or what are you afraid of?'

Hilja's hand clutched the knife. 'It was this afternoon. I was in the forest, collecting herbs for my mother. I often do that, it's nice and calm among the trees. But this time I heard shouting coming from the village. It was very strange, those angry voices, so I hid under the large yew at the end of the village, where I could see without being seen. There were strange soldiers, six men in red uniforms, with big swords, and a priest.

'Their tongue was harsh and hard to understand and their faces were covered in marks like mine. It seemed my father knew them, for he was afraid.' She looked around. 'I had never seen him afraid before. The soldiers told everybody to stand in front of their houses.' Then she gasped, her eyes large and full of horror. 'They killed my dad, because of the mark on his cheek. Traitor, they called him.'

Tears ran down her face. 'My mother screamed and one of the soldiers hit her in the face with his ax.

'They had torches and fired our house and then they threw my parents inside. My mother wasn't dead yet -- I heard her. The priest said something to Barat, the village elder. I don't know what it was, but the priest didn't like his answer, for he yelled some orders and the soldiers killed the other people. They laughed!' She shivered. 'I crept away and fled to hide here in the Old Emperor's temple. Karos protects us, said my father always. And he did! He sent you here.'

'Fynni?' said Tuuri, shocked at her tale. 'Here, too?'

The girl didn't answer and they sat in silence for a moment.

'Do you have food?' asked she. 'I haven't eaten for ages.'

Tuuri shook his head. He hadn't had much to eat himself since his escape two days ago. 'Not much,' he said. 'Like you, I'm a fugitive.' All at once, he felt the need to unburden himself. There, by the light of a small spark, he told her of Rannar and his bid for the throne of the Norden, of his own adventures and how he'd managed to escape from Holder Kjelle's grasp.

When he was done, there was a long silence, as the girl stared at him and Tuuri wondered how much of it she had understood.

'Fynnikin,' said she finally. 'Is that what I am, too? And those Fynni sound like the men who killed my parents.' Then she sighed deeply and went on to more practical things. 'We can go to our village. Perhaps not everything is burned.'

'Show me the way.' Tuuri sprang up. 'All at once I'm feeling starved.'

Outside, the thunder hadn't died down, but the thought of food made braving the weather easier. They ran, keeping as much as possible in the minimal shelter of the trees, until Tuuri noticed the pungent smell of burned wood. The rain had all but extinguished the worst fires; the ruined houses glowed in the dark of the night. 'Can you see anything?' he said, pulling the girl back.

'Not much,' she said. 'It's so awfully dark. Why?'

Tuuri tried not to look at the diagonal crosses, each bearing a headless, mutilated corpse. 'Those soldiers did things to the people you'd better not see,' he said.

He felt her stiffen. 'What have they done?'

'They've beheaded the people and some have been... cut.' Gutted, he thought, like whitings in a fishmonger's stall. 'Let's concentrate on food.'

'This way,' said the girl. Then she cried out. 'A dead soldier!'

Tuuri hurried over. He saw not one, but five dead soldiers. And a way beyond a man in a dark robe, with his skull split. All soldiers wore red-painted armor. 'Were they the enemy?'

'Yess,' the girl's voice sounded gleeful. 'It's them. Someone killed them!' She started to laugh, hiccoughing, without being able to stop until Tuuri shook her. Enough!' he said sharply.

With a last cough, she collapsed in his arms, senseless to the world. There he stood, feeling awkward with an unconscious girl against his breast. He stared at nearest dead soldier and wondered who had killed those murderous bastards. His ears picked up the sound of voices at the other side of the village. Tuuri took Hilja in his arms and disappeared among the trees. From behind some bushes he looked back.

Four people he counted, and... His breath seemed to stop. *It's them! Mighty Ullr, it's that Kjelle and his tame Völva. How did they come here? They must've passed me on the road.* He felt Hilja stir in his arms and clamped a hand over her mouth. 'Enemies!' he whispered, and he felt her freeze. She nodded once, and carefully he removed his hand. His blood ran as a swift mountain brook through his veins, making his heart pump madly. Afraid to move, he stood there, clasping a trembling girl to his breast. Finally, the four from Eidungruve turned away, their words inaudible in the rustling rain. They left and sometime later he heard the faint scrunching of their horses on the stony path. When he was sure they were gone, he heaved a deep sigh and let go of the girl in his arms.

'It was him,' he said, 'Lord Kjelle. He must have killed those murderers.'

Hilja brushed the strands of wet hair from her face. 'He did? Then he can't be all bad.'

Tuuri gave a lopsided grin. 'That's the point, he isn't bad at all. He is a good, honorable man.'

'Then why run away from him?'

'Because when he catches me, he will hang me. He and his lord are the enemies of my lord. That makes us enemies, too.'

The girl shook her head. 'I don't understand.' She wiped her nose on her sleeve and looked up at him, her face dripping with rain and soot from the fires. 'What will you do now?'

'I'm going south. That was in my orders, to go south and catch another enemy.'

'In the south? Do you know where?'

Tuuri nodded. 'That's the one thing I kept from Kjelle and his Völva. It was in Vulf's orders. There is a mountain pass across the Barrier Alps into Falrom, near a village called Olhorec in southern Gaul. That's where I must go. What will you do?'

She shrugged. 'I don't know. The only people I knew are dead.'

For a moment there was silence.

'You can come with me,' said Tuuri. He stiffened at his own words. What did he say? Take her with him? But she would be a burden.

'Thanks, but you don't really want me to,' said Hilja. 'I'll stay here and make do. I know the area; I'll be all right, really.'

'No,' he said, 'You can't stay here all alone. Come, you won't be in the way.'

'You sure?'

'Of course I'm sure,' said Tuuri, shouting down his own objections. 'Besides, we Fynnikin should stick together.'

He bent and grabbed a fallen sword from the ground. Swiftly, he took a scabbard from the dead soldier and hung it on his own belt. Sheathing the sword, he sighed. 'That's better. Now, we were going to look for food. Where would be the best place?'

'Come,' she said. 'I'll show you.'

The barn had been forcibly opened, but the contents, all that was left of the village's winter stock, were intact.

'Lord Kjelle came just in time to kill those bastards,' said Tuuri, with his mouth full of salted ham. 'They didn't have time to take or spoil anything.' He spat out a piece of bone and burped. 'Now we only need a horse. I'm afraid I'll have to steal one somewhere, but on foot we'll never get to the Barriers in time.' He dug into a tub still half filled with wrinkled apples and sought for one of the freshest.

When he turned, Hilja was gone. He frowned and stepped outside, looking around. 'Hilja?' he called. He was answered by the whinny of a horse.

Moments later, the girl was back, leading an old dappled grey mare. 'This is Mai,' she said. 'Elder Barat's horse. She was in her little paddock, as calm as you please. There's no saddle and tack, though; the elder always took that home with him.

'I can ride without,' said Tuuri. 'It's a wonder she survived. Thank you, it's a great gift.'

With old sacks and some ends of rope he improvised two saddlebags and filled them with foodstuffs. 'Shall we go?' he asked.

Hilja looked around, and now her tears returned. She nodded violently. 'Yes, please. I don't want to be here anymore.'

At the burned-out ruins of a small house she stopped and said something, too soft for Tuuri to hear her words. Then she turned and ran off to the path.

Tuuri gripped the horse by its mane and hurried after her. Near the road, she waited for him. He looked at her drawn face and thought it better to ask no questions. 'We'll have to ride double,' he said. 'Luckily neither of us is very heavy.'

She blinked against her tears. 'I don't know how. She's very big, isn't she?'

'I'll mount first and you'll sit behind me.' He put his hands on the horse's spine and jumped onto her back. 'Now you mount from the side, never from behind. Even an old nag like this can kick.'

Awkwardly, Hilja got up behind him and put her arms around his middle.

'Ready?' Tuuri moved his knees and slowly the horse started to walk.

CHAPTER 21 – TO GAUL

For the second time Muus took his leave. Only now he couldn't just slip away unnoticed, for all the druids came to wish him well.

Nothing disturbed their journey now and late that night they arrived in Bythern, a bustling harbor town. They slept the night in the local Hall.

The next morning they went looking for a boat to the mainland. They found a willing skipper, owner of a local merchant vessel, who had done this before. There wasn't a ship large enough to take the horses, so they sold them for a tidy sum to the local horse-coper. After two days, they finally arrived in Harflot, two months later than planned.

The merchant captain landed them close to the fishing harbor. 'I'm not going south,' the man had said. 'Best you ask a coastal fisher to take you part of the way. Hopping from harbor to harbor may sound slow, but I'd say it was a lot faster than walking. It's a mighty long way to Baian and many merchants avoid it because of the Bay.'

'What is wrong with the Bay?' said Muus.

The skipper looked at him. 'Ne'er heard of the Bay of Storms? It's a mortal danger, traveler. Terrible winds, crosscurrents, thunderstorms in winter, heavy fog for the rest of the year. Great risk of bumpin' into one of them giant fish. I'm not sailin' there for all the riches in Espayne.'

With that he took his leave, to catch the tide back home.

'Giant fish?' whispered Geir.

'Whales,' said Moirra. 'They're said to be very big.'

'I've heard of them.' Ottil gave Geir a poke. 'Don't look so scared, they're just fish.'

Geir sighed. 'I'm not scared; it's just that there are so many terrible things in the world.'

'It's all right,' said Ottil soothingly. 'You're with me; I'll take care of it.'

It took them all afternoon, but they managed to find a southward-bound ship to take them as far as Lannuon, in Armorica. It was a small vessel, built for speed, on the same lines as the Nordish drakkar. They had to take their own provisions, for the crew was too small to take care of passengers. But the winds were favorable and they made good speed. Sailing only by day and spending the nights in small coves along the coast, they reached their next port on the third day.

Lannuon's port lay a bit inland, on a broad river amid dark woods.

'Here you'll have to find someone reckless enough to carry you across the Bay of Storms,' said the skipper. 'May the Gods be with you, travelers.'

In spite of the man's gloomy warnings, the first sailor they accosted immediately pointed them to the dark bulk of a cog, a medium sized ship, at the far end of the quay. 'That's the man to ask, stranger,' said the sailor. 'Capt'n Kireg will sail you to the end of the world for a bit of gold.'

Kireg was a tall man, stooped from ducking beneath his own rigging. Unshaven, longhaired and dressed in dirty leather, he didn't make a very good impression. But his ship was clean and well cared for. Now Muus understood what the rune of Tongues did, for it helped him understand the vile dialect the captain spoke, a local patois even Moirra couldn't follow.

'Bring you to Baian, no problems. Gods of Bay quiet, no storm, no angry weather. Good, good. Sail when Sun is highest, be on board then.'

He was as good as his word, for at noon the black cog ship left the harbor. Two hours later they rounded the Armorican headland and the captain pointed forward. 'The Bay of Storms,' he said, smiling a toothless smile. 'Ships buried there, thousands of ships. All drowned.' His tone was mournful and gave them goose bumps.

'Freyr aid me,' muttered Geir, after Ottil had translated.

That day the two boys spend most of their time at the railing, staring out over the sea.

'What they doing?' asked the captain. 'Looking for storm?'

Muus smiled. 'They're hoping to see a whale.'

Kireg's face grew long. 'Whales are big, bring bad luck. They will see them, hope not too close. Big hungry, the whales are.'

The next morning, the boys got what they wanted.

'Look!' cried Geir. A spout of water rose from the sea, not far from the ship. Then he screamed as a dark shape appeared alongside, half as long again as their vessel and nearly as high as the railing. On the afterdeck, the captain swore as the ship heaved on the disturbances the whale had caused.

One eye, calm and deep blue, stared at the boys. Then, as serenely as it had come, the whale disappeared beneath the waves.

'Damn you calling whales!' screamed the captain. 'Monster nearly sank us.'

'She wanted to look at the boys,' said Muus soothingly. 'She was just curious.'

'You not know. Whales are hungry, eat ships whole.'

Muus' face was full of wonder. 'This one wasn't hungry. I heard her, the voice was too thin for our ears but I heard her. They speak with the mind, you know, and somehow she had picked up the boy's longing to see her, so she came. Now she's gone again, back to down below.'

'How you know?' said Kireg suspiciously.

Muus let a bit of flames appear at his fingertips. 'I am a Runemaster.'

The captain blanched and backed off. 'Sorcerie,' he gasped, and retired to the afterdeck.

It was clear that their relationship with the crew had deteriorated. Wherever they went, they only got black looks and sullen mutterings from the sailors. When they reached Roian that night, a large port on two-thirds of the route, captain Kireg confronted Muus, his arms crossed over his breast.

'You leave ship,' said he. 'No sorceries on board. You go, take whale boys.'

Muus fastened his eye on the man, feeling his anger grow. 'We paid you to take us to Baian. You agreed and took our money.' Small lightning leaked from his hand as he pointed at the captain. 'You will bring us to Baian, is that clear?'

The captain gave a sullen nod. 'We sail now,' he said. 'You be in Baian tomorrow, then leave.' Turning around, he screamed orders at his crew, shouting down their protests, and with all sails set the ship raced back into the Bay.

That night and all morning the cog ship ran as she had never before, skipping over the waves like a hurrying albatross. Around noon they came to the mouth of the Ador. With a mad cry the captain sent two men to the bow. 'Warn me for the sandbanks.' Then, with a long, rending sound, the cog ran aground. Crew and passengers tumbled around the deck and when they'd picked themselves up, the deck lay at a slight angle, rock solid still.

His face livid, the captain turned on Muus. 'Curse you!' he said.

'You went in too fast,' said Muus. 'That's not my fault. Lower your boat and bring us to the harbor. You can wait until high tide to float off.'

'My bottom!' cried the captain. 'My planks will be sprung, my seams leak, and we'll sink.'

'Just lower your boat, Captain,' said Muus tiredly, 'and we'll leave.'

'Yes, yes, leave!' Kireg shouted for a boat to be lowered and his men obeyed reluctantly. The looks with which they regarded their captain promised a lot of trouble.

'Stop howling,' said one of the men. 'If we sink, you're in trouble, Captain. Don't lose our share in the ship or pay it out now.'

'Damn you! Bring them sorcerers ashore and come back help pull ship to the beach. We'll careen and look for damage, but those cursed sorcerers away first.'

The sailors swore and lowered the ship's boat. Putting their backs into it, they rowed to the beach.

'You gotta walk to Baian, Runemaster.' The sailor spat in his hands. 'It's all of six miles into town. You can hire transport here at the village that's faster than us rowing you. We must keep an eye on that rotten bastard that calls hisself captain. We bought a share in 'is ship, you see.'

Muus lowered himself in the icy water. It came to halfway his chest. 'I wish you luck with repairing the ship.' With a nod he started to wade toward the beach.

Behind him, he heard an oath and a lot of splashing. It was Ottil, who had lost his footing and struggled to reach the beach. 'Now I can swim,' he declared, sloshing over the pebbles toward the grass.

'Like a drowning cat,' said Hraab. 'Watch Geir, he knows how.'

'I was born on a river,' said the boy defensively. 'Our farm is on a slope that ends in the water. When I was small, I rolled down so often that Olf taught me how to swim.'

Ottil snorted. 'I was borne at the seaside. But my mother thought it too dangerous and far too cold.'

They came to a small village. Moirra approached three men leaning on a wooden gate. 'Good day. Would there be somebody here who could drive us to town?'

Slowly, the men looked at each other. The first two turned their eyes back to the sea, but the third pointed. 'Small house with the cart.'

It wasn't much, a one-roomed cottage, but when they entered there was a fire burning and wet as they were they welcomed the warmth. Moirra repeated her question to the woman of the house, who nodded. 'Me husband. Dry yerself first, you're drippin' all over.' Muus wanted to say something, but she didn't listen and walked to the door. She gave a shout and went back to her cooking. Some five minutes later the husband entered and Muus heard Ottil snicker behind his back. He was the same man who had pointed them to the cottage in the first place.

'You're off the fool ship,' he said by way of greeting. 'Saw 'er strike, comin' in so fast. Then you were rowed to the beach, so I 'alf 'n 'alf expected you, me being the only one with a cart hereabouts. For one gold piece I'll bring you to town if that's what you want.'

'Yes please,' said Muus and the man nodded wisely.

'Thought so. The moment I saw you splashin' through the sea I thought, them youngsters are wantin' to go to town. You must have business there.'

'You're a clever man,' said Moirra.

The woman stirring her pot made a small sound, but she didn't say anything.

'Does the town have a druid?' asked Moirra.

'Baian? There are three of them, an old woman and two young men. Their temple is on the market square. I can bring you straight to their door if that's your wish.'

Some hours later the garrulous man dropped them off in the town center.

'Nice place,' said Ottil, looking around at the stone houses with their slate roofs and stout doors. 'Nidros should be like this, too. Not that primitive collection of hovels my unrespected father made of it.'

Geir whispered something.

'Yes, but you never knew my father,' said the Prince testily. 'He was a fool.'

Moirra stepped up to a door with a large tree painted upon it. 'This must be the temple.' She pushed the door open and led them into a hallway. Left and right was a corridor and straight ahead a walled garden with a large ash tree. 'A moment,' she said vaguely and went to stand with the tree. Some minutes passed, while the others patiently waited. Finally she sighed and stepped backwards.

'Welcome, sister,' said a voice, and an old druidess left the shadow of the corridor. 'I am Athona, of the Circle of Baian.'

'Moirra of the Un-a-Dach. I am with Runemaster Terrel on his quest. With us are Hraab, Ottil and Geir.'

'A Runemaster of your people! You must be a powerful man, friend Terrel.'

Muus spread his hands. 'Not powerful enough for what I have to do, druidess. That's why I had to come to Baian.'

'Tell me presently, but first the important things. Have you eaten? Rested?' Athona looked at each of them. 'You haven't. I sense weariness. Come, and we will see to it.'

The corridor circled the garden and brought them to a large room, in which a younger man sat staring at the flames of the hearth.

'This is Fynch,' said the old druidess. 'He will arrange some food for you all.'

The young man rose and bowed in Gaullish fashion. 'Welcome to our Circle,' said he. 'Sit and rest yourself, while I get something to fill your bellies.'

'If you please,' said Ottil. 'The grumbling you hear is not a piglet, but my stomach.'

'You're in dire need then,' said Fynch. 'I'll not tarry, friend.'

'What brought you to our town, Runemaster?' said Athona.

'In order to fulfill the task the Gods laid on me, I need first to collect a series of fingerbones that contain master runes. Fjinge's Knucks they are called and it is said that one of them must be in this town.'

'Of Fjinge's bones I have heard, vaguely, for rune mastery is far from my area of knowledge. But here?'

'We were told a legend of some centuries ago. The Oaken Bard told us of one Sarrias the Thief, who had the trick of disappearing at will. He was nevertheless caught somehow and immured in some place here in Baian. It is possible his trick was achieved by one of the Knucks.'

'We will have to ask Fynch; he is local. I come from the north and our second brother hails from Espayne. Whence do you come?'

'We were last at the Great Temple,' said Moirra.

'Yes, we defeated the leader of the Grim Doubh worshipers,' said Ottil proudly.

Moirra sighed. 'You, of all people, should know how to be discreet, Ottil. This is not a subject for polite conversation.'

Druidess Athona gave her a sharp glance. 'Grim Doubh, the boy said?'

'There was a priest who styled himself the Caller of Earth. His followers strove for the return of the Old Ones. He had made his lair in the sphere of Earth, so we followed and the Runemaster killed him.'

'That was a good deed. We know of such people too. Not here, but further to the East they dwell, trying to do the unspeakable. They are called Chastigants.'

Druid Fynch came in with food and drink. 'Here is enough to fortify yourselves with,' said he. 'May it bless you with its wholesomeness.'

'Thank you for your efforts and good wishes,' said Muus, and he set spoon to bowl. It was a thick soup, rich with good meat and brown peas he couldn't put a name to. The bread that accompanied it was crusty and came with a thick slice of salted ham. To drink there was a heady red wine. They ate in silence and Muus was glad of the quiet.

Finally he had eaten enough. Cradling his wine cup in his hand, he thanked his hostess for the meal.

'Do not thank me, Runemaster,' the druidess said with a smile. 'We must thank you for ridding us of our enemies. Now, let me show you a room. We will talk again when you have rested.'

CHAPTER 22 – TRADE AGENCY

The next afternoon, Muus talked with druid Fynch, a tall, bone-thin fellow with a permanent stoop.

'The druidess tells me you are the local man?' said Muus. 'Have you heard the story of Sarrias the Thief, who lived some centuries ago?'

Fynch eyed him in surprise. 'Of course, it's a local tale. But what is there to interest a Runemaster from far Brytanna?'

'The secret of his stealth,' said Muus with a smile. 'I believe he could make himself invisible at will?'

Fynch pulled at his nose. 'So we are told. But whether it be true I can't tell you.'

'There is a certain rune I seek that has the power.'

Fynch raised his brows. 'A rune of stealth? That could come in handy. But Sarrias has been dead a long time.'

'He was immured, I believe? Would you know where?'

'Yes, but the knowledge won't help you much. The tower that used to serve as the town prison is now the Baljaren Trade Agency, almost straight across from here. But you won't ever get inside. They're a suspicious bunch who hate druids, and they don't trust anyone who's not a Baljaren.'

'Why are they here then?' said Ottil. 'If they don't like it here?'

Fynch laughed. 'They like our gold. Their Agent here trades with Aquitaine and with Espayne. It must be big business. The talk is, the former prison cells bulge with trade goods. Nobody knows, of course. I'm afraid they'll never let you see them.'

Hraab snorted. 'Any idea of the layout of those cells?'

The druid stared at him. 'You seem pretty sure of yourself, youngster. Are you some kind of burglar?'

'Who, me?' said Hraab innocently. 'Nah... How do I find that bricked up place?'

Fynch grinned. 'Down the stairs, left, at the end of the corridor. They just walled off a few feet of the hallway, with the thief inside. The bricklayers did leave a window of about a foot open, to gloat at him.'

'They would,' muttered Hraab. 'Silly spectacle. Why didn't they just kill him?'

'It's in our character, I'm afraid,' said Fynch, with a slight smile. 'We're a vengeful people.'

'It's a weakness. Well, no sense in waiting. I'll go and scout around a bit.' Hraab looked at Ottil. 'No. I must do this alone. It just wouldn't work dragging you along. Geir, you still got that rope you and Ottil were practicing knots with?'

The boy blushed and nodded. He lifted his tunic and unwound a sizeable length of tarred ship's rope from his middle.

'Where did you get that?' Muus asked, surprised.

Geir's blush deepened.

'He just cut it off somewhere,' said Ottil, defending his hirdman. 'Don't worry; it wasn't keeping the sails up or anything like that. Besides, we didn't like captain Kireg.'

'Nor did I,' said Hraab. 'May I keep it for a bit?'

Geir handed him the rope.

'Right, be back later.' With that, Hraab slipped from the room.

The tower was easy to find, a solid-looking, square building at the end of a small, lightless bystreet. Even its present use as a trader's headquarters hadn't quite erased the old air of despair typical of prisons. It lay on one side of a small square. Next to the entrance was a rather neglected garden full of shrubs and weeds. Hraab, only a shadow in the dusk, moved stealthily forward, and entered the garden. It didn't look like anyone ever came there, making it a perfect hiding place. Through a hole in the surrounding hedge he could see the front of the tower, and he waited.

The shadows were lengthening towards evening when suddenly someone left the tower, a large boy of some fifteen years, with curly hair, wearing a fine, dark-blue tunic. He said something to someone inside and strolled away, towards where Hraab was waiting. As he passed the entrance to the garden, Hraab whispered 'Hey!'

The boy turned his head and showed a plump face with suspicious eyes. 'What?' Then he opened his mouth to shout, but Hraab jumped up, clasped a hand over the boy's mouth and dragged him into the garden. His knife glittered in Sun's departing light and the boy started to sweat. 'You...' he began, but Hraab prodded him with the point of his knife. 'Quiet!'

'You're making a mistake,' whispered the boy. 'If you're a robber, I have no money on me. And you're in big trouble. I'm the Agent's son. He will ruin this town if anything happens to me.'

'What should I care?' said Hraab in a hollow voice he was very proud of. 'I don't live here. And Agent's sons die just as easily as any others. I don't want your money, fatso. Take your clothes off.'

'What? Why?'

Hraab pulled the boy's head backwards and laid the knife edge along his throat.' 'No – questions. Just do as I say.'

'But... but...' With shaking fingers, the boy began to unfasten his tunic.

Deftly, Hraab transferred his knife to the boy's groin. 'Just take it off, without any sudden moves. You don't want me to unman you.'

The boy gasped. 'No!' A few heartbeats later he stood naked in the garden.

'You really should exercise more,' said Hraab critically. 'You're way too fat.' He pressed his foot hard in the inside of his victim's knee and the boy went down, with Hraab on top. 'Now tell me something. The way to the prison cells.'

The boy shivered, stretched out naked on the rocky ground. 'You're going to kill me.'

'I'm going to kill you – if you don't answer my questions or if you lie to me. Now speak. The way to the prison cells.'

'That's easy.' The boy's teeth chattered from fear or cold. 'The stairs down are directly opposite the door.'

'Any guards I need to watch out for?'

The boy's eyes got crafty. 'No.'

Hraab smiled, and with the point of his knife, made a small scratch in the boy's skin, right over his heart. A few droplets of blood welled up and the boy's eyes grew wild.

'Don't!'

'You lied to me. Try it again. Any guards?'

'One, next to the door,' gasped the boy.

'That's all?'

'That's all, I swear it.'

Hraab nodded and started to truss his prisoner up. The boy moaned all the time, tears running down his shaking cheeks. Finally Hraab ripped the boy's fine silk sash in two and bound one half tightly across his victim's mouth, silencing him. Then he donned the fine tunic and stood still for a moment. His face shimmered and seemed to change into the boy's plump countenance. His victim on the ground lay still and his eyes almost bulged out of his head. Hraab looked at him and nodded. 'I'm a mighty sorcerer,' he said in a sepulchral tone. 'Behave and you might survive.' Disgust filled his face as he saw the boy on the ground wetting himself. 'Cowardly pig.' Then he stooped and with the butt of his knife knocked the boy unconscious.

Walking sedately, he went to the tower and entered. In a small room next to the door sat a guard, who looked up as he entered. 'Back already, master Belsarios?' he called, in a bored tone.

Hraab just waved at him and walked on into the corridor. Directly opposite the entrance was a doorway. Quickly he went through it and onto a stone stair leading down.

A guard sat on a stool, concentrating on the wooden image of a pretty young girl he was carving. *Damn!* As Hraab came down the stair, the man looked up. 'Hey,' he said. 'You're not...' He dropped the carving and went for his sword. Hraab jumped at him and his thin knife entered the guard's jugular. Blood spattered all over the blue tunic as Hraab caught the dead man in his arms and laid him softly down. 'Sorry, friend,' he said. 'You were not supposed to be here.' Then he went on down the corridor. To the left and right were cells, locked with rusty iron grills. Only in the first two were some cases and bales, the rest were empty. No loads of precious goods, no treasures. Hraab sighed sadly.

At the end was a stone wall with a small window. The opening was too high for Hraab, so he hurried back and returned with the dead guard's stool. Standing on it, he could see inside the narrow space and and spied the bones of some unhappy prisoner lying in a disjointed heap against the wall. The skull had rolled away and stared emptily at the ceiling. Wrapped round the upper vertebrae of the spine was a leather cord with a knuckle bone, as proof that this had indeed been Sarrias the Thief. Now came the difficult part. *Iowynh?*

The piece inside him moved slightly. *No.*

Iowynh, there's nobody to see it. We need that bone, dear God.

I can't.

Iowynh, please?

The God cursed. *Whaddayawant?*

I must get through that hole and back out.

You're a damned nuisance, kid.

I know, it wasn't my idea.

No. Grmbl. You got ten minutes.

Hraab felt himself grow insubstantial. He lost weight, the feel of his body, the shadow of his hand on the wall. As a wisp he slipped through the hole and down to the ground. Swiftly he took the bone from around the thief's spine, pleased he could somehow grasp the thing. *Thank you, Sarrias,* he thought and then his eye fell on the letters written on the wall. Reddish-brown they looked in the dim light, as if written in blood. 'Bugger you.' Hraab laughed softly as he went back through the hole. That thief must've been some guy. Then he went up the stairs and out of the tower.

Back in the garden, the Baljaren boy had come to and was furiously trying to get free from the ropes. He stopped struggling as Hraab's nebulous shade looked down at him. There was fear in the boy's face, but also something else. Anger, disgust.

Slowly Hraab felt himself solidify and after a few moments the spell had gone. Quickly he took off the blue tunic. 'Here it is, slightly blood-spattered.' He knelt next to the boy and removed the gag. 'You lied. There was a second guard, downstairs. I hadn't wanted to kill him, but he attacked me. Pity, he was a good carver.'

'Annios!' spat the boy. 'He was always shirking his duties for his damn fool woodwork. He won't be missed.'

Hraab thought back to the delicate statuette. A pity the man had chosen the wrong job. And with such a heartless bastard as this spoiled brat. 'You're Belsarios.' It was a statement rather than a question.

The boy nodded quickly. 'How do you know?'

Hraab's grin was mocking. 'I know all. Now I'll leave you here. If you're lucky they'll find you before you die from the cold.' Quickly, he re-gagged the boy. Then he left the garden and hurried through the dark back to the Circle house.

Muus heaved a sigh of relief as Hraab entered. 'There you are,' he said. 'I was worried about you.'

'I've got your knuckle, here it is, but we must leave immediately. I stupidly let my disguise slip. Then I ran into a guard who shouldn't have been there, and I killed him. I'm sure they'll come searching for us.'

'Did you have to kill him?' said Muus, frowning.

'He attacked me,' said Hraab. 'It was in defense, but I still hate it.'

Ottil looked sharply at him. 'You mean that.'

Hraab pressed his lips together. 'Yes,' he said. 'He was just doing his job.'

'Was this burglary necessary?' Druidess Athona frowned down at Hraab. 'We of the Circle don't hold with taking life.'

'Nor do I,' said the boy bitterly. 'Especially not on that day Fynni took the lives of my family. But the Runemaster needs that knuckle bone for the good of the Circle, and that makes it all necessary.'

Athona nodded. 'I accept your reasoning. Well, they won't dare come in here. Not into the Druid house.'

'I'm not so sure about that,' said Hraab. 'I, eh, had to rough up the Agent's son a bit, too.'

'You didn't harm him?' said Moirra, shocked.

'Nope, but the kid will be very upset with me.'

'That fat piece of arrogance,' said Fynch with some satisfaction. 'Nobody is going to mind your bashing him.'

'Except for his father,' said Muus. 'Where can we get horses?'

'Two miles out of town, on the southern road, you'll find a man named Hanoris. He breeds horses, both for the king's riders and for farmers all over Aquitaine. I'll walk with you.' Fynch rose and fastened his hood over his head.

Muus thanked the old druidess, and with her blessing they followed Fynch into the night. It was quiet in the market square. The houses had their shutters closed against the cold and it had started to rain. Behind them they heard a sudden, rattling sound behind them. Looking over his shoulder, Muus saw armed men walking towards the temple they'd just left.

'Soldiers,' said Hraab softly.

Fynch glanced at the men and frowned. 'Town guards. They're quicker than I expected.'

'Perhaps Baljaren's money helps them walk faster,' said Hraab.

Fynch gave a short laugh. 'Could well be.' Walking quickly, they left town.

It was dark at the horse farm when they arrived. The druid walked up to the door and banged on the wood. After some heartbeats a voice grunted: 'Who's there?'

'It's me, Fynch, from the temple. Got a customer for you, Hanoris.'

The door opened and a suspicious face appeared. 'At this time of night? Come back tomorrow.'

'Sorry,' said Muus. 'We need them now. Five horses.'

'Five, eh...' The man stepped from the house and peered at each of them. 'Young people, late at night. With plenty of money.'

'And plenty of defenses,' said Hraab.

'That's good,' said the coper. 'There's foul folk abroad, these nights. Come.' He led them to a large field with some twenty horses of all sizes. 'There'ye are. Choose and I'll tell you their cost.'

'Bring me out the five best ones,' said Muus. 'And mind you, I'll know when you are cheating me. I have the power.'

Hanoris looked at him and grumbled. Then he slouched into the field and led five of the animals forward. 'These are me best.'

'Let's take them one by one,' said Muus with a smile. He pointed at a tall, dark horse. 'Is this one sound, healthy and of your best?'

'Yes,' said the man.

The second was smaller, of a grayish color that looked pale green in Moon's light. 'And this one?'

'Yes.'

The third horse appeared slightly nervous. 'This one?'

The man sniffed. 'Yes.'

False, said a voice in Muus head.

'You're having me on,' said Muus sternly. 'This one's lacking, friend.'

Muttering, Hanoris exchanged the nervous animal for an older brown beast. That one and the remaining two passed muster, and after some haggling over the price, including elementary harness, some gold changed hands.

'Pleasure doing business with you,' said Muus politely.

'Sure,' said the coper. 'Don't lame them with any wild capers, lad.' Then he hurried back inside, out of the steady drizzle.

Muus held out his hand. 'Thanks for your help,' said he to Fynch.

'May the Gods be with you, Runemaster,' said the druid. 'And with you, sister, and the boys.' He turned and walked away in the darkness.

'Right,' said Hraab, still unusually grim. 'Let's get away from here.'

'You seem worried,' said Ottil.

'I'm angry.' Hraab looked over his shoulder. 'I hadn't wanted to kill that guard. The fool had slipped away to do a quiet bit of woodworking. Perhaps I should've waited a few hours, till everyone slept.' He sighed. 'I was too hasty.'

'Nice to know you can make mistakes too,' said Ottil, in an attempt to cheer his friend up.

Hraab sighed. 'Don't be daft. Well, it's done now.' He turned and went to check his new horse.

'We go west,' said Muus. 'We need to stay within sight of those mountains in the distance.'

'Why?' said Ottil.

'Those are the mountains the High Druid said we should follow. Fois must be somewhere in front of us.'

They rode away through the rain, with the snow topped peaks to the right and the Ardor River to the left. This was a different land from what Muus had seen in Brytanna, different too from the Norden. It was open, dotted with villages and small towns. The hills bore wakening vineyards and meadows with early spring flowers. The weather was mild. The people they met were friendly at first, but the nearer they came to Fois, the more silent and morose villagers became. At last it was as if a nameless fear lay over the hills and permeated everything.

CHAPTER 23 – ANOTHER CALLER

After a sevenday, Muus came to a village, a collection of farms like many others they'd passed. Here, they were stopped by a small group of locals, armed with pitchforks and rusty weapons, guarding the road.

'Halt,' said one of them, a thickset, graying farmer. 'Go back where you came from. We don't want no strangers here.'

Moirra raised her hand in greeting and pushed past Muus. 'Good day to you, friends. I am the druidess Moirra.'

'A druidess!' said the spokesman. 'All the druids that have come here have died. Even our own, who lived here all his life, has disappeared. You had better flee too, before you suffer misfortune.'

'You said all druids. How many have there been here?' said Muus.

'Many, stranger. They came, passed our houses, and never returned. Then our druid went to see where they had gone. That was the last we've seen of him.'

'Was there something strange about those druids?'

Moirra gave Muus a sharp look, but the farmer nodded. 'They were painted, with blue markings over their faces and hands. Never seen a druid with such symbols.'

Behind them, Ottil grunted. 'Grim Doubh?'

'Are there secret places in the neighborhood?' said Muus. 'Places people can hide?'

'There be the caves,' said one of the men hesitantly. 'Those where the old ones dwelled. Many could hide there forever.'

'That sounds promising. Where can we find those caves?'

'There are several between here and the Count's town,' said the farmer. 'The closest one is past the village, across the little bridge and left at the old oak. It leads to the next village, Ennovicce. There's an old trail that never grows over, ending up right in front of the cave mouth.'

'Right,' said Muus. 'We'll go and have a look.'

The locals stepped aside to let them pass. 'I hope you know what you're doing, stranger. There are weird things going on in those old holes.'

The old oak was swiftly found and so was the trail.

'Many people have come this way recently,' said Hraab.

Ottil stared at the muddy path and the countless footsteps. 'Your wisdom is amazing.'

Suddenly the trail ended at a grass-grown pit that led to a hole in the hillside. The grass was flattened, with tracks entering the cave.

They left the horses tied to a tree and followed the footsteps into the hill. Inside, it was musty and dark.

'Muus, can't you make a light or something?' whispered Ottil.

Can you make light, A'lin? Muus thought. Immediately the corridor shone with the light of a thousand torches. *Not so bright! Just a tiny flame to see where we're going.* The light dimmed to a single candle.

Straight ahead, there was a bend in the tunnel, leading downward. Cautiously, they went on, stopping every few heartbeats to listen. It was quiet; only the faint rustle of a small animal now and then.

A rending scream shocked them nearly witless; a cry of fear, followed by the shouts of children's voices and the rattling of bars.

Through a small passage, they ran into a torch-lit cave, with animal paintings moving on the walls. Part of the cave was closed off by a rusty grate door, behind which children were screaming and shaking the bars. In the cave itself, two cloaked shapes were trussing up another child, a boy, who was wailing like a demented animal.

'At them!' Ottil rushed forward, with Geir following him blindly and - after a small hesitation, Hraab. The two cloaked men were completely surprised and died before they realized what was happening.

'Stop screaming,' said Ottil testily to the writhing child. 'You're saved.'

The boy closed his mouth with a snap and stared at the Prince, who had started to untie the ropes that bound the boy. He stammered something Ottil didn't understand.

'Speak Gaullish; I don't know your barbarian dialect.'

'Who're you?' repeated the boy obediently. 'Are you with... them?'

'Don't be daft! Would we kill them if we were?' Ottil handed the rope to Geir. 'Here, keep this for me.'

In the meantime, Hraab had searched the fallen enemies.

'They're Grim Doubh for sure,' said he, pointing at the nude painted bodies underneath the cloaks. Then he picked something up from the floor. 'A key.' He turned to the children in the cage. 'Do you want out?'

'Please,' said one of them, a blonde girl. 'Of course we want out. We want to go home.'

Hraab bowed. 'As you command, m'lady.' Then he unlocked the cage door and swung it open. 'There y'are.'

The girl looked at him. 'You're strange. But you're nice, thank you.'

'Where are you from?' said Muus.

'From Ennovicce,' said the girl. She pointed towards the dark. 'The cave opens not far from our village.' She started to cry. 'We were all working in the common garden when they came. They looked like druids, but they weren't. They were false, painted men like the ones you killed. There were many of them and they caught us all. We screamed, but no one heard us.'

'Won't your fathers be looking for you?' said Muus surprised.

The girl's face worked as she shook her head. 'They dare not. The false druids came to our village earlier on and forbade all to come near any of the caves. They... killed some people to show they meant it. My poor uncle Jehan, and old Margui, they just b-burned them with their magic. Now no one can leave the village, because all roads go through the caves. We... we thought the garden was safe, but it wasn't.'

'Which one of you can show me the way to the other caves?' said Muus.

'I will,' said the girl without hesitation. 'But there are many of the bad ones there.'

'Don't worry,' said Hraab with one of his broad grins. 'We've done this before.'

'Best you other children stay where you are for the moment. Here, you have the key to the cell door. We'll come back when we've done away with those painted animals. Don't show yourselves outside, no one needs to know you're free.' He handed the key to the boy they'd freed first.

'Yes, Lord,' said the boy. 'We'll stay inside an' be as quiet as mice. But please do hurry; this is a terribly wicked place.'

'We'll do our best,' said Muus. And to the girl, 'What's your name?'

'Ciadra, m'lord. My father is the village smith.'

'Right, Ciadra, show us the way out.'

Quickly, the girl guided them from the cave on the opposite side of the hill. Before them stretched a broad valley of meadows and fields. There was no one in sight.

'They'll all be home,' said the girl. 'Staying inside and talking. They always talk.' She said it as a matter of fact, without any condemnation. Country folk lived with death and danger all their lives and it wouldn't surprise Muus if their parents had already counted the abducted children as dead.

Past a swift-flowing river they went, and where going through a small field of twisted apple trees when a shout alerted them.

'It's one of them,' said Ciadra shakily.

'What are you doing here?' shouted the false druid. 'We ordered you all to stay inside. Now you'll die, fools.'

'Let me,' murmured Hraab, and now for the first time he showed how well he could throw his little hawk. A swift twist of his wrist sent the ax spinning, and before the man could finish his spell, blood gushed all over his face and he tumbled backwards to lie twitching in the grass.

'Yes!' shouted the girl, pummeling Hraab's shoulder. 'You got him!'

Hraab smiled and hurried over to retrieve his weapon.

Further down the road was the second cave mouth, smaller than the first one. Half naked, painted men were dragging in freshly slaughtered sheep, still dripping blood.

'They're stealing our sheep,' whispered the girl, flushed with anger. 'How will we get through the next winter? We'll starve.'

Ottil drew his sword, but Muus shook his head. 'Too many.'

He raised his hands. *Kill them.* Lights flashed and one by one the sheep stealers tumbled down.

Ciadra looked at Muus, her eyes round and her hands covering her mouth. 'What magic is that?'

'The power of the runes,' said Hraab curtly. 'Magic letters he wears around his neck. Muus is a Runemaster and very powerful.'

Powerful was not how Muus felt. Every time he used the runes it left him spent. 'Inside,' he said, and stepped over the carcasses into the cave. It was cool inside and the sound of dripping water made him think of that walk through the mountain at Eidungruve. Just as in the first cave, the walls were covered with strange pictures of animals. Wooly wisents like the ones in the Norden that would suffocate from the heat here in the South of Gaul. Deer with enormous antlers, hunted by little men with spears. He shook his head. It wasn't the work of the Old Ones; the pictures felt normal, human, but very old.

The cave was empty of life, so they hurried on to the third one, halfway across the valley. Here the entrance was large enough for four wagons to enter side by side. A huge pile of wood near the entrance reminded Muus of the large fires he had seen at the Grim Doubh camps.

Moirra's strained, 'Let's be careful' told him she'd thought the same. This must be the main cave, where the ceremonies were held. It all looked familiar. Whether the worshippers called themselves Grim Doubh or Chastigants, they were one and the same cult. He had to stop them, had to deny the Gods Before entry to the world, for it was better not to recharge the Kalmanir than to let those primitives return to terrorize humanity.

The burning land appeared in his mind and a terrible pain gripped him. 'Muus!' He felt Moirra's arms encircling him. *Stop it!* he thought at the skyshard, grabbing at the rough cave wall. *It was the Gods who sent you, not those Old Ones. Do you* want *our Gods to be hunted, exiled, destroyed? It that what you came for? Are you a traitor, stone?* An explosion of light made him cry out and then all was right again. *Fine. Shall we proceed then?*

A sense of impatience made itself felt and he grinned. He took Moirra's hand. 'Don't worry. Our friend didn't understand what we were doing. I told him I couldn't go to Falrom as long as these Grim Doubh were trying to get their own Gods back. He didn't like that, but now he understands the need. That shard is powerful, but not very... smart.'

'If he was smart, they wouldn't need you,' said Hraab.

'Am I supposed to be glad?' Seeing Ciadra's face, Muus threw their young guide a wink. 'Not to worry, girl. There are things happening, but they don't concern you. Let us exterminate these false druids, then you all can be safe again.'

Ciadra shook her blonde hair. 'I don't want to know these things; they frighten me. I want to feel safe, that's all.'

'Smart girl. Let's go.'

The inside of the cave was enormous. The ceiling was lost in darkness, massive dripping stones reached up and down, as if they were in the mouth of a gigantic monster. Slowly they walked on, till a scream rent the air. 'Intruders!'

A horde of naked, painted men and women ran past the teeth stones, brandishing long staves, knives and curious stone axes.

Ottil yelled, dropping his sword and falling under the feet of the onrushing idolaters. Geir shouted and ran to him, covering the Prince's body with his own. Muus saw it happen and a fierce hatred flamed up in him.

Screaming, the naked bodies dropped left and right, falling where they ran, tumbling over each other, piling up. Muus scrambled over them towards the center. There, in front of a golden stool, stood a beautiful woman. She had not the magnificent build of the priestess at the abandoned hill fort, nor was she a giant like the Caller of Earth. This one was almost petite, with silver hair hanging down to shapely buttocks; she had big, firm breasts and a graceful carriage. 'Why do you kill my people?' she said, sounding sorrowful. 'Why do you come? Is it... for me?'

Her voice took Muus' breath away and he relaxed. *She's so beautiful, so innocent...*

'I like you, handsome Un-a-Dach,' she murmured. 'Come to me, let me heal the hurt inside you.'

Hurt... Muus did a step forward. *Heal my hurt.*

Then Moirra was onto him, hands clawing. 'Fool,' she shouted. 'She's as false as the others! She's Grim Doubh.' With the flat of her hand, she gave Muus a stinging slap across the face. Tears sprang to his eyes and he felt blood coming from his nose. *She's right*, said a voice inside him. *Where's all your big talk now? Kill her, idiot.*

He looked at the silver-haired girl, saw the sharp angles under her fine cheekbones, the wrinkled skin camouflaged by magic, the palsy her image hid, and he shuddered. 'Enough,' he said. 'Who are you?'

'I'm the Caller of Sky, handsome.' The pretty smile made him want to puke.

'You're the second Caller I will kill,' said Muus conversationally. 'Earth was first.'

The shapely face twisted into something horrible. 'You won't,' she screeched.

Let her die, snarled Muus.

Flashing light burned the silver hair away, the fair skin melted like hot butter, bones crackled and blackened as without another word the Caller died.

Muus turned around to Moirra, let his hands fall to his side and bowed his head. 'I'm sorry,' he said.

Moirra pulled his head towards her. 'I know, it was her strongest spell. It doesn't matter, Muus. It really doesn't matter.' She kissed him lightly on the lips.

'Moirra,' called Hraab. 'I need your help.'

The urgency in his voice reminded them of Ottil and Geir and they hurried to where Hraab and Ciadra sat.

Falling on her knees beside them, Moirra put a hand on each of the boys' foreheads. 'They live. Ottil's heart is beating soundly, but Geir's is fluttering like a trapped bird. I need your strength, Muus.'

'What's left of it is yours.' Muus put his hands on Moirra's shoulders. *Help her.*

The thoughts in his mind said *'Why?'*

Muus sighed. 'Don't always be so obtuse,' he said aloud. 'Because I ask it of you.'

They're just boys. They're nothing to us.

'They are to me. Now hurry up.'

Grumbling, the shard fell silent. Muus felt power streaming through his hands into Moirra. 'Go ahead.'

Softly, the druidess started to sing, words Muus didn't know - and with the knucklebones concentrating on helping Moirra, the rune of Tongues didn't translate. Her song took away bruises and despair, and went round and round the two boys under her hands. After a few bars, Ottil opened his eyes and lay still but aware. Geir didn't stir. Without looking at the prince, Moirra pulled her left hand away from him and laid it by her right hand on Geir's head. The boy's eyelashes twisted, as if trying to remember how to open. Then Geir sighed and his head fell aside.

Moirra broke away from Muus' hands and with a bump the Shardheld sat down. He had never felt as empty as this.

'The boy sleeps, and that is well,' said Moirra softly. 'Now, Ottil.'

'I'm all right,' said the prince. 'Just got a bump on the head, that's all. Damned stone axes. What's wrong with Geir?'

'He protected you with his body,' said Moirra. 'It was very brave of him and they hurt him badly. But he will heal, how fully I don't know.'

'Geir did?' The prince's voice was full of wonder. 'But he's so slight. Damn it, they could've killed him.' He tried to sit up. 'I must make him free then. Saving my life ends all his obligations. I'll tell him he is free to go.'

'It's not a reward to give somebody what he doesn't want to have.'

Ottil looked puzzled. 'What do you mean?'

Moirra smiled. 'Geir is proud to serve you. It means something to him. If you take that away, he'll be lost.'

Ottil stared at his hands. 'I never thought of that. All right, I won't tell him. He can have his freedom whenever he wants it.'

Hraab had gone over the dead bodies and was prowling around the cave now. 'Hullo,' he said through the near dark. 'What's this? Two chests full of gold? Them naked bastards were rich.'

Ottil heaved himself upright and groaned. 'Stand still, world,' he said. 'Damn headache.' Then he joined Hraab and whistled. 'Booty!'

Muus came over, walking slowly, like an old man. He rubbed his eyes and yawned. He seemed so tired, as if no gold could gladden him. 'We'll take one chest.' He turned. 'Ciadra, would a chest of this help your village repairing the damage?'

The girl hurried to them and stared at the gold, reflecting warmly in Muus' small light. 'Oh, it's so much. What can you buy with that?' Then she looked at Muus. 'Would you... would you give us some? Just like that?'

Muus smiled. 'We can't take all of it. So yes, I'll give you one of the chests to pay for damages.'

Ciadra gripped his hand and stared at him. 'Thank you,' she said simply. 'You must be a God, come to help us.'

Hraab cracked a laugh. 'Ha! Muus, she saw through your disguise.' Somehow the notion seemed to please him.

'I'm no God, but why wouldn't I help you? I hate those idolaters, they're even worse than you think and we don't want them anywhere in the world. And gold is the least of my concerns.' Again he yawned. 'There's one more cave. Is it far from here?'

'About half an hour,' said the girl, eyeing him anxiously. 'You look awful tired.'

Muus nodded 'I am. Those spells take out a lot of me. Are you fit to go back and tell those children to go home? Hraab will go with you. Ask some of them to bring our horses.'

Ciadra looked at Hraab and colored slightly. 'I can go back.'

The boy's eyes sparkled. 'Let's go, then.'

Muus went back to Moirra.

'The girl was right, you look awful,' said the druidess. 'Go lie down a bit; Ottil and I will keep guard.'

Muus sat down. 'I'm sorry, I'm beat.' He stretched out on the stone floor and the world went out.

CHAPTER 24 – ESCAPE

Some two sevendays after they left the burned village, Tuuri and Hilja came to a stone road. The girl was bone-weary, but she didn't complain. Tuuri had seen her grow thinner, though, her face getting more and more peaked and her nightly dreams too fevered to let her rest. The horse, bless her strong back, plodded on between the two walls of forest on either side.

Around a sharp bend the woods opened onto a small town of some twenty dwellings, built around a wooden castle on the banks of a river. A few outlying farms were the scene of much activity.

'They're expecting trouble,' said Tuuri. Peasants who should've been at work in the fields were pushing carts, loaded with meager possessions. Young boys drove thin cows and sheep, or carried baskets of terrified chickens, while girls carried toddlers or even babes in their arms. All had but one goal, the small, palisaded castle on its low hill.

'What town is this, friend?' Tuuri asked a watchman at the gate.

The man eyed him suspiciously. 'This is Count Dagiberh's township of Divion. Who are you that you don't know this?'

Tuuri frowned at the man's tone. 'I am Tuuri Little Knife of Westhal,' he said sternly. 'I'm a nobleman of the Norden. I'm travelling south to see the Fire Mountains.'

'Your pardon, m'lord,' said the watcher, with something of a salute. 'We're not happy with strangers just now, y'see. We expect an attack at any moment.'

Tuuri looked at the heavy gate and the stout wooden enclosure. 'Who would attack a castle this strong?'

Something of fear crept over the soldier's face. 'We don't rightly know, m'lord. They wear red armor and they are led by...' He lowered his voice. 'Magicians, Lord. They burned the township of Tulla, to the west, a week ago.'

Tuuri felt Hilja stir. 'Who is in charge here?'

'The marshal, Lord; the count being still a minor. You'll find him on the walls, should you wish to confer with him.'

'We need to know more.' Tuuri said over his shoulder. 'What do you think?'

Hilja looked uncertain. 'You're asking me? I would run away from here, but I'm so tired. I can't go on; I just can't.'

'Then we'll stay the night.' Kjelle sighed. 'The marshal's on the walls, you said?'

The watcher nodded. 'Yes, Lord. You'll recognize him easily by his white hair.'

They found the marshal staring out over the wide fields. He was a tall man, broad of shoulders, with long, wavy white hair. And he looked at least eighty years old. The boy at his side was perhaps eight or nine years, clad in miniature leather armor and armed with a long hunting knife. He turned around at their coming.

'I don't know you,' he said. 'Are you an enemy?'

Tuuri smiled. 'No, I am an ally of your people.'

'That is good, then I don't have to kill you,' said the boy seriously. 'I am a famous warrior, you see.'

'Of course you are,' said Hilja, hiding a snicker. 'Are you Dagiberh?'

'Count Dagiberh, girl. I rule this town.' The boy stuck his chest out. 'I am a nobleman.'

'Show you manners, boy,' said the marshal. 'Always be polite to strangers.' His clear blue eyes looked his unexpected guests over. 'Under better circumstances I would welcome you to Divion, but not now. If you stay, I cannot guarantee you will leave again.'

'Your man at the gate said the same, marshal. You expect an assault?'

'We do, though we do not know by whom. For weeks now, an army of red clad warriors has been terrorizing the province. Our neighbor town of Tulla has already fallen, and I am afraid it will be our turn next.'

'We saw soldiers dressed in red near Malbeck in the north,' said Kjelle. 'The Blodward, they called themselves, and they were followers of the Gods Before.'

The marshal eyed him curiously. 'How did you escape?'

'We evaded them. They were busy burning down a village, so they didn't notice us.' He gave a short bow. 'I am Tuuri, a lord of Westhal, in the Norden, and my sister is Hilja. We escaped those ruffians only to be attacked by wolves. My sister's horse and my

226

servant were killed, but I have business in the south, so I decided to continue our journey. We need a good night's sleep and then we'll depart again in the morrow.'

'We are all out of beds, Lord Tuuri,' said the marshal dubiously. 'With all the townsfolk inside our walls, we're full up. The old grain loft at the south wall, that's the only place left. It's straight across from here.'

'That will be fine,' said Tuuri. 'As long as it is dry, we will not complain. Thank you for your hospitality.'

The grain loft was an old tower overhanging the castle wall. A large door on both sides of the loft showed that the townspeople used to hoist the grain into the tower from outside the walls. It was a drafty place now, probably full of mice, but it was private and indeed dry.

'Are you really a lord?' said Hilja as they were inside.

Tuuri shrugged. 'My mother was a noblewoman, my father a Fynni priest. I serve Jarl Rannar and that makes me nobleman enough.'

'You're a good tale-teller.' The girl laughed a little. 'Am I your sister now?'

'What else? You're too young for my wife, and all other things would be... indecent.'

'I'm not too young to marry; I'll be fifteen this summer.'

'Then you're still five years my junior. This is the best solution.'

The girl snickered. 'As you say, my brother.' She sat down and rolled herself in her cloak. 'Let's hope the enemy will leave us alone tonight.' Without another word, she slept.

Tuuri looked down at her for a moment. Then he lay down beside her.

Some hours later, a crashing sound woke them up. The grain loft shook and ages-old dust rained down on them.

'Quick, get your things together!' Tuuri opened the door to the castle courtyard wide enough to look through. 'Damn!' he said, 'They're inside already.' His eyes widened. 'There are Fynni among them!'

A screaming child's voice came up the ladder to their loft. 'They're here, they're here!' It was young Dagiberh, wild-eyed and disheveled. He clung to Tuuri. 'The enemy is inside! They crashed the gate with magic. The marshal is dead and... and... They're killing everyone!'

'Quiet,' said Tuuri. 'They must not hear us!'

He pushed the boy into Hilja's arms. 'Hold him.' Then he hurried to the other side and opened the blinds to the fields. 'Nobody, that's our luck.' He looked up at the old wooden hoist. There was still a rope attached to it, but it hung over a roof beam, way out of reach. 'Dago, come here,' he said. 'And stop sniveling; we noblemen never cry.'

The boy wiped his nose. 'They're killing people.'

'I know,' said Tuuri. 'I'll lift you onto my shoulders; see if you can pull down that rope. You understand?'

The boy nodded. Tuuri grabbed the little count under his armpits and swung him up. With some difficulty, the boy managed to stand up, while Tuuri held him by his middle.

'I can't,' sobbed the boy. 'It's...' Then he jumped, grabbed the rope and fell, bringing Tuuri down as well. They crashed to the floor in a heap.

'Well done!' said Tuuri, fingering the place where the boy's irontoed shoe had kicked his cheek. 'You did great.' He opened the blinds far enough to let him pass. 'I'll go down first,' he said to Hilja. 'Then you'll throw down the baggage. Dagi goes second and you last. Don't be afraid; should either of you fall, I'll catch you.'

He gripped the rope and tugged. It was old and worn, and the beam it was attached to creaked, but it held. Quickly he threw it over the edge; it ended a manlength above the ground. Swiftly he climbed down and at the end, let himself drop. Then followed their packs. Hardly had he put them out of the way, before the small shape of Dagiberh appeared, climbing down easily. Hilja followed last, and that was too much for the ancient rope. It broke as she was half-way and with a smothered cry she fell. Tuuri stretched up his arms, but the girl was heavier than the little count, and for the second time he went down. A blinding pain shot through his leg. 'Damn! My ankle.' He heard voices overhead, and fear made him disregard the pain. 'Let's get out of here.' As fast as he could he hobbled towards the edge of the forest, with Hilja and Dagi carrying the packs. When they reached the darkness among the trees, he stopped. 'We did it,' he said to the others.

'And so you did,' said a familiar voice.

Tuuri turned around. From the shadows stepped the massive, white-haired figure of Rannar, Westhal's Jarl. Behind his back two empty-eyed Fynni guards stared at the young Fynnikin.

Tuuri gaped at his master. 'Lord!' said he finally. 'I am doing your will. How comes you here?'

'I ask of you the same, messenger,' said Jarl Rannar coldly. 'Why do you live, while Vulf and his force are dead? Did you sell me out? Was Dettrich a better lord than I?'

Tuuri blanched. 'No, Lord. I don't know Dettrich. I wouldn't betray you, Lord. I have ever been loyal.'

'Your acts don't show that, messenger. I am no longer sure of you.' Rannar beckoned to his guards. 'Bind him and the girl. I will interrogate them tomorrow, when Rev is back.'

'Lord...' Tuuri fell silent as Rannar turned his back on him. Rough hands took his weapons and bound his hands on his back. Beside him, Hilja screamed. The Fynni guards laughed as they made short work of her struggles and pushed their captives towards a small camp, where they tied them to a tree just outside the circle of tents.

'Be silent,' said a guard. 'Or we come and hurt you.' Then they left.

'Sha'akaii,' whispered Tuuri. 'Come and help us.' But his totem bear didn't answer. Tiredly, he led his head slump to his chest, while beside him Hilja sobbed softly.

Hours passed and night fell over the camp. From the distance came the sounds of revelry, as the Blodward were plundering the town. In the camp, all was silent. Tuuri hadn't seen Jarl Rannar again, nor his men. Rannar here, with a Fynni force, plundering an innocent town. Pictures flashed through his mind of his youth at the Jarl's court; of the way his lord had always been there to help him. He remembered the years he had served Rannar as page; how proud he had been to be named the Jarl's Messenger. Then he thought of King Vidmer's murder, of treason and rebellion. Belisheim and Eidungruve. The Fynni cruelty. Rannar's Fynni's... Slowly, his loyalty crumbled and fell to pieces around him. Lord Kjelle had been right; his master was an honorless villain. He couldn't serve such a one any longer; he... he'd rather die. As he probably would. He shivered.

Something moved in the undergrowth. Something dark... a wolf? Hilja had seen it too, and her face was strangely intent. The small shadow crept towards him and then he recognized Dagiberh. Gods! he'd completely forgotten the little fellow. The boy's eyes were large with fear, but his face was determined and so was the knife in his hand. Swiftly he cut Tuuri's bonds and hurried on to Hilja.

Tuuri moved his arms and only just suppressed a groan as his cramped muscles stretched. The boy motioned them to follow him and low against the ground they crept away. Arrows of pain shot through Tuuri's leg from his hurt ankle, but he clamped his teeth and followed Dagi to the wood's edge. There grazed two horses, saddled and bridled. Tuuri stared at them. 'Where...' he whispered, but the boy shook his head. 'Found them wandering!' spelled his lips. 'Let's run.' Quickly, the boy climbed into the saddle. Dagi's feet couldn't reach the stirrups, but he didn't seem to care. As Tuuri mounted the other horse, the tearing pain in his ankle made him gasp.

'You all right?' asked Hilja softly. When he nodded, she quickly scrambling up behind him. Dagiberh walked his horse out of the trees and then spurred her on, away from his burning town. Tuuri followed, still stiff and confused, but with a strange elation in his heart. All at once, he felt free. Not only from his captivity, but also from everything that had bound his life. His allegiance to Jarl Rannar, his bonds with the Fynni, they were gone. He was Tuuri, a free man of the Norden. Plans bubbled up in him like water from a well. He would go south, see if he could find that guy everyone was looking for, and warn him of Rannar's plans. Then he'd make his peace with Lord Kjelle and go... Well, he'd see that when it came. First they needed a safe place to hole up till his ankle was better. He felt Hilja's arms around his middle and wanted to sing.

CHAPTER 25 – THE LITHAN

'That's where the Lithan lives,' said Elbrich, pointing at the central mountain in the snowy range before them. 'The Pillar of Memories'.

'Those passes look pretty steep,' said Ajkell.

The young Niflung smiled. 'They are nothing. Wait till you see the path to the summit.'

'To the summit?' Kjelle stared. 'You mean the top of that mountain?'

'Close to it.' Elbrich spread his hands. 'I've never been there, but that's what our Wisemen say. The path winds upwards to end at the Lithan's domain, there where the snow begins.'

Kjelle saw the snow line and groaned. 'Just like those stairs inside the Wederer.'

The Mastersmith coughed. 'This path is on the outside.'

'It will be cold, then and...'

'Gods, Kjelle, let's move! Talking won't get us there.' With an angry shake of her head, Birthe started on the path that would lead them to the lowest pass.

Without another word or glance, the other three followed her.

A sevenday later, they arrived at the foot of the Pillar. Closer up, the climb looked even more daunting, but a glance at Birthe's face told Kjelle that he had better be silent. Ever since had they left Almansford, her moods had been like the ebb and flow in the fjords of the Norden, but ever since their fight at that nameless burning village, her temper had grown worse. Something was spurring her on to greater hurry and she was irritated at every delay.

'It's a stiff trail,' said Ajkell. 'And we haven't got much food left.'

Birthe gave him a dirty glance, but the bear warrior returned her gaze calmly and she looked away. 'I know,' she said. 'There hasn't been much prey for my bow, lately.'

'We just have to make do.' Kjelle took a deep breath. The path was no more than a small ledge clinging to the rocky wall of the mountain. It seemed hardly broad enough for a mountain goat, so they would have to leave the horses below. *Thor, give us a clear day,* he prayed. Resolutely he turned to the others. 'We need safety lines that bind us together.'

Ajkell nodded and took a long rope from his saddle. .

Walking wasn't easy. The ascent was steep and loose gravel on the path made it treacherous. Hour after hour they went on, pausing regularly to regain their breath.

'Damn,' said Kjelle. 'Breathing's never been so difficult.'

'It's the thin air.' Elbrich stretched and inhaled deeply. 'It is pure and clear, as it ought to be. The air down on the ground is heavy and stultifying. Here, a man can breathe.'

Kjelle's face clouded over. 'Feeling superior, little man?'

Elbrich looked at him. 'You're always towering over me in your big bodies. Aren't you feeling superior then, with your great strength and long reach?'

Kjelle touched the Niflung's arm. 'You're right. Apologies, it was a stupid thing to say.'

A smile lit up Elbrich's thin face. 'Don't worry. It's the lack of air speaking.'

The wind rose, howling around them, tugging on cloaks, bodies and horses, deafening the ears, making nose and ears painful to the touch. They still made progress, however slowly, through a world of silence, where the only voice was that of the wind.

Suddenly Ajkell, walking at the rear, stumbled. His foot slipped and, slowly as in a bad dream, he went over the edge.

Birthe, the next in line, screamed and Kjelle turned in time to see what was happening. He braced himself, feeling his heart beating like a war drum. *Cut the line!* he wanted to yell. *Cut it, before we all go down!* But he said nothing. In silence, he watched while Birthe rode out the shock of catching Ajkell's full weight. She stood leaning backwards, pressing her spine hard into the mountain side, gripping the taut rope in both hands.

Kjelle gaped at her. His love was a Nord and a well-made girl, but she had never before shown the strength she demonstrated now. She pulled the safety line, like a fjord fisherman roping in a caught shark. The veins on her forehead stood out while she fought the rope and Ajkell's weight, all the while chanting something Kjelle couldn't understand. Ajkell managed to get first his left hand on the ledge and then his right. His head, purpled from strain, rose above the edge and with an audible grunt, he placed first one arm on the path and then the other. He pushed himself up and placed a knee between his hands. With a last heave, Birthe dragged him away from the edge and stood there, panting. Ajkell rose painfully to his feet and embraced her as she clung to him, sobbing.

'Thanks,' he said, his voice rough. And with a look at the ragged rocks below, 'It's a long way down.' Then he turned white and sat down with a bump, resting his head between his knees.

Kjelle, red with guilt, touched Ajkell's shoulder. 'Well done, mate!' Then he turned to Birthe. 'You make me feel ashamed,' he said softly. 'But I'm so damned proud of you.'

The girl looked at him. 'I couldn't let him go. He's a friend.'

It was such an innocent remark, but Kjelle felt his cheeks glow in embarrassment. Hurriedly, he nodded. 'I know.' Then he turned away and stared out over the grim mountains.

Two hours later, emotionally and physically exhausted, they reached the abode of the Lithan. The entrance was a large cave, lit by glowing bulbs on the walls. Inside, they were met by a stout woman in a sober gray dress. She was small and stern, her apple-cheeked face unsmiling and her eyes critical. Her accent, when she spoke seemed strange, as if she wasn't used to speaking. 'You expected were.'

Birthe saw the woman's glance inspecting them from top to toe, starting with Kjelle, and she smiled grimly at her love's unhappy face. *Let him suffer awhile,* she thought. She understood his indecision when Ajkell fell; it was a part of him he would never lose. But the time of making up wasn't yet.

The woman seemed of her mind, for she rejected Kjelle as a person of no consequence, while Ajkell got a vague smile. 'The Fates good to you were, warrior. But now sleep you need. I'll you show a room, if you will a minute wait.'

Birthe met her eyes and for the first time the woman smiled slightly. 'Lady Völva, you expected were. The Lithan wishes to see you. And you, Mastersmith. Please, follow me, all of you.'

She led them into a large, round hall, with more lights all over the walls.

'Beautiful,' sighed Elbrich.

'Fifty years the masters needed to arrange it thus,' said the woman as she brought them to a room. 'The efforts it was of four generations.'

To Birthe she said, 'Alas, you never see will how magnificent it is. I so you half blind humans pity.'

A faint voice sounded from within, drifting on the air. The woman bowed and looked abashed. 'I stand corrected, Lithan. Your pardon, Völva. I let my bias show; that is a personal failing of mine you should not suffer for.' She seemed upset, and Birthe smiled soothingly.

'I think we all understand. My countrymen have done your peoples great harm. It is a goal of us all here to put that to right.' She hesitated, but decided. 'Lord Kjelle here has invited the Un-a-Rhan of Wederer Mountain to his own minehold already.'

'He did?' The woman gave Kjelle a straight look. 'I underrated you then, Lord. That is a noble thing to do.'

'I was honored the Mistress of Wederer accepted,' said Kjelle. 'To have the craftsmen of her clan run our silvermine will be mutually profiting.'

'As it should be, of course. But we keep the Lithan waiting. Step inside, if you please.' And with a show of fussiness, 'Yes, yes, all of you. I was mistaken. Don't tarry now.'

The Lithan was ancient. *That's how Muus would look, if he was several hundreds of winters old,* thought Kjelle. His skin was translucent as clear ice, so the white of his skin had turned to pink. His hair was still a full mop, but pale blue. He sat in a tall chair and around him was a vague mist that enveloped him completely.

'Welcome.' His voice was as a soft flute, clearly audible but ethereal. He lifted his right hand in greeting, without moving even the wrist and the arm. 'Your arrival came to me in a dream. I have always dreamed much about the sorrow of my peoples. I remember how it used to be, in the lands you call Alfheim. How we lived peacefully side by side, Dachi and Rhani, making magic and precious objects, minding our business, living our lives. Till you Nords came, with your superstition and your fear. We had to leave, all of us, and our hearts died with our going. To save my people, I bear most of this pain, so that they can live in strange lands.'

'And for that you have our eternal gratitude, my Father,' said Elbrich softly.

'There is no need,' said the Lithan. 'I am the Son of Dach, who was first of us all. It is my duty as well as my wish to carry this burden.' With a shake of his head, he stilled Elbrich's words. 'If you are sincere in your words, Holder of Eidungruve, if you really want us to return to the North, that will be the saving of us all. For you must know my time is nearly done. And after my going, the Dachi and Rhani will have to carry their own burden. That will prove too heavy for many. Knowing that to return home is possible, even that would be enough for most to go on living. That thought made me agree to receiving you.'

'My words were truth, Lithan,' said Kjelle. 'We made a promise to the Mistress of Wederer Mountain, and the Lady Völva signed a solemn contract with her in my name. We will make all possible effort to get the king-to-be, Prince Ottil, to agree to the return of you all to the Norden. You have my oath.'

'Then we just have to make sure this Prince prevails,' said the Lithan with a slight smile. 'This will not be an easy task.' He fell silent and his eyes closed, whether in sleep or thought, Kjelle didn't know.

'Lady Völva, come hither, please.' The Lithan spoke without opening his eyes. 'Come and enter my peoples' dreams. Use theirs to dream yours, Lady, stronger than you'd ever be able to.'

Without hesitation, Birthe stepped forward and let the thin mist cover her. She had never before attempted a dream without her dream wine, and it surprised her how easy it was. She was a bird, a sharp-eyed eagle, flying high over the world. The world was round, just like her father had told her once, and she flew around it effortlessly.

Then she saw him -- the terrible, scarred face of Rev. He sat in a tent, in a forest. He wasn't alone. Jarl Rannar was there, and Swinne. For a moment, her wings faltered. Swinne... Asgisla's murderer.

Around them were Fynni soldiers, their souls as empty as sucked eggs. Her eyes focused on Rev. On the little prayer doll around his neck that held the shadows which were driving him. Four shadows, the doll contained, a thumb-less hand from which a line grew.

She followed the line with her eyes and her wings, flying higher and higher, till she reached the blue bowl of the sky. A small piece was missing -- was that the skyshard? Effortlessly she passed through the blue shell and came to a dark one, empty and lightless. On she flew, till she reached a cave. And there they were, the Gods Before. Dark the Bashing Wind, looking like a molting crow, with bare patches of skin visible through his feathers. Orwang the Drowner Giant, a cadaverous turtle, his shell barnacled with rotting shellfish. Urus the Destroyer, like a rock with eyes that leaked molten tears. Klabang the Decapitator, a misshapen giant, clad in rusty pieces of armor and armed with a wooden club.

They were terrible in their ugliness, their hunger and their power. The line Birthe had followed sprang from within the four Gods. It was their power, she knew, the last of their Godly power. Above them she saw a glass bottle in which something writhed and squirmed. It was Rev's soul, hanging by a chain from the cave's roof. Instead of his soul, the four foul Gods animated Rev through the doll he wore. Should the doll die, the Gods Before would be diminished. For this must be their last gamble. To make them fail, Rev must die.

The world pulled her back down, through the lightless infinity, through the blue bowl that protected the earth, through the air, no longer as a bird, but as a thought, and as a thought she returned to her body.

Kjelle was just in time to catch her as she stumbled backwards. 'Are you all right?'

'I saw him.' Birthe gripped his arm. 'Rev. He is only a tool of the Gods Before. They keep his soul and rule him through a little prayer doll he wears. We must destroy that doll to end all those Fynni and their killing. Only then can we free the Norden.'

The Lithan laid his hands on Birthe's head, and she felt her heartbeat return to normal. 'Thus you know your purpose, Lady

Völva,' he said gently. 'You must destroy Rev and sever the link between our plane and the Gods Before.'

'What!' cried Kjelle. 'She can't! I... She is... I love her,' he ended unhappily.

'A proper admission, Lord Kjelle,' said the Lithan with a smile. 'Your love will be vital in strengthening her. But the Lady Birthe must destroy Rev to save the life of Muus and the purpose of the Shardheld.'

'Muus?' cried Kjelle. 'He only has to bring that cursed stone to Falrom.'

'*Only* is an inappropriate word for the Shardheld, Lord Kjelle,' said the Lithan. 'On Muus's shoulders rest the safety of the world. He must reach the Kalmanir and we have to prevent him from falling into the hands of Rev. Should the skyshard be joined with the Gods Before, our world would cease to exist. For now, the Shardheld is battling his way through the world, just like you. He is killing the Old Ones' minions and thus weakening the Gods Before.'

'How is he?' asked Birthe, feeling peaceful and detached under the Lithan's touch.

'The Shardheld is well, although the weariness is pulling at him. And it is Moirra who goes with him. My granddaughter, who is a rock in times of need.'

'So Muus found one, too.' said Kjelle with a soft smile.

The Lithan's light eyes sought Kjelle's face. 'You, a Nord, know your weakness and you accept it? How surprising.'

'Muus taught me my worst failings,' said Kjelle. 'I see them, though I can't always conquer them. But I have my rock in times of my own need.'

The Lithan laughed, a sound that brought the woman who had received them back into the room. 'You give me hope for the future,' he said. 'But now you must sleep. There are rooms where you can rest and eat before you leave. We will speak again.'

'I haven't heard him laugh for – oh so long,' said the woman as they went back in the hall. 'You surely must have brought good news.' At a brisk pace she led them to a small corridor. 'Here is a sleeping room,' she said. 'Master Elbrich, you want a room of your own, of course.'

The young smith shook his head. 'I'll stay with my friends,' he said. 'I've gotten used to sleeping in company by now.'

The woman shook her head. 'As you wish.'

'If we wish to return north,' said Elbrich seriously, 'we must learn to mix with other peoples. We can't afford to keep out distance like we used to in the old days, lest history repeat itself.'

'That is a wise thought,' said Birthe after the woman had left. 'The more we know of each other, the better it is for all of us.'

'I have a confession to make,' said Elbrich. 'When you fell, Ajkell. If Birthe had been unable to drag you back, I would have burned the rope through.'

The bear warrior's look was calm. 'I would have done the same.'

Kjelle gaped at him. 'You... I thought it, but that thought shamed me.'

Ajkell shrugged. 'There's no use in you all being dragged down. Still, it was a fabulous feat of strength. You do have the power, Birthe.'

'It's a trick. As a hunter, I was dragging around cadavers every day. You learn how to handle dead weights. If you had panicked and struggled, I would have cut that rope myself.'

The woman returned with a trio of children, small and black-haired like herself, all carrying baskets of food and drink. The little ones clearly had not seen strangers before, but they weren't shy, only curious. 'You're no Dachi,' said the smallest. 'And you're not bald, so you're no Rhani either. What are you?'

'I'm a Nord,' said Ajkell.

'Nords are bad people,' said the child, frowning heavily.

'Not us, kid. We are friends of your people.'

'Friendly Nords?' This seemed a big bite to chew, for the child fell still and only stared at the bear warrior.

When the woman and her little helpers had left, Kjelle and his companions sat down on their cots and ate.

'We need to plan,' said Birthe, waving a chicken leg. 'We must find Rev and kill that doll of his. But how?'

'Tomorrow,' said Kjelle firmly. 'I know how eager you are, but today we eat and sleep.'

Birthe set her teeth in the chicken leg and was silent.

CHAPTER 26 - DALLYW

Muus woke up at the sound of excited children's voices and of horse hooves on the stone ground. Groaning, he struggled to his feet as some of the older children entered the main cave. They shrieked with glee and clapped their hands at the sight of the dead idolaters. The boy they had saved first broke into a run and started to kick the dead bodies one by one, tears streaming down his face.

Hraab, in the meantime, had with Ciadra's help cut up some false druid cloaks into squares and poured a handful of gold onto each of them. After binding them tightly, he presented them to Muus. 'Here you are. A bag for each of us.'

'Just put them in our saddlebags, will you?' said Muus. The lure of gold left him completely untouched. He stepped over the dead bodies to pick up the boy, who had stopped kicking and now stood among the dead, bawling his heart out. 'It's all right, lad. You're all safe again. The bad people are dead. You can go home and tell everybody how terribly brave you are.'

The boy nodded, and wiped his face with the back of his hand before joining his friends.

Not much later the parents arrived -- the mothers first, crying harder than their offspring, clasping them as if they'd never let them go.

Ciadra looked at all the happy reunions. 'My mother is dead. I've been my own mother for years.'

'I know how it feels,' said Moirra. 'I never knew mine. It's very lonely sometimes, being always grown up.'

'Yes,' said the girl. And wistfully, 'I can't go with you, I suppose.'

Moirra shook her head. 'I'm sorry. What we must do is very dangerous. We follow Runemaster Terrel. Every one of us is connected with his task somehow, so we have to risk it. We wouldn't want you killed for something you are not part of.'

Ciadra sighed. 'You won't mind my offering to the Gods now and then? For your safety?'

'It would be a great honor if you did.'

'Then that must be enough. It won't be, but I'll pretend it is.'

Moirra hugged the girl for a moment and then they sat in silence.

Ottil came up to Muus, pulling him away from the grateful mothers. 'I found a dead man.'

For a moment Muus didn't understand him. 'What do you mean?'

'I found a dead man, not one of those idiots.'

Muus noticed the Prince seemed a bit ill. 'He wasn't a Grim Doubh?'

'No, and he had no heart.'

'Show me.'

They walked past the dead bodies, past the husk of the silver-haired priestess, to a dark corner beyond.

'Here,' said Ottil.

Muus immediately understood Ottil's queasiness. The naked body was of a man of middle age, of slight build, with a graying beard. His chest had been opened, not by a sharp knife, but by something that made a ragged, gaping wound.

'There's a stone knife over there,' said the Prince. 'Looking at him, he wasn't dead when they... they opened him.'

Muus agreed with him. The frozen agony on the man's face was indescribable and his fingers were red and bloody from clawing something hard, like a stone altar.

'This must be the missing druid.' The Prince shivered. 'The one from the first village. Better the children don't see this. It's what those monsters were going to do to them, too.'

'Stay near here and keep them away,' said Muus. 'All of them. I'll ask one of the elders to take care of him.'

'All right, but make it quick, I puked my stomach empty already.'

Sometime later the men arrived, armed with pitchforks, spades and other farming implements.

'Ciadra!' A burly man in a smith's apron opened his arms and the girl ran into them, hugging him tightly. 'You're safe, girl!'

'She's been a great help,' said Muus. 'She guided us to three caves as fearless as a royal paladin. You must be very proud of her.'

'I am,' said the man simply. 'I always was. After her mother died, she ran our household like she was born to it. Never a complaint, though she must have hated it sometimes. And now this!' His eyes sought his daughter, his emotion raw on his face. 'I thought I'd lost her, too.'

'The Runemaster saved us,' said Ciadra. 'He killed all the false ones with lightning. It was great. Better than the fireworks the druids do at Fois castle. He saved us all, he and the druidess Moirra and... Hraab. And the two boys, of course. One of them is hurt, father. We must take him in till he's better. This cold cave isn't good for him.'

'Of course, my daughter. We couldn't do less.'

'A word with you, smith,' said Muus. 'Ciadra, would you stay with Geir for a moment?'

Out of earshot he said, 'We found a dead man who could be the druid of the neighboring village. He went missing. Those idolaters offered him to their Gods and, well, it's no pleasant sight, I warn you.'

The smith swallowed a few times as he gazed at the dead man. 'Aye, it is him. I knew him well enough. We all did; seeing we've no druid of our own, he held many a ceremony here. He was a good man. What were those bastards? Why did they do this?'

'They're followers of the Gods Before,' said Muus. 'They want to bring them back into the world.'

The smith shuddered. 'That would be bad.'

'It would. But we've also good news for you.' He led the smith to the alcove with the gold.

'We found their trove. We've already taken our share, and what's left here is for the villagers. Perhaps it'll help compensate for your losses.'

'You mean it?' Ciadra's father looked at Muus in utter astonishment. 'There's more gold there than we would see in a hundred years. And you're just giving it to us?'

Muus smiled. 'We can't take it with us, I've no time to bother about it and you need it more than we do. So please use it for those brave children of yours.'

'We cannot repay this,' said the smith worriedly. 'You leave us with a load of debt, Runemaster.'

Moirra slipped out of the darkness to stand next to Muus. 'These caves are large,' she said. 'Send someone to the High Temple in Brytanna and invite them to build a center here for study and repose.

They know well the dangers of the Grim Doubh. Their presence can protect you, their knowledge can help you, it'll repay your debt, and it'll give your daughter something else to do apart from filling her mother's shoes.'

The smith gaped at her. 'Ciadra? My daughter a druidess?'

Moirra smiled. 'She has some vestiges of power. How much I can't ascertain, but it will be better for her to channel it. Untrained power tends to make people very unhappy.'

'A Druid Circle. It would make Ennovicce famous, like Lorda.'

'Tell the High Druid that you were sent by Moirra of the Un-a-Dach. He knows me well.'

The smith bowed. 'I will. Thank you, Wisdom, and you, Runemaster, for your aid and counsel.' He rubbed his hands. 'It will be good to see Ciadra better herself. She is such a clever girl and I'd hate to see her wasted working on a farm.'

'If you were to go to Brytanna,' said Muus, 'why not take her along? The High Druid would certainly like to test her and the journey would take her mind off things. You have gold enough now to hire some guards and travel in safety.'

'Yes, yes, she would love that. I'll tell her, she'll be happy.' Hurriedly, he left.

Moirra turned to Muus. 'Luckily he didn't ask about what 'things' you meant. So you saw it too?'

'That she has a crush on Hraab? Yes. And that's unsuitable, under the circumstances.'

'Very unsuitable,' said Moirra, laughing.

The villagers went and brought a cart to carry the body of the murdered druid and the chests of gold to the village. They dressed the dead man in one of the discarded robes they found in the cave and sent a messenger with the bad news to the neighboring village. The gold was locked away in the smith's house, to be shared out when the village elders had ascertained everybody's losses. Young Geir was brought on a litter and put to bed on a heap of straw in the smith's room. The boy slept and didn't even once wake during transport. Ottil sat down next to him.

'He looks so thin,' he said, with a worried face.

Moirra smiled at him. 'That's because he is tired. The healing I did on him not only used a lot of Muus' energy, but also at lot of Geir's own. He must sleep a long time before we can see how fit he is.'

The Prince nodded. 'I'll stay here for a bit, if you don't mind.'

When Muus later that afternoon came to check on the patient, he found Ottil asleep beside Geir, holding his hirdman's hand. After looking for Geir's firm breathing, he tiptoed out of the room again. 'They're both sleeping,' he said, smiling.

'Ottil's worn out too,' said Moirra. 'Though he would never admit it. Our prince is tough, but he is only a boy after all.'

'Prince?' said Ciadra, looking up from the dough she was kneading.

Moirra gave her a stern look. 'It is a secret,' she said. 'Ottil is a prince. There's trouble at his home and for the moment it is safer for him to be away. But when he returns, he will be a king.'

For a moment the girl stood still. The she realized what she was doing and hastily went on with her work. 'I don't understand what's going on,' she said. 'Those painted beasts, then you and the druidess, so different from the druids I've met, and now a real prince in our house?' She smiled suddenly, a bright, happy smile. 'And father told me we'll go to Brytanna, he and I. If the village council agrees. All the way to Brytanna! I can't believe it, I was so terribly bored here.'

'Your council will agree,' said Moirra confidently. 'We will convince them, Muus and I.'

And agree they did. More than that, they were ecstatic over the idea. That those musty old caves could be used for good after all!

'Shouldn't we notify the count in Fois?' said a farmer.

'Nonsense!' The smith towered over him. 'The count for all his airs is no more than the military commander. He's supposed to defend us, but where was he when the painted beasts came? No, Ennovicce's a free village under the king's rule. And Leodowric don't care as long as we pay our taxes. Besides, think of the faces those good folk at Lorda will pull when they get competition – from the holy High Temple itself!'

That clincher made them banging the table.

While they waited for Geir to get better, they searched the four caves from bottom to top, but nowhere was any sign to be found of the druid Dallyw. Finally, Muus had to conclude that this wasn't the place where the man from Brytanna had disappeared. So they relaxed, loafed around and slept a lot.

Ottil sat besides the makeshift bedding and looked at Geir. The boy was restless, moving his head, his hands fluttering over his chest. On impulse, the Prince bent over him. 'Geir?'

Almost immediately, the boy quieted. 'Here, Highness,' he whispered. Then he opened his eyes and tried to focus. Ottil gripped the boy's hands. 'How do you feel?'

'Fine,' said the boy. 'Now I'm fine.'

'That was a daft thing you did, trying to protect me. Them beasts trampled all over you.'

'You're my prince, I must protect you.'

'But they nearly killed you.'

'They didn't kill you,' said Geir mulishly. 'It's my duty as hirdman.'

'I don't want you killed, silly.' Ottil couldn't say any more. Geir was right. He had named the boy hirdman, his personal guard.

'I live to protect you.' The boy closed his eyes. 'My father couldn't feed me, my brother died, you took me on. You're my prince, my duty. What other purpose have I?'

'You could... you could be my friend,' said Ottil awkwardly.

'You're the Prince, I'm a farm boy. It wouldn't... work.'

'Damn it, we're both Nords. We're not that formal.'

'Not from where you sit.' Geir tried to smile. 'That wasn't nice, sorry. Let me be what I am, Highness. Please?'

'Of course,' said Ottil stiffly. 'If that's how you want it.' He rose. 'I'll call Moirra. She'll want to check you up.'

'Highness?' The boy looked up at him. 'Are you mad at me?'

'Damn, now you sound like Hraab,' said Ottil, and he laughed. 'No, of course I'm not mad. Just try not to die, will you?' Then he hurried from the room, calling for Moirra.

After this, Geir's recovery went fast. Through Moirra's healing powers and his own resilience, he started to walk again and after a sevenday was deemed fit enough for them to continue their journey.

'We're leaving tomorrow,' said Hraab.

'I heard,' said Ciadra, hanging out the washing for Sun to dry. 'Next sevenday father and I will go away, too. I'll miss you.'

'It wouldn't have worked,' said Hraab softly.

Ciadra shrugged. 'I know.' Then she bent over the mount of fresh laundry in her arms and kissed him lightly. 'Thank you, anyhow.'

'For what?'

'For letting me dream.'

For once Hraab was at a loss for words, while the girl went on hanging the washing.

The day of departure had arrived and the whole village gathered to see them off.

'Have a safe journey,' said the smith. 'May your path be clear and let you find what you seek.'

'You, too, on your going to Brytanna,' said Muus.

He noticed Hraab's face as he took his leave from Ciadra. His relief at her decorum in just shaking hands was manifest, and the girl smiled. She threw her arms around Muus. 'Thank you again. I'll pray for your safety every day of my life. Without you, this day would have been grim and filled with grief. Now there is hope.'

Moirra she embraced as a sister. 'I'm so glad to know you. You're so wise. I hope I'll grow up looking like you.'

'Well, not looking like me,' said Moirra with a laugh. 'You wouldn't want to become a Un-a-Dach. But thanks, it was kindly said.'

'And tell Hraab I'll keep his secrets safe forever. All of them.'

Moirra held her at arm's length and studied her face. 'Well, well, your eyes are clear enough. Yes, your discretion is appreciated. And your not asking any questions, too.'

The girl sighed. 'I'll never forget you all.'

Then they rode off, with Geir sitting a bit hunched. His body hurt him still, but he had insisted on their leaving and got very upset at the thought of the others delaying their journey only for him. So they passed through the fourth cave, followed all the way by some of the boldest children. Only when they had left the cave mouth for the lands beyond, were they finally alone.

The day was fine, this late spring. The land basked in Sun's light, with all the flowers open to her glory.

After about two hours they saw in the distance the castle of Fois on its high rock. A high, walled donjon, looking nigh on untakable, it watched over the surrounding countryside. At the foot of the rock huddled the town, with a palisade guarding stone houses with red roofs, and a stone bridge across the river.

'Let us see if there is a Druid Circle here,' said Moirra. 'If the cave we want is around here, the local temple is the first place to ask.'

'The druids,' said the guard at the gate. 'But of course. Make your way to the foot of the Rock. There, guarding the road to the castle, you'll find the Circle house. Wisdom Landronis is the senior.'

Through the small streets they went, following the sheer wall of the rock that bore the castle, till they came to a tall house, half hidden by trees.

Druid Landronis proved to be a youngish man, rather stiff, both in limbs and in character. 'Ah, druidess Moirra, welcome. Master Terrel, you're a Runemaster? One of the Older Folk too, I surmise?'

Moirra smiled, but Hraab sniffed audibly. No Un-a-Dach liked to be called Older Folk, as if they were svartalves or some such.

'We would appreciate a meal and a night's lodging, Landronis. Our journey is long and one of us was recently wounded.'

'Of course,' said their host without enthusiasm. 'You're from the High Temple? Well, I was trained at the temple in Boyocasse. Not everybody can study at the top.'

'I've heard the High Druid mentioning Boyocasse with respect,' said Moirra at her most innocent.

Landronis visibly relaxed. 'Is that so? Well, eh, it is a proper temple, after all.'

'I am sure,' said Moirra. 'And Fois is an important location; you must be getting many visitors?'

'Ah, some, some. But you are the first in a long time from far Brytanna.'

'That is actually why we came here. Some eighty years ago the then High Druid sent a druid named Dallyw this way to search for a cave where strange beasts had been sighted. He never returned. Would you have any knowledge or records of him?'

Landronis frowned. 'The name means nothing to me, it's so long ago. Perhaps druid Rochis would know. He has lived here forever. But his mind is wandering and I'm not sure how much he'll remember.' He rose. 'I'll show you to his room.'

They followed the druid to the second floor.

'He can't leave his chamber anymore,' said Landronis. 'One of us visits him twice a day to feed and clean him up.' He looked at the boys. 'Better you three wait in the corridor, he gets flustered with too many people around.'

Druid Rochis was indeed old. His hair was white and very thin, his skin a collection of lines and wrinkles, and his toothless mouth a gaping hole. Landronis bend over him. 'Rochis, some visitors for you.'

Slowly, the old eyes opened. 'Aneeta? Is that you, Aneeta? And you brought your husband, that no-good. A pity you married him, Aneeta. Still, you always were a headstrong girl.'

'How are you?' said Moirra, taking one of the thin hands in hers.

'Alive,' said the druid. 'Only the Gods know how... and why.' He laughed softly. 'Them and their mysteries. They never really tell us anything.'

'No,' said Moirra. 'I had noticed.'

The old eyes stared at her face. 'Aye, you would. Y'always were a clever girl, Aneeta. Why did you come?'

Moirra didn't even blink at the abrupt question. 'Remember Dallyw? That druid from the High Temple?'

'Dallyw. The cave man.'

'He was searching for a cave, yes.'

'I remember him. Tall fellow, very hoity-toity. A fool he was, with all his high learning. Lookin' for fancy monsters. Here, as if we were in Espayne or some such low place. Idiot.'

'It sounds strange, yes,' said Moirra, smiling at the old man. 'Had he found his cave?'

'Oh, yes, he did. Was goin' to search the hole at Eubona, to the south of here. Probably didn't find anything, for he never came back to crow about it. Silly guy.'

Muus threw Landronis a quick glance and the man nodded.

'There won't be any monsters here,' said Moirra. 'With such a stout castle.'

'Castle, bah! 'Tis not the count that keeps the monsters away. It's the land itself. The good soil of Gaul that keeps them at bay. The Gods bless Gaul and King Helderic.'

'You must not agitate yourself, Rochis. Sleep, the lady has to leave.'

Moirra touched the old man's cheek. 'The Gods will always protect Gaul, rest assured.'

'They will,' mumbled the old man, and closed his eyes again.

'I am sorry about that,' said Landronis, once they were on the landing. 'Aneeta was his daughter. As far as I know she died sixty years ago.'

'King Helderic, too,' said Moirra with a wink at Ottil. 'He was the present king's great-grandfather, I believe.'

'He was,' said Ottil surprised. 'Why?'

Moirra shook his head. 'Druid Rochis' mind lives in days long past.'

'Is he that old?' said the Prince awe-struck.

'About a hundred and twenty,' said Landronis. 'Some of us are so blessed.'

'You know this place he mentioned?' said Muus.

'Eubona? Yes, it is to the southeast, one of those small villages; very lonely. Bear country, I've been told.'

'Bear!' said Ottil breathlessly. 'I have never hunted bear yet.'

'And you won't now, if I can help it,' said Muus. 'We're not on a hunting trip, young man.'

'Spoilsport,' said Ottil.

'Yeah,' said Hraab. 'He wants to be the youngest Nord ever to do his manhood Test.'

Ottil colored slightly. 'I must set an example.'

Muus frowned. 'Would you really encourage your subjects to start fighting bears at twelve years old?'

'Why not?' said the Prince. He turned to Geir, 'Would you go and kill a bear?'

'If you wanted me to, Highness,' said the boy.

'You would attack a bear if Ottil said so?' Muus stared at the boy. 'Why?'

Geir pressed his lips together. 'He's my prince.'

'That is a very great responsibility, Ottil,' said Muus.

Ottil blinked. 'How so? I wouldn't have him do things I wouldn't do myself.'

'Nords!' said Muus exasperated. 'Pigheaded fools, all of them.'

'But you can't deny they're brave,' said Hraab, grinning broadly.

'Pigheaded and foolhardy, then,' said Muus with disgust.

The next morning they left early, heading towards the village of Eubona, where the cave they sought would be. They rode into the foothills of the Pyrenes: stony terrain, sparsely covered with trees and small shrubs. Rocky peaks grew around them, shaped like wolf's teeth; seemingly close. Far away rose the snow-covered massif of the mountains proper.

It was pleasant so to ride, thought Muus. No worries, no hurry for a while. A faint glow of fiery lava tried to intrude, but he pushed the image away. *Leave me some peace.* The path they walked was mostly broad enough for a drawn cart, although they met no one. Finally they reached a clutch of houses built from local stone. In front of one of them sat an old man.

'Good day,' called Muus. 'Is this Eubona?'

The man stared at him but didn't react. From the house came a stout woman, wiping her hands on her faded gown.

'No use talking to him,' said she. 'Grandfa's both deaf and lost in 'is mind. You were wantin' sumpthing?'

'If you please,' said Muus. 'This is Eubona?'

'Indeed it is, segnor. What could we have of interest for one like you?'

'A cave,' said Muus, with a smile.

'But yes, a cave.' The woman's face grew suspicious. 'There is one nearby, segnor. What might be yer business with it?'

'The druids' business, mistress,' said Moirra softly.

The woman's mouth formed a surprised 'oh'. 'Yer pardon, Wisdom, I hadn't seen yer calling. Druids' business, of course. The Circle has been interested in our cave before. Grandfa used to tell about the druid he guided to the cave when he was but a lad. He brought him hither and somehow lost him inside. It was strange, said Grandfa. One moment the druid was there. He said sumpthing about water, and when Grandfa turned around, the man was gone. Grandfa searched, of course, and later the men of the village too, but they ne'er found no trace of 'im. A terrible thing, that was.'

'Where can we find this cave, mistress?'

'It's close by, segnor. You follow the path till the next bend. Then there's a trail to the left that leads you directly to it. Don't know how the goin' is, nobody's been there in a long time.'

Muus thanked the woman. and following her instructions they reached the trail at the bend easily enough.

'Not very horse-friendly,' said Muus. 'No sense in risking a strained leg or worse; you can hardly see where the trail goes.'

So they hitched their mounts to a tree and continued on foot. The path was a tangle of briars and overhanging branches, heavy going, but finally they reached the cave's mouth.

Here they paused for a while, catching their breath. The sun shone through the new leaves of the beech tree at the entrance and somewhere a bird sang. Then they stepped inside, intp near-complete darkness. Hurriedly, Muus asked the runes for a light and had it spring from his hand almost instantly. The space they were in was large, the size of High King Cucharann's hall in Kings' Lud. Strewn around were countless bones, large and small, and some of them human. It made Muus think of the encounter, ages ago, with the snowwolf whose tail still adorned the coat he wore. As they slowly walked deeper into the cave, the sight of the bones kept him extra alert

'Bear signs,' said Moirra. 'We'd best be careful.'

'I hope that druid isn't one of these,' said Ottil staring at the bones.

'There wasn't a bear here when he disappeared,' said Hraab. 'That woman would have told us.'

'There isn't one now, either,' said Ottil, sounding slightly disappointed.

'Be glad there isn't,' said Muus sourly.

They walked on, towards the sound of running water. The light that sprang from Muus's fingers grew brighter with the size of the cave, which was now an enormous vault through which, some lengths below them, a small river ran. Muus felt a strange, pulling sensation. It wasn't the same feeling as when the skyshard pulled at him. This was more intimate, as from a child pulling your sleeve. 'There is something nearby,' said he. 'The runes want me to go somewhere.'

'Well, follow them,' said Hraab.

'It goes down towards the river. I'm not planning to jump, if you don't mind.'

Hraab went down on all fours and crept to the edge of the rock. Peering down, he said: 'There is something there. I see a skull and some bones.'

'How are we going to get down there?'

'Geir has a rope,' said Ottil. 'I will climb down, if you want me to.'

'There's no place to fasten the rope to,' said Muus. 'We'll lower the lightest of us by hand.'

'That's me,' said Hraab.

'I think Geir.' Ottil looked critically at his hirdman. 'He's really thin.'

Hraab grinned. 'Let him go; I'm better at not dropping him halfway.'

Geir's color had heightened. 'I'll do it if you want me to, Highness,' he said stiffly.

'That's settled, then,' said Ottil. 'Give me the rope.'

Hurriedly, Geir unwound the rope from his middle and handed it over. Ottil began to lay two hand loops in the rope.

'Where did you learn that?' said Muus surprised.

'From the *Madgund's* sailors,' said the Prince. 'While you were all talking and loafing about I was studying seamanship. It's not good to let your hands get idle, my mother used to say.' After making the loops, he laid a big knot in the end of the rope. 'There you are,' he said finally. 'You put your hands through the loops and set your feet on this ball at the end. No sweat, we'll do all the work.'

Geir stared at the rope. Then he swallowed and nodded.

Muus looked over the knots, but they seemed solid enough to him. 'Ready?' They all gripped the rope and hung it over the edge.

'First your hands in the loops,' commanded Ottil. "Now step over the side and put your feet on the ball.'

Geir took a deep breath and closed his eyes as he hung by his arms. For a moment his legs milled around.

'Take it easy,' said Ottil.

Then Geir found the big knot and opened his eyes.

'You ready?'

Geir nodded again, blinking a tear away.

Gently, the others lowered the rope, until the boy was on the ledge with the skeleton.

'I'm down,' shouted Geir. And a few moments later: 'It's a lot of bones in a druid's robe. There's a little finger on a silver cord, with a rune on it. I... Aaah! Damn.'

'What is it?' said Ottil.

'Damn! A frog jumped out of the skull,' Geir's voice sounded hoarse.

'A frog!' Ottil started to laugh. 'Priceless! Now, if you've got the rune, get onto the rope and we'll pull you back up.'

'Yes! Please yes!'

A few minutes later, the boy was back on the ledge. He was shivering uncontrollably. His hands with the fingerbone were shaking and his teeth were chattering.

'You're cold!' said Moirra.

'I stood half in the w-water,' said Geir. 'Damn.' He started to cry.

Moirra looked at Muus. 'It's the shock,' she said softly. 'Let's get him outside, into the sun.'

Ottil put his arm around the trembling boy. 'You were great,' he said awkwardly. 'Sorry I laughed about the frog, I would have yelled too.'

'It was so s-stupid,' said Geir. 'That stupid skull lay there, next to the rest of the bones, grinning at me. I grabbed the rune and then that f-frog jumped out of an eye hole right into me face. I...' He folded double and began to vomit. After a while his heaving stopped. He wiped his mouth on his sleeve. 'Sorry, it g-got me for a moment.'

'We go back to the Circle house in Fois and put you to bed,' said Moirra. When Geir started to protest, she raised her hand. 'You're simply overtired, and you're going to sleep it off.'

That evening they sat round the fire in the druids' common room.

'We found him all right,' said Muus, warming the cup of wine in his hands. 'The remains are at the bottom of a ledge over an underground river. We spoke with a woman in the village whose grandfather as a boy had accompanied Dallyw to the cave. The druid had disappeared while he and the boy were talking. He must have misjudged the distance to the edge and fallen to his death. He lay on a small ridge above the water level, hidden from view from the top. Any searchers will have missed him. It's awful dark there.'

'He must be brought back, I suppose,' said druid Landronis rather stiffly. It was clear he wasn't looking forward to it.

'Some people with ropes and a sheet can do it.'

'And you found what you were looking for?'

Muus nodded. 'The object is safe. It's only a tiny thing, just a rune I need. But I'm glad we found it.'

'Then all ends well, thanks to the Gods.'

'I'll pass on your thanks,' said Hraab.

Landronis frowned, as if he suspected flippancy, but the boy only smiled politely.

Three days passed, in which Muus took it upon himself to lift the remains of druid Dallyw from the cave. Some stout farmers from Eubona village assisted, spurred on by the woman whose Grandfa had been with Dallyw when he disappeared from life.

'So he's been there all the time,' she'd said when Muus told her of their findings. 'Poor man. Pity Grandfa won't understand it anymore; it always was a great mystery to him.'

They buried Dallyw in the woods, at the foot of an ancient oak, symbol of wisdom and life, with a full ceremony led by Landronis and Moirra, and with all the folk of Eubona in attendance.

The next morning they left. Geir was still not fully fit, but he was fretting so much over his weakness holding up his prince, that Moirra thought it better to continue their journey.

And so, after days of traveling east, they reached a plateau overgrown with wild flowers. Here, the road went sharply down to a small harbor town, white against the sparkly expanse of blue sea and blue sky.

'Levastra,' said Muus. 'Now we need to find a ship that can take us to Kartakos.'

'The sea again,' said Geir, half to himself. His tone wasn't enthusiastic.

Ottil slapped his shoulder. 'You don't have to work this time. A few days of sleeping and loafing about. Perhaps do some fishing over the side. It's perfect.'

His hirdman nodded, but he didn't seem convinced.

Muus didn't listen. He stared out over the sea. There, far away on the horizon, he saw a fiery glow. There was what he feared most of all -- the burning lands of Falrom, where the Kalmanir waited.

LIST OF WORDS

Bondsman	freeman who is a farmer or artisan
Cog (ship)	medium-sized ship from Gaul or Brytanna
Draug	walking dead (plural: draugar)
Dvergar	forefather of the Niflunger
Freedman	former slave now freed but bound to the Hold.
Freeman	freeborn Nord (male or female)
Fynni	shamanic people of the Ostmark
Fynnikin	half-breed Fynni/Ostmarker
Headman	captain of a Hold's warriors
Hird	private fighting force of a Lord, Jarl or King
Hirdman	personal follower of a king or jarl
Hold	the property of a Holder
Holder	Nordish rank (Baron), lord of a Hold
Holderling	the male heir to a Hold
Karl	freeman who is both farmer and fighter
Lendmann	councilor to king or jarl
Lightalves	golden haired alves (hist.)
Long Night, the	Polar Night, the
Ostmark	the eastern part of the Norden; barbaric lands
Ovate	druidic rank; senior student
Rest	measure of distance: a two-hour walk
Rune magic	male magic commanding runes and elements
Runemaster	man practicing rune magic (high level)
Sa'aman	shamanic priest of the Fynni
Sa'amaniman	the shamanic chief priest of the Fynni
Seidr magic	female magic with songs, chants, prophecies
Sevenday	period of 7 days, a week.
Svartalf	forefather of the Un-a-Dach
Tarkynn	Fynni shamanic warleader
Tennight	period of ten nights
Thing	legislative meeting of all freemen of a place
Thrall	slave
Ulvhednar	Fynni wolf berserkers (singular & plural)
Völva	woman practicing seidr magic (high level)
Wise(wo)man	person practicing magic (low level)

LIST OF NAMES

Aeylla, (D) Muus's mother
Ajkell Gudrofsen, bear warrior
Alman, (D) Holder of Eidungruve; Kjelle's father
Annawn, Bryttic Goddess of Healing
Annios, Byzanten Trade Agency guard
Annlith, girl healer from Wedeler Mountain
Arawan, Bryttic God of the Death
Arkenhapt, Mistress of Wederer Mountain
Arraw, High Druid of the Inner Circle
Asgar, Lord, a Nord Holder of Dalland
Asgisla (D), Völva of Belisheim
Athona, senior Druidess of Baian Circle
Barn (D), Birthe's first husband, Búi's father
Barulf Gudrofsen, Holder of Leidwald
Belsarios Nefaristos, son of the Baljaran Trade Agent at Baian
Bemm, leader of ten, warrior of the Niflung from Wederer Mountain
Birthe Gudesdotter, Völva and Huntmaster
Brundal, Jarl; Landesregent
Búi Birthesen, Birthe's baby son (D)
Cardoc, chief of Windiss village, Brytanna
Cucharann, High King of Brytanna
Dagiberh, Count of Divion
Dallyw (D), an historic druid
Darh the Bashing Wind (Sky), one of the four Gods Before
Dettrich, Jarl of Dalland
Elbrich of the Silver Mountain, a Niflung mastersmith
Elward, watchman of Eidungruve
Ema, Kjelle's *amour* at Eidungruve
Ewynn, druid of Windiss
Fardoragh, archdruid
Frey, Nordish/Gaullish God of male magic, etc.
Freya, Nordish/Gaullish Goddess of female magic, etc.
Fynch, a Druid of Baian Circle
Gillach, son of Cardoc of Windiss village
Göll Haldisdottr, archer at Almansford
Gude the Viking, (D) Birthe's father
Gunthchramn, captain of the *Madgrun*
Hagen (D), a warrior of Eidungruve
Hanoris, horse-coper near Baian

Harald Enske, foreman of Eidungruve
Hilja, village girl in Lotharn
Hraab (Raaf), a boy
Iowynh, Bryttic God of Magic and Tricks
Jarrol, a man of Eidunsgruve and Almansford
Kireg, a ship's captain from Roian
Kjelle Almansen; Holderling of Eidungruve
Klabang the Decapitator (Fight), one of the four Gods Before
Kremmendor, a warrior of Wederer Mountain, the Mistress'nephew
Leocastre of Gaul, Queen of the Norden, mother to Prince Ottil
Leodowric, King of Gaul
Logmar, one of King Vidmer's Councillor's
Mawgann, Bryttic Goddess of War and Prophecy
Meili Brandrsen (D), Thegnling of Leidwald
Muus (Terrel); slave, Un-a-Dach, runemaster, Shardheld.
Niord (Stiller-of-Storms), Nordish God of Sea and Storms
Odin, the Allfather, chief God of the Nordish pantheon
Olf Gormsen (D), Geir's second brother
Orlach, Warleader of Ad-Cadol, Brytanna
Orwang the Drowner Giant (Sea), one of the four Gods Before
Ottil Vidmersen, Prince of de Norden
Radgundis de Megern, wife to Dettrich Jarl of Dalland
Rannar Walesen, Jarl of Westhal
Rev, the sa'amaniman, the Fynni chief high priest.
Rodolf Utharsen, Jarl of Haugland
Sarrias the Thief (D), hist.
Sha'akaii, Tuuri's totem bear
Siga, wisewoman of Eidungruve
Skid Largassen *Bearjaw*, the Viking of Helmshaven
Slade (D), Muus/Terrel's father, a druid
Swinne (Swine), follower of Rannar, a Fynni tarkynn
Thor, Nordish/Gaullish God of War and Battle, Thundergod
Tuuri Little Knife, Rannar's messenger.
Tyllas, Royal Druid of Brytanna
Ullr, Nordish God of Archery and Winter, Ostmark god
Urus the Destroyer (Earth), one of the four Gods Before
Uthar, Warleader of Dynar Byn, Brytanna
Valiantrude de Vergy, Paladin of the Court of Gaul
Vectitos, Captain of the garrison at Parisi Isles
Vidmer II (D); King of de Norden; Ottil's father
Vyvain, the Oaken Bard of the Druid Circles

Vulf (Wolf), follower of Rannar, a Fynni tarkynn
Waldrich, Jarl of Herigel
Welddich, Guardmaster of Wederer Mountain

AUTHOR'S LETTER

Dear Reader,

Thank you for reading my work.
I hope you found as much enjoyment in it as I found in writing the story. If not, I apologize for failing you...

I have a request.
Would you, dear Reader, tell the world whether or not you liked this book?
If so, would you write a small review of it at Amazon, Smashwords, Goodreads or wherever you bought it?
Should you like the story, I won't mind your jubilant opinion. And if you don't, well, I'll hope you won't hesitate to say so. Perhaps then I can do better next time. Positive or negative, your opinion is of great value to me.

And should you have any questions about the book or the story, you can always find me at pehorsman@gmail.com. I promise to answer any questions you might have.

Thank you for your input!

ZIHAEN

If you enjoyed this book, perhaps you would be interested in my other fantasy adventure, The Shadow of the Revenaunt-series:

How did his parents and brothers die? Was their death really an accident, or were they killed? This question the young Ghyll Hardingraud must answer before he can ascend Rhidauna's throne. His search for the truth leads him and his companions on a journey back to the past and he slowly unravels a dark conspiracy.

To give you a taste, here are the first pages of Zihaen, The Shadow of the Revenaunt, Chapter 1, in which Ghyll, his foster brother Olle and their friends go out to discover the truth behind the accidents that killed Ghyll's brothers and parents.

PAUL E. HORSMAN

THE SHADOW OF THE REVENAUNT

Book 2

ZIHAEN

CHAPTER 1 - RHIDAUN-LORN

Ghyll lay on his stomach on the sheets, naked and vulnerable. Wide-eyed, he stared at the priest beside his bed. 'I'll stay crippled?'

The healing priest's round face was professional, expressionless, without pity. 'I'm sorry, Baron. The chirurgeon and I came to the same conclusion. The damage to your leg muscles is permanent. Not even our combined powers could restore the destroyed tissues.' As he spoke, he rubbed sour smelling ointment into the scar on Ghyll's back. 'This should reduce the swelling.' His deft fingers placed a linen bandage over the painful area. 'It does not smell pleasant and I will not tell you what it is made of, but it is effective. You can dress now.' The priest wiped his fingers on a cloth his acolyte handed him. 'There's some good news as well, your broken nose is almost healed. I will leave off the dressing. You should be cautious; the cartilage is still somewhat vulnerable.' He paused and looked down at Ghyll. 'I have one last bit of advice.' For a moment, the healer's contempt broke through his mask of objectivity. 'Keep your sword in its sheath and avoid new honor fights.' With a nod, he strode from the room with his helper.

Ghyll stared at the ceiling, too shocked for words. *Honor fights!*

The door opened and Olle came. 'How is it?'

Ghyll looked at his anxious face. 'The healer thought I had gotten my wounds in a duel.'

Olle growled. 'What an idiot. Was that all he had to say?'

'My nose is almost better.' Ghyll sat up and leaned his head against one of the bedposts. 'Only the limp won't go away.'

'That bastard Vasthul!' snapped Olle, his dark skin coloring deep red in anger. 'You're a soft fool, Ghyll. You should have cut that sorcerer's throat when you had the chance.'

Ghyll spread his hands. 'I know. But that's not what Uncle Jadron taught us.'

Olle's eyebrows shot up. 'No? I've always understood differently.' His deep eyes studied Ghyll from head to toe and he shook his head. 'You're not hard enough.'

'I'm already harder than I was,' said Ghyll annoyed. 'Harder than I ever wanted to be. Let's drop it. I can walk and ride with this leg. I'll have to get used to it.' He touched his nose with two fingers. 'Leave me be for a while, I have some thinking to do.'

Olle nodded. 'Don't worry too much. If you need anything, I'm with the others.'

Left alone, Ghyll stared at the dancing motes in the narrow beam of sunlight escaping the curtains. *Crippled at twenty. All because of that cursed Dar'khamorth sorcerer, Vasthul.* In his mind, he saw himself walking around. Step, bonk, step, bonk; like Grogar, the blacksmith of Castle Tinnurad. Only Grogar was dead as the two hundred others were. Images of their burning keep forced upon him, memories of triumphal firebirds above Tinnurad's collapsing tower. Slowly he began to dress.

A soft knock on the door drove the hateful birds from his thoughts. 'There is a messenger asking for you, my lord.' The footman sounded awed. 'He comes from the Palace.'

Ghyll started buttoning his shirt. 'Let him come in.'

The courier, an older man in the blue-and-silver livery of House Hardingraud, entered the room and bowed. He took a sealed document from the briefcase on his hip. 'By the hand of His Grace the Regent,' he said in a tone meant to bring the recipient in a state of deep humility.

Ghyll thanked him and opened the missive. It contained only a few lines, written in a robust script.

If you wish to meet the Crown Prince of Opit, he is with me. His Highness has information that may be of interest to you. Kyssander.

Ghyll smiled. Clear and concise. The regent was not a flowery writer. He stood up. 'Tell His Grace I will be with him shortly.'

A slight frown crossed the face of the courier at Ghyll's casual reply. He bowed and departed in dignified silence.

Ghyll went to the bell rope. 'Tell the stable to bring my horse,' he said to the servant who answered. He walked into the living room, where his friends were gathered. 'I have to go to the palace. The regent needs me.'

'You'll not go alone,' said Olle. 'I...'

'I'll go with him,' cried Torril. 'I can protect Ghyll as well as anyone.' Challengingly he looked around the circle.

Olle opened his mouth, but Ghyll was first. 'Make it quick then, I shall not wait for you.'

Torril jumped up, grabbed his ax from the weapon rack and his cloak from its peg. Shouting for a horse, he ran out the door.

Olle snorted. 'Young monkey. Why aren't we all going?'

Ghyll's mouth twisted. On the threshold, he paused. 'Brother mine, I'll be damned to hide behind your back. Torril will be enough.' He closed the door and limped downstairs.

Zinobad, Prince of Opit and Mandaba, was young and round. In a wide Opitian dress, decorated with embroidered gold elephants, and on his head a turban with swaying feathers, he shone as a purple pug in the cool throne room. His eyes laughed when he answered Ghyll's bow, clearly aware of the impression he made. 'Ooh, the mysterious Baron Halwyrd,' he said. 'His Grace insisted I meet you.'

'It is an honor, Highness,' said Ghyll.

'The prince told me something that will interest you,' said the regent as they sat down. 'It touches your recent fights with golems.'

'Golems,' cried Torril. 'Where?' His fingers drummed on the handle of his ax while he gave the young exquisite a hard stare.

The prince blinked. 'Not here. I must disappoint you.'

Ghyll clenched his fists. 'Torril and I have met those makemen before, Highness. He reacts a bit more impulsively than I would, but our sentiments are the same.'

'Exterminate them all,' said the young Nhael eagerly.

Zinobad's chubby face clouded over. 'Duke Kyssander said your golems appeared warriors in black armor, and that they were oblivious to fire. It made me think of my father. You see, nine years ago he was killed by such beings.'

His words struck Ghyll like a fist. Had there been golems in Opit, even them? 'Prince, we need to talk.' His gaze slid over the elegant throne room with everywhere shadows, niches and obscure corners. 'May I invite you to our inn? Our rooms there are safe from listening ears. Besides, my Companions will want to hear your story too. If the Duke does not mind I rob him of his guest?'

The regent cast Ghyll a sharp glance. 'It is unfortunate,' he said with a straight face. 'But I resign myself to it. May I suggest you tell His Highness the truth?'

Ghyll spread his hands. 'Nothing but the truth, Duke.'

Zinobad looked from one to the other. 'The truth?' he asked with raised eyebrows.

The regent stood up. 'Baron Halwyrd's secret,' said he. 'May I present you to His Royal Highness, Ghyllander III of the House of Hardingraud?'

The look of bewilderment on Zinobad's round face was almost comical.

'The King arrived at court only yesterday, after an adventurous journey,' said the regent. 'It is his wish not to make his arrival known to the people at this moment.'

The prince took a deep breath and bowed to Ghyll. 'What a surprise! King Ghyllander, on behalf of my brother Mojalman I'm happy to congratulate you upon your return.'

Ghyll's color heightened. 'Not many people know it yet, Prince. Outside my faithful friends, you are the third. I will explain everything at the inn.'

'What a secret!' said Zinobad and his eyes gleamed.

'We princes are good at secrets.' Torril straightened his tunic and grinned.

Zinobad looked at him. 'We princes?'

Ghyll chuckled. 'Our young friend here reminds me I should reveal his secret as well. This is Prince Torril Nikkelsen, second heir to the Nhael.'

Prince Zinobad's mouth fell open. 'The Nhael! Ooh, Rhidauna has signed peace at last?'

Ghyll looked at the regent, but when the duke shook his head, he said, 'Not yet; Prince Torril is here in a personal capacity. As a friend rather than as a representative of his country.'

'Let's go,' said Zinobad urgently. 'If I don't get the whole story soon, I'll die of curiosity.'

When they left the throne room, it became clear the prince had not arrived in Rhidauna unaccompanied. He was met at the door by a pair of elderly men in dark robes, a two-man honor guard in ceremonial cuirasses, and a trumpeter, whom he all ignored. On the driveway, a private groomsman waited with the prince's mount to the door.

Torril's mouth fell open. 'Drakes get me,' he said, coloring bright red. 'What ís that stupid beast?'

'That, young barbarian, is called a camel,' said Zinobad stern-faced, but the smile in his eyes betrayed him. 'Caravel of the desert. Carries twice the load of a horse and can go a week without water. A noble animal, my friend.'

'Precious!' Torril burst out laughing. 'He looks as stuck-up as the footmen at the inn!'

The animal sank to his front legs. Ignoring the offered knee of his little groom the prince hoisted his rotund self into the saddle. Rocking, the camel came up until Zinobad towered above Ghyll. Rhidaun-Lorn was a cosmopolitan city, used to visitors of many cultures. But Opit's crown prince in his baggy clothing of royal purple and gold, with the plumes on his headdress moving in the languid breeze, was a sight to make people stop and stare. Now the reason for the two soldiers became clear. Their whips cracked, their voices roared, and slowly the awed mob parted. The trumpeter added his strident call and a small lane opened to let the prince and Ghyll ride forward.

www.ingramcontent.com/pod-product-compliance
Lightning Source LLC
Chambersburg PA
CBHW070549130626
46556CB00001B/76